The Second Penguin Book of
MODERN WOMEN'S SHORT STORIES

The Second Penguin Book of
Modern Women's Short Stories

AN ANTHOLOGY

Selected and introduced by Susan Hill

MICHAEL JOSEPH
LONDON

MICHAEL JOSEPH LTD

Published by the Penguin Group
27 Wrights Lane, London w8 5tz, England
Viking Penguin Inc., 375 Hudson Street, New York, New York 10014, USA
Penguin Books Australia Ltd, Ringwood, Victoria, Australia
Penguin Books Canada Ltd, 10 Alcorn Avenue, Toronto, Ontario, Canada m4v 3b2
Penguin Books (NZ) Ltd, 182–190 Wairau Road, Auckland 10, New Zealand

Penguin Books Ltd, Registered Offices: Harmondsworth, Middlesex, England

First published 1997
1 3 5 7 9 10 8 6 4 2

This selection and introduction copyright © Susan Hill 1997

The acknowledgements on page vii constitute an extension of this copyright page

Set in 11.5/14pt Monotype Garamond
Typeset by Rowland Phototypesetting Ltd,
Bury St Edmunds, Suffolk
Printed in England by Clays Ltd, St Ives plc

A CIP catalogue record for this book is available from the British Library

ISBN 0-7181-3931-3

Contents

Acknowledgements vii
Introduction ix

ANDREA BARRETT
The English Pupil 1

ITA DALY
The Lady With the Red Shoes 14

JULIA DARLING
The Street 26

ANITA DESAI
Private Tuition by Mr Bose 34

JOAN DIAMOND
The Dowry 43

HELEN DUNMORE
Girls on Ice 49

PENELOPE FARMER
In a German Pension (Munich 1957) 56

PENELOPE FITZGERALD
The Axe 80

SUSAN GLASPELL
A Jury of Her Peers 89

CARSON McCULLERS
The Haunted Boy 113

KATHERINE MANSFIELD
The Doll's House 128

EMILY MEIER
Watching Oksana 137

CATHERINE MERRIMAN
The Experiment 160

NAOMI MITCHISON
The Hostages 175

JULIA O'FAOLAIN
Under the Rose 186

WENDY PERRIAM
Angelfish 202

E. ANNIE PROULX
The Unclouded Day 216

MICHÈLE ROBERTS
The Bishop's Lunch 229

ROXANA ROBINSON
Mr Sumarsono 235

TERESA WAUGH
Somewhere Out of This World 250

EUDORA WELTY
The Key 257

Acknowledgements

The publishers wish to thank the copyright holders of the following stories for permission to reprint them in this volume:

Andrea Barrett: to David Higham Associates Ltd for 'The English Pupil' from SHIP FEVER AND OTHER STORIES (W.W. Norton, 1996)

Julia Darling: to the author for 'The Street' from BLOODLINES (Panurge Publishing, 1995)

Anita Desai: to the author c/o Rogers, Coleridge & White Ltd, 20 Powis Mews, London W11 1JN for 'Private Tuition by Mr Bose' from GAMES IN TWILIGHT (William Heinemann). Copyright © Anita Desai, 1978

Joan Diamond: to Curtis Brown Ltd for 'The Dowry'. Copyright © Joan Diamond, 1996

Helen Dunmore: to A.P. Watt Ltd for 'Girls on Ice'

Penelope Farmer: to Deborah Owen (Literary Agency) for 'In A German Pension (Munich 1957)' (Gollancz, 1987). Copyright © Penelope Farmer, 1987

Penelope Fitzgerald: to Random House UK Ltd for 'The Axe' from THE TIMES ANTHOLOGY OF GHOST STORIES (Jonathan Cape)

Emily Meier: to *Stand* Magazine for 'Watching Oksana' (*Stand*, Vol. 37, No. 2, Spring 1996)

Catherine Merriman: to Curtis Brown Ltd for 'The Experiment' from SILLY MOTHERS (Honno, 1991). Copyright © Catherine Merriman, 1991

Naomi Mitchison: to David Higham Associates Ltd for 'The Hostages'

Julia O'Faolain: to Rogers, Coleridge & White Ltd, 20 Powis Mews, London W11 1JN, for 'Under the Rose' (first published in *The New Yorker*). Copyright © 1994 Julia O'Faolain

Wendy Perriam: to the author and Curtis Brown Group Ltd for 'Angelfish' from TWENTY STORIES, edited by Francis King (Secker & Warburg, 1985)

Michèle Roberts: to Little, Brown (UK) Ltd for 'The Bishop's Lunch' from DURING MOTHER'S ABSENCE (Virago Press)

Roxana Robinson: to Peters, Fraser & Dunlop Group Ltd for 'Mr Sumarsono' from ASKING FOR LOVE (Bloomsbury Publishing)

Teresa Waugh: to Peters, Fraser & Dunlop Group Ltd for 'Somewhere Out Of This World' (published in *The Oldie*)

Eudora Welty: to Marion Boyars Publishers Ltd for 'The Key' from THE COLLECTED STORIES OF EUDORA WELTY

In spite of all efforts to acknowledge Ita Daly, Susan Glaspell, Carson McCullers and E. Annie Proulx, this hasn't proved possible. The editor would be grateful if they or their estates (as appropriate) would contact the publishers, so that these ommissions can be rectified in any future editions.

Introduction

In compiling this third collection of short stories by women writers my chief criterion, as before, has been literary excellence, and I found it. But for the first time, I invited submissions, principally from authors' agents, and in particular of stories by little- or un-known women, whose work would nevertheless be good enough to sit alongside some of the major names of the twentieth century – Katherine Mansfield, Carson McCullers, Eudora Welty. It ought not to matter whose name is attached to which story; in theory, it would have been possible to have scrambled them in a hat and then re-assigned them, in order to focus the reader's attention not on the name and relative fame of the writer but on the work itself.

Outlets for short stories get fewer and fewer. Occasional anthologies such as this one are compiled, though not all use much work by new writers; one or two small magazines, with very modest circulations, struggle bravely on, publishing new short stories – the esteemed *London Magazine* and *Stand*, and *Panurge*, from the north of England, but few large circulation magazines and journals publish any fiction. Radio Four is one of the last bastions of good short story broadcasting but there is too little of it. In spite of this, huge numbers of people, and particularly women, continue to write short stories, without much hope of having them published, no matter how good they may be. I was inundated with entries for this collection, even after they came sifted initially by established agents, and anyone who runs or judges a short story competition knows that they are letting themselves in for not hundreds but thousands of submissions. Would-be writers, it seems, are not daunted or discouraged by the paucity of outlets for their work. It is the act of writing that is important, not the going into print or the opinion of others.

But quantity is one thing, quality quite another. Really excellent stories such as those here are rare and precious as jewels and dazzle with a similar brightness. When you read such a story, the writer's absolute sureness of touch, the strength and beauty of the prose, its versatility, its shapeliness, its grace, arrest and impress at once. And every one has that extra quality which is so hard to analyse or pin down; the originality of the writers. No one reading these short stories several times over, as I have, could fail to learn from them as well as to enjoy and admire them. They extend one's literary horizons, and deepen one's understanding of the human heart. They make an impact. They are memorable. There is nothing small-scale or miniature or trivial about them. Above all, they are so wide-ranging, so varied in setting and approach, scope and character that they give the lie to any remaining prejudice about women short story writers being concerned with trivial matters, domestic minutiae, or pleasant but ephemeral footnotes to important human and public affairs.

A Japanese man visits a close-knit, all-female family, in small-town America during the 1950s and changes them forever. The eighteenth-century scholar Linnaeus is wonderfully brought to life in his extreme old age in ice-bound Scandinavia. Sister Josephine of the Holy Face is the heroine of a trenchant, hilarious piece of black comedy. A young boy tells of his last weeks as a slave of the conquering Roman army, while an adolescent American boy bluffs desperately to save his face and his mother's pride in front of a cynical friend. A sailor in Odessa fantasizes about the little daughter he abandoned, and whom he imagines as the world-famous skater he sees on a flickering foreign television screen. An experienced hunter in the American outback is obliged to teach a rich boor to shoot. The themes and settings could not be more unusual or more varied. The past, the present, imaginary

countries, real people, the historical dead, inarticulate and vulner-
able children and rough men, remote, exotic places, extremes of
weather, wit, humour, suppressed violence, nostalgia, wistfulness,
sadness, betrayal, disappointment, age, youth, fame, obscurity.
This is the stuff of all literature. There are moments which move
one to tears, moments of terror, incidents which provoke cries
of protest, of pain, of recognition, or anger, in the reader who
becomes deeply, passionately involved in the world of one short
story for one short space of time. Intense relationships are held
briefly under a spotlight, under a microscope, up to our scrutiny
and our judgement. The styles vary, from the relaxed to the
violently compressed, the lyrically descriptive to the terse, the
sardonic and light to the poetically allusive.

Here are women writing wonderfully, women of many ages
and countries with a wealth of real, and imagined experience,
famous women, little-known women. The short story form is, for
reasons I do not fully understand, much practised by women.
But, much more important, is the fact that these are stories written
by fine writers. For, just as one might have juxtaposed the names,
perhaps one could have changed them to male ones without
anyone knowing the difference. This happens to be a collection
of short stories written by women because that seems to me to
be as good a way as any other of making a collection, in order to
introduce fine writing to an interested audience. But the truth is
that, when it is a simple question of literary excellence, gender
is immaterial.

The English Pupil

ANDREA BARRETT

Andrea Barrett lives in New York and has just received the prestigious National Book Award for her fiction.

Outside Uppsala, on a late December afternoon in 1777, a figure tucked in a small sleigh ordered his coachman to keep driving.

'Hammarby,' he said. 'Please.'

The words were cracked, almost unintelligible. The coachman was afraid. At home he had a wife, two daughters, and a mother-in-law, all dependent on him; his employers had strictly forbidden him to take the sleigh beyond the city limits, and he feared for his job. But his master was dying and these afternoon drives were his only remaining pleasure. He was weak and depressed and it had been months since he'd voiced even such a modest wish.

How could the coachman say no? He grumbled a bit and then drove the few miles across the plain without further complaint.

It was very cold. The air was crisp and dry. The sun, already low in the sky, made the fields glitter. Beneath the sleigh the snow was so smooth that the runners seemed to float. Carl Linnaeus, wrapped in sheepskins, watched the landscape speeding by and thought of Lappland, which he'd explored when he was young. Aspens and alders and birches budding, geese with their tiny yellow goslings. Gadflies longing to lay their eggs chased frantic herds of reindeer. In Jokkmokk, near the Gulf of Bothnia, the local pastor had tried to convince him that the clouds sweeping over the mountains carried off trees and animals.

He had learned how to trap ptarmigan, how to shoot wolves with a bow, how to make thread with reindeer tendons, and how to cure chilblains with the fat that exuded from toasted reindeer cheese. At night, under the polar star, the sheer beauty of the natural world had knocked him to the ground. He had been twenty-five then, and wildly energetic. Now he was seventy.

His once-famous memory was nearly gone, eroded by a series of strokes – he forgot where he was and what he was doing; he forgot the names of plants and animals; he forgot faces, places, dates. Sometimes he forgot his own name. His mind, which had once seemed to hold the whole world, had been occupied by a great dark lake that spread farther every day and around which he tiptoed gingerly. When he reached for facts they darted like minnows across the water and could only be captured by cunning and indirection. Pehr Artedi, the friend of his youth, had brought order to the study of fishes, the minnows included. In Amsterdam Artedi had fallen into a canal after a night of beer and conversation and had been found the next morning, drowned.

The sleigh flew through the snowy landscape. His legs were paralyzed, along with one arm and his bladder and part of his face; he could not dress or wash or feed himself. At home, when he tried to rise from his armchair unaided, he fell and lay helpless on the floor until his wife, Sara Lisa, retrieved him. Sara Lisa was busy with other tasks and often he lay there for some time.

But Sara Lisa was back at their house in Uppsala and he was beyond her reach. The horses pulling him might have been reindeer; the coachman a Lapp dressed in fur and skins. Hammarby, the estate he'd bought as a country retreat years ago, at the height of his fame, was waiting for him. The door leading into the kitchen was wide and the sleigh was small. Linnaeus gestured for the coachman to push the sleigh inside.

The coachman was called Pehr; a common name. There had been Artedi, of course, and then after him all the students named Pehr; Pehr Lofling, Pehr Forskal, Pehr Osbeck, Pehr Kalm. Half of them were dead. This Pehr, the coachman Pehr, lifted Linnaeus out of the sleigh and carried him carefully into the house. The kitchen was clean and almost bare; a rough table, a few straight chairs.

Pehr set Linnaeus on the floor, propped against the wall, and then he went back outside and unhitched the horses and shoved the sleigh through the door and in front of the stone fireplace. He was very worried and feared he had made a mistake. His master's face was white and drawn and his hand, gesturing from the sleigh to the door again and again, had been curled like a claw.

'Fire?' Linnaeus said, or thought he said. At certain moments, when the lake receded a bit and left a wider path round the shore, he was aware that the words coming out of his mouth bore little resemblance to the words he meant. Often he could only produce a syllable at a time. But he said something and gestured towards the fireplace, and Pehr had a good deal of sense. Pehr lifted Linnaeus back into the sleigh, tucked the sheepskins around his legs and his torso, and then built the fire. Soon the flames began to warm the room. The sky darkened outside; the room was dark except for the glow from the logs. Pehr went to tend to the horses and Linnaeus, staring into the flames, felt his beloved place around him.

He'd rebuilt this house and added several wings; on the hill he'd built a small museum for his herbarium and his insect collection and his rocks and zoological specimens. In his study and bedroom the walls were papered from ceiling to floor with botanical etchings and prints, and outside, among the elms and beyond the Siberian gardens, the glass bells he'd hung sang in the wind. In his youth, he had heard the cries of ptarmigan, which had sounded like a kind of laughter. The fire was warm on his face and his hands, and when Pehr returned from the horses Linnaeus gestured towards his tobacco and pipe.

Pehr filled the pipe, lit it and placed it in his master's mouth. 'We should go back,' he said. 'Your family will be worried.' Worried was a kind word, Pehr knew; his master's wife would be raging, possibly blaming him. They were an hour late already and the sun was gone.

Linnaeus puffed on his pipe and said nothing. He was very pleased with himself. The fire was warm, his pipe drew well, no one knew where he was but Pehr and Pehr had the rare gift of silence. A dog lying near the hearth would have completed his happiness. Across the dark lake in his mind he saw Pompey, the best of all his dogs, barking at the water. Pompey had walked with him each summer Sunday from here to the parish church and sat in the pew beside him. They'd stayed for an hour, ample time for a sermon; if the parson spoke longer they rose and left anyway. Pompey, so smart and funny, had learned the pattern if not the meaning. When Linnaeus was ill, Pompey left for church at the appropriate time, hopped into the appropriate bench, stayed for an hour and then scampered out. The neighbours had learned to watch for his antics. Now he was dead.

'Sir?' the coachman said.

His name was Pehr, Linnaeus remembered. Like Osbeck and Forskal, Lofling and Kalm. There had been others, too; those he had taught at the university in Uppsala and those he had taught privately here at Hammarby. Germans and Danes, Russians and Swiss, Finns and a few Norwegians; a Frenchman, who had not worked out, and an American, who had; one Englishman, still around. And then there were those he had hardly known, who had come by the hundreds to the great botanic excursions he'd organized around the city. Dressed in loose linen suits, their arms full of nets and jars, they had trailed him in a huge parade, gathering plants and insects and herding around him at resting places to listen to him lecture on the treasures they'd found. They were young, and when he was young he had often kept them out for twelve or thirteen hours at a stretch. On their return to the Botanic Gardens they had sometimes been hailed by a kettledrum and French horns. Outside the garden the band had stopped and cheered; *Vivat scientia! Vivat Linnaeus!* Lately there were those who attacked his work.

4

The coachman was worried, Linnaeus could see. He crouched to the right of the sleigh, tapping a bit of kindling on the floor. 'They will be looking for you,' he said.

And of course this was true; his family was always looking for him. Always looking, wanting, needing, demanding. He had written and taught and lectured and tutored, travelled and scrabbled and scrambled; and always Sara Lisa said there was not enough money, they needed more, she was worried about Carl Junior and the girls. Carl Junior was lazy, he needed more schooling. The girls needed frocks, the girls needed shoes. The girls needed earrings to wear to a dance where they might meet appropriate husbands.

The three oldest looked and acted like their mother; large-boned, coarse-featured, practical. Sophia seemed to belong to another genus entirely. He thought of her fine straight nose, her beautiful eyes. When she was small he used to take her with him to his lectures, where she would stand between his knees and listen. Now she was engaged. On his tour of Lappland, with the whole world still waiting to be named, he'd believed that he and everyone he loved would live forever.

Now he had named almost everything and everyone knew his name. How clear and simple was the system of his nomenclature! Two names, like human names; a generic name common to all the species of one genus; a specific name distinguishing differences. He liked names that clearly described a feature of the genus; *Potamogeton*, by the river; *Drosera*, like a dew. Names that honoured botanists also pleased him. In England the King had built a huge garden called Kew, in which wooden labels named each plant according to his system. The King of France had done the same thing at the Trianon. In Spain and Russia and South America plants bore names that he'd devised, and on his coat he wore the ribbon that named him a Knight of the Polar Star. But his monkey Grinn, a present from the Queen, was dead; and also Sjup the raccoon and the parrot who had sat on his shoulder at meals and the weasel who wore a bell on his neck and hunted rats among the rocks.

There was a noise outside. Pehr leapt up and a woman and a man walked through the door. Pehr was all apologies, blushing, shuffling, nervous. The woman touched his arm and said, 'It wasn't your fault.' Then she said, 'Papa?'

One of his daughters, Linnaeus thought. She was pretty, she was smiling; she was almost surely Sophia. The man by her side looked familiar, and from the way he held Sophia's elbow Linnaeus wondered if it might be her husband. Had she married? He remembered no wedding. Her fiancé? Her fiancé, then. Or not: the man bent low, bringing his face down to Linnaeus's like the moon falling from the sky.

'Sir?' he said. 'Sir?'

One of those moments in which no words were possible was upon him. He gazed at the open, handsome face of the young man, aware that this was someone he knew. The man said, 'It's Rotheram, sir.'

Rotheram. Rotheram. The sound was like the wind moving over the Lappland hills. Rotheram, one of his pupils, not a fiancé at all. Human beings had two names, like plants, by which they might be recalled. Nature was a cryptogram and the scientific method a key; nature was a labyrinth and this method the thread of Ariadne. Or the world was an alphabet written in God's hand, which he, Carl Linnaeus, had been called to decipher. One of his pupils had come to see him, one of the pupils he'd sent to all the corners of the world and called, half-jokingly, his apostles. This one straightened now, a few feet away, most considerately not blocking the fire. What was his name? He was young, vigorous, strongly built. Was he Lofling, then? Or Ternstrom, Hasselquist, Falck?

The woman frowned. 'Papa,' she said. 'Can we just sit you up? We've been looking everywhere for you.'

Sophia. The man bent over again, sliding his hands beneath Linnaeus's armpits and gently raising him to a sitting position. He was Hasselquist or Ternstrom, Lofling or Forskal or Falck. Or he was none of them, because they were all dead.

Linnaeus's mind left his body, rose and travelled along the paths his apostles had taken. He was young again, as they had been; twenty-five, thirty, thirty-five, the years he had done his best work. He was Christopher Ternstrom, that married pastor who'd been such a passionate botanist. Sailing to the East Indies in search of a tea plant and some living goldfish to give to the Queen, mailing letters back to his teacher from Cadiz. On a group of islands off Cambodia he had succumbed to a tropical fever. His wife had berated Linnaeus for luring her husband to his death.

But he was not Linnaeus. He was Frederik Hasselquist, modest and poor, who had landed in Smyrna and travelled through Palestine and Syria and Cyprus and Rhodes, gathering plants and animals and keeping a diary so precise that it had broken Linnaeus's heart to edit it. Twice he had performed this task, once for Hasselquist, once for Artedi. After the drowning, he had edited Artedi's book on the fish. Hasselquist died in a village outside Smyrna, when he was thirty.

Of course there were those who had made it back; Pehr Osbeck, who had returned from China with a huge collection of new plants and a china tea-set decorated with Linnaeus's own flower; Marten Kahler, who'd returned with nothing. Kahler's health had been broken by the shipwreck in the North Sea, by the fever that followed the attack in Marseilles, by his endless, grinding poverty. The chest containing his collections had been captured by pirates long before it reached Sweden. Then there was Rolander. Daniel Rolander – was that the man who was with him now?

But he had said Ro ... Ro ... *Rotheram, that's who it was, the English pupil.* Nomenclature is a mnemonic art. In Surinam the heat had crumpled Rolander's body and melted his mind. All he brought home was a lone plant of Indian fig covered with cochineal insects, which Linnaeus's gardener had mistakenly washed away. Lost insects and a handful of grey seeds, which Rolander claimed to be pearls. When Linnaeus gently pointed out the error, Rolander had left in a huff for Denmark, where he was reportedly living on charity. The others were dead; Lofling, Forskal and Falck.

7

Sophia said, 'Papa, we looked all over – why didn't you come back?'

Pehr the coachman said, 'I'm sorry, he begged me.'

The pupil – *Lofling?* said, 'How long has he been weeping like this?'

But Pehr wasn't weeping, Pehr was fine. Someone, not Pehr or Sophia, was laughing. Linnaeus remembered how Lofling had taken dictation from him when his hands were crippled by gout. Lofling was twenty-one, he was only a boy; he had tutored Carl Junior, his lazy son. In Spain Lofling had made a name for himself and had sent letters and plants to Linnaeus; then he'd gone to South America with a Spanish expedition. Venezuela; another place Linnaeus had never been. But he had seen it, through Lofling's letters and specimens. Birds so brightly coloured they seemed to be jewelled and rivers that pulsed, foamy and brown, through ferns the height of a man. The letter from Spain announcing Lofling's death from fever had come only months after little Johannes had died.

There he sat, in his sleigh in the kitchen, surrounded by the dead. 'Are you laughing, Papa?' Sophia said. 'Are you happy?'

His apostles had gone out into the world like his own organs; extra eyes and hands and feet, gathering, naming. Someone was stroking his hands. Pehr Forskal, after visiting Marseilles and Malta and Constantinople, reached Alexandria one October and dressed as a peasant to conceal himself from marauding Bedouins. In Cairo he roamed the streets in his disguise and made a fine collection of new plants; then he travelled by Suez and Jedda to Arabia, where he was stricken by a plague and died. Months later, a letter arrived containing a stalk and a flower from a tree that Linnaeus had always wanted to see; the evergreen from which the Balm of Gilead was obtained. The smell was spicey and sweet but Forskal, who had also tutored Carl Junior, was gone. And Falck, who had meant to accompany Forskal on his Arabian journey, was gone as well – he had gone to St Petersburg instead, and then travelled through Turkestan and Mongolia. Lonely and lost and sad in Kazan, he had shot himself in the head.

Outside the weather had changed and now it was raining. The pupil; Falck or Forskal, Osbeck or Rolander – *Rotheram, who had fallen ill several years ago, whom Sophia had nursed, who came and went from his house like family* – said, 'I hate to move you, sir; I know you're enjoying it here. But the rain is ruining the track. We'll have a hard time if we don't leave soon.'

Rolander? There was a story about Rolander, which he had used for the basis for a lecture on medicine and, later, in a paper. Where had it come from? A letter, perhaps. Or maybe Rolander had related it himself, before his mind disintegrated completely. On the ship, on the way to Surinam, he had fallen ill with dysentery. Ever the scientist, trained by his teacher, he'd examined his faeces and found thousands of mites in them. He held his magnifying glass to the wooden beaker he'd sipped from in the night, and found a dense white lime of flour mites down near the base.

Kahler lashed himself to the mast of his boat, where he remained two days and two nights without food.

Hasselquist died in the village of Bagda.

Pehr Kalm crossed the Great Lakes and walked into Canada.

In Denmark, someone stole Rolander's grey seeds, almost as if they'd been truly pearls.

Generic names, he had taught these pupils, must be clear and stable and expressive. They should not be vague or confusing; neither should they be primitive, barbarous, lengthy, or difficult to pronounce. They should have significant metaphorical or historical associations with the character of the genus. Another botanist had named the thyme-leaved bell-flower after him; *Linnaea borealis*. One June, in Lappland, he had seen it flourishing. His apostles had died in this order; Ternstrom, Hasselquist, Lofling, Forskal, Falck, and then finally Kahler, at home. His second son, Johannes, had died at the age of two, between Hasselquist and Lofling; but that was also the year of Sophia's birth. Once, when Sophia had dropped a tray full of dishes, he had secretly bought a new set to replace them, to spare her from her mother's wrath.

His apostles had taken wing like swallows, but they had failed to return. Swallows wintered beneath the lakes, or so he had always believed. During the autumn, he had written, they gather in large groups in the weeds and then dive, resting beneath the ice until spring. An English friend – Collinson, Peter in his own tongue, but truly Pehr, and also dead – had argued with him over this and begged him to hold some swallows under water to see if they could live there. Was it so strange to think they might sleep below the water above which they hovered in summer? Was it not stranger to think they flew for thousands of miles? He knew another naturalist who believed that swallows wintered on the moon. But always there had been people, like his wife, who criticized his every word.

He had fought off all of them. The Queen had ennobled him; he was Carl von Linné now. But the pupils he'd sent out as his eyes and ears were dead. During his years in Uppsala he had written and lectured about the mud iguana of Carolina and Siberian buckwheat and bearberries; about lemmings and ants and a phosphorescent Chinese grasshopper. Fossils, crystals, the causes of leprosy and intermittent fever – all these things he had known about because of his pupils' travels. Over his bedroom door he'd inscribed this motto; 'Live blamelessly; God is present.'

A group of men had appeared to the left of the fire. Lofling, Forskal, Falck he saw, and also Ternstrom and Hasselquist. And another, whom he'd forgotten about; Carl Thunberg, his fellow Smalander.

Thunberg was back then? Thunberg, the last he had heard, was still alive. From Paris Thunberg had gone to Holland. From Holland he had gone to the Cape of Good Hope, and then to Java and finally to Japan. In Japan he had been confined to the tiny island of Deshima, isolated like all the foreigners. So desperate had he been to learn about the Japanese flora that he had picked daily through the fodder the servants brought to feed the swine and cattle. He had begged the Japanese servants to bring him samples from their gardens.

Of all his pupils, Thunberg had been the most faithful about sending letters and herbarium specimens home. He had been scrupulous about spreading his teacher's methods. 'I have met some Japanese doctors,' he'd written. 'I have been teaching them botany and Linnean taxonomy. They welcome your method and sing your praises.' He had also, Linnaeus remembered, introduced into Japan the treatment of syphilis by quick-silver. He had left Japan with crates of specimens; he'd been headed for Ceylon. But here he was, sharp-featured and elegant, leaning on the mantelpiece and trading tales with his predecessors.

'The people are small and dark and suspicious of us,' he was saying. 'They find us coarse. But their gardens are magnificent, and they have ways of stunting trees that I have never seen before.'

'In Palestine,' Hasselquist replied, 'the land is so dry that the smallest plants send roots down for many feet, searching for buried water.'

'The tropics cannot be described,' Lofling said, 'the astonishing fertility, the way the vegetation is layered from the ground to the sky, the epiphytes clumped in the highest branches like lace . . .'

'Alexandria,' Forskal said, 'everything there is so ancient, so layered with history.'

'My health is broken,' Falck said; and Kahler said, 'I walked from Rome almost all the way to Sweden.'

In Lappland, Linnaeus said silently, *a grey gnat with striated wings and black legs cruelly tormented me and my most miserable horse.* His apostles did not seem to hear him. *A very bright and calm day,* he said, *the great Myrgiolingen was flying in the marshes.*

'We'll go home now, Papa,' the tall woman said. 'We'll put you to bed. Won't you like that?'

Her face was as radiant as a star. What was her name? Beside her, his apostles held leaves and twigs and scraps of blossoms, all new and named by them with their teacher's advice. They were trading these among themselves. A leaf from a new succulent for a spray from a never-seen orchid. Two fronds of a miniature fern for a twig from a dwarf evergreen. They were so excited that their voices were rising; they might have been playing cards, laying down plants for bets instead of gold. But the woman and the other pupil didn't seem to notice them. The woman and the other pupil were wholly focused on helping Pehr the coachman push the sleigh back outside.

The woman opened the doors and held them. Pehr and the pupil pushed and pulled. The crisp, winy air of the afternoon had turned dank and raw, and a light rain was turning the snow to slush. Linnaeus said nothing, but he turned and gazed over his shoulder. The group gathered by the fireplace stepped back, displeased, when Pehr returned and doused the fire. Thunberg looked at Linnaeus and raised an eyebrow. Linnaeus nodded.

In the hands of his lost ones were the plants he had named for them; *Artedia*, an umbelliferous plant, and *Osbeckia*, tall and handsome; *Loeflingia*, a small plant from Spain; *Thunbergia*, with its black eye centred in yellow petals, and the tropical *Ternstroemia*. There were more, he couldn't remember them all. He'd named thousands of plants in his life.

Outside, the woman and the pupil separated. *Sophia? Sophia, my favourite.* Sophia bundled herself into the borrowed sleigh in which she'd arrived; the pupil wedged himself into Pehr's sleigh, next to Linnaeus. In the dark damp air they formed a line that could hardly be seen; Pehr's sleigh, and then Sophia's, and behind them, following the cunning signal Linnaeus had given, the last sleigh filled with his apostles. Pehr huddled into his coat and gave the signal to depart. It was late and he was weary. To their left, the rain and melting snow had turned the low field into a lake. Linnaeus looked at his pupil – *Rotheram? Of course it was him; the English pupil, the last one, the one who would survive him* – and tried to say, 'The death of many whom I have induced to travel has turned my hair grey, and what have I gained? A few dried plants, accompanied by great anxiety, unrest and care.'

Rotheram said, 'Rest your head on my arm. We will be home before you know it.'

The Lady With the Red Shoes

ITA DALY

Ita Daly was born in Co. Leitrim in 1944, and lives in Dublin. Her short stories have been published widely in Ireland, the UK and America, and in her collection The Lady With the Red Shoes. *She has written five novels.*

The West of Ireland, as every schoolboy knows, is that part of the country to which Cromwell banished the heretical natives after he had successfully brought the nation to heel. Today, it is as impoverished and barren as ever it was, bleak and lonesome and cowering from the savagery of the Atlantic which batters its coastline with all the fury that it has gathered in over three thousand miles. But the West of Ireland can also be heartbreakingly beautiful; and on a fine April morning with the smell of gorse and clover filling the air and the bees showing the only evidence of industry in a landscape that is peopleless as far as the eye can see – on such a morning in the West of Ireland you can get a whiff of Paradise.

It is an irony which pleases me mightily that we as a family have such a strong attachment to the West. Our ancestors, you see, came over with Cromwell, footsoldiers who fought bravely and were rewarded generously and have never looked back since. And every Easter we leave Dublin and set out westwards where we spend a fortnight in McAndrews Hotel in North Mayo. It is a family tradition, started by my grandfather, and by now it has achieved a certain sacredness. Nothing is allowed to interfere with the ritual, and so when I married Judith one April day, some twenty-five years ago, it seemed quite natural that we should spend our honeymoon there. We have gone there every Easter since and if Judith has found it somewhat dull on occasion, she accepts gracefully the period of boredom in the knowledge that it gives me so much pleasure, while I in turn have been known to accompany her to Juan-les-Pins. An experience which, however, I have not been foolish enough to repeat.

McAndrews is one of the puzzles of the world. Built on the outskirts of Kilgory, looking down on the hamlet and on the sea, it dates back to the late nineteenth century. A large, square house, red-bricked and turreted, it is a reminder of the worst excesses of the Gothic revival, and every time I see its monstrous outline, lonely on the hill, my heart bounds and my pulse quickens. Nobody knows whether it was there before Kilgory and the village grew up around it or whether Kilgory was there first. But certainly it seems an odd place to have built a hotel, miles from a town, or a church, or even a beach. It is situated on a headland overlooking the Atlantic, but the cliffs are so steep and the sea so treacherous here that there is neither boating nor swimming available. Strange to build a hotel in such a place, stranger still that there have been enough eccentrics around to keep it in business for almost a century. My father, as a boy, used to arrive by train. The main line ran from Dublin to Westport and from there a branch line went to the hotel – not to Kilgory, mark you, but to the actual hotel grounds. 'Any guests for McAndrews?' the porters used to shout as one disembarked at Westport and was ushered on to a toy train with its three or four first-class carriages, to be shunted along the fifteen miles and deposited a stone's throw from the grand front door of McAndrews with its noble stone balustrade.

The toy station is still there, although nowadays the guests arrive by motor. I am always glad when I see my Daimler disappearing into the cavernous garages, and most of the other guests seem to experience a similar sense of relief, for though they arrive in motor cars, they continue thereafter on foot and the grounds and environs are delightfully free of petrol fumes. We are of a kind, McAndrews clientele, old-fashioned, odd perhaps; some would say snobbish. Well, if it is snobbish to exercise one's taste, then I admit I am a snob. I do not like the bad manners, the insolence of shop assistants and taxi-drivers which passes for egalitarianism in this present age; I resent chummy overtures from waiters who sometimes appear to restrain themselves with difficulty from slapping one on the back. I am irritated by cocktail bars and at a loss in the midst of all that bright and fatuous chatter. I like peace and quiet and reserve in my fellow man – decent reserve, which appears to be the *raison d'être* of McAndrews. I know most of my fellow-guests' names – like me they have been coming here since they were children – yet can rest assured that when I meet any of them again in any part of the hotel, I shall be spared all social intercourse apart from a civil word of greeting. Such respect for dignity and personal privacy is hard to come by in commercial establishments these days.

This year, Judith was ill and did not accompany me. To say that she was ill is something of an exaggeration, for if she had been, I would certainly not have left her. But she was somewhat under the weather, and as her sister was in Dublin from London, she decided to stay there with her while I went to Mayo alone. In truth I was somewhat relieved, for I am only too aware of how difficult it must be for Judith, gay and outgoing, to be married to a dry stick like myself all these years. I am glad when she gets the opportunity to enjoy herself and I had no doubt that Eleanor and she would be much happier without my inhibiting presence. Still, I was going to miss her, for like many solitary people I am very dependent on the company of those few whom I love.

But the magic of McAndrews began to re-assert itself as soon as I got down to breakfast the first morning and found Murphy, with his accustomed air of calm and dignity, presiding over the dining-room. Murphy has been head-waiter here for over thirty years now, although I always see him as more a butler, a loyal family retainer, than as a smart *maître d'hôtel*. His concern for each guest is personal and his old face is suffused with genuine pleasure when he sees you again each year. He came forward to greet me now. 'Good morning, sir.'

'Good morning, Murphy. Nice to see you again.'

'And you, sir, always such a pleasure. I'm sorry Mrs Montgomery will not be with us this year, sir?'

'Afraid not.'

'Nevertheless, I hope you will have a pleasant stay. May I recommend the kippers this morning, sir? They are particularly good.'

Such exchanges would be the extent of my intercourse with the world for the next fortnight – formal, impersonal, remote, and totally predictable. I have always found it a healing process, part of the total McAndrews experience, helping one to relax, unbend, find one's soul again.

I quickly re-established my routine, falling into it with the ease and gratitude one feels on putting on again an old and much-worn jacket. Breakfasts were latish but hearty, then a walk as far as the village and back. Afterwards an hour or two spent in the library in the delightful company of Boswell, a man to be enjoyed only in leisurely circumstances – I never read him in Dublin. Lunch and an afternoon in a deckchair in the gardens, looking out to sea, dozing, dreaming, idling. After dinner, another walk, this time more strenuous, perhaps two miles along the coast road and then back to McAndrews for a final glass of port followed by early bed with a good detective novel. The bliss of those days is hard to convey, particularly the afternoons, when it never seemed to rain. I would take my deckchair and place it in a sheltered spot and sit, hour upon hour, and watch the Atlantic at its ceaseless labours. I'd watch as the light changed – from blue to green and from green to grey – until an occasional seagull would cut across my line of vision and I would raise my eyes and follow its soaring flight to the great vault of heaven. A couple of afternoons like that and things were back in perspective. The consciousness of one's encroaching age, the knowledge that one is regarded as a has-been, became less painful, and there, on the edge of the Atlantic, a peace began to make itself felt.

But then I have always been out of step with the world and even as a young man McAndrews was a retreat, a haven for me. However, as I grow older and my unease increases, McAndrews becomes more precious. Here I can escape from all those aggressive young men with their extraordinary self-confidence and their scarlet-nailed women and their endless easy chatter. My son, Edward, who is married to a beautician – a profession which, I am assured, has some standing in this modern world – this son of mine tells me that my only problem is that I am a nasty old snob. This apparently puts me completely beyond the pale, and he views me as a pariah, almost as someone who should be put down. But we are all snobs of one variety or other, and what he really means is that my particular brand of snobbery has gone out of fashion. He has working-class friends and black friends, but no stupid friends; he would not dream of spending his holidays in such a bastion of privilege as McAndrews, but then neither would he think of going to the Costa Brava; he drinks pints of Guinness but abhors sweet wine. And he tells me that the difference between us is that he has discernment and I am a snob.

The generation gap is what any modern sociologist would inelegantly and erroneously call it, for, as I have said, there has always been as big a gap between me and most of my own generation as there is between me and Edward's. It is a painful sensation, constantly feeling that the time is out of joint, although as I sit sipping my sherry in McAndrews, in the pleasant expectation of a good dinner, I can laugh at my own foolishness and that of my son, and indeed, at the general idiocy of the human animal. This is what makes McAndrews so dear to me, but it is also what makes each leave-taking so difficult. I grow increasingly apprehensive before every return to the world, and as this holiday drew to a close and I finally sat waiting for dinner on the last evening, I was aware of my mounting nervousness and depression. I decided to console myself with that nectar of so many ageing men – a bottle of vintage claret. Now as I sought Murphy's advice, I ignored, with unaccustomed recklessness, both the price and the knowledge that if I drank a whole bottle, I would undoubtedly spend a sleepless night. There were worse things than insomnia.

By dinner-time the light had changed outside and a soft blue opacity was flooding in from the Atlantic through the great windows of the dining-room. This is the Irish twilight, most beautiful of times and that part of the day I missed most during those few years I spent in West Africa as a young man. It is a time that induces a half-wilful melancholia – helped no doubt by the glass in one's hand – and in McAndrews they respect this mood, for the curtains are never drawn nor the lights switched on until darkness finally descends. As I moved through the flickering pools of yellow light – for there were many diners already present and many candles lit – I was struck again by the solemnity of the room. Years and years of ritual have given it a churchlike quiet, a hint of the ceremony and seriousness with which eating is invested by both guests and staff. I took my usual seat against the wall, facing out towards the sea, and as Murphy murmured, priest-like, over the wine, we were both startled by a raised and discordant voice. 'Waiter, come here please.'

Together we turned towards the voice, both acutely conscious of the solecism that had been committed in referring to Murphy as 'Waiter'. The offender was sitting about six feet away at a small table in the middle of the room. It was an unpopular table, unprotected, marooned under the main chandelier, seldom occupied, except when the hotel was very busy. I guessed now that some underling, flustered by the novelty of the situation, had forgotten himself to such an extent as to usher this person to it without first consulting Murphy. And the arrival of this new diner *was* a novelty. She was not a resident, which was odd in itself, for McAndrews has never been the sort of place to seek out a casual trade; then she was alone, unescorted, a sight which was not only odd, but simply not done; ladies, one feels, do not dine alone in public. But the most striking thing of all about our newcomer was her appearance. She was in her fifties, maybe sixty, with hair and dress matching, both of a indeterminate pink. She wore spectacles which were decorated with some kind of stones along the wings. These shone and sparkled as she moved her head, but no more brightly than her teeth, which were of an amazing and American brightness. She flashed them up at Murphy now, and as he shied away from their brilliance, I could see that for once he was discomposed. But Murphy is a gentleman and within seconds he had himself again in hand. Stiffening his back, he bowed slightly in the direction of the teeth. 'Madam?' he enquired, with dignity.

'Could I have a double Scotch on the rocks, and I'd like a look at the menu.' Her voice had that familiarity which so many aspects of American life have for Europeans who have never even crossed the Atlantic. I don't think I have ever met an American but I have a great fondness for their television thrillers and I immediately identified the voice as a New York voice, tough New York, like so many of my favourite villains. Proud of my detective work, I sat back to listen.

The whisky had appeared with that speed to which we McAndrews guests are accustomed, and if Murphy disapproved of this solitary diner, his training was too perfect even to suggest it. He hovered beside her now, solicitously, as she studied the menu, and as she turned it over and turned it back again I noticed her face grow tight and apprehensive. I should say here that McAndrews does not have a menu in the usual commercial sense of that word. Mrs Byrne, who has been cooking there for the past thirty years, is an artist, and it would offend her artistic sensibility, and indeed equally displease the guests, if she were asked to produce the commonplace, vast à la carte vulgarity that one finds in so many dining rooms today. For festive occasions she will prepare a classic dish in the French tradition, and otherwise she keeps us all happy cooking simple but superb dishes using the local fish and meat and the vegetables which grow a couple of hundred yards away. She is a wonder certainly, but I can perfectly understand that one used to the meaningless internationalism of the modern menu might find Mrs Byrne's hand-written and modest proposals something of a puzzle. One would look in vain for the tired Entrecôte Chasseur or the ubiquitous Sole Bonne Femme in this dining room and be somewhat at a loss when faced with the humble, boiled silverside of beef followed by stewed damsons with ginger.

I could see that this was precisely the position in which our lady diner now found herself. She toyed with the piece of paper and looked up helplessly at Murphy. Murphy coughed encouragingly behind a genteel hand and began, 'Perhaps, Madam, I could recommend tonight the –' But she gathered her shoulders together and threw back her head. 'No, you could not, waiter. I know exactly what I want.' Her voice had taken on an added stridency. 'I want a filet mignon with a green salad. Surely a place like this can produce that – huh?'

'It is not on the menu, Madam, but certainly if that is what you require, we can arrange it.' I thought I noticed a hint of disapproval in Murphy's silky tones.

'Yeah, that's what I want. Nothing to start and I want the steak medium-rare. All you Irish overcook meat.'

I thought for a moment that Murphy was going to lose control, that years of training and polish would at last begin to give way before this latest onslaught of rudeness, but again he recovered himself. For a second he paused over his order and then looked up again and said, still politely, 'And to drink, Madam, would you like something?' The lady looked at him, genuinely puzzled as she held up her whisky glass. 'I've gotten it already – remember?' It was now Murphy's turn to look puzzled and I could see him struggling mentally before the implication of her remark became clear to him. This extraordinary person intended to drink whisky with her filet mignon!

As I watched my fellow-diner I wondered how on earth she had ever found her way to McAndrews. It was not a fashionable spot, not the sort of place that attracted tourists. There was a hideous motel only ten miles away, much smarter than McAndrews, flashing neon lights, full of Americans, supplying what they called an ensemble for the gratification of their guests. Surely this woman would have been much more at home in such a place? But as I studied her, I began to realize that this strange creature was actually impressed by McAndrews. I was sure now that she hadn't accidentally happened upon it as I had at first surmised, but that for some unknown reason she had chosen it deliberately. And I saw too that her apparent rudeness was no more than awkwardness, an effort to hide her awe and inexperience in such surroundings. My daughter-in-law – the beautician – when she visited me here once, gave a display of genuine rudeness, authentic because it was based on contempt, for Murphy, for me, for our kind of world. She shouted at Murphy because she saw him as an inefficient old fogey. But he didn't impinge at all on her world and was only a nuisance to her because he did not mix her cocktail in the correct proportion. This woman, however, was different, although I saw that Murphy didn't think so – indeed, whereas he was prepared to make excuses for Helen, as one of the family, I could tell that he had put up with as much as he was going to from an outsider. As the waiter placed the steak in front of her, Murphy approached, disapproval in every line of his stately person. 'Medium-rare, as you required,' he said, and even I, sitting some distance away, drew back from the sting of his contempt.

Other guests were taking notice now, attracted perhaps by Murphy's slightly raised voice, a unique occurrence in this dining-room. I could feel a current of mild disapproval beginning to circulate and I saw that the lady was noticing something too. She was looking discomfited but bravely she took up her knife and fork and tucked in her chin. I was beginning to admire her pluck.

Decency demanded that I leave her some privacy to eat so reluctantly I looked away. Soon, I was glad to see, the other guests lost interest in her, and when after a safe interval I glanced back at her table, she had finished her meal and was wiping her mouth with an air of well-being and relaxation. It must have been a satisfactory filet mignon. When Murphy brought the menu again she actually smiled at him. 'No, no,' she said, waving it away, 'nothing more for me. We women have to watch our figures – eh?' And as she glanced at him archly, I thought for an awful moment that she was going to dig him in the ribs. Murphy looked at her coldly, making no effort to return her smile. 'Very well, Madam.' The words hung between them and as she sensed his unfriendliness, indeed hostility, the smile, still awkward upon her lips, became transfixed in an ugly grimace. 'I guess you'd better bring me another Scotch.' Defeat was now beginning to edge out defiance in her voice. She grasped her drink when it arrived, and gulped it, as a drowning man gulps air. This seemed to steady her somewhat and taking another, slower sip, she drew out a cigarette from her bag and lit it. It was then that she discovered, just as Murphy was passing on his way towards my table, that there was no ashtray. 'Excuse me,' she sounded embarrassed, 'could you bring me an ashtray please?' Murphy turned slowly in his tracks. He looked at her in silence for fully five seconds. 'I am sorry, Madam' – and it seemed to me now that the whole dining-room was listening to his even, slightly heightened tones. 'I am sorry, but our guests do not smoke in the dining-room.' In essence this is true, it being accepted among the guests that tobacco is not used in here – a measure of their consideration for each other as smoke fumes might lessen someone's enjoyment of an excellent meal. I thoroughly approve of this unwritten rule – it seems to me to be eminently civilized – but I know well that on occasion, people, newcomers for example, have smoked in McAndrews dining-room, and Murphy, though perhaps disapproving, has never demurred. I looked at him now in amazement and maybe he caught my expression of surprise, for he added, 'Coffee is served in the blue sitting-room, Madam, there are ashtrays there. However, if you'd prefer it, I can –' The woman stood up abruptly almost colliding with Murphy. Her face and neck were flooded with an ugly red colour and she seemed to be trying to push him away. 'No. Not at all, I'll have the coffee,' and she blundered blindly towards the door. It seemed a long, long journey.

I finished my cheese and followed her thoughtfully into the sitting-room. All evening, something had been niggling me, something about that voice. I have a very sensitive ear I believe – I am rather proud of it – and although, as I had noticed, this woman spoke with an American accent, there was some underlying non-American quality about it. Something familiar but different about those vowels and th's. Now as I sat and lit my cigar, I realized that it was – it was so obvious that I had missed it until now. Her voice, of course, was a local voice, a North Mayo voice with that thick and doughy consistency that I was hearing around me since I had come down. It had become Americanized, almost completely so, but to my ear its origins were clear. I could swear that that woman had been born within ten miles of this very hotel.

We both sipped our coffee, the tinkle of coffee spoons falling between us. I watched her as she sat alone, isolated and tiny in the deep recess of the bay window, looking out at the darkening gardens. Beyond, there were still some streaks of light coming from the sea, and I knew that down below on the rocks the village children would be gathering the final bundles of seaweed before heading off home to bed. The seaweed is sold to the local factory where it is turned into fertilizer of some kind and the people here collect it assiduously, sometimes whole families working together, barefooted, for the salt water rots shoe-leather. Even the little ones have hard and calloused feet, sometimes with ugly cuts. Life is still hard in the West of Ireland. I looked across at my lady – *her* feet were encased in red high-heeled shoes with large platform soles. Her face, as she gazed out unseeing, was sad now, sad and crumpled-looking. I recalled again her voice, and as we sat there, drinking our coffee, I suddenly knew without a shadow of a doubt what she was doing there. I knew *her* intimately – her life was spread out in front of me. I could see her as a little girl, living nearby in some miserable cottage. Maybe, when I was out walking as a child with my Mama, I had even passed her, not noticing the tattered little girl who stood in wonder, staring at us. McAndrews must have been a symbol to her, a world of wealth and comfort, right there on the doorstep of her own poverty-stricken existence. Perhaps she had even worked in the hotel as a maid, waiting to save her fare to America, land of opportunity. And in America, had she been lonely, frightened by that alien place, so different from her own Mayo? Had she wept herself to sleep many nights, sick for a breath of home? But she had gone on, sent money back and always, all those years, she had kept her dream intact; one day she would return home to Kilgory, a rich American lady, and she would go into McAndrews Hotel, not as a maid this time but as a guest. She would order a fine dinner and impress everyone with her clothes and her accent and her wealth.

She sat now, a rejected doll in her pink dress and red shoes, for tonight she had seen that dream disintegrate like candy-floss. I wanted to go to her, to tell her, explain that it didn't matter any more – the world itself was disintegrating. She should realize that places like McAndrews weren't important any longer, people only laughed at them now. She had no need to be saddened, for she, and all those other little Irish girls who had spent their days washing other people's floors and cooking other people's meals, they would inherit the earth. The wheel had come round full circle.

Of course I didn't approach her. I finished my coffee and went straight to bed thinking how the world is changing, my world, her world. Soon McAndrews itself will be gone. But for me, this landscape has been caught forever – caught and defined by its heroine, the lady with the red shoes. Of course, you, on reading this, are going to see me as a sentimental old codger, making up romantic stories about strangers, because I am lonely and have nothing better to do. But I know what I know.

The Street

JULIA DARLING

Julia Darling has written stories for Stand, Writing Women *and Women's Press anthologies. Her book,* Bloodlines, *was broadcast on Radio Four's 'Woman's Hour' in February 1997.*

I can tell a good sausage from a poor one by putting it to my ear.

I was in the sausage shop when a stranger glided in. He said he was after a woman called Amy Steel, and that's me.

I didn't like the look of him. He smelt of brown paper envelopes, and civic corridors. I shook my head at the butcher and he told the visitor that he didn't know me. Also, I don't like meeting strangers in my slippers, and if I was in trouble, I wanted time to get ready. I turned and ran back home and put on support tights and pearl lipstick and sat waiting, pursing my furry old lips and looking out of the window that overlooks my street. It was unusually quiet. The dogs weren't barking, the babies weren't yelling.

I held my front door keys firmly in my hand, which is my way of being alert, and wondered what was about to happen. I'm known as a trouble-maker. Every day I complain about something. There's no shortage of matters to complain about. No one ever listens, and the more silent the officials are the more I complain. Perhaps this has finally dawned on the men in suits, hence the visitor.

Whenever I sit down, which isn't often, I consider the past. It's like a jigsaw that I'm always trying to get straight. I could see one of my nieces lifting her nets and staring at me. I had a feeling she was whispering about me to someone else. I closed my eyes and thought.

The street is long. Once it was a dirt track with a few rotting houses propped up either side. Now it's brick and mortar, and I oversee the cleaning of the pavement and the polishing of the windows. I was born here. A wild bull ran up my mother's stairs and got into bed with her. I am the result of that union. That's what makes me different. If it wasn't for me there wouldn't be a street, every single person in this row has some of my blood in them.

I complain about the state of the pavements, the wildness of the dogs, and the scruffy street sign that hangs off the house at the end. Sometimes I feel that my life has been a battle against abandonment, against the clouds of dust that keep settling over and over again, and against men and destruction. It seems to me that there are two kinds of woman; mad or bad. I am the second kind.

I was born before multi-storeys existed, when schools were inkwells, and women wrapped sticks into bundles and exchanged them for meat bones.

I'm so old now that my face is an ordnance survey map. You could find your way home by it. It's full of streets and hills and valleys and chimneys. I was the oldest child of thirteen children, which makes me special. I've been looking after babies since I was a baby myself.

They told me I was clever at school, but I knew that I must fail at arithmetic and English and geography, because there was no room for those things in my life. If I had passed and tried to continue with my education then it would have been no use. Ma would have rolled my schoolbooks into fire-lighters, and the words would have become smoke smogging up the sky.

I left school at fourteen and went away, to work at a hospital in the countryside. It was a place for poor women who were trying to forget. We did a lot of sluicing, and because we were young, we larked about, as there was nothing else to do in the country. All you could see through the windows was fields. I came home sometimes on the bus, which was filled with young girls who were maids and farmhands, and who carried parcels of food home to their hungry families. Some of the food was the leavings of rich people. I remember a girl showing me the teeth marks of a baroness on a pork chop.

It was alright at the hospital until one night when me and the other girls broke out and squeezed ourselves through the bars. I still have dents on my breasts to this day. We went to a bar in the countryside where cows were tied up outside and the villagers danced about like pigs. I drank six green beers and was sick all over a young farmer. When we got home the matron caught us hanging off the drainpipes, and I got sacked for being the ring-leader and bending hospital property.

All this time I read romantic books. I love books. I don't care what they're about, I just like the place they take me to. It's a room with big windows. When I was young the man who Ma slept with hated that room and would knock the book out of my hand. He even blew out the candles and the gaslight so I couldn't see, so half the time we grew up in the dark.

When I was fifteen I got disgusted with my Ma. She kept on having babies. They wouldn't stop coming out. I didn't agree with children then. All they did was eat. I liked the women in films who didn't have them; who lay about in floaty nighties and smoked in bed. I lost my temper with her and threw my keys at her man who dropped down unconscious. When he came round he was impotent.

He never spoke to me again, just wrote me orders on brown paper bags. There were no more babies.

I open my eyes. The stranger must have got lost. Ha Ha.

I feel as if everyone in my street is staring at me, and that something unusual is about to happen. I don't like it, my webby hands start to shake. I shut my eyes again and think.

*

When I was sixteen I started courting. I know for a fact that a lot of boys were scared of me and hid when they saw me coming. I wasn't slow in coming forward even then. I judged a man by his mother. If she was slovenly, or over-loving, or mean, I knew he would be no good, and that the sparkle in his eyes was as temporary as fairy lights from a market stall. Also I had a beautiful scarlet dress that I had handsewn myself, that was so silky it felt like running water in your fingers, and I didn't want it besmirched, so I was picky.

I was standing on the corner and waiting for a girlfriend when I met Billy. He came swaggering up and asked me for a kiss, so I hit him with my keys and cut him on the forehead. Later on he came round with a bandage on his head and asked me out to see Seventh Heaven at the Gaiety. That was more like it. The gas meter ran out when he was standing there and he gave my Ma a shilling and the lights went on for a long, long time and I confused this with love, or perhaps that's what love is, illumination.

Also, Billy told me his mother was a hairdresser, and an agoraphobic, and this worked in his favour.

He was a handsome man then. People thought he was foreign, because he'd been in India and he had dark skin and a jaunty moustache. His fingers were like a girl's, with delicate fingernails and thin wrists. It would have all been hunky dory if the army hadn't taken him off, and there hadn't been a war.

I'd hardly got to know him when he got sent to fight, and by the time he came back he was different. He had become a desert rat, and he had seen the insides of men's hearts strewn in the sand.

And he had lost his legs.

I would like to sue someone for what they did to Billy. I have written more letters than I care to count, but all you get back is regret letters.

We regret to say.

With our deepest regret.

Regretfully.

I hate that word.

One of my grandchildren bangs on the window pane and I open one eye. She looks like she's going to a party. She's wearing a pink dress with a bow at the back. I got her that dress. No one told me about any party. She is smiling at me and saying something about a surprise. Her mother comes running out and tugs her away, without even looking at me. A year ago I would have chased her down the street, but I'm tired. I don't even know how old I am anymore, I've lied about it so many times. I must be getting on. I was one of the older ones in the war when Billy was away.

I was a welder down at the shipyard. I've got scars round my eyes from the sparks. I built battleships. There was a whole lot of us. Women with flanks like horses and merciless wit. Most of them are dead now, or invisible. I see them sometimes in supermarkets, picking out the dented cans and pulling their hats down over their faces. I see them alright, but no bugger else does. We worked day and night, and never stopped until those ships steamed away up the river.

I reckon, after we got laid off, the whole enterprise went downhill. We even had to put on our own leaving do, with a couple of bottles of yellow gin off the black market. We had it in the engine room of a ship, and stripped off to our underwear and sang our heads off.

After we left the yards it was as if our time there was an embarrassment, because it was never mentioned. We had grown too big for our kitchens, and we couldn't work out how to be in them for a while. But I had a husband with no legs and that was that.

I couldn't have managed Billy if it hadn't been for his mother, Lotty, who lived a few miles up the hill. You see, Billy was mad. A lot of men were mad. The women ignored it and just carried on, but after the war we were basically living in one great open air asylum, with no drugs to hand. If it hadn't been for the allotment society it would have been even worse.

Billy's madness was religious. He took up chanting, and would hobble down the street in a pair of orange calcutta pyjamas. After I had the children he made them chant too. Nobody said anything, they were too busy coping with husbands and fathers who thought they were birds, or that they were being followed, or that they were still in the trenches, or the desert. We formed all kinds of sewing groups and jam-making societies just to get away from them. And we locked them in sheds in the garden, and I still say that no woman's life is her own without a shed and a stout padlock.

The men who went back to work were better off. They could hide in shadows of the shipyards and the mines, and the noise drowned their nightmares, but there was a time when if you walked the street at night all you could hear was bad dreams, flying about like bombs over your head.

I am sure I can smell meat pies. Something's cooking. I don't like waiting, and I don't like silence. It reminds me of death.

When Billy's mother died I cried for a whole month, and you can still see the ditches down my cheeks from the tears.

Her hairdressing business was in her front room, and it was one of the safe places for a lot of women. Nothing bad could happen to you there. It smelt of ammonia and burnt plastic, and there was always biscuits and gossip, and women's business to sort out (and I'm not talking about recipe swapping, I'm talking life and death). Lotty gave me free perms and rinses, and if Billy was bad all I had to do was wave a hair roller at him to shut him up.

When Lotty died we found her sat in the salon with a woman's magazine on her lap with an article in it on 'How To Deal With Bereavement'. Even in death she was considerate. At the church the pews were filled with women whose hair had been tamed by her clever fingers, and I couldn't help wondering what would happen to the appearance of the area now she had gone. I for one went downhill, and never got the hang of home rinses.

The stranger turns the corner. I can see him clearly now. He walks along my street, looking at the doors one by one. I squeeze my keys.

As he strolls along all my family start stepping out of the houses and standing on the pavement.

There's a lot of laughter in the air. I feel left out.

The stranger rings the doorbell. I slowly walk to the door.

'Yes,' I say. Stern. I built battleships.

'Are you Mrs Steel?'

I look beyond his cardboard features to the crowd of relatives who have gathered outside. My daughters are smiling and nodding their heads. Is it my birthday?

'Congratulations,' he smiles.

'What's going on?' I bellow. I am getting really mad. The bull in me is showing the whites of its eyes.

'You've lived here all your life haven't you?' A camera flashes.

'Watch it!' I snort. My keys are in my fist.

'And this is your family?'

I step backwards.

'We have a surprise for you.'

I take a swing at him. He tumbles backwards. Unfortunately I miss his head. He lies on the rosebeds shaking his bureaucratic head, and a dog licks his ear.

'What is it?' I say abruptly.

At this my eldest daughter steps out holding what looks like a plank under her arm. She holds it up. I squint. My eyes aren't good and a sudden ray of sunshine obscures my vision. Then I see it. It's a fucking street sign, and it's my name. They are going to name the street after me. Amy Street.

A lot of thoughts flash through my head then. People say before they die they see their lives, like a film, flashing in front of them. Everyone was waiting for me to be pleased, and to be polite.

But one thing I don't have in my blood is gratefulness. I take the sign. I look at it without smiling and then frown into the eyes of the local press photographer who waits for a sweet old granny to brush the tears from her eyes.

I think, 'Is this the prize at the end? Is this all? A bloody sign.'

The stranger knows he isn't wanted. He staggers to his feet, and mutters something aggressive in my daughter's ear, then stamps off down Amy Street looking for his lost face.

The ceremony ends awkwardly.

But when they've gone, and I see my people standing in the street, looking disappointed, I stamp my foot and let a smile winch up the corners of my mouth. It's about time, I thought. About time a woman left her bloody mark.

And then we have a party, and I get mortal drunk and tell them the story of my life.

Private Tuition by Mr Bose

ANITA DESAI

Anita Desai was born in Mussoorie, India, in 1937, and since the publication of her first novel in 1963 has won several prestigious literary awards. Among her novels are Fire on the Mountain *and* Clear Light of Day, *and she has also written children's books, including the bestselling* The Village by the Sea.

Mr Bose gave his private tuition out on the balcony, in the evenings, in the belief that, since it faced south, the river Hooghly would send it a wavering breeze or two to drift over the rooftops, through the washing and the few pots of *tulsi* and marigold that his wife had placed precariously on the balcony rail, to cool him, fan him, soothe him. But there was no breeze: it was hot, the air hung upon them like a damp towel, gagging him and, speaking through this gag, he tiredly intoned the Sanskrit verses that should, he felt, have been roared out on a hill-top at sunrise.

'*Aum. Usa va asvasya medhyasya sirah . . .*'

It came out, of course, a mumble. Asked to translate, his pupil, too, scowled as he had done, thrust his fist through his hair and mumbled:

'Aum is the dawn and the head of a horse . . .'

Mr Bose protested in a low wail. 'What horse, my boy? What horse?'

The boy rolled his eyes sullenly. 'I don't know, sir, it doesn't say.'

Mr Bose looked at him in disbelief. He was the son of a

34

Brahmin priest who himself instructed him in the Mahabharata all morning, turning him over to Mr Bose only in the evening when he set out to officiate at weddings, *puja* and other functions for which he was so much in demand on account of his stately bearing, his calm and inscrutable face and his sensuous voice that so suited the Sanskrit language in which he, almost always, discoursed. And this was his son – this Pritam with his red-veined eyes and oiled locks, his stumbling fingers and shuffling feet that betrayed his secret life, its scruffiness, its gutters and drains full of resentment and destruction. Mr Bose suddenly remembered how he had seen him, from the window of a bus that had come to a standstill on the street due to a fist fight between the conductor and a passenger, Pritam slipping up the stairs, through the door, into a neon-lit bar off Park Street.

'The sacrificial horse,' Mr Bose explained with forced patience. 'Have you heard of Asvamedha, Pritam, the royal horse that was let loose to run through the kingdom before it returned to the capital and was sacrificed by the king?'

The boy gave him a look of such malice that Mr Bose bit the end of his moustache and fell silent, shuffling through the pages. 'Read on, then,' he mumbled and listened, for a while, as Pritam blundered heavily through the Sanskrit verses that rolled off his father's experienced tongue, and even Mr Bose's shy one, with such rich felicity. When he could not bear it any longer, he turned his head, slightly, just enough to be able to look out of the corner of his eye through the open door, down the unlit passage at the end of which, in the small, dimly lit kitchen, his wife sat kneading dough for bread, their child at her side. Her head was bowed so that some of her hair had freed itself of the long steel pins he hated so much and hung about her pale, narrow face. The red border of her sari was the only stripe of colour in that smoky scene. The child beside her had his back turned to the door so that Mr Bose could see his little brown buttocks under the short white shirt, squashed firmly down upon the woven mat. Mr Bose wondered what it was that kept him so quiet – perhaps his mother had given him a lump of dough to mould into some thick and satisfying shape. Both of them seemed bound together and held down in some deeply absorbing act from which he was excluded. He would have liked to break in and join them.

Pritam stopped reading, maliciously staring at Mr Bose whose lips were wavering into a smile beneath the ragged moustache. The woman, disturbed by the break in the recitation on the balcony, looked up, past the child, down the passage and into Mr Bose's face. Mr Bose's moustache lifted up like a pair of wings and, beneath them, his smile lifted up and out with almost a laugh of tenderness and delight. Beginning to laugh herself, she quickly turned, pulled down the corners of her mouth with mock stern-ness, trying to recall him to the path of duty, and picking up a lump of sticky dough, handed it back to the child, softly urging him to be quiet and let his father finish the lesson.

Pritam, the scabby, oil-slick son of a Brahmin priest, coughed theatrically – a cough imitating that of a favourite screen actor, surely, it was so false and over-done and suggestive. Mr Bose swung around in dismay, crying, 'Why have you stopped? Go on, go on.'

'You weren't listening, sir.'

Many words, many questions leapt to Mr Bose's lips, ready to pounce on this miserable boy whom he could hardly bear to see sitting beneath his wife's holy *tulsi* plant that she tended with prayers, water-can and oil-lamp every evening. Then, growing conscious of the way his moustache was agitating upon his upper lip, he said only, 'Read.'

'*Ahar va asvam purustan mahima nvajagata . . .*'

Across the road someone turned on a radio and a song filled with a pleasant, lilting *weltschmerz* twirled and sank, twirled and rose from that balcony to this. Pritam raised his voice, grinding through the Sanskrit consonants like some dying, diseased tram-car. From the kitchen only a murmur and the soft thumping of the dough in the pan could be heard – sounds as soft and comfortable as sleepy pigeons'. Mr Bose longed passionately to listen to them, catch every faintest nuance of them, but to do this he would have to smash the radio, hurl the Brahmin's son down the iron stairs ... He curled up his hands on his knees and drew his feet together under him, horrified at this welling up of violence inside him, under his pale pink bush-shirt, inside his thin, ridiculously heaving chest. As often as Mr Bose longed to alter the entire direction of the world's revolution, as often as he longed to break the world apart into two halves and shake out of them – what? Festival fireworks, a woman's soft hair, blood-stained feathers? – he would shudder and pale at the thought of his indiscretion, his violence, this secret force that now and then threatened, clamoured, so that he had quickly to still it, squash it. After all, he must continue with his private tuitions: that was what was important. The baby had to have his first pair of shoes and soon he would be needing oranges, biscuits, plastic toys. 'Read,' said Mr Bose, a little less sternly, a little more sadly.

But, 'It is seven, I can go home now,' said Pritam triumphantly, throwing his father's thick yellow Mahabharata into his bag, knocking the bag shut with one fist and preparing to fly. Where did he fly to? Mr Bose wondered if it would be the neon-lit bar off Park Street. Then, seeing the boy disappear down the black stairs – the bulb had fused again – he felt it didn't matter, didn't matter one bit since it left him alone to turn, plunge down the passage and fling himself at the doorposts of the kitchen, there to stand and gaze down at his wife, now rolling out *purees* with an exquisite, back-and-forth rolling motion of her hands, and his son, trying now to make a spoon stand on one end.

She only glanced at him, pretended not to care, pursed her lips to keep from giggling, flipped the *puree* over and rolled it finer and flatter still. He wanted so much to touch her hair, the strand that lay over her shoulder in a black loop, and did not know how to – she was so busy. 'Your hair is coming loose,' he said.

'Go, go,' she warned, 'I hear the next one coming.'

So did he, he heard the soft patting of sandals on the worn steps outside, so all he did was bend and touch the small curls of hair on his son's neck. They were so soft, they seemed hardly human and quite frightened him. When he took his hand away he felt the wisps might have come off onto his fingers and he rubbed the tips together wonderingly. The child let fall the spoon, with a magnificent ring, onto a brass dish and started at this discovery of percussion.

The light on the balcony was dimmed as his next pupil came to stand in the doorway. Quickly he pulled himself away from the doorpost and walked back to his station, tense with unspoken words and unexpressed emotion. He had quite forgotten that his next pupil, this Wednesday, was to be Upneet. Rather Pritam again than this once-a-week typhoon, Upneet of the flowered sari, ruby earrings and shaming laughter. Under this Upneet's gaze such ordinary functions of a tutor's life as sitting down at a table, sharpening a pencil and opening a book to the correct page became matters of farce, disaster and hilarity. His very bones sprang out of joint. He did not know where to look – everywhere were Upneet's flowers, Upneet's giggles. Immediately, at the very sight of the tip of her sandal peeping out beneath the flowered hem of her sari, he was a man broken to pieces, flung this way and that, rattling. Rattling.

Throwing away the Sanskrit books, bringing out volumes of Bengali poetry, opening to a poem by Jibanandan Das, he wondered ferociously: Why did she come? What use had she for Bengali poetry? Why did she come from that house across the road where the loud radio rollicked, to sit on his balcony, in view of his shy wife, making him read poetry to her? It was intolerable. Intolerable, all of it – except, only, for the seventy-five rupees paid at the end of the month. Oranges, he thought grimly, and milk, medicines, clothes. And he read to her:

> *'Her hair was the dark night of Vidisha,*
> *Her face the sculpture of Svarasti . . .'*

Quite steadily he read, his tongue tamed and enthralled by the rhythm of the verse he had loved (copied on a sheet of blue paper, he had sent it to his wife one day when speech proved inadequate).

> *' "Where have you been so long?" she asked,*
> *Lifting her bird's-nest eyes,*
> *Banalata Sen of Natore.'*

Pat-pat-pat. No, it was not the rhythm of the verse, he realized, but the tapping of her foot, green-sandalled, red-nailed, swinging and swinging to lift the hem of her sari up and up. His eyes slid off the book, watched the flowered hem swing out and up, out and up as the green-sandalled foot peeped out, then in, peeped out, then in. For a while his tongue ran on of its own volition:

> *'All birds come home, and all rivers,*
> *Life's ledger is closed . . .'*

But he could not continue – it was the foot, the sandal that carried on the rhythm exactly as if he were still reciting. Even the radio stopped its rollicking and, as a peremptory voice began to enumerate the day's disasters and achievements all over the world, Mr Bose heard more vigorous sounds from his kitchen as well. There too the lulling pigeon sounds had been crisply turned off and what he heard were bangs and rattles among the kitchen pots, a kettledrum of commands, he thought. The baby, letting out a wail of surprise, paused, heard the nervous commotion continue and intensify and launched himself on a series of wails.

Mr Bose looked up, aghast. He could not understand how these two halves of the difficult world that he had been holding so carefully together, sealing them with reams of poetry, reams of Sanskrit, had split apart into dissonance. He stared at his pupil's face, creamy, feline, satirical, and was forced to complete the poem in a stutter:

> *'Only darkness remains, to sit facing*
> *Banalata Sen of Natore.'*

But the darkness was filled with hideous sounds of business and anger and command. The radio news commentator barked, the baby wailed, the kitchen pots clashed. He even heard his wife's voice raised, angrily, at the child, like a threatening stick. Glancing again at his pupil whom he feared so much, he saw precisely that lift of the eyebrows and that twist of a smile that disjointed him, rattled him.

'Er – please read,' he tried to correct, to straighten that twist of eyebrows and lips. 'Please read.'

'But you have read it to me already,' she laughed, mocking him with her eyes and laugh.

'The next poem,' he cried, 'read the next poem,' and turned the page with fingers as clumsy as toes.

'It is much better when you read to me,' she complained impertinently, but read, keeping time to the rhythm with that restless foot which he watched as though it were a snake-charmer's pipe, swaying. He could hear her voice no more than the snake could the pipe's – it was drowned out by the baby's wails, swelling into roars of self-pity and indignation in this suddenly hard-edged world.

Mr Bose threw a piteous, begging look over his shoulder at the kitchen. Catching his eye, his wife glowered at him, tossed the hair out of her face and cried, 'Be quiet, be quiet, can't you see how busy your father is?' Red-eared, he turned to find Upneet looking curiously down the passage at this scene of domestic anarchy, and said, 'I'm sorry, sorry – please read.'

'I have read!' she exclaimed. 'Didn't you hear me?'

'So much noise – I'm sorry,' he gasped and rose to hurry down the passage and hiss, pressing his hands to his head as he did so, 'Keep him quiet, can't you? Just for half an hour!'

'He is hungry,' his wife said, as if she could do nothing about that.

'Feed him then,' he begged.

'It isn't time,' she said angrily.

'Never mind. Feed him, feed him.'

'Why? So that you can read poetry to that girl in peace?'

'Shh!' he hissed, shocked, alarmed that Upneet would hear. His chest filled with the injustice of it. But this was no time for pleas or reason. He gave another desperate look at the child who lay crouched on the kitchen floor, rolling with misery. When he turned to go back to his pupil who was watching them interestedly, he heard his wife snatch up the child and tell him, 'Have your food then, have it and eat it – don't you see how angry your father is?'

He spent the remaining half-hour with Upneet trying to distract her from observation of his domestic life. Why should it interest her? he thought angrily. She came here to study, not to mock, not to make trouble. He was her tutor, not her clown! Sternly, he gave her dictation but she was so hopeless – she learnt no Bengali at her convent school, found it hard even to form the letters of the Bengali alphabet – that he was left speechless. He crossed out her errors with his red pencil – grateful to be able to cancel out, so effectively, some of the ugliness of his life – till there was hardly a word left uncrossed and, looking up to see her reaction, found her far less perturbed than he. In fact, she looked quite mischievously pleased. Three months of Bengali lessons to end in this! She was as triumphant as he was horrified. He let fall the red pencil with a discouraged gesture. So, in complete discord, the lesson broke apart, they all broke apart and for a while Mr Bose was alone on the balcony, clutching at the rails, thinking that these bars of cooled iron were all that were left for him to hold. Inside all was a conflict of shame and despair, in garbled grammar.

But, gradually, the grammar rearranged itself according to rule, corrected itself. The composition into quiet made quite clear the exhaustion of the child, asleep or nearly so. The sounds of dinner being prepared were calm, decorative even. Once more the radio was tuned to music, sympathetically sad. When his wife called him in to eat, he turned to go with his shoulders beaten, sagging, an attitude repeated by his moustache.

'He is asleep,' she said, glancing at him with a rather ashamed face, conciliatory.

He nodded and sat down before his brass tray. She straightened it nervously, waved a hand over it as if to drive away a fly he could not see, and turned to the fire to fry hot *purees* for him, one by one, turning quickly to heap them on his tray so fast that he begged her to stop.

'Eat more,' she coaxed. 'One more' – as though the extra *puree* were a peace offering following her rebellion of half an hour ago.

He took it with reluctant fingers but his moustache began to quiver on his lip as if beginning to wake up. 'And you?' he asked. 'Won't you eat now?'

About her mouth, too, some quivers began to rise and move. She pursed her lips, nodded and began to fill her tray, piling up the *purees* in a low stack.

'One more,' he told her, 'just one more,' he teased, and they laughed.

The Dowry

JOAN DIAMOND

Joan Diamond divides her time between the Alexander Technique and writing; she is currently completing her first novel. She lives between London and the Lake District.

Lucia sits in the courtyard of her grandmother's house. She embroiders the last pillowslip of her dowry. The fountain whispers to her as it plays low over broad green leaves. She listens and lets her soft back rest and seep into the thick stone walls. Her body is a part of this house and cannot leave.

In the old Jewish quarter, the carved wooden door is bolted.

Outside, in another quarter of Cordoba, she knows that Rodrigo's mother is setting her table with the best silver. Tonight they are to celebrate.

Lucia's black hair rests on her shoulder, shining like a raven's wing.

Last night in her troubled sleep, a grey cat entered her dreams. It perched on the high wall of the courtyard. As the full moon came closer, the cat turned to silver and began to wail. Soon the wailing changed into the deep round voice of a contralto. The cat turned to her with tender longing in her eyes and Lucia knew this was her mother singing to her. All night she strained to understand the words and then finally, as she lifted out of her dream, she heard them clearly:

'We are sisters, sister, sisters.'

How can my mother be my sister, Lucia wonders now as she

stitches blue leaves around a pink sunflower. At seventeen she still has not given up her childlike habit of making nature over into her own colours.

Of course my mother can come to me, she thinks, because she is already dead and the dead can travel. Everyone knew that. The bell towers had no glass in their windows so the dead could come and go as they pleased. Lucia left her window ajar at night in the hope that her mother might visit.

But in all this time her mother had never come and now, just as she was about to be married, she came and sang to her.

'We are sisters, sisters, sisters.'

She takes a lilac thread and starts to make a fish in the sky above the pink sunflower. Yes, certainly it is a riddle, she thinks.

Lucia had been raised by her grandmother, who is Catholic.

'Your mother is with the angels, very safe, very safe,' she assured her granddaughter a long time ago.

Lucia's grandmother is a plump and practical Catholic who talks to God whenever she wishes, mostly while ironing. Inside the house through the open shutters, Lucia sees her grandmother ironing and by the constant movement of her mouth she knows that the late afternoon conversation with God has begun.

As a small child, Lucia often watched her grandfather come into the courtyard at dawn. He started praying to God in a language she did not understand. The old man rocked back and forth on the bench in the courtyard.

The same stone bench she is sitting on now. She rocks herself a while.

But her grandfather put his hands over his head and wept. Why did this have to happen? Later he stopped weeping and returned to his study. Simple food was brought to him there. He never ate with the rest of the household.

'Why does grandfather weep and hold his head?' she asked her grandmother when she was still a child.

'Because God is telling him too many things at once,' her grandmother said.

'Why does he stay in his study all day and eat alone?' she asked.

'Because he is very busy writing down everything God said.'

Carved deep in the stone lintel above the door is a star of David. As a child Lucia thought that maybe God could see this star and it guided Him to the house and into the courtyard at dawn to speak to her grandfather.

She takes a yellow thread and begins to sew little eyes on the purple fish. She will never understand why her grandfather wept so much.

She remembers the one time she entered his study. Her grandmother was nowhere to be seen and Lucia followed the servant woman through the house, stepping quietly behind her skirts as she carried the tray of food to the furthest room in the courtyard.

Inside the walls were lined with old books and her grandfather sat at his table, his long white hair brushing his shoulders.

He caught sight of her as she peered around from behind the servant woman's skirts. His eyes were the palest green, like a cat and she saw that they had a fire in them.

He reached out one long bony hand to her across his table covered in books and papers.

'My child, my child, you have come to me at last,' then he wept and covered his head with his hands.

Not long after that her grandfather died. They buried the casket of his ashes under the stone bench in the courtyard.

Lucia feels better about her grandfather now that he has stopped weeping.

The purple fish is covered in yellow eyes. She ties off the thread and cuts it. As she searches through her basket for a certain deep blue, she wants to make a raven in flight, she thinks of what she will wear tonight for the celebration. Deep blue for the sadness she feels at all she is to lose, and amber for her trapped spirit. They will find her elegant in those colours but she will know their meaning. The amber belongs to her grandmother.

She puts down her sewing and walks into the cool house through the polished tiled hallway to her grandmother's room. On the low mahogany dresser sits the carved jewellery box. It still smells of cedar as she picks it up and presses it to her face.

As she lifts off the roof of the casket she sees a folded letter under the little roof. That's something new.

The amber necklace lies sleeping and glinting in the deep velvet of the casket along with other treasures in ivory and silver. But she puts them all down and takes the letter.

Lucia sits on the edge of her grandmother's four-poster bed, careful not to rumple the lace counterpane.

On the letter head are two angels intertwined and the heading:

SISTERS OF MERCY.

My dearest Mother,

Thank you for the news of Lucia's coming engagement, I praise the Mother of us all that we have been so absolved. I am fearful. They say that the children of incest bear offspring with tails. They say the sins of the fathers travel down unto the third generation. For my daughter's sake, tell her the truth.

I trust in God for your judgement.

Your ever obedient daughter,

Rachael.

She folds the letter noticing an address in Granada. She puts the little roof back on the casket, returning the amber to the darkness.

Quietly, she walks back to the courtyard and sits down with her sewing. She takes up her small scissors and cuts an empty window into the sky above the purple fish with yellow eyes. Then she puts the scissors into her pocket and walks through the silent tiled hallways to her room.

Below her window is the cedar chest with her dowry. She lifts the lid and takes out the first set of linens. In each napkin she cuts an open window and then in the table cloth. She continues through the pillow slips, the sheets, the counterpanes until the whole dowry lies like snowy mountains around her knees.

She puts the little scissors back into her pocket and takes the money saved in gold coins from underneath her carpet.

Empty handed she walks through the house to where her grandmother stands ironing and talking to God. She is thanking Him for the fine match he has granted Lucia and is telling him what a fine dowry she has made; the best in Cordoba.

'I have run out of black thread,' she interrupts her grandmother. 'I'll go quickly myself to the market.'

Her grandmother smiles and nods.

'You can wear my amber necklace tonight,' she promises.

Lucia walks into the bright street and down the hill to the open market place. She crosses the market place to the far end where the horses are sold.

'Is one of you returning to Granada?' she asks the traders.

The one with the beard up to his eyes nods to her in silence.

She takes a gold coin and holds it out to him.

'Will you conduct me safely to the Sisters of Mercy?'

He nods again.

Lucia rides behind the trader on a grey mare. In the fields the wheat has been harvested. Further along, silver oaks clasp the low-lying hills with their gnarled claws. Gradually the rising hills give way to mountains until finally she sees snow on the jagged peaks of the Sierra. Each night she cuts a little more of her raven's hair off and buries it where she sleeps.

*

By the time she stands in front of the small door of the Sisters of Mercy, her head is as cropped as the wheat fields she left behind.

'I am Lucia. I have come to join my sister,' she says.

'Yes, we knew you would come.'

The old nun leads her into the cloisters.

'They are all sleeping now. They have been praying,' the nun explains.

Lucia follows her over the stone corridors and into a room. They sit at a wooden table where a bowl of figs and a jug of water stand.

'Here.' The nun offers her figs. 'They come from our courtyard.'

Lucia dives deep into her pocket and takes out the scissors and the gold coins.

'I ruined my dowry,' she says.

'It was already ruined,' the old nun answers, 'but you can still sew.'

Girls on Ice

HELEN DUNMORE

Helen Dunmore's novel, A Spell of Winter, *won the first Orange Prize for women's fiction in 1996, and* Talking to the Dead *was published in the same year. She is also a poet, and her collection of short stories is forthcoming.*

Ulli has studied the brackish waters of the Baltic in high school science. She remembers field trips when she had to sample and test sea water before reading up on experiments which reported the leeching of DDT from the shores of our great neighbour into the tissues of Baltic herring. Our great neighbour. That was what they'd called the Soviet Union then. Ironic, defensive. That was the way to survive. There are no national borders as far as pollution is concerned, their teacher had emphasized. They should arm themselves with information. It was their future.

But there were so many campaigns. Campaigns against heart disease. Campaigns to solve the energy crisis. Campaigns against alcoholism. They'd been bored kids in caps with ear-flaps, trawling the water to see how many life-forms it supported, looking sideways at each other, grinning and giggling. The environment was less fashionable then. She recalls the very words, held in the glassy tissue of boredom like flies in amber. The relatively shallow, brackish waters of the Baltic freeze easily. Leaving aside, as someone had whispered, the fact that it's fucking freezing anyway.

Girls by the Sea

There's a good title for a painting. Or it could be a chapter heading for a novel perhaps? But not a good title for a poem. Girls by the sea. No, it definitely wouldn't work for a poem. You would begin to think of something sad, something elegaic, something long-gone. Long-gone good times.

Girls on Ice

No better. Trying to be ambiguous. Trying too hard. Can anybody trust a story which starts by shoring itself up with double meanings? Perhaps it's only by not having a title at all that you can hold on to the itch of the moment.

It's very cold. A yellow snow-laden wind is just veering round from north to north-east. Ulli and Edith are walking south-west over the ice, out to sea, and now the wind's blowing directly behind them, butting them along, wrapping their long coats around their thighs and knees so it's hard to walk straight. Edith clutches her fur cap down with both hands. She wears a very soft pair of fur-lined leather gloves which once belonged to her grandmother. The surface of the leather is finely crazed with age, but the gloves are supple and warm. Edith can remember holding her grandmother's hand and stroking the fur cuffs of the gloves. Now her own fingers have replaced her grandmother's.

Ulli's family does not have such things to hand on. Gloves made of the finest leather that could be bought. Made to last. And a bargain, really, if you look at it the right way; once acquired, they last through generations, just like money does.

Ulli is all in brilliant Inca wools; a cap of layered colours, a long scarf which she's crossed over her chest and knotted at her back, and a pair of mittens in ochre and terracotta. Her coat is a heavy secondhand wool greatcoat from a church used-goods store. She has dragged it in at the waist with a wide leather belt, and its skirts flap round her ankles. She likes the contrast between her own narrow waist and the wide swirls of heavy cloth.

Both girls wear laced leather boots with strong crêpe soles which grip well on the ice. The boots are a neat matt black, and they fit tightly around the ankles. They look rather like Edwardian skating boots, the kind with holes in the bottom into which you screw the blades. The girls share a detestation for parkas in muddy primaries, for built-up snow-boots and thermal caps with ear-flaps, for mittens with strings which run through the armholes, for padded vests and all-in-one zip-up suits in scarlet or turquoise. In fact they avoid all sensible practical outdoor clothing of the type listed as suitable for high-school, cross-country ski trips. Edith will spend hours washing lace in weak tea until it acquires just the right patina of age. Ulli has spent a fortune on silk thermal underwear so that she need not mummify herself in heavy jumpers all through the winter.

Girls on Ice

Here and there the ice surface is churned by tyres. Away to their right a yellow Saab is nosing its way out, squat as a pig truffling for fish. As far as they can see the Baltic has just stopped still as if a traffic policeman has put his hand up.

'It depends on what you mean by love,' says Edith, skirting a Sitka spruce someone has dragged out here with the idea of lighting a bonfire on the ice. But the fire must have fizzled out, or perhaps someone else put a stop to it. One branch of the spruce is charred, that's all, and the ice is puckered up where the fire has touched it.

Ulli pretends not to hear what Edith has said. She wishes she'd never brought up the subject. They've had this conversation so many times. Is Jussi getting hurt, is Edith responsible for this, is there anything anybody can do about it, ought Edith to pull out of the relationship even if it makes Jussi unhappier than ever in the short term . . .

And whatever anybody says it doesn't make the slightest

difference to Edith. That's just not the way she thinks. From her point of view, everything's fine. Jussi's having a good time. He must be, or else why would he stay with Edith? After all, Jussi's free to do as he pleases, isn't he? Nobody is making him stay. Certainly not Edith. People should relax more, Edith thinks. Why are they always talking about relationships? Either you are having a good time with somebody, or you aren't. If you aren't, talking about it doesn't help. And besides, Jussi is so moody these days. No fun to be with at all.

And Ulli can't help feeling that there's a great deal in what Edith says, even though it does make some of her friends so indignant that they stop discussing relationships with Edith and start shouting instead. There's certainly something lacking in Edith, they say to one another afterwards.

Edith is a fashion student. She's set up her loom in the house where she lives with four other students and she weaves marvellously rough bright cloth out of which she cuts jackets and coats. One boutique is taking her clothes already, though their mark-up is scandalous, Edith says. In a year or two, when she's built up her stock, Edith's going to open a shop of her own, in partnership with two other final-year students. There's no doubt that Edith's going to make it. This winter she's trying out a technique she calls scrap-weaving, and the room where she sleeps is covered with pieces of experimental cloth. She's making up small, close-fitting jackets, like skating jackets. There's a woman in England who breeds a particular type of long-haired sheep, and Edith's got some wool samples from her, Jacobs, the sheep are called. Edith is making drawings of brief, smooth, long-haired skirts.

Girls in Short Skirts

They could walk on the ice in their short skirts, with thick tights and legwarmers and boots. Why not? They'd love that nipped-in Russian look, that lovely balance of torso and leg, but they'd gain something nice. The sense of striding out.

Men Looking at their Legs

Yes, there'd be that of course. Does Ulli mind? Does Edith mind? Their legs are bold in dark green thick-ribbed tights and diamond-patterned Inca leg-warmers. Their legs are not anybody's easy meat. They have no desire to wear glossy nylon and to strip off their frozen skin along with their tights.

It's nearly too cold to think. They go on squeaking over the ice, not wanting to turn back and walk into the wind. When they look back, the wind slashes at their eyelids until they brim with tears. A curd of snot freezes from Ulli's nostrils to her lips. The shore is so far away. How far they've come, much farther than they meant. The town is just a little clutch of houses, humped round by low hills. Ulli feels as if she's swimming miles out. She'd like to float on her back as close as possible to the surface of the water and to the warm sun. She must block out of her mind the dark depths of the water heaving underneath her. When she looks back to shore she feels a shiver of fear, emptiness and weakness, as if her blood is pouring out of her.

Girls on Ice

The only ones out here now. The yellow Saab has crawled back to its heated garage, and the kids who were practising ice hockey and shrieking across the bay to one another have all gone back home to drink hot chocolate and make up their team lists. Because soon it's going to be dark. Already the horizon is folding in all around them. Already the reed banks have gone, and the spruce plantation behind the reeds. Blink, and the dusk thickens. Two soft round lights come on where the town is, and then there are more and more, coming on in warm rooms, as distant and inaccessible as the lights of a liner passing close inshore with a long moo from its foghorn. Blink, and you'll miss the way home.

'We'd better go back,' says Edith.

They turn, and the wind bites into them, glazing each particle of exposed flesh with frozen tears. Ulli's greatcoat flaps open and a knife of wind slides up the inside of her thighs. She trips, and barges into Edith. They just can't walk fast enough. The wind is shoving them offshore, like a flat hand saying BACK, BACK! But they are glad of its noise as it whines and buffets past their ears. They know for sure that they are too far out. The sound of the wind will hide from them what they are afraid to hear; the slow creak and unzipping of the ice. No good telling them now that the ice is solid from here to Ahvennanmaa. Out here you have to believe in ghosts and ice-spirits and broad-backed monsters breaking the surface with their snouts.

The girls link arms. This way it's easier to walk against the wind. They have to keep their heads down.

'Don't keep staring at your boots,' shouts Ulli. 'It'll send you to sleep!'

God, that is the last thing she needs. A sleeping Edith, keeled over on the ice, confident that everything's going to be all right.

It depends on what you mean by love.

A cuff of wind blows the girls sideways. Now there are particles of ice in it. The air's blurring. And surely it isn't quite so cold? The temperature's going up quickly towards freezing point.

'I think it's going to snow,' says Edith.

'You don't need to shout about it,' says Ulli. She doesn't want to give the weather any more ideas than it seems to have already. Now she remembers someone telling her that there's a current around here. It curves past the headland and then sweeps in close to shore. You want to watch that you don't get caught. But she didn't take much notice at the time. Who was it told her? It must have been some time last summer. They must have been going swimming, or perhaps Birgit had planned to take the boat out? They hadn't taken any notice. Birgit knew the coast like the back of her hand.

Now Ulli looks up and sees the snow coming from the north-east. The snow rushes towards them like the great filtering mouth of a whale. A ribbed curtain, swaying as it gains on them. The town lights have gone, but Ulli still knows where they were. She clings on to knowing where they were as the snow closes in on Edith and Ulli and wipes out the colours of cap and greatcoat, scarf and bold bottle-green tights until it's all one whirlpool of white. Ulli thinks of the current, a long smooth muscle flexing itself under them. Edith's cap has been torn off by the wind, and her wild brown hair flares upward, crusted with snow, snaking and streaming above her head like the locks of a Medusa. Edith's mouth is wide and her teeth are bared and white. Surely, thinks Ulli, she can't be laughing?

Girls on Ice

If you were to take a photograph of Edith and Ulli now, they would be dots. Black and white, merging to grey. Look closely and you won't see their images at all, just two darker splodges on a pale background, like a graze on the paper. They'll look as accidental and as unconvincing as those photographs taken to prove the appearance of ghosts.

Enlarged, Edith and Ulli would be cell-like clumps of dots, like embryos held together in the loose grip of one particular moment before the wind changed, before the snow covered them or stopped falling, before they reached or failed to reach the shore.

In a German Pension (Munich 1957)

PENELOPE FARMER

Penelope Farmer's first book, a collection of mock fairy stories, was published when she was twenty-one, and the first of her four novels for adults in 1984. Her best-known children's book, Charlotte Sometimes, *was taken as inspiration by the pop group The Cure, for their song of the same name.*

'Oh, to tell the truth, the plain truth, as only a liar can' – Katherine Mansfield's problem I see as my own, precisely.

Let me, however, begin at the beginning. Let me state an even more fundamental problem, which is that they don't make girls like me any more. At least I *hope* they don't. In those days, when they had not yet finished putting Munich back together again after its wartime battering, I used to walk to the Englischer Garten down street after street of façades with nothing behind them, whereas I was quite the opposite, my seething depths protected only by a veneer of solid English convention grafted on them, not very effectively, by my upbringing and education.

At the bottom of my suitcase, for instance, unused and disregarded, lay the card given me by the man I had met on the train before I even left England. (In those days you couldn't take a plane across Europe, you took a berth on a transcontinental express; to embark in one country, go to sleep in another, wake up in a third, gave you more sense from the beginning of just how far from home you were.) This man had urged me, with fervour, to call on himself and his wife. So why didn't I call on them, I wondered? Who knows what interesting people I might have encountered at their house. But I could not bring myself to do it. Probably I dared not, having still too vivid, too uncomfortable a memory of the shame and irritation, the unnameable, yet utterly frustrated longing I had felt that first night on the train, lying on my bunk, after he had visited me; after he had so abruptly gone away.

Such an innocent, boring little man, no doubt; whom all the same I saw as what – seducer? – rapist? – bringer of adventure? – though he was, in retrospect, as frightened as I was, if much more pleased with himself. His first overtures distracted me, had he but known it, not from the German grammar lying ostentatiously open on my lap, but from an ecstatic perusal of the Kentish countryside, in which churches and oasthouses stuck up little horns like snails, only a moment or so before the train had sped out of the interminable tunnel beneath the North Downs before Dunton Green. The last straggling houses of London finally left behind, this space of sky and land, its familiar contours defined by the shimmering colours of the amazing blue-green cabbage field, seemed every time I attained it to offer me the whole wide world I longed for, with a longing so vast these days it felt as if it would burst out of my chest and fly away like an eagle, like a dove at the very least.

'So you are trying to learn German?' he enquired with a kindly smile. Did it do, I wondered, mumbling a reply, to talk to strange men in railway carriages? No, of course it did not do. On the other hand, my mother had a vast store of anecdotes concerning *her* encounters on European trains, and it was, after all, such a particularly harmless question. And from a foreigner too, a species I felt obliged, this still being England, to put at his ease if I could. (English shoes never had such thick stitching round the uppers; Englishmen never wore such rimless spectacles as hid this man's pale, blinking eyes.) He was older than me, of course, but not that old. Indeed most likely, I realize suddenly, he'd be alive somewhere now, a thought I find more disturbing than comforting. Till this moment I've imagined him safely embalmed, like my seventeen-year-old self, in that distant time and space.

Actually he was much less interested in my learning German, I soon realized, than in practising upon me his mainly scientific English. A geneticist, on his way home from a conference in Cambridge, he had reached some pinnacle of ambition in meeting at this conference, being photographed with, two descendants of Charles Darwin. He informed me of it several times in both languages, before rummaging in his suitcase and searching for the photograph in question. Thereafter he launched into a lecture on genetics that I almost certainly could not have followed had his native language been English. I did my best to understand, however. I was interested in everything then, when allowed to be, well-qualified or not.

Indeed by now, sitting in that railway carriage, anxiously clutching the bag containing my passport and my tickets, my traveller's cheques, my German marks, I was beginning to say ecstatically to myself (and a bit contentiously to my mother, whom I had only left behind me in the purely physical sense), 'I've been picked up. *I've* been picked up.' I was also wondering, rather anxiously, what exactly I was going to do about it. Fortunately, when we reached Dover and the customs hall, my German friend had to go through the channels designated for aliens; they swallowed him without trace, leaving me free for the next part of the journey to sit in the sun, watching the gulls perform their joyful and noisy gyrations above the viridescent curves of the steamer's wake, while I wove fantasies round our meeting, a much more entertaining pursuit than listening to the German himself lecturing me on the subject of genetics in his almost indecipherable English. The trance into which I fell stayed with me afterwards. By the time I'd fought my way across quays, in and out of official sheds, through all the awkwardness of finding porters and small change and foreign phraseology, I'd almost forgotten the man who'd helped me induce it.

Indeed it was only much later, in the sleeping-car – so thoroughly had I forgotten about him or any other possible interruption, I had not even bothered to hide myself from the corridor by pulling down the blind – that I heard an unexpected knock upon the door of my compartment. I looked up startled from my book, to see the pale round face of the geneticist staring in at me. In one hand he was waving what looked like a photograph.

I felt I had no choice but to let him in. 'You see I found my photo,' he said, beaming at me mildly. The next moment he was sitting on the bunk beside me, jabbing his finger at several rows of people – mostly male, I observed, without surprise or rancour – standing on a lawn in front of a large porticoed building; so many of them in fact it was hard to identify any individual features. Invited to pick out my companion I could not begin to. Nor could I see anything distinctive in the two descendants of Darwin. Though I might have been more impressed had I not, all at once, become conscious of the fact that I was sitting, alone, on a bed, in a strange country, my head, my whole body in disquietingly close – worse, excitingly close – proximity to that of a strange man.

The scientist also realized it, and as suddenly, judging by the manner in which he snatched the photograph from me, by the haste with which he rose to his feet, brushing himself down, his gestures much too extravagant to suit him. He was shuffling his feet meanwhile in their undeniably foreign shoes. What round cheeks he has, I thought; what pale eyebrows; the way it catches on his specs, one whole eye is drowned in light; only a moment ago I could see the very flecks in the iris; I could see the little beads of sweat upon his forehead; was even close enough to scent, very faintly, the peppery smell of his shaving soap, the smell that always reminds me of my father.

'This must not do; not at all,' he was crying out. 'You nice, are you not nice young girl?' gesturing at the bunk behind me in a way that made me wonder if I was a nice young girl after all, or if I wanted to be. My curiosity was no less strong than my alarm and my embarrassment. Indeed, at this moment, he seemed much the more embarrassed of the two. Thrusting out a small white card, he gabbled something to the effect that he and his wife would be so pleased to see me in München, would I be so kind as to take his card. But he threw the card in my direction rather than handed it; our flesh did not touch in any way. At once, he scuttled out, sliding the door to with a bang.

Such an undignified anti-climax still qualified, I felt, as an adventure of sorts. It left me prey, moreover, to all kinds of indecent feelings which did not go away no matter how firmly I pulled down the blind on my window, looping the cords round the little hook provided for that purpose. Given the lack of likely and suitable people, the most unlikely, not to say unsuitable, one could arouse in me those days such strange, unfamiliar sensations I was ashamed to mention them to anyone. Yet it was undoubtedly a delicious as well as disturbing shame I felt as I took my clothes off and climbed into my bunk.

Over the years I've come to see the paradox in the way middle-class girls of my generation were treated in our youth. On the one hand we were considered helpless children, the responsibility of our fathers until the day we got married. ('I was relieved when you took her off my hands,' my father said to my first husband, years later. 'I never could manage her.' 'And can *you* manage me?' I'd asked, between rage and exasperation when he recounted it. 'My dear girl, I wouldn't try,' he said smoothly. (Who in fact spent all our lives together trying to do little else; something I could only combat, effectively, the day I understood it, the day I took my decision to walk out.)

On the other hand it was our fathers (and our mothers), precisely, who thrust us out of childhood by means much more ruthless than I would ever apply to any daughter of mine. Aged fifteen or so, along with most of my contemporaries, I had been marched off to have my hair permed, to be squeezed into a roll-on, a process from which I emerged looking like a podgy, elderly version of my mother. Two years later, my stay in Munich, at

Viktorin Strasse 23, was part of that even more painful process, as innocently connived at by its victims, known as 'being finished'. Which meant letting yourself be uprooted from friends, family, everything familiar, and dumped down alone in a foreign city with little grasp of the language and even less grasp of what you were doing there.

Twenty-five years before, my mother had been ecstatically happy in this very household to which she had sent me. But that was the precise reason, I thought, that I was not, since not only my mother but also my hosts, Baron and Frau Baronin von Kramer, were twenty-five years older, and their guests, elderly for the most part, seemed to have been chosen to match. If my youth roused kindly feelings in some of them, surrogate aunts and uncles were not what I needed in those days. What I needed were friends on the one hand, would-be lovers on the other.

I blamed myself, of course, for my failure, so far, to attract either. In particular, I blamed myself for my failure to interest, let alone attract, a French youth, called Alex, the von Kramers' only other lodger at all close in age to me. Not that Alex's lack of interest surprised me – from the start I could see our hopeless incompatibility. After a few days I became incapable of weaving the smallest fantasy round the young man's presence at the dinner table. Languid, seemingly supercilious, always dressed neatly à l'anglais in tweed jacket, white shirt, a paisley scarf tucked nonchalantly in at the neck, his light hair was licked back in a way no proper English boy would have countenanced for a moment. It was even a relief in some ways that he chose to ignore me, flirting instead, his charm apparently well-practised, with Frau Erna Wilhelm, a somewhat ripe, somewhat leonine redhead of forty or so. For how on earth was I, the plump English schoolgirl, to compete with her? A mere glance at her delicately hennaed hair, her sly smiles, her well-shaped bosom, discreetly, but not too discreetly, veiled by a brilliant silk scarf of abstract design, convinced me that I didn't want to compete, even if I could have done. I much preferred to try out my German on the eight-year-old son who visited her once (she was divorced, I discovered; the first divorced woman I'd probably ever met), or on the other guests at the Frau Baronin's dining-table; a fat little doctor from Hamburg; a withered Herr Professor of some undisclosed academic subject; finally an elderly widow called Frau Seyffertitz, never seen without two cloth bags, one stuffed with half-finished embroideries and other sewing gear, the other, much smaller, containing supplies of pretzels and breadsticks at which she constantly nibbled.

She had a stomach problem, Frau Seyffertitz told us, patting her plump belly often, as if it was a little dog. Her means of treating this problem apart from the pretzels and breadsticks was to eat heartily from every dish offered to her by the Frau Baronin, the wife of our host the Herr General Baron von Kramer, an ex-general in the German army. A white-haired yet ruddy and vigorous woman, who wore a black mourning dirndl throughout my visit (for whom she was in mourning was never, to my memory, disclosed), she seemed, unfortunately, to regard it as her duty to make Alex and me, the two foreigners, practise their German. It was also she who turned the conversation, whenever her husband, the ex-general, leaned towards one of us and in pursuit of some argument or other whispered hoarsely (he had had some recent operation to his throat), 'Wenn wir den Krieg gewonnen hätten', adding sometimes to me, to reinforce the point, 'If we had *von* the var.'

I don't think the Baron meant it aggressively. I really think he saw this remark as small talk only. My mother told me that he had used to say the same thing to her all those years ago, meaning the First World War in that case; he was sixty if he was a day, even seventy possibly. All these people were sixty if they were a day apart from Frau Wilhelm and Alex, whom as I said I gave up on first sight. So how could I make friends with them in any way I needed? Least of all, how could I take up the fat little doctor's offer of friendship? Having told me at length about his butterfly collection, he begged me over and over to call him Onkel Doktor.

I never could get my tongue round that, though I knew he was, genuinely, trying to be kind; so kind sometimes that in the fact of my failure, observing that he too appeared no less lonely than I, my eyes would fill with tears.

But that was how it was; I explored Munich by myself that wet and windy April, nearly thirty years ago, wrapped in scarves and a big coat the cut of which I cannot remember, let alone the colour. And for a week or two I scarcely cared if anyone loved me, let alone if I loved them. I loved a city and that was, for the moment, enough. I loved the churches, I loved the museums, I loved the pictures and statues and porcelain figures. I even loved the heavenly Konditoreien. Though I had no money to squander on their wares, the smell was almost enough for me, as I jammed my nose against their windows, admiring the spiced strudel on one tray, the caramel glaze of the pastries on another. The sweet ooze of the cream, the thick layer of the chocolate on the Sacher-torte might have been caressing my tongue already. With the same sensual joy I snuffed up all the unfamiliar smells that surrounded me; the reek of sausage and garlic and piss and God knows what else that made it clear, should I have doubted it, that this place wasn't England; that I had left home at last.

It is hard, trying to recreate that city I left so long ago – the tourist maps and guides to Munich cannot begin to fill the gaps in my memory. The names remain the same of course; as I work my way across the map the litany returns in a way that first pleases, then discomforts me. After a while I find myself chanting those once familiar names: Ludwigstrasse – Leopoldstrasse – Odeons-platz, Theatinerkirche – thereby raising, less by design than accident, a whiff of the same elation and despair that they once used to engender, that all cities where one walks as a stranger engender, though not always, thank God, with such exhausting intensity; to which the facile enthusiasms of Baedeker or Michelin, Blue Guide or Berlitz, are, of course, no useful guide whatever.

What can such guides tell me anyway about the postwar city

in which I found myself, with its discreetly fenced gaps and ruins, past which I used to tramp? Not only had they not yet rebuilt the Residenz, the ghost of Hitler hung over everything, though I do not know how aware of it I was; any more than I know if the sour miasma that as the weeks went by crept ever more pervasively between the paving stones was engendered by me or the place.

In the end, all I can say for certain is that most days I took the bus down to Leopoldstrasse, past the university, to Odeonsplatz. And that from thence I plunged into the city; where, indefatigable, I explored everything – which street or church or museum was which I scarcely remember, let alone where it was. I read, for instance, in the little Berlitz guide that I bought only yesterday morning, hoping to jog my memory, that Rubens is 'magnificently represented in the Alte Pinatotek by a vast panoply of talents'. Yet to my recollection, he was not in the Alte Pinatotek at all, rather in the Haus der Kunst, the house that Hitler built at the edge of the Englischer Garten, room after room of him, looming above my head. I daresay it doesn't matter if I remember rightly or not. The fact is that out of all the pictures in Munich, it's not the Memling or the Brueghel or the Raphael I remember, not the Giorgione, or the early Leonardo da Vinci (whose work I assumed that I adored; being too green as yet to consciously distrust those smooth surfaces; those ambiguous curves; those equally ambiguous smiles). What I remember, what I can see to this day, are the gigantic Rubens, even though I did not think I liked them very much.

Both my like or dislike are irrelevant I think. What is relevant is the exalted state in which I dwelt those days. Thus exalted how could I not admire – here adore may be the more appropriate word – the lush vigour of all that lively flesh, the tender tones in which Rubens described it? In those heaving breasts and buttocks, just as in a grassy field painted by some impressionist or other I could discern every tint, every colour under the sun. It was a lie of course, if ever there was one. Even I knew, even then, that Western flesh was various kinds of pink and nothing else. Yet this lie made so satisfactorily, such an archetypal, fleshly, decidedly curvaceous truth.

Indeed, nothing could satisfy me at that time, it seemed, except curves of one kind or another. The severe Gothick lines of the Marienkirche altogether failing to please me, I embraced, instead, for the first time in my life, half gladly, half uneasily, the ubiquitous Baroque. Its gaudy gilt, its sunbursts, its proliferation of limbs and torsos, its writhings as of man Laocoöns bound up in the coils of serpents, made me feel like Laocoön myself after a while, no less inextricably entangled. All the more so, paradoxically enough, when I discovered near the gilt altar in the Peterskirche a glass case in which a skeleton, its eyes and teeth replaced by jewels, was laid out on a velvet cushion.

To this day I can't be sure whose skeleton it was; I can hardly even be sure that I saw it – yet I must have done; I know there was a skeleton, as I also know there had to be one. Flesh is godlike; flesh is also grass; I was beginning to know that all too well. And in less hectic, gayer moods, I preferred I will admit the more delicate amusements of the Theatinerkirche, no less fantastic it is true, like a whipped cream confection from one of the Konditorei in some street nearby. On my way to the Ludwigstrasse I passed it almost every day; more often than not I went in and more often than not came out reminded of Mozart for some reason, soothed and with a lighter heart.

All the same I soon began to learn – could not avoid learning – that art is not everything; that a body fed with Rubens is all very well but does not make up for the lack of a body fed with other things. Love would solve everything, I thought, if I could find it – a dangerous belief at the best of times, and an inconvenient one, given the lack of love to be had. The letters from my family detailed a world once familiar, now as if irrevocably torn from my grasp. I knew nothing at that time in human terms except the central hallway at the heart of Viktorin Strasse 23, on to which all rooms led, including mine. A dark and gloomy place, the one small window obscured by a huge and flowerless plant, its walls were dominated by a twisted Christ on a crucifix, hung over a black sideboard where a bowl of glass fruit, placed dead centre of a long lace runner, was flanked by a row of napkins belonging to us, the von Kramers' lodgers. From there we fetched them at the beginning of each meal. Not till we held them in our hands did we begin our ruthless manoeuvres round the oval table which took up the rest of the room.

The little doctor, for instance, tried as hard to win a seat near me as I, even more singlemindedly, tried to avoid him; not because I disliked him, but because I did not want to have to pronounce those dreadful words 'Onkel Doktor'. Just so Alex, in a half-hearted way that would have been less insulting if he had taken more trouble over it, attempted to put the width of the table between me and himself, directing what energy he could muster to finding a seat by the voluptuous Frau Wilhelm. She aided and abetted his efforts on some occasions. On others, for reasons of her own, she removed herself, sat as far away from him as she could get.

All these manoeuvres I could understand more or less. What did baffle me in the beginning was the eager way in which each one of the guests, except for me and Alex, competed for seats next to the General Baron, or if not him, the Frau Baronin. Considering the problems of conversing with a man lacking half his throat, I failed to understand how anyone could want to spend a meal alongside the Baron.

I did not then, naturally, appreciate the significance of his rank, let alone understand that though our host and hostess had been reduced to running a boarding house for the past thirty years or so, it still, in Bavaria, counted for everything. The most exalted of the Hapsburg nobility, I was to discover, had sunk to such activities since the First World War, let alone the Second, without it having shifted one jot the universal reverence for the Almanach de Gotha. I was to meet, for instance, not so very long after, the then Emperor of Austria, father of a pale-eyed brood of chinless Hapsburg children, who also, like the von Kramers, kept a boarding house (in his case beside some Bavarian lake) at which carefully selected guests not only queued up to stay, they murmured 'Eure Kaiserliche Hoheit' when he supervised their breakfast in the morning. When he appeared at the dinner table some of them curtseyed; some of them even ventured to kiss his hand.

No one, it is true, tried to kiss the Herr General Baron's hand. As for trying to kiss the Frau Baronin's hand, she was much too busy trying to organize us two young foreigners into sitting either by her husband or herself, so that they could supervise the improvement of our German.

'And so, Elinor, where did you go this morning?' she would ask me at the start of every lunchtime, as she ladled out soup from the huge white china tureen.

'I went to the Haus der Kunst, Frau Baronin.'

'And which artists did you see? Which one did you like best?'

'I looked at Rubens today.'

'Elinor, why did you not go to the zoo? You will learn much German if you go to the zoo,' the Herr General Baron would roar from his end of the table. But I did not want to learn German; by now I had decided that if there was any language under the sun I did not want to know, it was German. Equally I did not want to go to the zoo or anywhere near it. I wanted to bury myself in Rubens, so bury myself I did, and when they asked what I was doing, declared it. In a little while my love of art became a standing joke, raising guffaws from the whole table – how could anyone, they demanded, want to see so many pictures, so many statues? Only Onkel Doktor from Hamburg did not tease or admonish me. He even ventured sometimes to make comparisons between Rubens, say, and Rembrandt, speaking to me in English at such times and ignoring both benevolently and blandly the frowns and admonitions he received from everyone else at the table.

His kindness often made my eyes fill with tears. Feeling I could not bear it, I hated him more than anyone else in the room, at the precise moment that I felt I ought to love him. Pretending I could not understand a word he said, I'd bend my face relentlessly to my Bratwurst or Rindfleisch, until at last, with a hurt but cheerful look, he went back to sprinkling wheatgerm on his meat from one of the innumerable bags containing vitamins and so forth that he set beside his place.

Later I would note, between pain and embarrassment, the way Frau Wilhelm – Alex had taken to calling her Erna these days – tapped her admirer playfully on the arm; as I would also note the disapproving look given both of them by the Frau Baronin. Frau Seyffertitz, meanwhile, kept nibbling away at pretzels like a squirrel. She was just like a squirrel, I decided. Her flesh curved as neatly and roundly as the tails of the red squirrels in the Englischer Garten, that another old lady, much thinner and spryer, used to feed every afternoon at precisely three o'clock. (I went often, these days, to walk in the Englischer Garten.) Opposite her the scrawny Herr Professor, who ate so fast his plate was always empty long before anyone else's, fired some question at me, scowled at the way I stumbled over every elementary phrase in my attempts to answer him, and all the time kept polishing his plate with his bread until it shone. Frau Wilhelm and Alex, meanwhile, would fall to discussing in French, oblivious of the rest of us, the poor dress sense of English women. They exempted me, of course, from their condemnations the moment they saw that I observed them, but only by the most perfunctory of gestures.

What an unseasonable April it was, the Frau Baronin had taken to proclaiming to the table at large. They were even, she suggested one evening, giving her husband an anxious smile, they were even forecasting snow. This led to the Herr Professor informing Onkel Doktor with notably sour triumph that he would have to wait longer to see his butterflies this year, which in its turn gave Onkel Doktor yet another excuse to describe to the assembled company the glories of his collection. He had not finished by the time pudding appeared, had only just come to a halt when it had been eaten and Frau Seyffertitz and the Herr Professor were laying competitive eyes on the last apricot, the solitary Zwetschgen-knödeln. (How did the Herr Professor remain so thin, I used to wonder enviously, when he ate twice as much as everyone else at the table, while the doctor from Hamburg, who only picked ruefully at the dishes set in front of him, remained as round as a plum?) Not that such a pressing concern could prevent the Professor from starting to bewail yet again his days at the university, or Frau Seyffertitz from complimenting the Herr Baron at every turn. One day she had even offered to embroider his family motto, went so far as to pull a range of embroidery silks from her bag in order that he should choose the colours.

As time went on, much as I despised my elders' greed, I found myself understanding it all too well; beginning to fear that I too, like them, would end my life unloved once art ceased to be sufficient nourishment, what then was left for me but food? While I could not actually bring myself to compete for the remaining dumpling or pancake, meals all too soon became the highlights of my days. Between while I sat alone in my room off the dining-hall, with its two beds, only one of them slept in, writing an interminable diary, laying bare my puny soul, and equally interminable letters to my parents and anyone else I could think of. I also struggled to compose some children's stories. But all such things sucked nourishment from me rather than replenished it. They did not warm me any way that I could tell.

These days instead of rationing myself to a single roll at breakfast, I took two or even three. I accepted second helpings whenever they were offered, and far from declining puddings as I had done in the beginning, pretending I wasn't hungry, I devoured every crumb of every last one of them, cakes, pancakes, Aprikosen-zwetschgenknödeln. Sometimes I even bought the cakes I could not rightly afford from the Konditorei in the next door street, and gorged, trembling, alone in my room, eating so fast I barely tasted them. In much the same way I would have masturbated, I daresay, had I known what masturbation was or what it could do for me – as guiltily and with as furtive, not very pleasurable, pleasure.

I put on weight of course. Given the lack of long mirrors in the von Kramer establishment, I registered the fact from the tightness of my clothes. Though I attempted sometimes to counter my suspicions – hadn't that skirt, for instance, been tight when I bought it? – furtive glances in the shop windows that I passed always confirmed my fears instead of denying them.

I also grew constipated. For a whole week once, weighed down miserably by Schinken and Schlachplatten, by Knödeln and Kartoffeln, I did not succeed in evacuating my bowels. As ashamed and embarrassed as if I had been trying to buy contraceptives I took to haunting chemists' shops in search of laxatives. Though I pretended to look for shampoo and face cream, I would always be forced in the end, my German dictionary lacking all the words I needed, to point at this shelf or that, meanwhile muttering approximations to some incomprehending assistant. 'You mean –?' he or she would say at last, shouting the word or brand name to the shop at large; whereupon I would scuttle home blushing, to gobble up, privately, the pills or the granules or the syrup, whatever they provided.

Of the three brands I bought with my fast shrinking funds, only the third proved effective, so effective in fact, that I was forced to haunt for most of a morning one of the two lavatories that the pension boasted, my recalcitrant bowels griping with a viciousness that made me retch with pain. The violence in which they finally exploded left me sitting on the seat for quite ten minutes after, gasping and faint. My head bowed to my lap, I felt more wretched and lonely than in the whole of my previous life; so wretched and so lonely, that the sound of some other would-be user rattling at the lavatory door with ever-increasing frenzy, made no sense to me at all.

Two days later I dared think the worst was over. It was fortunate for me perhaps that I did not know that it actually only heralded the beginning of the worst when the Frau Baronin ushered into my room a tall, limp, rather sulky-looking English girl, wearing a regulation school coat made of blue tweed, a brown velvet beret plonked firmly on the middle of her head. I did not mind in the least having to share my room. I not only found friendship in the sulky girl. At one remove, which was really about as near as I wanted, if I am honest, I found something like love itself.

This girl, it so happened – wasn't her name Catrina? – she had a Scots name, certainly; her father, unlike mine, was definitely very rich – had been sent to Munich to keep her from the arms of some unsuitable, that is to say, poor, lover, a music student, her relationship with whom she described each night in passionate whispers after we had put out our light. I in my narrow bed lay avid for details, trying not to appear so, she in hers seemed equally anxious to divulge them, if only in her own good time.

It lasted for perhaps three or four days, this glorious friendship. No longer did I struggle at the dinner table to convey platitudinous thoughts in my halting German. Catrina was not only impervious to all attempts to make us sit separately, she was equally impervious to the frowns of the Herr General Baron and the Frau Baronin; she and I giggled together in English from the beginning of each meal to the end. I gave only the briefest of pitying thoughts to my abandoned Onkel Doktor, even if I did try now and then to soften Catrina's all too obvious amusement at his butterfly collections, at his packets of wheatgerm, vitamins and bran.

The very weather improved those days as I remembered it. On the third day the sun came out, we took a tram from the Hauptbahnhof, and went to Nymphenberg to look at the park and the palace and the china makers, whose white figures had bowed and simpered in my mother's most treasured cabinets all the days of my life. 'Aren't they *ghastly*?' Catrina dismissed them so cheerfully I was disconcerted, even a little hurt. What did it matter if I loved them mainly because my mother did? I was in Munich mainly to follow in my mother's footsteps. 'You can't really like them?' Catrina persisted, scornfully, in a way which was the beginning of the end, had I but known it. Since I did not know it, the whole place, the fountains, the canals, the gravel walks, filled me with such acute yet subtle pleasure that for once

I did not crave the less disciplined, more English arrangements of my favourite Englischer Garten.

That night Alex invited Catrina and me to a Bierkeller in the Ludwigstrasse. This extraordinary event did not surprise Catrina in the least; she grimaced a little before accepting his invitation. I was baffled on the other hand. Alex, to my relief, had ignored Catrina till now no less assiduously than he had persisted in ignoring me. It was only when the three of us were sitting in our little stall with mugs of lager before us, that it occurred to me that he might be as alarmed by Catrina and me, individually, as I was alarmed by him; and that it was only there being two of us made either one a safe companion.

A little later – our mainly gloomy silence had been made all the gloomier by the accordion which suddenly struck up, setting two men in lederhosen to perform a thigh-slapping dance – it occurred to me, also for the first time, that despite the dinner-table flirtations, I had never seen Alex in the company of Frau Wilhelm on any other occasion; I had never, come to think of it, seen him in the company of anyone. Could he in fact be as lonely as I? Not that such an insight did me the slightest good. When I mentioned it to Catrina later, she accused me of self-pity. I do not know what, if anything, I had said to offend her, but something seemed to have done, judging by the fact that those were almost the last words she addressed to me for the whole of the remaining time during which she shared my room, apart from the suggestion, once, that I could do with losing weight.

Though exchanging scowls with Catrina, I did not find it in me to blame her. I do not blame her now, much. I daresay she was missing her lover as painfully as I was missing my family. Taking it in turns to beat at the window of our little room like birds penned in my sky, we were both of us at that time, I think, exiled from our proper place, at least temporarily crazy.

After a week she went quite as suddenly as she'd come. The first I knew of it was when, giving me a triumphant and defiant look – puzzled, I returned the defiance, if not the air of triumph – she heaved her suitcase down from the narrow wardrobe in which our clothes had been competing for space and dumped it on her bed. Shortly after she walked out, without even saying good-bye. Though that was the last I saw or heard of her, I wondered occasionally if she had used that iron will, hidden so guilefully beneath the limp, schoolgirl exterior, to get herself reunited with her lover.

She had, in some way, wounded me beyond endurance; the exhilaration of my defiance faded as soon as she departed and how I hung on to things I really do not know. Day by day the streets seemed bleaker and colder. Though I took up once again my indefatigable explorations, penetrating deeper and deeper into the map of the ruined city, I only reached places bound to exacerbate my grief. One day for instance, in the pouring rain, I found myself confronting the fascist spaces of Hitler's Königsplatz. Its vast perspective gleamed at me like steel under the frigid sky; the pitiless spears of rain seemed to spring back up at me from every stone they pelted.

But the museum to which I ran for shelter did not treat me any better. It was not the fault of the Blaue Reiter group that I encountered it at such a time – to this day I don't know if its screams of colour really were as chaotic as I thought. I only knew that I ran from them no less frantically than I had run from the relentless space laid down by the same Adolf Hitler who had named such painting decadent; he could call it as far as I was concerned any name he liked – he could call *anything* any name he liked. I could not even endure Rubens any more, the Baroque seemed at once both corrupt and overdone; the Theatinerkirche itself was like nothing so much as an over-iced wedding-cake.

All I wanted these days was England; that was why I kept fleeing to the Englischer Garten, though I could see the irony even then. Having dreamed of escaping England all my adolescent years, I discovered that what I'd actually wanted to escape was myself, and since this was not possible – quite the contrary in fact – redirected all my yearnings to the country I'd disowned. Which now, it seemed, I passionately loved. Not in a patriotic way exactly; more in an aesthetic, even a sensuous one. I would lie in bed, for instance, conjuring up detail by detail the view from the train beyond Dunton Green tunnel, and hugging it to me like a long lost lover. As I would also conjure up and embrace the view from my bedroom window at home, the elm tree they had had to cut down a year ago, and beyond the sweep of hill, dotted with Friesian cows, among which stood a stone folly of some kind, part Gothick, part cupola, mad, sorry and joyful all at once. (There was a cupola, too, in the Englischer Garten; but not far away from it ran the cold, green Isar, that most central European, most un-English of rivers.)

It snowed at last; it snowed for two whole days. Though it did not settle, I kept myself indoors. On the third day when it ceased, more or less, I went out for a while, and returned to Viktorin Strasse 23 to find there was sauerkraut for lunch, the one thing that in all my craving for food I had never learned to love. Fortunately even my lust for food had left me by now. Gone way beyond I thought, despairingly, the lovelessness of the thin Herr Professor or the plump Frau Seyffertitz, I no longer cared whose turn it was to win the last slice of meat, the remaining apricot.

'Well, Elinor,' cried the Frau Baronin as I pushed my fork around my plate, picking out caraway seeds and eating them with almost masochistic pleasure – I'd already learned that by stirring up one hurt you could distract yourself from another – 'Well, Elinor and what did you do with yourself this morning?'

'I looked at pictures,' I said as usual; though actually I had no more taste for pictures. Defiantly, staring them all out, I added, 'I went once more to see the Rubens.'

Onkel Doktor at my side knew how unhappy I was I am certain, the way he touched my arm. The very clock on the wall – I mean the clocks, there were several – ticked in self-righteous, not entirely unanimous sorrow. I wanted to shout at them, 'Will you kindly shut up,' or rather just 'Shut *up*.' All I did, however, was thrust

Onkel Doktor's hands from my arm, or try to. In the end I found no energy even for that. It was the first time he had touched me. As I looked at him with swimming eyes his face swung to and fro before me. 'No,' I said beneath my breath. 'No, no, no.' But I do not think anybody heard, maybe not even him.

'So many pictures, Elinor,' someone was saying. 'Do you never get tired of pictures?'

And now the Herr General Baron was puffing up the bellows in his mutilated throat. He was leaning forward, the stubble on his neck as unrelenting as the grey hairs that sprouted from his ears and from his nose, as unsightly as the sinister brown speckles scattered across his face and neck. He was saying, his voice between a whisper and a croak, 'Why not visit the zoo? At the zoo, Elinor, you will much German learn.'

My tears fled from whence they had come. I regarded him coldly, my eyes dry as a bone. 'How is that?' I enquired, in my best German. At each word my voice grew louder. 'How is that, Herr General? Do even the animals speak German? Is it only me who does not?'

I spat out the last words. At once I jumped to my feet. I said in English to the Frau Baronin – I actually liked the Frau Baronin, so forgave her, mostly, for her attempts to make me speak her awful language – 'I'm not hungry. Please excuse me.' And then, evading her concerned look, I fled, grabbing my coat from the little entrance hall, and running most of the way to the folk museum on the far side of the Englischer Garten, full of Nymphenberger figures on the one hand, dark Bavarian carving on the other; the first frivolous and inane, the second not only crude but cruel. I wandered between them weeping, not caring in the least who saw me. At last when I had sucked the remaining life from me, I fled this place, too; I fled right away down a gravel path and on to a wooden bridge across the Isar. Here I paused to catch my breath, gazing down from the wooden rail on to the almost opaque, celadon-green water. I had never seen a river so cold and fast; I had never seen water such a colour, I decided, imagining myself as one of the twigs being swept along it, scarcely raising an eddy; though the water did break here and there, mysteriously, in sulky yellow ripples.

And so we come to it at last. To the deathly experience I have been trying, vainly, to define ever since. 'An adolescent anxiety crisis,' my second husband, a doctor and a Jew, declared crisply, when I once described the event to him. 'I experienced the death of God,' was how I myself put it that same evening. A good little Christian I went on, 'It was as if Jesus had never been conceived,' scoring out those words immediately in the embarrassment of one taught to avoid excess at all costs. For it was excessive, undoubtedly. The whole thing was excessive. In that, Daniel, certainly, was right.

Yet I still think I may have been right in a way – if you feel the absence of something, the implication is that it may at one time have been present. And don't all such quasi-mystic experiences – adolescent anxiety, crisis or not, what happened in the Englischer Garten has always seemed to me like a quasi-mystic experience – result from some kind of deprivation or other? Might you not in such circumstances catch a glimpse of some essential matter? I'm sure that's why I keep obsessionally, every few years or so, trying to describe what happened; because it was somehow essential, and essences are in the end the only things I am willing to pursue. The problem is to work out how, precisely, to entrap them. Lying in this case, far from telling the plain truth seems, if anything, to lead farther from it.

I could, for instance, create a much more interesting drama by claiming to have seen a dead body in the Isar; I could maybe say it was that which drove me briefly from my mind. But not only would that be a lie, it sounds too much like one to be of any use. So I will state, categorically, that all I saw after I'd run on to the bridge like a madwoman, my feet clattering on the wooden boards, my hair awry, the tears streaming, was a tangle of twigs being carried away at speed downriver. Even so it halted me for some reason, as if something much more sinister was there. Hanging over the railing for a while, I kept staring at the water with such appalled intensity that I succeeded finally in stupefying myself. Then and only then, placing my feet carefully, scarcely making a sound on the hollow boards, did I leave the wooden bridge. After passing among some trees, just coming into leaf, I walked out into the wide green spaces of the garden.

It was a Saturday afternoon; though the time was only half-past two, the spry woman with small fur boots and tight grey hair, who waited usually till its stroke of three, was already feeding the squirrels from her hand. Behind her lay the empty lake. To one side the grass swept up to a slope upon which stood the cupola or folly, the one that always reminded me of the view from my bedroom window. A family was walking across the grass towards me. It was a very neat family; father, mother, three children, all three wearing dazzlingly white socks and holding each other carefully by the hand. I walked towards them, my footsteps ever slower and slower. Until at last I stopped walking altogether; at the same time as I was continuing to walk. At least I think I was both stopping and continuing to walk; I think that was the curious vision that I had.

Of course impressionable girls of seventeen or so have always tended to have visions of one kind or another; healthy visions of the Virgin Mary, usually; not seemingly barren ones like mine. Would I rather have seen the Virgin Mary? No, certainly, I would not. I wasn't Catholic, for a start, besides, I only ever said my prayers when I felt I needed to – lately, I had not felt able to say my prayers at all. What good, anyway, could such a vision of purity have done me? With the feelings I was prey to, that I welcomed more often than not, who was I to invoke it?

So no, I did not see the Virgin Mary in Munich that afternoon, any more than I saw a dead body in the Isar. Which brings me back to the hard fact that there are no words to describe what actually did occur; that I lie, for instance, when I say it occurred in every fibre of my body; in my eyes, my ears, my nose, in all my bones and organs, in every furthest atom of my flesh. Though it was like that, though I did feel it like that, I still lie when I say I did.

Because how could it have happened? How *could* everything have stopped? Yet it did stop, I swear it, the world no less than I; for there was no separation between the world and I, we were equally motionless and meaningless. It is true that for the whole interminable, momentary moment, I did actually go on walking. Yet I did not know I did because the movement was meaningless; because there was no movement; because the graininess of things was just grain and nothing more, formed no connection, was going nowhere; because the only way I could describe it was to write that God was dead; that Jesus had never been conceived.

Yet that was it. Almost before I knew that things had stopped, they began again like a motor picking itself up. The woman fed her squirrels. The unred and the unwhite, the unarms and the unlegs, became red sweaters and white socks, became arms and legs and torsos, walked towards me once again, was a respectable family taking a weekend walk, among other families pushing bicycles or prams or simply walking and talking with each other. Even the sun was coming out. My body regained itself; I had skin and flesh, I had breasts, I had a belly; better still I had my own arms and legs and was using them efficiently to propel myself across the grass. I was dazed yet whole; trembling yet alive, terrified and yet not quite dead of terror.

I did not run yet. I did not dare to. I walked like someone whose limbs had gone to sleep, and now, all pins and needles, was coming to life again. I felt an agony of sorts; but did not, would not – did not know how to – show it. I walked as steadily and neatly as my German fellow-walkers, past the trees and squirrels, on to the path that was leading out of the garden, among trees and through a gate, into the street that was all façades with nothing whatever behind them. Coming towards me was a pram in which a fat baby with a yellow bobble hat, waving an oversize toy rabbit, was being pushed by a fattish and sandy woman;

alongside it, not quite as tall as her, walked a balding, thickset young man with metal-rimmed spectacles.

If it was he – most likely it was not – the young man I'd met on the train, I did not want to know it. I took to my heels and ran as if all the hounds of hell were after me. When, briefly, I looked back, the man, the woman and the baby were staring open-mouthed as if the hounds of hell were actually after me. For how could they know, any more than I did, that I was running home to write that God had died. And thereafter, getting used to the idea, to go on telling story after story?

The Axe

PENELOPE FITZGERALD

Penelope Fitzgerald is one of England's most respected and admired authors. Three of her novels, The Bookshop, The Beginning of Spring, *and* The Gate of Angels, *have been shortlisted for the Booker Prize, which she won in 1981, with* Offshore. *Her most recent novel,* The Blue Flower, *won the 1996 Heywood Hill Prize, and she has also written several biographies.*

. . . You will recall that when the planned redundancies became necessary as the result of the discouraging trading figures shown by this small firm – in contrast, so I gather from the Company reports, with several of your other enterprises – you personally deputed to me the task of 'speaking' to those who were to be asked to leave. It was suggested to me that if they were asked to resign in order to avoid the unpleasantness of being given their cards, it might be unnecessary for the firm to offer any compensation. Having glanced personally through my staff sheets, you underlined the names of four people, the first being that of my clerical assistant, W. S. Singlebury. Your actual words to me were that he seemed fairly old and could probably be frightened into taking a powder. You were speaking to me in your 'democratic' style.

From this point on I feel able to write more freely, it being well understood, at office-managerial level, that you do not read more than the first two sentences of any given report. You believe that anything which cannot be put into two sentences is not worth attending to, a piece of wisdom which you usually attribute to the late Lord Beaverbrook.

As I question whether you have ever seen Singlebury, with whom this report is mainly concerned, it may be helpful to describe him. He worked for the Company for many more years than myself, and his attendance record was excellent. On Mondays, Wednesdays and Fridays, he wore a blue suit and a green knitted garment with a front zip. On Tuesdays and Thursdays he wore a pair of grey trousers of man-made material which he called 'my flannels', and a fawn cardigan. The cardigan was omitted in summer. He had, however, one distinguishing feature, very light blue eyes, with a defensive expression, as though apologizing for something which he felt guilty about, but could not put right. The fact is that he was getting old. Getting old is, of course, a crime of which we grow more guilty every day.

Singlebury had no wife or dependants, and was by no means a communicative man. His room is, or was, a kind of cubby-hole adjoining mine – you have to go through it to get into my room – and it was always kept very neat. About his 'things' he did show some mild emotions. They had to be ranged in a certain pattern in respect to his in and out trays, and Singlebury stayed behind for two or three minutes every evening to do this. He also managed to retain every year the complimentary desk calendar sent to us by Dino's, the Italian café on the corner. Singlebury was in fact the only one of my personnel who was always quite certain of the date. To this too his attitude was apologetic. His phrase was, 'I'm afraid it's Tuesday.'

His work, as was freely admitted, was his life, but the nature of his duties – though they included the post-book and the addressograph – were rather hard to define, having grown round him with the years. I can only say that after he left, I was surprised myself to discover how much he had had to do.

Oddly connected in my mind with the matter of the redundancies is the irritation of the damp in the office this summer and the peculiar smell (not the ordinary smell of damp), emphasized by the sudden appearance of representatives of a firm of damp eliminators who had not been sent for by me, nor is there any record of my having done so. These people simply vanished at the end of the day and have not returned. Another firm, to whom I applied as a result of frequent complaints by the female staff, have answered my letters but have so far failed to call.

Singlebury remained unaffected by the smell. Joining, very much against his usual habit, in one of the too frequent discussions of the subject, he said that he knew what it was; it was the smell of disappointment. For an awkward moment I thought he must have found out by some means that he was going to be asked to go, but he went on to explain that in 1942 the whole building had been requisitioned by the Admiralty and that relatives had been allowed to wait or queue there in the hope of getting news of those missing at sea. The repeated disappointment of these women, Singlebury said, must have permeated the building like a corrosive gas. All this was very unlike him. I make it a point not to encourage anything morbid. Singlebury was quite insistent, and added, as though by way of proof, that the lino in the corridors was Admiralty issue and had not been renewed since 1942 either. I was astonished to realize that he had been working in the building for so many years before the present tenancy. I realized that he must be considerably older than he had given us to understand. This, of course, will mean that there are wrong entries on his cards.

The actual notification to the redundant staff passed off rather better, in a way, than I had anticipated. By that time everyone in the office seemed inexplicably conversant with the details, and several of them in fact had gone far beyond their terms of reference, young Patel, for instance, who openly admits that he will be leaving us as soon as he can get a better job, taking me aside and telling me that to such a man as Singlebury dismissal would be like death. Dismissal is not the right word, I said. But death is, Patel replied. Singlebury himself, however, took it very quietly. Even when I raised the question of the Company's Early Retirement pension scheme, which I could not pretend was over-generous, he said very little. He was generally felt to be in a state of shock. The two girls whom you asked me to speak to were quite unaffected, having already found themselves employment as hostesses at the Dolphinarium near here. Mrs Horrocks, of Filing, on the other hand, *did* protest, and was so offensive on the question of severance pay that I was obliged to agree to refer it to a higher level. I consider this as one of the hardest day's work that I have ever done for the Company.

Just before his month's notice (if we are to call it that) was up, Singlebury, to my great surprise, asked me to come home with him one evening for a meal. In all the past years the idea of his having a home, still less asking anyone back to it, had never arisen, and I did not at all want to go there now. I felt sure, too, that he would want to reopen the matter of compensation, and only a quite unjustified feeling of guilt made me accept. We took an Underground together after work, travelling in the late rush-hour to Clapham North, and walked some distance in the rain. His place, when we eventually got to it, seemed particularly inconvenient, the entrance being through a small cleaner's shop. It consisted of one room and a shared toilet on the half-landing. The room itself was tidy, arranged, so it struck me, much on the lines of his cubby-hole, but the window was shut and it was oppressively stuffy. This is where I bury myself, said Singlebury.

There were no cooking arrangements and he left me there while he went down to fetch us something ready to eat from the Steakorama next to the cleaners. In his absence I took the opportunity to examine his room, though of course not in an inquisitive or prying manner. I was struck by the fact that none of his small store of stationery had been brought home from the office. He returned with two steaks wrapped in aluminium foil, evidently a special treat in my honour, and afterwards he went out on to the landing and made cocoa, a drink which I had not tasted for more than thirty years. The evening dragged rather. In the course of conversation it turned out that Singlebury was fond of reading. There were in fact several issues of a colour-printed encyclopaedia which he had been collecting as it came out, but unfortunately it had ceased publication after the seventh part. Reading is my hobby, he said. I pointed out that a hobby was rather something that one did with one's hands or in the open air – a relief from the work of the brain. Oh, I don't accept that distinction, Singlebury said. The mind and the body are the same. Well, one cannot deny the connection, I replied. Fear, for example, releases adrenalin, which directly affects the nerves. I don't mean connection, I mean identity, Singlebury said, the mind is the blood. Nonsense, I said, you might just as well tell me that the blood is the mind. It stands to reason that the blood can't think.

I was right, after all, in thinking that he would refer to the matter of the redundancy. This was not until he was seeing me off at the bus-stop, when for a moment he turned his grey, exposed-looking face away from me and said that he did not see how he could manage if he really had to go. He stood there like someone who has 'tried to give satisfaction' – he even used this phrase, saying that if the expression were not redolent of a bygone age, he would like to feel he had given satisfaction. Fortunately we had not long to wait for the 45 bus.

At the expiry of the month the staff gave a small tea-party for those who were leaving. I cannot describe this occasion as a success.

The following Monday I missed Singlebury as a familiar presence and also, as mentioned above, because I had never quite realized how much work he had been taking upon himself. As a direct consequence of losing him I found myself having to stay late – not altogether unwillingly, since although following general instructions I have discouraged overtime, the extra pay in my own case would be instrumental in making ends meet. Meanwhile Singlebury's desk had not been cleared – that is, of the trays, pencil-sharpener and complimentary calendar which were, of course, office property. The feeling that he would come back – not like Mrs Horrocks, who has rung up and called round incessantly – but simply come back to work out of habit and through not knowing what else to do, was very strong, without being openly mentioned. I myself half expected and dreaded it, and I had mentally prepared two or three lines of argument in order to persuade him, if he *did* come, not to try it again. Nothing happened, however, and on the Thursday I personally removed the 'things' from the cubby-hole into my own room.

Meanwhile in order to dispel certain quite unfounded rumours I thought it best to issue a notice for general circulation, pointing out that if Mr Singlebury should turn out to have taken any unwise step, and if in consequence any inquiry should be necessary, we should be the first to hear about it from the police. I dictated this to our only permanent typist, who immediately said, oh, he would never do that. He would never cause any unpleasantness like bringing police into the place, he'd do all he could to avoid that. I did not encourage any further discussion, but I asked my wife, who is very used to social work, to call round at Singlebury's place in Clapham North and find out how he was. She did not have very much luck. The people in the cleaner's shop knew, or thought they knew, that he was away, but they had not been sufficiently interested to ask where he was going.

On Friday young Patel said he would be leaving, as the damp and the smell were affecting his health. The damp is certainly not drying out in this seasonably warm weather.

I also, as you know, received another invitation on the Friday, at very short notice, in fact no notice at all; I was told to come to your house in Suffolk Park Gardens that evening for drinks. I was not unduly elated, having been asked once before after I had done rather an awkward small job for you. In our Company, justice has not only not to be done, but it must be seen not to be done. The food was quite nice; it came from your Caterers Grade 3. I spent most of the evening talking to Ted Hollow, one of the area sales-managers. I did not expect to be introduced to your wife, nor was I. Towards the end of the evening you spoke to me for three minutes in the small room with a green marble floor and matching wallpaper leading to the ground-floor toilets. You asked me if everything was all right, to which I replied, all right for whom? You said that nobody's fault was nobody's funeral. I said that I had tried to give satisfaction. Passing on towards the washbasins, you told me with seeming cordiality to be careful and watch it when I had had mixed drinks.

I would describe my feeling at this point as resentment, and I cannot identify exactly the moment when it passed into unease. I do know that I was acutely uneasy as I crossed the hall and saw two of your domestic staff, a man and a woman, holding my coat, which I had left in the lobby, and apparently trying to brush it. Your domestic staff all appear to be of foreign extraction and I personally feel sorry for them and do not grudge them a smile at the oddly assorted guests. Then I saw they were not smiling at my coat but that they seemed to be examining their fingers and looking at me earnestly and silently, and the collar or shoulders of my coat was covered with blood. As I came up to them, although they were still both absolutely silent, the illusion or impression passed, and I put on my coat and left the house in what I hope was a normal manner.

I now come to the present time. The feeling of uneasiness which I have described as making itself felt in your house has not diminished during this past weekend, and partly to take my mind off it and partly for the reasons I have given, I decided to work overtime again tonight, Monday the 23rd. This was in spite of the fact that the damp smell had become almost a stench, as of something putrid, which must have affected my nerves to some extent, because when I went out to get something to eat at Dino's I left the lights on, both in my office, and in the entrance hall. I mean that for the first time since I began to work for the Company I left them on deliberately. As I walked to the corner I looked back and saw the two solitary lights looking somewhat forlorn in contrast to the glitter of the Arab-American Mutual Loan Corporation opposite. After my meal I felt absolutely reluctant to go back to the building, and wished then that I had not given way to the impulse to leave the lights on, but since I had done so and they must be turned off, I had no choice.

As I stood in the empty hallway I could hear the numerous creakings, settlings and faint tickings of an old building, possibly associated with the plumbing system. The lifts for reasons of economy do not operate after 6.30 p.m., so I began to walk up the stairs. After one flight I felt a strong creeping tension in the nerves of the back such as any of us feel when there is danger from behind; one might say that the body was thinking for itself on these occasions. I did not look round, but simply continued upwards as rapidly as I could. At the third floor I paused, and could hear footsteps coming patiently up behind me. This was not a surprise; I had been expecting them all evening.

Just at the door of my own office, or rather of the cubby-hole, for I have to pass through that, I turned, and saw at the end of the dim corridor what I had also expected, Singlebury, advancing towards me with his unmistakable shuffling step. My first reaction was a kind of bewilderment as to why he, who had been such an excellent timekeeper, so regular day by day, should become a creature of the night. He was wearing the blue suit. This I could make out by its familiar outline, but it was not till he came halfway down the corridor towards me, and reached the patch of light falling through the window from the street, that I saw that he was not himself – I mean that his head was nodding or rather swivelling irregularly from side to side. It crossed my mind that Singlebury was drunk. I had never known him drunk or indeed seen him take anything to drink, even at the office Christmas party, but one cannot estimate the effect that trouble will have upon a man. I began to think what steps I should take in this situation. I turned on the light in his cubby-hole as I went through and waited at the entrance of my own office. As he appeared in the outer doorway I saw that I had not been correct about the reason for the odd movement of the head. The throat was cut from ear to ear so that the head was nearly severed from the shoulders. It was this which had given the impression of nodding, or rather, lolling. As he walked into his cubby-hole Singlebury raised both hands and tried to steady the head as though conscious that something was wrong. The eyes were thickly filmed over, as one sees in the carcasses in a butcher's shop.

I shut and locked my door, and not wishing to give way to nausea, or to lose all control of myself, I sat down at my desk. My work was waiting for me as I had left it – it was the file on the matter of the damp elimination – and, there not being anything else to do, I tried to look through it. On the other side of the door I could hear Singlebury sit down also, and then try the drawers of the table, evidently looking for the 'things' without which he could not start work. After the drawers had been tried, one after another, several times, there was almost total silence.

The present position is that I am locked in my office and would not, no matter what you offered me, indeed I could not, go out through the cubby-hole and pass what is sitting at the desk. The early cleaners will not be here for seven hours and forty-five minutes. I have passed the time so far as best I could in writing this report. One consideration strikes me. If what I have next door is a visitant which should not be walking but buried in the earth, then its wound cannot bleed, and there will be no stream of blood moving slowly under the whole width of the communicating door. However I am sitting at the moment with my back to the door, so that without turning round, I have no means of telling whether it has done so or not.

A Jury of Her Peers

SUSAN GLASPELL

Born in Davenport, Iowa in 1882, Susan Glaspell was the author of novels, including Fidelity, Brook Evans *and* The Fugitive's Return. *She also wrote plays, among them* Alison's House, *which won a Pulitzer Prize. She died in 1948.*

When Martha Hale opened the storm door and got a cut of the north wind, she ran back for her big woolen scarf. As she hurriedly wound that around her head her eye made a scandalized sweep of her kitchen. It was no ordinary thing that called her away – it was probably further from ordinary than anything that had ever happened in Dickson County. But what her eye took in was that her kitchen was in no shape for leaving: her bread all ready for mixing, half the flour sifted and half unsifted.

She hated to see things half done, but she had been at that when the team from town stopped to get Mr Hale, and then the sheriff came running in to say his wife wished Mrs Hale would come too – adding, with a grin, that he guessed she was getting scary and wanted another woman along. So she had dropped everything right where it was.

'Martha!' now came her husband's impatient voice. 'Don't keep folks waiting out here in the cold.'

She again opened the storm door, and this time joined the three men and the one woman waiting in the big two-seated buggy.

After she had the robes tucked around her she took another look at the woman who sat beside her on the back seat. She had met Mrs Peters the year before at the county fair, and the thing she remembered about her was that she didn't seem like a sheriff's wife. She was small and thin and didn't have a strong voice. Mrs Gorman, sheriff's wife before Gorman went out and Peters came in, had a voice that somehow seemed to be backing up the law with every word. But if Mrs Peters didn't look like a sheriff's wife, Peters made it up in looking like a sheriff. He was to a dot the kind of man who could get himself elected sheriff – a heavy man with a big voice, who was particularly genial with the law-abiding, as if to make it plain that he knew the difference between criminals and noncriminals. And right there it came into Mrs Hale's mind, with a stab, that this man who was so pleasant and lively with all of them was going to the Wrights' now as a sheriff.

'The country's not very pleasant this time of year,' Mrs Peters at last ventured, as if she felt they ought to be talking as well as the men.

Mrs Hale scarcely finished her reply, for they had gone up a little hill and could see the Wright place now, and seeing it did not make her feel like talking. It looked very lonesome this cold March morning. It had always been a lonesome-looking place. It was down in a hollow, and the poplar trees around it were lonesome-looking trees. The men were looking at it and talking about what had happened. The county attorney was bending to one side of the buggy, and kept looking steadily at the place as they drew up to it.

'I'm glad you came with me,' Mrs Peters said nervously, as the two women were about to follow the men in through the kitchen door.

Even after she had her foot on the doorstep, her hand on the knob, Martha Hale had a moment of feeling she could not cross that threshold. And the reason it seemed she couldn't cross it now was simply because she hadn't crossed it before. Time and time again it had been in her mind, 'I ought to go over and see Minnie Foster' – she still thought of her as Minnie Foster, though for twenty years she had been Mrs Wright. And then there was always something to do and Minnie Foster would go from her mind. But *now* she could come.

The men went over to the stove. The women stood close together by the door. Young Henderson, the county attorney, turned around and said, 'Come up to the fire, ladies.'

Mrs Peters took a step forward, then stopped. 'I'm not – cold,' she said.

And so the two women stood by the door, at first not even so much as looking around the kitchen.

The men talked for a minute about what a good thing it was the sheriff had sent his deputy out that morning to make a fire for them, and then Sheriff Peters stepped back from the stove, unbuttoned his outer coat, and leaned his hands on the kitchen table in a way that seemed to mark the beginning of official business. 'Now, Mr Hale,' he said in a sort of semiofficial voice, 'before we move things about, you tell Mr Henderson just what it was you saw when you came here yesterday morning.'

The county attorney was looking around the kitchen.

'By the way,' he said, 'has anything been moved?' He turned to the sheriff. 'Are things just as you left them yesterday?'

Peters looked from cupboard to sink; from that to a small worn rocker a little to one side of the kitchen table.

'It's just the same.'

'Somebody should have been left here yesterday,' said the county attorney.

'Oh – yesterday,' returned the sheriff, with a little gesture as of yesterday having been more than he could bear to think of. 'When I had to send Frank to Morris Center for that man who went crazy – let me tell you, I had my hands full *yesterday*. I knew you could get back from Omaha by today, George, and as long as I went over everything here myself . . .'

'Well, Mr Hale,' said the county attorney, in a way of letting what was past and gone go, 'tell just what happened when you came here yesterday morning.'

Mrs Hale, still leaning against the door, had that sinking feeling of the mother whose child is about to speak a piece. Lewis often wandered along and got things mixed up in a story. She hoped he would tell this straight and plain, and not say unnecessary things that would just make things harder for Minnie Foster. He didn't begin at once, and she noticed that he looked queer – as if standing in that kitchen and having to tell what he had seen there yesterday morning made him almost sick.

'Yes, Mr Hale?' the county attorney reminded.

'Harry and I had started to town with a load of potatoes,' Mrs Hale's husband began.

Harry was Mrs Hale's oldest boy. He wasn't with them now, for the very good reason that those potatoes never got to town yesterday and he was taking them this morning, so he hadn't been home when the sheriff stopped to say he wanted Mr Hale to come over to the Wright place and tell the county attorney his story there, where he could point it all out. With all Mrs Hale's other emotions came the fear that maybe Harry wasn't dressed warm enough – they hadn't any of them realized how that north wind did bite.

'We come along this road,' Hale was going on, with a motion of his hand to the road over which they had just come, 'and as we got in sight of the house I says to Harry, "I'm goin' to see if I can't get John Wright to take a telephone." You see,' he explained to Henderson, 'unless I can get somebody to go in with me they won't come out this branch road except for a price *I* can't pay. I'd spoke to Wright about it once before; but he put me off, saying folks talked too much anyway, and all he asked was peace and quiet – guess you know about how much he talked himself. But I thought maybe if I went to the house and talked about it before his wife, and said all the womenfolks liked the telephones, and that in this lonesome stretch of road it would be a good thing – well, I said to Harry that that was what I was going to say – though I said at the same time that I didn't know as what his wife wanted made much difference to John –'

Now there he was! – saying things he didn't need to say. Mrs Hale tried to catch her husband's eye, but fortunately the county attorney interrupted with, 'Let's talk about that a little later, Mr Hale. I do want to talk about that, but I'm anxious now to get along to just what happened when you got here.'

When he began this time, it was very deliberately and carefully. 'I didn't see or hear anything. I knocked at the door. And still it was all quiet inside. I knew they must be up – it was past eight o'clock. So I knocked again, louder, and I thought I heard somebody say, "Come in." I wasn't sure – I'm not sure yet. But I opened the door – this door,' jerking a hand toward the door by which the two women stood, 'and there in that rocker' – pointing to it – 'sat Mrs Wright.'

Everyone in the kitchen looked at the rocker. It came into Mrs Hale's mind that that rocker didn't look in the least like Minnie Foster – the Minnie Foster of twenty years before. It was a dingy red, with wooden rungs up the back, and the middle rung was gone, and the chair sagged to one side.

'How did she – look?' the county attorney was inquiring.

'Well,' said Hale, 'she looked – queer.'

'How do you mean – queer?'

As he asked it he took out a notebook and pencil. Mrs Hale did not like the sight of that pencil. She kept her eye fixed on her husband, as if to keep him from saying unnecessary things that would go into that notebook and make trouble.

Hale did speak guardedly, as if the pencil had affected him too.

'Well, as if she didn't know what she was going to do next. And kind of – done up.'

'How did she seem to feel about your coming?'

'Why, I don't think she minded – one way or other. She didn't pay much attention. I said, "Ho' do, Mrs Wright? It's cold, ain't it?" And she said, "Is it?" – and went on pleatin' at her apron. Well, I was surprised. She didn't ask me to come up to the stove, or to sit down, but just set there, not even lookin' at me. And I said, "I want to see John."

'And then she – laughed. I guess you would call it a laugh.

'I thought of Harry and the team outside, so I said, a little sharp, "Can I see John?" "No," says she – kind of dull like. "Ain't he home?" says I. Then she looked at me. "Yes," says she, "he's home." "Then why can't I see him?" I asked her, out of patience with her now. "Cause he's dead," says she, just as quiet and dull – and fell to pleatin' her apron. "Dead?" says I, like you do when you can't take in what you've heard.

'She just nodded her head, not getting a bit excited, but rockin' back and forth.

'"Why – where is he?" says I, not knowing *what* to say.

'She just pointed upstairs – like this' – pointing to the room above. 'By this time I didn't know what to do. I walked from there to here; then I says, "Why, what did he die of?"

'"He died of a rope round his neck," says she; and just went on pleatin' at her apron.'

Hale stopped speaking, and stood staring at the rocker, as if he were still seeing the woman who had sat there the morning before. Nobody spoke; it was as if everyone were seeing the woman who had sat there the morning before.

'And what did you do then?' the county attorney at last broke the silence.

'I went out and called Harry. I thought I might – need help. I got Harry in, and we went upstairs.' His voice fell almost to a whisper. 'There he was – lying over the –'

'I think I'd rather have you go into that upstairs,' the county attorney interrupted, 'where you can point it all out. Just go on now with the rest of the story.'

'Well, my first thought was to get that rope off. It looked –'

He stopped, his face twitching.

'But Harry, he went up to him, and he said, "No, he's dead all right, and we'd better not touch anything." So we went downstairs.

'She was still sitting that same way. "Has anybody been notified?" I asked. "No," says she, unconcerned.

' "Who did this, Mrs Wright?" said Harry. He said it businesslike, and she stopped pleatin' at her apron. "I don't know," she says. "You don't *know*?" says Harry. "Weren't you sleepin' in the bed with him?" "Yes," says she, "but I was on the inside." "Somebody slipped a rope round his neck and strangled him, and you didn't wake up?" says Harry. "I didn't wake up," she said after him.

'We may have looked as if we didn't see how that could be, for after a minute she said, "I sleep sound."

'Harry was going to ask her more questions, but I said maybe that weren't our business; maybe we ought to let her tell her story first to the coroner or the sheriff. So Harry went fast as he could over to High Road – the Rivers' place, where there's a telephone.'

'And what did she do when she knew you had gone for the coroner?' The attorney got his pencil in his hand all ready for writing.

'She moved from that chair to this one over here' – Halc pointed to a small chair in the corner – 'and just sat there with her hands held together and looking down. I got a feeling that I ought to make some conversation, so I said I had come in to see if John wanted to put in a telephone; and at that she started to laugh, and then she stopped and looked at me – scared.'

At sound of a moving pencil the man who was telling the story looked up.

'I dunno – maybe it wasn't scared,' he hastened; 'I wouldn't like to say it was. Soon Harry got back, and then Dr Lloyd came, and you, Mr Peters, and so I guess that's all I know that you don't.'

He said that last with relief, and moved a little, as if relaxing. Everyone moved a little. The county attorney walked toward the stair door.

'I guess we'll go upstairs first – then out to the barn and around there.'

He paused and looked around the kitchen.

'You're convinced there was nothing important here?' he asked the sheriff. 'Nothing that would – point to any motive?'

The sheriff too looked all around, as if to reconvince himself.

'Nothing here but kitchen things,' he said, with a little laugh for the insignificance of kitchen things.

The county attorney was looking at the cupboard – a peculiar, ungainly structure, half closet and half cupboard, the upper part of it being built in the wall, and the lower part just the old-fashioned kitchen cupboard. As if its queerness attracted him, he got a chair and opened the upper part and looked in. After a moment he drew his hand away sticky.

'Here's a nice mess,' he said resentfully.

The two women had drawn nearer, and now the sheriff's wife spoke.

'Oh – her fruit,' she said, looking to Mrs Hale for sympathetic understanding. She turned back to the county attorney and explained. 'She worried about that when it turned so cold last night. She said the fire would go out and her jars might burst.'

Mrs Peters' husband broke into a laugh. 'Well, can you beat the women! Held for murder, and worrying about her preserves.'

The young attorney set his lips.

'I guess before we're through with her she may have something more serious than preserves to worry about.'

'Oh well,' said Mrs Hale's husband, with good-natured superiority, 'women are used to worrying over trifles.'

The two women moved a little closer together. Neither of them spoke. The county attorney seemed suddenly to remember his manners – and think of his future.

'And yet,' said he, with the gallantry of a young politician, 'for all their worries, what would we do without the ladies?'

The women did not speak, did not unbend. He went to the sink and began washing his hands. He turned to wipe them on the roller towel – whirled it for a cleaner place.

'Dirty towels! Not much of a housekeeper, would you say, ladies?'

He kicked his foot against some dirty pans under the sink.

'There's a great deal of work to be done on a farm,' said Mrs Hale stiffly.

'To be sure. And yet' – with a little bow to her – 'I know there are some Dickson County farmhouses that do not have such roller towels.' He gave it a pull to expose its full length again.

'Those towels get dirty awful quick. Men's hands aren't always as clean as they might be.'

'Ah, loyal to your sex, I see,' he laughed. He stopped and gave her a keen look. 'But you and Mrs Wright were neighbors. I suppose were friends, too.'

Martha Hale shook her head.

'I've seen little enough of her of late years. I've not been in this house – it's more than a year.'

'And why was that? You didn't like her?'

'I liked her well enough,' she replied with spirit. 'Farmers' wives have their hands full, Mr Henderson. And then –' She looked around the kitchen.

'Yes?' he encouraged.

'It never seemed a very cheerful place,' said she, more to herself than to him.

'No,' he agreed. 'I don't think anyone would call it cheerful. I shouldn't say she had the homemaking instinct.'

'Well, I don't know as Wright had, either,' she muttered.

'You mean they didn't get on very well?' he was quick to ask.

'No. I don't mean anything,' she answered, with decision. As she turned a little away from him, she added, 'But I don't think a place would be any the cheerfuller for John Wright's bein' in it.'

'I'd like to talk to you about that a little later, Mrs Hale,' he said. 'I'm anxious to get the lay of things upstairs now.'

He moved toward the stair door, followed by the two men.

'I suppose anything Mrs Peters does'll be all right?' the sheriff inquired. 'She was to take in some clothes for her, you know – and a few little things. We left in such a hurry yesterday.'

The county attorney looked at the two women whom they were leaving alone there among the kitchen things.

'Yes – Mrs Peters,' he said, his glance resting on the woman who was not Mrs Peters, the big farmer woman who stood behind the sheriff's wife. 'Of course Mrs Peters is one of us,' he said, in a manner of entrusting responsibility. 'And keep your eye out, Mrs Peters, for anything that might be of use. No telling; you women might come upon a clue to the motive – and that's the thing we need.'

Mr Hale rubbed his face after the fashion of a showman getting ready for a pleasantry.

'But would the women know a clue if they did come upon it?' he said; and, having delivered himself of this, he followed the others through the stair door.

The women stood motionless and silent, listening to the footsteps, first upon the stairs, then in the room above them.

Then, as if releasing herself from something strange, Mrs Hale began to arrange the dirty pans under the sink, which the county attorney's disdainful push of the foot had deranged.

'I'd hate to have men comin' into my kitchen,' she said testily – 'snoopin' round and criticizin'.'

'Of course it's no more than their duty,' said the sheriff's wife, in her manner of timid acquiescence.

'Duty's all right,' replied Mrs Hale bluffly, 'but I guess that deputy sheriff that come out to make the fire might have got a little of this on.' She gave the roller towel a pull. 'Wish I'd thought of that sooner! Seems mean to talk about her for not having things slicked up, when she had to come away in such a hurry.'

She looked around the kitchen. Certainly it was not 'slicked up'. Her eye was held by a bucket of sugar on a low shelf. The cover was off the wooden bucket, and beside it was a paper bag – half full.

Mrs Hale moved toward it.

'She was putting this in there,' she said to herself – slowly.

She thought of the flour in her kitchen at home – half sifted, half not sifted. She had been interrupted, and had left things half done. What had interrupted Minnie Foster? Why had that work been left half done? She made a move as if to finish it – unfinished things always bothered her – and then she glanced around and saw that Mrs Peters was watching her – and she didn't want Mrs Peters to get that feeling she had got of work begun and then – for some reason, not finished.

'It's a shame about her fruit,' she said, and walked toward the cupboard that the county attorney had opened, and got on the chair, murmuring, 'I wonder if it's all gone.'

It was a sorry enough looking sight, but 'Here's one that's all right,' she said at last. She held it toward the light. 'This is cherries, too.' She looked again. 'I declare I believe that's the only one.'

With a sigh, she got down from the chair, went to the sink, and wiped off the bottle.

'She'll feel awful bad, after all her hard work in the hot weather. I remember the afternoon I put up my cherries last summer.'

She set the bottle on the table, and, with another sigh, started to sit down in the rocker. But she did not sit down. Something kept her from sitting down in that chair. She straightened – stepped back, and, half turned away, stood looking at it, seeing the woman who had sat there 'pleatin' at her apron'.

The thin voice of the sheriff's wife broke in upon her. 'I must be getting those things from the front-room closet.' She opened the door into the other room, started in, stepped back. 'You coming with me, Mrs Hale?' she asked nervously. 'You – you could help me get them.'

They were soon back – the stark coldness of that shut-up room was not a thing to linger in.

'My!' said Mrs Peters, dropping the things on the table and hurrying to the stove.

Mrs Hale stood examining the clothes the woman who was being detained in town had said she wanted.

'Wright was close!' she exclaimed, holding up a shabby black skirt that bore the marks of much making over. 'I think maybe that's why she kept so much to herself. I s'pose she felt she couldn't do her part; and then, you don't enjoy things when you feel shabby. She used to wear pretty clothes and be lively – when she was Minnie Foster, one of the town girls, singing in the choir. But that – oh, that was twenty years ago.'

With a carefulness in which there was something tender, she folded the shabby clothes and piled them at one corner of the table. She looked up at Mrs Peters, and there was something in the other woman's look that irritated her.

'She don't care,' she said to herself. 'Much difference it makes to her whether Minnie Foster had pretty clothes when she was a girl.'

Then she looked again, and she wasn't so sure; in fact, she hadn't at any time been perfectly sure about Mrs Peters. She had that shrinking manner, and yet her eyes looked as if they could see a long way into things.

'This all you was to take in?' asked Mrs Hale.

'No,' said the sheriff's wife. 'She said she wanted an apron. Funny thing to want,' she ventured in her nervous little way, 'for there's not much to get you dirty in jail, goodness knows. But I suppose just to make her feel more natural. If you're used to wearing an apron – She said they were in the bottom drawer of this cupboard. Yes – here they are. And then her little shawl that always hung on the stair door.'

She took the small gray shawl from behind the door leading upstairs, and stood a minute looking at it.

Suddenly Mrs Hale took a quick step toward the other woman.

'Mrs Peters!'

'Yes, Mrs Hale?'

'Do you think she – did it?'

A frightened look blurred the other thing in Mrs Peters' eyes.

'Oh, I don't know,' she said, in a voice that seemed to shrink away from the subject.

'Well, I don't think she did,' affirmed Mrs Hale stoutly. 'Asking for an apron and her little shawl. Worryin' about her fruit.'

'Mr Peters says —' Footsteps were heard in the room above; she stopped, looked up, then went on in a lowered voice, 'Mr Peters says — it looks bad for her. Mr Henderson is awful sarcastic in a speech, and he's going to make fun of her saying she didn't — wake up.'

For a moment Mrs Hale had no answer. Then, 'Well, I guess John Wright didn't wake up — when they was slippin' that rope under his neck,' she muttered.

'No, it's *strange*,' breathed Mrs Peters. 'They think it was such a — funny way to kill a man.'

She began to laugh; at sound of the laugh, abruptly stopped.

'That's just what Mr Hale said,' said Mrs Hale, in a resolutely natural voice. 'There was a gun in the house. He says that's what he can't understand.'

'Mr Henderson said, coming out, that what was needed for the case was a motive. Something to show anger — or sudden feeling.'

'Well, I don't see any signs of anger around here,' said Mrs Hale. 'I don't —'

She stopped. It was as if her mind tripped on something. Her eye was caught by a dish towel in the middle of the kitchen table. Slowly she moved toward the table. One half of it was wiped clean, the other half messy. Her eyes made a slow, almost unwilling turn to the bucket of sugar and the half-empty bag beside it. Things begun — and not finished.

After a moment she stepped back, and said, in that manner of releasing herself, 'Wonder how they're finding things upstairs? I hope she had it a little more redd up up there. You know' — she paused, and feeling gathered — 'it seems kind of *sneaking*, locking her up in town and coming out here to get her own house to turn against her!'

'But, Mrs Hale,' said the sheriff's wife, 'the law is the law.'

'I s'pose 'tis,' answered Mrs Hale shortly.

She turned to the stove, saying something about that fire not being much to brag of. She worked with it a minute, and when she straightened up she said aggressively, 'The law is the law – and a bad stove is a bad stove. How'd you like to cook on this?' – pointing with the poker to the broken lining. She opened the oven door and started to express her opinion of the oven; but she was swept into her own thoughts, thinking of what it would mean, year after year, to have that stove to wrestle with. The thought of Minnie Foster trying to bake in that oven – and the thought of her never going over to see Minnie Foster –

She was startled by hearing Mrs Peters say, 'A person gets discouraged – and loses heart.'

The sheriff's wife had looked from the stove to the sink – to the pail of water which had been carried in from outside. The two women stood there silent, above them the footsteps of the men who were looking for evidence against the woman who had worked in that kitchen. That look of seeing into things, of seeing through a thing to something else, was in the eyes of the sheriff's wife now. When Mrs Hale next spoke to her, it was gently. 'Better loosen up your things, Mrs Peters. We'll not feel them when we go out.'

Mrs Peters went to the back of the room to hang up the fur tippet she was wearing. A moment later she exclaimed, 'Why, she was piecing a quilt!' and held up a large sewing basket piled high with quilt pieces.

Mrs Hale spread some of the blocks on the table.

'It's log-cabin pattern,' she said, putting several of them together. 'Pretty, isn't it?'

They were so engaged with the quilt that they did not hear the footsteps on the stairs. Just as the stair door opened Mrs Hale was saying, 'Do you suppose she was going to quilt it or just knot it?'

The sheriff threw up his hands.

'They wonder whether she was going to quilt it or just knot it!'

There was a laugh for the ways of women, a warming of hands over the stove, and then the county attorney said briskly, 'Well, let's go right out to the barn and get that cleared up.'

'I don't see as there's anything so strange,' Mrs Hale said resentfully, after the outside door had closed on the three men – 'our taking up our time with little things while we're waiting for them to get the evidence. I don't see as it's anything to laugh about.'

'Of course they've got awful important things on their minds,' said the sheriff's wife apologetically.

They returned to an inspection of the block for the quilt. Mrs Hale was looking at the fine, even sewing, and preoccupied with thoughts of the woman who had done that sewing, when she heard the sheriff's wife say, in a queer tone, 'Why, look at this one.'

She turned to take the block held out to her.

'The sewing,' said Mrs Peters, in a troubled way. 'All the rest of them have been so nice and even – but – this one. Why, it looks as if she didn't know what she was about!'

Their eyes met – something flashed to life, passed between them; then, as if with an effort, they seemed to pull away from each other. A moment Mrs Hale sat there, her hands folded over that sewing which was so unlike all the rest of the sewing. Then she had pulled a knot and drawn the threads.

'Oh, what are you doing, Mrs Hale?' asked the sheriff's wife, startled.

'Just pulling out a stitch or two that's not sewed very good,' said Mrs Hale mildly.

'I don't think we ought to touch things,' Mrs Peters said, a little helplessly.

'I'll just finish up this end,' answered Mrs Hale, still in that mild, matter-of-fact fashion.

She threaded a needle and started to replace bad sewing with good. For a little while she sewed in silence. Then, in that thin, timid voice, she heard, 'Mrs Hale!'

'Yes, Mrs Peters?'

'What do you suppose she was so – nervous about?'

'Oh, *I* don't know,' said Mrs Hale, as if dismissing a thing not important enough to spend much time on. 'I don't know as she was – nervous. I sew awful queer sometimes when I'm just tired.'

She cut a thread, and out of the corner of her eye looked up at Mrs Peters. The small, lean face of the sheriff's wife seemed to have tightened up. Her eyes had that look of peering into something. But next moment she moved, and said in her thin, indecisive way, 'Well, I must get those clothes wrapped. They may be through sooner than we think. I wonder where I could find a piece of paper – and string.'

'In that cupboard, maybe,' suggested Mrs Hale, after a glance around.

One piece of the crazy sewing remained unripped. Mrs Peters' back turned, Martha Hale now scrutinized that piece, compared it with the dainty, accurate sewing of the other blocks. The difference was startling. Holding this block made her feel queer, as if the distracted thoughts of the woman who had perhaps turned to it to try and quiet herself were communicating themselves to her.

Mrs Peters' voice roused her.

'Here's a birdcage,' she said. 'Did she have a bird, Mrs Hale?'

'Why, I don't know whether she did or not.' She turned to look at the cage Mrs Peters was holding up. 'I've not been here in so long.' She sighed. 'There was a man round last year selling canaries cheap – but I don't know as she took one. Maybe she did. She used to sing real pretty herself.'

Mrs Peters looked around the kitchen.

'Seems kind of funny to think of a bird here.' She half laughed – an attempt to put up a barrier. 'But she must have had one – or why would she have a cage? I wonder what happened to it.'

'I suppose maybe the cat got it,' suggested Mrs Hale, resuming her sewing.

'No. She didn't have a cat. She's got that feeling some people have about cats – being afraid of them. When they brought her to our house yesterday, my cat got in the room, and she was real upset and asked me to take it out.'

'My sister Bessie was like that,' laughed Mrs Hale.

The sheriff's wife did not reply. The silence made Mrs Hale turn around. Mrs Peters was examining the birdcage.

'Look at this door,' she said slowly. 'It's broke. One thing has been pulled apart.'

Mrs Hale came nearer.

'Looks as if someone must have been – rough with it.'

Again their eyes met – startled, questioning, apprehensive. For a moment neither spoke nor stirred. Then Mrs Hale, turning away, said brusquely, 'If they're going to find any evidence, I wish they'd be about it. I don't like this place.'

'But I'm awful glad you came with me, Mrs Hale.' Mrs Peters put the birdcage on the table and sat down. 'It would be lonesome for me – sitting here alone.'

'Yes, it would, wouldn't it?' agreed Mrs Hale, a certain determined naturalness in her voice. She had picked up the sewing, but now it dropped in her lap, and she murmured in a different voice, 'But I tell you what I *do* wish, Mrs Peters. I wish I had come over sometimes when she was here. I wish – I had.'

'But of course you were awful busy, Mrs Hale. Your house – and your children.'

'I could've come,' retorted Mrs Hale shortly. 'I stayed away because it weren't cheerful – and that's why I ought to have come. I' – she looked around – 'I've never liked this place. Maybe because it's down in a hollow and you don't see the road. I don't know what it is, but it's a lonesome place, and always was. I wish I had come over to see Minnie Foster sometimes. I can see now –' She did not put it into words.

'Well, you mustn't reproach yourself,' counseled Mrs Peters. 'Somehow, we just don't see how it is with other folks till – something comes up.'

'Not having children makes less work,' mused Mrs Hale, 'but it makes a quiet house – and Wright out to work all day – and no company when he did come in. Did you know John Wright, Mrs Peters?'

'Not to know him,' said Mrs Peters. 'I've seen him in town. They say he was a good man.'

'Yes – good,' conceded John Wright's neighbor grimly. 'He didn't drink, and kept his word as well as most, I guess, and paid his debts. But he was a hard man, Mrs Peters. Just to pass the time of day with him –' She stopped, shivered a little. 'Like a raw wind that gets to the bone.' Her eye fell upon the cage on the table before her, and she added, almost bitterly, 'I should think she would've wanted a bird!'

Suddenly she leaned forward, looking intently at the cage. 'But what do you s'pose went wrong with it?'

'I don't know,' returned Mrs Peters, 'unless it got sick and died.'

But after she said it she reached over and swung the broken door. Both women watched it as if somehow held by it.

'You didn't know – her?' Mrs Hale asked, a gentler note in her voice.

'Not till they brought her yesterday,' said the sheriff's wife.

'She – come to think of it, she was kind of like a bird herself. Real sweet and pretty, but kind of timid and – fluttery. How – she – did – change.'

That held her for a long time. Finally, as if struck with a happy thought and relieved to get back to everyday things, she exclaimed, 'Tell you what, Mrs Peters, why don't you take the quilt in with you? It might take up her mind.'

'Why, I think that's a real nice idea, Mrs Hale,' agreed the sheriff's wife, as if she too were glad to come into the atmosphere of a simple kindness. 'There couldn't possibly be any objection to that, could there? Now, just what will I take? I wonder if her patches are in here – and her things.'

They turned to the sewing basket.

'Here's some red,' said Mrs Hale, bringing out a roll of cloth. Underneath that was a box. 'Here, maybe her scissors are in here – and her things.' She held it up. 'What a pretty box! I'll warrant that was something she had a long time ago – when she was a girl.'

She held it in her hand a moment; then, with a little sigh, opened it.

Instantly her hand went to her nose.

'Why –'

Mrs Peters drew nearer – then turned away.

'There's something wrapped up in this piece of silk,' faltered Mrs Hale.

'This isn't her scissors,' said Mrs Peters, in a shrinking voice.

Her hand not steady, Mrs Hale raised the piece of silk. 'Oh, Mrs Peters!' she cried. 'It's –'

Mrs Peters bent closer.

'It's the bird,' she whispered.

'But, Mrs Peters!' cried Mrs Hale. '*Look* at it! Its *neck* – look at its neck! It's all – other side *to.*'

She held the box away from her.

The sheriff's wife again bent closer.

'Somebody wrung its neck,' said she, in a voice that was slow and deep.

And then again the eyes of the two women met – this time clung together in a look of dawning comprehension, of growing horror. Mrs Peters looked from the dead bird to the broken door of the cage. Again their eyes met. And just then there was a sound at the outside door.

Mrs Hale slipped the box under the quilt pieces in the basket, and sank into the chair before it. Mrs Peters stood holding to the table. The county attorney and the sheriff came in from outside.

'Well, ladies,' said the county attorney, as one turning from serious things to little pleasantries, 'have you decided whether she was going to quilt it or knot it?'

'We think,' began the sheriff's wife in a flurried voice, 'that she was going to – knot it.'

He was too preoccupied to notice the change that came in her voice on that last.

'Well, that's very interesting, I'm sure,' he said tolerantly. He caught sight of the birdcage. 'Has the bird flown?'

'We think the cat got it,' said Mrs Hale, in a voice curiously even.

He was walking up and down as if thinking something out.

'Is there a cat?' he asked absently.

Mrs Hale shot a look up at the sheriff's wife.

'Well, not *now*,' said Mrs Peters. 'They're superstitious, you know; they leave.'

She sank into her chair.

The county attorney did not heed her. 'No sign at all of anyone having come in from the outside,' he said to Peters, in the manner of continuing an interrupted conversation. 'Their own rope. Now let's go upstairs again and go over it, piece by piece. It would have to have been someone who knew just the –'

The stair door closed behind them and their voices were lost.

The two women sat motionless, not looking at each other, but as if peering into something and at the same time holding back. When they spoke now it was as if they were afraid of what they were saying, but as if they could not help saying it.

'She liked the bird,' said Martha Hale, low and slowly. 'She was going to bury it in that pretty box.'

'When I was a girl,' said Mrs Peters, under her breath, 'my kitten – there was a boy took a hatchet, and before my eyes – before I could get there –' She covered her face an instant. 'If they hadn't held me back I would have' – she caught herself, looked upstairs where footsteps were heard, and finished weakly – 'hurt him.'

Then they sat without speaking or moving.

'I wonder how it would seem,' Mrs Hale at last began, as if feeling her way over strange ground – 'never to have had any children around?' Her eyes made a slow sweep of the kitchen, as if seeing what that kitchen had meant through all the years. 'No, Wright wouldn't like the bird,' she said after that – 'a thing that sang. She used to sing. He killed that too.' Her voice tightened.

Mrs Peters moved uneasily.

'Of course we don't know who killed the bird.'

'I knew John Wright,' was Mrs Hale's answer.

'It was an awful thing was done in this house that night, Mrs Hale,' said the sheriff's wife. 'Killing a man while he slept – slipping a thing round his neck that choked the life out of him.'

Mrs Hale's hand went out to the birdcage.

'His neck. Choked the life out of him.'

'We don't *know* who killed him,' whispered Mrs Peters wildly. 'We don't *know*.'

Mrs Hale had not moved. 'If there had been years and years of – nothing, then a bird to sing to you, it would be awful – still – after the bird was still.'

It was as if something within her not herself had spoken, and it found in Mrs Peters something she did not know as herself.

'I know what stillness is,' she said, in a queer, monotonous voice. 'When we homesteaded in Dakota, and my first baby died – after he was two years old – and me with no other then –'

Mrs Hale stirred.

'How soon do you suppose they'll be through looking for the evidence?'

'I know what stillness is,' repeated Mrs Peters, in just that same way. Then she too pulled back. 'The law has got to punish crime, Mrs Hale,' she said, in her tight little way.

'I wish you'd seen Minnie Foster,' was the answer, 'when she wore a white dress with blue ribbons, and stood up there in the choir and sang.'

The picture of that girl, the fact that she had lived neighbor to that girl for twenty years, and had let her die for lack of life, was suddenly more than she could bear.

'Oh, I *wish* I'd come over here once in a while!' she cried. 'That was a crime! That was a crime! Who's going to punish that?'

'We mustn't take on,' said Mrs Peters, with a frightened look toward the stairs.

'I might 'a' *known* she needed help! I tell you, it's *queer*, Mrs Peters. We live close together, and we live far apart. We all go through the same things – it's all just a different kind of the same thing! If it weren't – why do you and I *understand*? Why do we *know* – what we know this minute?'

She dashed her hand across her eyes. Then, seeing the jar of fruit on the table, she reached for it and choked out, 'If I was you I wouldn't *tell* her her fruit was gone! Tell her it *ain't*. Tell her it's all right – all of it. Here – take this in to prove it to her! She – she may never know whether it was broke or not.'

She turned away.

Mrs Peters reached out for the bottle of fruit as if she were glad to take it – as if touching a familiar thing, having something to do, would keep her from something else. She got up, looked about for something to wrap the fruit in, took a petticoat from the pile of clothes she had brought from the front room, and nervously started winding that around the bottle.

'My!' she began, in a high, false voice. 'It's a good thing the men couldn't hear us! Getting all stirred up over a little thing like a – dead canary.' She hurried over that. 'As if that could have anything to do with – with – My, wouldn't they *laugh*?'

Footsteps were heard on the stairs.

'Maybe they would,' muttered Mrs Hale, 'maybe they wouldn't.'

'No, Peters,' said the county attorney incisively, 'it's all perfectly clear, except the reason for doing it. But you know juries when it comes to women. If there was some definite thing – something to show. Something to make a story about. A thing that would connect up with this clumsy way of doing it.'

In a covert way Mrs Hale looked at Mrs Peters. Mrs Peters was looking at her. Quickly they looked away from each other. The outer door opened and Mr Hale came in.

'I've got the team round now,' he said. 'Pretty cold out there.'

'I'm going to stay here awhile by myself,' the county attorney suddenly announced. 'You can send Frank out for me, can't you?' he asked the sheriff. 'I want to go over everything. I'm not satisfied.'

Again, for one brief moment, the two women's eyes found one another.

The sheriff came up to the table.

'Did you want to see what Mrs Peters was going to take in?'

The county attorney picked up the apron. He laughed. 'Oh, I guess they're not very dangerous things the ladies have picked out.'

Mrs Hale's hand was on the sewing basket in which the box was concealed. She felt that she ought to take her hand off the basket. She did not seem able to. He picked up one of the quilt blocks which she had piled on to cover the box. Her eyes felt like fire. She had a feeling that if he took up the basket she would snatch it from him.

But he did not take it up. With another little laugh, he turned away, saying, 'No. Mrs Peters doesn't need supervising. For that matter, a sheriff's wife is married to the law. Ever think of it that way, Mrs Peters?'

Mrs Peters was standing beside the table. Mrs Hale shot a look up at her, but she could not see her face. Mrs Peters had turned away. When she spoke, her voice was muffled. 'Not – just that way,' she said.

'Married to the law!' chuckled Mrs Peters' husband. He moved toward the front room, and said to the county attorney, 'I just want you to come in here, George. We ought to take a look at these windows.'

'Oh – windows,' said the county attorney scoffingly.

'We'll be right out, Mr Hale,' said the sheriff to the farmer, who was still waiting by the door.

Hale went to look after the horses. The sheriff followed the county attorney into the other room. Again – for one final moment – the two women were alone in that kitchen.

Martha Hale sprang up, her hands tight together, looking at that other woman, with whom it rested. At first she could not see her eyes, for the sheriff's wife had not turned back since she turned away at that suggestion of being married to the law. But now Mrs Hale made her turn back. Her eyes made her turn back. Slowly, unwillingly, Mrs Peters turned her head until her eyes met the eyes of the other woman. There was a moment when they held each other in a steady, burning look in which there was no evasion nor flinching. Then Martha Hale's eyes pointed the way to the basket in which was hidden the thing that would make certain the conviction of the other woman – that woman who was not there and yet who had been there with them all through that hour.

For a moment Mrs Peters did not move. And then she did it. With a rush forward, she threw back the quilt pieces, got the box, tried to put it in her handbag. It was too big. Desperately she opened it, started to take the bird out. But there she broke – she could not touch the bird. She stood there helpless, foolish.

There was the sound of a knob turning in the inner door. Martha Hale snatched the box from the sheriff's wife, and got it in the pocket of her big coat just as the sheriff and the county attorney came back into the kitchen.

'Well, Henry,' said the county attorney facetiously, 'at least we found out that she was not going to quilt it. She was going to – what is it you call it, ladies?'

Mrs Hale's hand was against the pocket of her coat.

'We call it – knot it, Mr Henderson.'

The Haunted Boy

CARSON McCULLERS

Carson McCullers was one of the most influential novelists of the American Deep South, and belonging to the school known as Southern Gothic. Her first novel, published when she was twenty-three, was The Heart is a Lonely Hunter; *others include* The Ballad of the Sad Café *and* The Member of the Wedding.

Hugh looked for his mother at the corner, but she was not in the yard. Sometimes she would be out fooling with the border of spring flowers – the candytuft, the sweet william, the lobelias (she had taught him the names) but today the green front lawn with the borders of many-coloured flowers was empty under the frail sunshine of the mid-April afternoon. Hugh raced up the sidewalk, and John followed him. They finished the front steps with two bounds, and the door slammed after them.

'Mama!' Hugh called.

It was then, in the unanswering silence as they stood in the empty, wax-floored hall, that Hugh felt there was something wrong. There was no fire in the grate of the sitting room, and since he was used to the flicker of firelight during the cold months, the room on this first warm day seemed strangely naked and cheerless. Hugh shivered. He was glad John was there. The sun shone on a red piece of the flowered rug. Red-bright, red-dark, red-dead – Hugh sickened with a sudden chill remembrance of 'the other time'. The red darkened to a dizzy black.

'What's the matter, Brown?' John asked. 'You look so white.'

Hugh shook himself and put his hand to his forehead. 'Nothing. Let's go back to the kitchen.'

'I can't stay but just a minute,' John said. 'I'm obligated to sell those tickets. I have to eat and run.'

The kitchen, with the fresh checked towels and clean pans, was now the best room in the house. And on the enamelled table there was a lemon pie that she had made. Assured by the everyday kitchen and the pie, Hugh stepped back into the hall and raised his face again to call upstairs.

'Mother! Oh, Mama!'

Again there was no answer.

'My mother made this pie,' he said. Quickly he found a knife and cut into the pie – to dispel the gathering sense of dread.

'Think you ought to cut into it, Brown?'

'Sure thing, Laney.'

They called each other by their last names this spring, unless they happened to forget. To Hugh it seemed sporty and grown and somehow grand. Hugh liked John better than any other boy at school. John was two years older than Hugh and compared to him the other boys seemed like a silly crowd of punks. John was the best student in the sophomore class, brainy but not the least bit a teacher's pet, and he was the best athlete too. Hugh was a freshman and didn't have so many friends that first year of high school – he had somehow cut himself off, because he was so afraid.

'Mama always has something nice for after school.' Hugh put a big piece of pie on a saucer for John – for Laney.

'This pie is certainly super.'

'The crust is made of crunched up graham crackers instead of regular pie dough,' Hugh said, 'because pie dough is a lot of trouble. We think this graham-cracker pastry is just as good. Naturally, my mother can make regular pie dough if she wants to.'

Hugh could not keep still; he walked up and down the kitchen, eating the pie wedge he carried on the palm of his hand. His brown hair was mussed with nervous rakings, and his gentle gold-brown eyes were haunted with pained perplexity. John, who remained seated at the table, sensed Hugh's uneasiness and wrapped one gangling leg around the other.

'I'm really obligated to sell those Glee Club tickets.'

'Don't go. You have the whole afternoon.' He was afraid of the empty house. He needed John, he needed someone; most of all he needed to hear his mother's voice and know she was in the house with him. 'Maybe Mama is taking a bath,' he said. 'I'll holler again.'

The answer to his third call too was silence.

'I guess your mother must have gone to the movie or gone shopping, or something.'

'No,' Hugh said. 'She would have left a note. She always does when she's gone when I come home from school.'

'We haven't looked for a note,' John said. 'Maybe she left it under the doormat or somewhere in the living room.'

Hugh was inconsolable. 'No. She would have left it right under this pie. She knows I always run first to the kitchen.'

'Maybe she had a phone call or thought of something she suddenly wanted to do.'

'She *might* have,' he said. 'I remember she said to Daddy that one of these days she was going to buy herself some new clothes.' This flash of hope did not survive its expression. He pushed his hair back and started from the room. 'I guess I'd better go upstairs. I ought to go upstairs while you are here.' He stood with his arm around the newel-post; the smell of varnished stairs, the sight of the closed white bathroom door at the top revived again 'the other time'. He clung to the newel-post, and his feet would not move to climb the stairs. The red turned again to the whirling, sick dark. Hugh sat down. *Stick your head between your legs*, he ordered, remembering scout first aid.

'Hugh,' John called. 'Hugh!'

The dizziness clearing, Hugh accepted a fresh chagrin – Laney was calling him by his ordinary first name; he thought he was a sissy about his mother, unworthy of being called by his last name in the grand, sporty way they used before. The dizziness cleared when he returned to the kitchen.

'Brown,' said John, and the chagrin disappeared. 'Does this establishment have anything pertaining to a cow? A white, fluid liquid. In French they call it *lait*. Here we call it plain old milk.'

The stupidity of shock lightened. 'Oh, Laney, I am a dope! Please excuse me. I clean forgot.' Hugh fetched the milk from the refrigerator and found two glasses. 'I didn't think. My mind was on something else.'

'I know,' John said. After a moment, he asked in a calm voice, looking steadily at Hugh's eyes: 'Why are you so worried about your mother? Is she sick, Hugh?'

Hugh knew now that the first name was not a slight; it was because John was talking too serious to be sporty. He liked John better than any friend he had ever had. He felt more natural sitting across the kitchen table from John, somehow safer. As he looked into John's gray, peaceful eyes, the balm of affection soothed the dread.

John asked again, still steadily: 'Hugh, is your mother sick?'

Hugh could have answered no other boy. He had talked with no one about his mother, except his father, and even those intimacies had been rare, oblique. They could approach the subject only when they were occupied with something else, doing carpentry work or the two times they hunted in the woods together – or when they were cooking supper or washing dishes.

'She's not exactly sick,' he said, 'but Daddy and I have been worried about her. At least, we used to be worried for a while.'

John asked, 'Is it a kind of heart trouble?'

Hugh's voice was strained. 'Did you hear about that fight I had with that slob Clem Roberts? I scraped his slob face on the gravel walk and nearly killed him sure enough. He's still got scars or at least he did have a bandage on for two days. I had to stay in school every afternoon for a week. But I nearly killed him. I would have if Mr Paxton hadn't come along and dragged me off.'

'I heard about it.'

'You know why I wanted to kill him?'

For a moment John's eyes flickered away.

Hugh tensed himself; his raw boy hands clutched the table edge; he took a deep, hoarse breath: 'That slob was telling everybody that my mother was in Milledgeville. He was spreading it around that my mother was crazy.'

'The dirty bastard.'

Hugh said in a clear, defeated voice: 'My mother *was* in Milledgeville. But that doesn't mean she was crazy,' he added quickly. 'In that big state hospital there are other buildings for people who are just sick. Mama was sick for a while. Daddy and me discussed it and decided that the best hospital in Milledgeville was the place where there were the best doctors and she would get the best care. But she was the furthest from crazy than anybody in the world. You know Mama, John.' He said once again: 'I ought to go upstairs.'

John said: 'I have always thought that your mother is one of the nicest ladies in this town.'

'You see, Mama had a peculiar thing happen, and afterward she was blue.'

Confession, the first deep-rooted words, opened the festered secrecy of the boy's heart, and he continued more rapidly, urgent and finding unforeseen relief. 'Last year my mother thought she was going to have a little baby. She talked it over with Daddy and me,' he said proudly. 'We wanted a girl. I was going to choose the name. We were so tickled. I hunted up all my old toys – my electric trains and the tracks ... I was going to name her Crystal – how does that name strike you for a girl? It reminds me of something bright and dainty.'

'Was the little baby born dead?'

Even with John, Hugh's ears turned hot; his cold hands touched them. 'No, it was what they call a tumour. That's what happened to my mother. They had to operate at the hospital here.' He was embarrassed and his voice was very low. 'Then she had something called change of life.' The words were terrible to Hugh. 'And afterward she was blue. Daddy said it was a shock to her nervous system. It's something that happens to ladies; she was just blue and run-down.'

Although there was no red, no red in the kitchen anywhere, Hugh was approaching 'the other time'.

'One day, she just sort of gave up – one day last fall.' Hugh's eyes were wide open and glaring; again he climbed the stairs and opened the bathroom door – he put his hand to his eyes to shut out the memory.

'She tried to – hurt herself. I found her when I came in from school.'

John reached out and carefully stroked Hugh's sweatered arm.

'Don't worry. A lot of people have to go to hospitals because they are run-down and blue. Could happen to anybody.'

'We had to put her in the hospital – the best hospital.' The recollection of those long, long months was stained with a dull loneliness, as cruel in its lasting unappeasement as 'the other time' – how long had it lasted? In the hospital Mama could walk around and she always had on shoes.

John said carefully: 'This pie is certainly super.'

'My mother is a super cook. She cooks things like meat pie and salmon loaf – as well as steaks and hot dogs.'

'I hate to eat and run,' John said.

Hugh was so frightened of being left alone that he felt the alarm in his own loud heart.

'Don't go,' he urged, 'let's talk for a while.'

Hugh could not tell him. Not even John Laney. He could tell no one of the empty house and the horror of the time before. 'Do you ever cry?' he asked John. 'I don't.'

'I do sometimes,' John admitted.

'I wish I had known you better when mother was away. Daddy and me used to go hunting nearly every Saturday. We *lived* on quail and dove. I bet you would have liked that.' He added in a lower tone: 'On Sunday we went to the hospital.'

John said: 'It's kind of a delicate proposition selling those tickets. A lot of people don't enjoy the high school Glee Club operettas. Unless they know someone in it personally, they'd rather stay home with a good TV show. A lot of people buy tickets on the basis of being public spirited.'

'We're going to get a television set real soon.'

'I couldn't exist without television,' John said.

Hugh's voice was apologetic. 'Daddy wants to clean up the hospital bills first, because as everybody knows sickness is a very expensive proposition. Then we'll get TV.'

John lifted his milk glass. 'Skoal,' he said. 'That's a Swedish word you say before you drink. A good-luck word.'

'You know so many foreign words and languages.'

'Not so many,' John said truthfully. 'Just "kaput" and "adiós" and "skoal" and stuff we learn in French class. That's not much.'

'That's *beaucoup*,' said Hugh, and he felt witty and pleased with himself.

Suddenly the stored tension burst into physical activity. Hugh grabbed the basketball out on the porch and rushed into the backyard. He dribbled the ball several times and aimed at the goal his father had put up on his last birthday. When he missed he bounced the ball to John, who had come after him.

It was good to be outdoors and the relief of natural play brought Hugh the first line of a poem. 'My heart is like a basketball, bounding with glee down the hall. How do you like that for the start of a poem?'

'Sounds kind of crazy to me,' John said. Then he corrected himself hastily. 'I mean it sounds – odd. Odd, I meant.'

Hugh realized why John changed the word, and the elation of play and poems left him instantly. He caught the ball and stood with it cradled in his arms. The afternoon was golden and the wisteria vine on the porch was in full, unshattered bloom. The wisteria was like lavender waterfalls. The fresh breeze smelled of sun-warmed flowers. The sunlit sky was blue and cloudless. It was the first warm day of spring.

'I have to shove off,' John said.

'No!' Hugh's voice was desperate. 'Don't you want another piece of pie? I never heard of anybody eating just one piece of pie.'

He steered John into the house and this time he called only out of habit because he always called on coming in. 'Mother!' He was cold after the bright, sunny outdoors. He was cold not only because of the weather but because he was so scared.

'My mother has been home a month and every afternoon she's always here when I come home from school. Always, always.'

They stood in the kitchen looking at the lemon pie. And to Hugh the cut pie looked somehow – odd. As they stood motionless in the kitchen the silence was creepy, and odd too.

'Doesn't this house seem quiet to you?'

'It's because you don't have television. We put on our TV at seven o'clock and it stays on all day and all night until we go to bed. Whether anybody's in the living room or not. There's plays and skits and gags going on continually.'

'We have a radio, of course, and a vic.'

'But that's not the company of a good TV. You won't know when your mother is in the house or not when you get TV.'

Hugh didn't answer. Their footsteps sounded hollow in the hall. He felt sick as he stood on the first step with his arm around the newel-post. 'If you could just come upstairs for a minute.'

John's voice was suddenly impatient and loud. 'How many times have I told you I'm obligated to sell those tickets. You have to be public-spirited about things like glee clubs.'

'Just for a second. I have something important to show you upstairs.'

John did not ask what it was and Hugh sought desperately to name something important enough to get John upstairs. He said finally: 'I'm assembling a hi-fi machine. You have to know a lot about electronics – my father is helping me.'

But even when he spoke he knew John did not for a second believe the lie. Who would buy a hi-fi when they didn't have television? He hated John, as you hate people you have to need so badly. He had to say something more and he straightened his shoulders.

'I just want you to know how much I value your friendship. During these past months I had somehow cut myself off from people.'

'That's okay, Brown. You oughtn't to be so sensitive because your mother was – where she was.'

John had his hand on the door and Hugh was trembling. 'I thought if you could come up for just a minute –'

John looked at him with anxious, puzzled eyes. Then he asked slowly: 'Is there something you are scared of upstairs?'

Hugh wanted to tell him everything. But he could not tell what his mother had done that September afternoon. It was too terrible and – odd. It was like something a *patient* would do, and not like his mother at all. Although his eyes were wild with terror and his body trembled he said, 'I'm not scared.'

'Well, so long. I'm sorry I have to go – but to be obligated is to be obligated.'

John closed the front door and he was alone in the empty house. Nothing could save him now. Even if a whole crowd of boys were listening to TV in the living room, laughing at funny gags and jokes, it would still not help him. He had to go upstairs and find her. He sought courage from the last thing John had said, and repeated the words aloud. 'To be obligated is to be obligated.' But the words did not give him any of John's thoughtlessness and courage; they were creepy and strange in the silence.

He turned slowly to go upstairs. His heart was not like a basketball but like a fast, jazz drum, beating faster and faster as he climbed the stairs. His feet dragged as though he waded through knee-deep water and he held on to the bannisters. The house looked odd, crazy. As he looked down at the ground-floor table with the vase of fresh spring flowers, that too looked somehow peculiar. There was a mirror on the second floor and his own face startled him, so crazy did it seem to him. The initial of his high school sweater was backward and wrong in the reflection and his mouth opened like an asylum idiot. He shut his mouth and he looked better. Still the objects he saw – the table downstairs, the sofa upstairs – looked somehow cracked or jarred because of the dread in him, although they were the familiar things of every day. He fastened his eyes on the closed door at the right of the stairs and the fast, jazz drum beat faster.

He opened the bathroom door and for a moment the dread that had haunted him all that afternoon made him see again the room as he had seen it 'the other time'. His mother lay on the floor and there was blood everywhere. His mother lay there dead and there was blood everywhere, on her slashed wrist, and a pool of blood had trickled to the bathtub and lay dammed there.

Hugh touched the doorframe and steadied himself. Then the room settled and he realized this was not 'the other time'. The April sunlight brightened the clean white tiles. There was only bathroom brightness and the sunny window. He went to the bedroom and saw the empty bed with the rose-coloured spread. The lady things were on the dresser. The room was as it always looked and nothing had happened . . . nothing had happened and he flung himself on the quilted rose bed and cried from relief and a strained, bleak tiredness that had lasted so long. The sobs jerked his whole body and quieted his jazz, fast heart.

Hugh had not cried all those months. He had not cried at 'the other time', when he found his mother alone in that empty house with blood everywhere. He had not cried but he made a scout mistake. He had first lifted his mother's heavy, bloody body before he tried to bandage her. He had not cried when he called his father. He had not cried those few days when they were deciding what to do. He hadn't even cried when their doctor suggested Milledgeville, or when he and his father took her to the hospital in the car – although his father cried on the way home. He had not cried at the meals they made – steak every night for a whole month, so that they felt steak was running out of their eyes, their ears; then they had switched to hot dogs, and ate them until hot dogs ran out of their ears, their eyes. They got in ruts of food and were messy about the kitchen, so that it was never nice except the Saturday the cleaning woman came. He did not cry those lonesome afternoons after he had the fight with Clem Roberts and felt the other boys were thinking queer things of his mother. He stayed at home in the messy kitchen, eating Fig Newtons or chocolate bars. Or he went to see a neighbour's television – Miss Richards, an old maid who saw old maid shows. He had not cried when his father drank too much, so that it took his appetite and Hugh had to eat alone. He had not even cried on those long, waiting Sundays when they went to Milledgeville and he twice saw a lady on a porch without any shoes on and talking to herself. A lady who was a patient and who struck at him with a horror he could not name. He did not cry when at first his mother would say: *Don't punish me by making me stay here. Let me go home.* He had not cried at the terrible words that haunted him – 'change of life' – 'crazy' – 'Milledgeville' – he could not cry at all during those long months strained with dullness and want and dread.

He still sobbed on the rose bedspread, which was soft and cool against his wet cheeks. He was sobbing so loud that he did not hear the front door open, did not even hear his mother call or the footsteps on the stairs. He still sobbed when his mother touched him and burrowed his face hard in the spread. He even stiffened his legs and kicked his feet.

'Why, loveyboy,' his mother said, calling him a long-ago child name. 'What's happened?'

He sobbed even louder, although his mother tried to turn his face to her. He wanted her to worry. He did not turn around until she had finally left the bed, and then he looked at her. She had on a different dress – blue silk it looked like in the pale spring light.

'Darling, what's happened?'

The terror of the afternoon was over, but he could not tell it to his mother. He could not tell her what he had feared, or explain the horror of things that were never there at all – but had once been there.

'Why did you do it?'

'The first warm day I just suddenly decided to buy myself some new clothes.'

But he was not talking about clothes; he was thinking about 'the other time' and the grudge that had started when he saw the blood and horror and felt *why did she do this to me?* He thought of the grudge against the mother he loved the most in the world. All those last, sad months the anger had bounced against the love with guilt between.

'I bought two dresses and two petticoats. How do you like them?'

'I hate them!' Hugh said angrily. 'Your slip is showing.'

She turned around twice and the petticoat showed terribly. 'It's supposed to show, goofy. It's the style.'

'I still don't like it.'

'I ate a sandwich at the tearoom with two cups of cocoa and then went to Mendel's. There were so many pretty things I couldn't seem to get away. I bought these two dresses and look, Hugh! The shoes!'

His mother went to the bed and switched on the light so he could see. The shoes were flat-heeled and *blue* – with diamond sparkles on the toes. He did not know how to criticize. 'They look more like evening shoes than things you wear on the street.'

'I have never owned any coloured shoes before. I couldn't resist them.'

His mother sort of danced over toward the window, making the petticoat twirl under the new dress. Hugh had stopped crying now, but he was still angry. 'I don't like it because it makes you look like you're trying to seem young and I bet you are forty years old.'

His mother stopped dancing and stood still at the window. Her face was suddenly quiet and sad. 'I'll be forty-three years old in June.'

He had hurt her and suddenly the anger vanished and there was only love. 'Mama, I shouldn't have said that.'

'I realized when I was shopping that I hadn't been in a store for more than a year. Imagine!'

Hugh could not stand the sad quietness and the mother he loved so much. He could not stand his love or his mother's prettiness. He wiped the tears on the sleeve of his sweater and got up from the bed. 'I have never seen you so pretty, or a dress or a slip so pretty.' He crouched down before his mother and touched the bright shoes. 'The shoes are really super.'

'I thought the minute I laid eyes on them that you would like them.' She pulled Hugh up and kissed him on the cheek. 'Now I've got lipstick on you.'

Hugh quoted a witty remark he had heard before as he scrubbed off the lipstick. 'It only shows I'm popular.'

'Hugh, why were you crying when I came in? Did something at school upset you?'

'It was only that when I came in and found you gone and no note or anything –'

'I forgot all about a note.'

'And all afternoon I felt – John Laney came in but he had to go sell Glee Club tickets. All afternoon I felt –'

'What? What was the matter?'

But he could not tell the mother he loved about the terror and the cause. He said at last: 'All afternoon I felt – odd.'

Afterward when his father came home he called Hugh to come out into the backyard with him. His father had a worried look – as though he spied a valuable tool Hugh had left outside. But there was no tool and the basketball was put back in its place on the back porch.

'Son,' his father said, 'there's something I want to tell you.'

'Yes, sir?'

'Your mother said that you had been crying this afternoon.' His father did not wait for him to explain. 'I just want us to have a close understanding with each other. Is there anything about school – or something that puzzles you? Why were you crying?'

Hugh looked back at the afternoon and already it was far away, distant as a peculiar view seen at the wrong end of a telescope.

'I don't know,' he said. 'I guess maybe I was somehow nervous.'

His father put his arm around his shoulders. 'Nobody can be nervous before they are sixteen years old. You have a long way to go.'

'I know.'

'I have never seen your mother look so well. She looks so gay and pretty, better than she's looked in years. Don't you realize that?'

'The slip – the petticoat is supposed to show. It's a new style.'

'Soon it will be summer,' his father said. 'And we'll go on picnics – the three of us.' The words brought an instant vision of glare on the yellow creek and the summer-leaved, adventurous woods. His father added, 'I came out here to tell you something else.'

'Yes, sir?'

'I just want you to know that I realize how fine you were all that bad time. How fine, how damn fine.'

His father was using a swear word as if he were talking to a grown man. His father was not a person to hand out compliments – always he was strict with report cards and tools left around. His father never praised him or used grown words or anything. Hugh felt his face grow hot and he touched it with his cold hands.

'I just want to tell you that, son.' He shook Hugh by the shoulder. 'You'll be taller than your old man in a year or so.' Quickly his father went into the house, leaving Hugh to the sweet and unaccustomed aftermath of praise.

Hugh stood in the darkening yard after the sunset colours faded in the west and the wisteria was dark purple. The kitchen light was on and he saw his mother fixing dinner. He knew that something was finished; the terror was far from him now, also the anger that had bounced with love, the dread and guilt. Although he felt he would never cry again – or least not until he was sixteen – in the brightness of his tears glistened the safe, lighted kitchen, now that he was no longer a haunted boy, now that he was glad, somehow, and not afraid.

The Doll's House

KATHERINE MANSFIELD

One of the finest and most important short-story writers in modern literature, Katherine Mansfield was born in New Zealand and died in France, from tuberculosis. She was married to the author and critic John Middleton Murry and was a friend of Virginia Woolf and others from the Bloomsbury Set in London. She published five collections of stories, but no other fiction.

When dear old Mrs Hay went back to town after staying with the Burnells she sent the children a doll's house. It was so big that the carter and Pat carried it into the courtyard, and there it stayed, propped up on two wooden boxes beside the feed-room door. No harm could come of it; it was summer. And perhaps the smell of paint would have gone off by the time it had to be taken in. For, really, the smell of paint coming from that doll's house ('Sweet of old Mrs Hay, of course; most sweet and generous!') but the smell of paint was quite enough to make anyone seriously ill, in Aunt Beryl's opinion. Even before the sacking was taken off. And when it was . . .

There stood the doll's house, a dark, oily, spinach green, picked out with bright yellow. Its two solid little chimneys, glued on to the roof, were painted red and white, and the door, gleaming with yellow varnish, was like a little slab of toffee. Four windows, real windows, were divided into panes by a broad streak of green. There was actually a tiny porch, too, painted yellow, with big lumps of congealed paint hanging along the edge.

But perfect, perfect little house! Who could possibly mind the smell? It was part of the joy, part of the newness.

'Open it quickly, someone!'

The hook at the side was stuck fast. Pat pried it open with his open knife and the whole house-front swung back and – there you were, gazing at one and the same moment into the drawing-room and dining-room, the kitchen and two bedrooms. That is the way for a house to open! Why don't all houses open like that? How much more exciting than peering through the slit of a door into a mean little hall with a hatstand and two umbrellas! That is – isn't it? – what you long to know about a house when you put your hand on the knocker. Perhaps it is the way God opens houses at dead of night when He is taking a quiet turn with an angel . . .

'O-oh!' The Burnell children sounded as though they were in despair. It was too marvellous; it was too much for them. They had never seen anything like it in their lives. All the rooms were papered. There were pictures on the walls, painted on the paper, with gold frames complete. Red carpet covered all the floors except the kitchen; red plush chairs in the drawing-room, green in the dining-room; tables, beds with real bedclothes, a cradle, a stove, a dresser with tiny plates and one big jug. But what Kezia liked more than anything, what she liked frightfully, was the lamp. It stood in the middle of the dining-room table, an exquisite little amber lamp with a white globe. It was even filled all ready for lighting, though, of course, you couldn't light it. But there was something inside that looked like oil, and that moved when you shook it.

The father and mother dolls, who sprawled very stiff as though they had fainted in the drawing-room, and their two little children asleep upstairs, were really too big for the doll's house. They didn't look as though they belonged. But the lamp was perfect. It seemed to smile at Kezia, and say, 'I live here.' The lamp was real.

The Burnell children could hardly walk to school fast enough the next morning. They burned to tell everybody, to describe, to – well – to boast about their doll's house before the school-bell rang.

'I'm to tell,' said Isabel, 'because I'm the eldest. And you two can join in after. But I'm to tell first.'

There was nothing to answer. Isabel was bossy, but she was always right, and Lottie and Kezia knew too well the powers that went with being the eldest. They brushed through the thick buttercups at the road edge and said nothing.

'And I'm to choose who's to come and see it first. Mother said I might.'

For it had been arranged that while the doll's house stood in the courtyard they might ask the girls at school, two at a time, to come and look. Not to stay to tea, of course, or to come traipsing through the house. But just to stand quietly in the courtyard while Isabel pointed out the beauties and Lottie and Kezia looked pleased.

But hurry as they might, by the time they had reached the tarred palings of the boys' playground the bell had begun to jangle. They only just had time to whip off their hats and fall into line before the roll was called. Never mind. Isabel tried to make up for it by looking very important and mysterious and whispering behind her hand to the girls near her. 'Got something to tell you at playtime.'

Playtime came and Isabel was surrounded. The girls of her class nearly fought to put their arms around her, to walk away with her, to beam flatteringly, to be her special friend. She held quite a court under the huge pine trees at the side of the playground. Nudging, giggling together, the little girls pressed up close. And the only two who stayed outside the ring were the two who were always outside, the little Kelveys. They knew better than to come anywhere near the Burnells.

For the fact was, the school the Burnell children went to was not at all the kind of place their parents would have chosen if there had been any choice. But there was none. It was the only school for miles. And the consequence was all the children in the neighbourhood, the Judge's little girls, the doctor's daughters, the storekeeper's children, the milkman's, were forced to mix together. Not to speak of there being an equal number of rude, rough little boys as well. But the line had to be drawn somewhere. It was drawn at the Kelveys. Many of the children, including the Burnells, were not allowed even to speak to them. They walked past the Kelveys with their heads in the air, and as they set the fashion in all matters of behaviour, the Kelveys were shunned by everybody. Even the teacher had a special voice for them, and a special smile for the other children when Lil Kelvey came up to her desk with a bunch of dreadfully common-looking flowers.

They were the daughters of a spry, hardworking little washer-woman who went about from house to house by the day. This was awful enough. But where was Mr Kelvey? Nobody knew for certain. But everybody said he was in prison. So they were the daughters of a washerwoman and a gaolbird. Very nice company for other people's children! And they looked it. Why Mrs Kelvey made them so conspicuous was hard to understand. The truth was they were dressed in 'bits' given to her by the people for whom she worked. Lil, for instance, who was a stout, plain child, with big freckles, came to school in a dress made from a green art-serge table-cloth of the Burnells', with red plush sleeves from the Logans' curtains. Her hat, perched on top of her high forehead, was a grown-up woman's hat, once the property of Miss Lecky, the post-mistress. It was turned up at the back and trimmed with a large scarlet quill. What a little guy she looked! And her little sister, our Else, wore a long white dress, rather like a nightgown, and a pair of little boy's boots. But whatever our Else wore she would have looked strange. She was a tiny wishbone of a child, with cropped hair and enormous solemn eyes – a little whiteowl. Nobody had ever seen her smile; she scarcely ever spoke. She went through life holding on to Lil, with a piece of Lil's skirt screwed up in her hand. Where Lil went our Else followed. In the playground, on the road going to and from school, there was Lil marching in front and our Else holding on behind. Only when she wanted anything, or when she was out of breath, our Else gave Lil a tug, a twitch, and Lil stopped and turned round. The Kelveys never failed to understand each other.

Now they hovered at the edge; you couldn't stop them listening. When the little girls turned round and sneered, Lil, as usual, gave her silly, shamefaced smile, but our Else only looked.

And Isabel's voice, so very proud, went on telling. The carpet made a great sensation, but so did the beds with real bedclothes, and the stove with an oven door.

When she finished Kezia broke in. 'You've forgotten the lamp, Isabel.'

'Oh, yes,' said Isabel, 'and there's a teeny little lamp, all made of yellow glass, with a white globe, that stands on the dining-room table. You couldn't tell it from a real one.'

'The lamp's best of all,' cried Kezia. She thought Isabel wasn't making half enough of the little lamp. But nobody paid any attention. Isabel was choosing the two who were to come back with them that afternoon and see it. She chose Emmie Cole and Lena Logan. But when the others knew they were all to have a chance, they couldn't be nice enough to Isabel. One by one, they put their arms round Isabel's waist and walked her off. They had something to whisper to her in secret. 'Isabel's *my* best friend.'

Only the little Kelveys moved away forgotten; there was nothing more for them to hear.

Days passed, and as more children saw the doll's house, the fame of it spread. It became the one subject, the rage. The one question was, 'Have you seen the Burnells' doll's house? Oh, ain't it lovely?' 'Haven't you seen it? Oh, I say!'

Even the dinner hour was given up to talking about it. The little girls sat under the pines eating their thick mutton sandwiches and big slabs of johnny cake spread with butter. While always, as near as they could get, sat the Kelveys, our Else holding on to Lil, listening too, while they chewed their jam sandwiches out of a newspaper soaked with large red blobs.

'Mother,' said Kezia, 'can't I ask the Kelveys just once?'

'Certainly not, Kezia.'

'But why not?'

'Run away, Kezia; you know quite well why not.'

At last everybody had seen it except them. On that day the subject rather flagged. It was the dinner hour. The children stood together under the pine trees, and suddenly, they looked at the Kelveys eating out of their paper, always by themselves, always listening, they wanted to be horrid to them. Emmie Cole started the whisper.

'Lil Kelvey's going to be a servant when she grows up.'

'O-oh, how awful!' said Isabel Burnell, and she made eyes at Emmie.

Emmie swallowed in a very meaning way and nodded to Isabel as she'd seen her mother do on those occasions.

'It's true – it's true – it's true,' she said.

Then Lena Logan's little eyes snapped. 'Shall I ask her?' she whispered.

'Bet you don't,' said Jessie May.

'Pooh, I'm not frightened,' said Lena. Suddenly she gave a little squeal and danced in front of the other girls. 'Watch! Watch me! Watch me now!' said Lena. And sliding, gliding, dragging one foot, giggling behind her hand, Lena went over to the Kelveys.

Lil looked up from her dinner. She wrapped the rest quickly away. Our Else stopped chewing. What was coming now?

'Is it true you're going to be a servant when you grow up, Lil Kelvey?' shrilled Lena.

Dead silence. But instead of answering, Lil only gave her silly shamefaced smile. She didn't seem to mind the question at all. What a sell for Lena! The girls began to titter.

Lena couldn't stand that. She put her hands on her hips; she shot forward. 'Yah, yer father's in prison!' she hissed spitefully.

This was such a marvellous thing to have said that the little girls rushed away in a body, deeply, deeply excited, wild with joy. Someone found a long rope, and they began skipping. And never did they skip so high, run in and out as fast or do such daring things as on that morning.

In the afternoon Pat called for the Burnell children with the buggy and they drove home. There were visitors. Isabel and Lottie, who liked visitors, went upstairs to change their pinafores. But Kezia thieved out at the back. Nobody was about; she began to swing on the big white gates of the courtyard. Presently, looking along the road, she saw two little dots. They grew bigger, they were coming towards her. Now she could see that one was in front and one close behind. Now she could see that they were the Kelveys. Kezia stopped swinging. She slipped off the gate as if she was going to run away. Then she hesitated. The Kelveys came nearer, and beside them walked their shadows, very long, stretching right across the road with their heads in the buttercups. Kezia clambered back on the gate; she had made up her mind; she swung out.

'Hullo,' she said to the passing Kelveys.

They were so astounded that they stopped. Lil gave her silly smile. Our Else stared.

'You can come and see our doll's house if you want to,' said Kezia, and she dragged one toe on the ground. But at that Lil turned red and shook her head quickly.

'Why not?' asked Kezia.

Lil gasped, then she said, 'Your Ma told our Ma you wasn't to speak to us.'

'Oh well,' said Kezia. She didn't know what to reply. 'It doesn't matter. You can come and see our doll's house all the same. Come on. Nobody's looking.'

But Lil shook her head still harder.

'Don't you want to?' asked Kezia.

Suddenly there was a twitch, a tug at Lil's skirt. She turned round. Our Else was looking at her with big, imploring eyes; she was frowning; she wanted to go. For a moment Lil looked at our Else very doubtfully. But then our Else twitched her skirt again. She started forward. Kezia led the way. Like two little stray cats they followed across the courtyard to where the doll's house stood.

'There it is,' said Kezia.

There was a pause. Lil breathed loudly, almost snorted; our Else was still as a stone.

'I'll open it for you,' said Kezia kindly. She undid the hook and they looked inside.

'There's the drawing-room and the dining-room, and that's the – '

'Kezia!'

Oh, what a start they gave!

'Kezia!'

It was Aunt Beryl's voice. They turned round. At the back door stood Aunt Beryl, staring as if she couldn't believe what she saw.

'How dare you ask the little Kelveys into the courtyard?' said her cold, furious voice. 'You know as well as I do, you're not allowed to talk to them. Run away, children, run away at once. And don't come back again,' said Aunt Beryl. And she stepped into the yard and shooed them out as if they were chickens.

They did not need telling twice. Burning with shame, shrinking together, Lil huddled along like her mother, our Else dazed. Somehow they crossed the big courtyard and squeezed through the white gate.

'Wicked, disobedient little girl!' said Aunt Beryl bitterly to Kezia, and she slammed the doll's house to.

The afternoon had been awful. A letter had come from Willie Brent, a terrifying, threatening letter, saying if she did not meet him that evening in Pulman's Bush, he'd come to the front door and ask the reason why! But now that she had frightened those little rats of Kelveys and given Kezia a good scolding, her heart felt lighter. The ghastly pressure was gone. She went back to the house humming.

When the Kelveys were well out of sight of Burnells', they sat down to rest on a big red drain-pipe by the side of the road. Lil's cheeks were still burning; she took off the hat with the quill and held it on her knee. Dreamily they looked over the hay paddocks, past the creek, to the group of wattles where Logan's cows stood waiting to be milked. What were their thoughts?

Presently our Else nudged up close to her sister. But now she had forgotten the cross lady. She put out a finger and stroked her sister's quill; she smiled her rare smile.

'I seen the little lamp,' she said, softly.

Then both were silent once more.

Watching Oksana

EMILY MEIER

Emily Meier lives in St Paul, Minnesota. Her fiction, which has received numerous awards, has been published widely in America. 'Watching Oksana' is her first publication in the UK.

Once upon a time in far-off Odessa there lived a man who abandoned his child. He had done so unwillingly in the process of leaving his wife, but the result was the same as if he had had intent; the child did not know the father or the father the child.

For this man, known as Aleksei, the break was excruciating. In letting go of his child he had not felt a gradual unlocking, as of hands unclasping for skaters to glide apart. He had felt a yank, a sudden splitting away that told him his daughter was wounded, cut to the green quick of her sapling growth. And yet for Aleksei there was no going back, no possible return to the anger that had been his marriage and his wife. He was left in a rage of nightmares – that his daughter, who at two had outgrown her pram, would, by her mother's carelessness, be sent hurling down the *Potemkin* steps. That she would be lost in the labyrinth of catacombs beneath Odessa. That she would not know the excitement of a name – the Black Sea – or its floating of ancient myths: Jason and the Argonauts, the Golden Fleece. That she would grow up without Pushkin's words spiralling on the page so that she must lift her eyes to breathe.

In darkness and distress Aleksei stowed away aboard a ship,

was caught, was made a soldier and sent overland until all he saw was the Khyber Pass.

And there, in 1980, the tale grows muddled, for Aleksei, as he was called only because the Soviet Army held the stowaway papers that named him Aleksei Smirnov, went crazy with a war that, for him, meant killing and seeing his fellows killed and yet not being killed himself. And when he was done being crazy, done with hospitals and war, he was left with a memory that was like so many strips of tattered cloth.

'You have a family?' the doctors asked him in Moscow, and when he could not answer his discharge papers were stamped for Minsk, the home of Aleksei Andreiovitch Smirnov. A train took him there through the Russian night. Alone in his hotel he studied the papers, and on the next morning left for Odessa.

'A holiday?' the stationmaster asked, and Aleksei nodded his head, putting down roubles.

He sat upright on the train, staring out through the window. When he smelled the sea he began to tremble, and when he arrived in Odessa he ate smoked sturgeon which he bought from a vendor and, looking up, saw the five domes of Uspensky Sobor rising into the sky. Walking unsteadily past the shops of Deribasovskaya Ulitsa he made his way there. He lit a candle. He prayed to Our Lady of Kasperovskaya, asking for the return of his daughter's face. He prayed for his name. When, after days, neither the face nor the name appeared, he looked out to sea. Standing at the top of Potyemkinskaya Lestnitsa he watched the big ships' cranes loading cargo in the harbour below. He looked to the steel line of the horizon. This time, with his soldier's scars, when his strength was back he left Odessa with the official papers that had been issued to him and as a sailor.

And so the man known as Aleksei Smirnov became a traveller along the great sea lanes of the world. With his taut, stitched-together body, neither big nor small, and with the blank spaces of memory that clustered around the bittersweet images of Odessa and a faceless, nameless child, he began a present he could make into a past. At Yalta he bought a balalaika and discovered his fingers knew how to play it. His sea-bag was full of books. They had come with him on the train from Moscow, their endpapers blank, and now he wrote the name Aleksei Andreiovitch Smirnov carefully inside each cover so that, should he misplace his life again, he could start over with something to go on.

'Aleksei Andreiovitch, he is the book man,' his shipmates said, but it was a light sort of teasing Aleksei knew, for he could beat them at cards, beat them at a fight because of his quickness, beat them with girls because of his lambent, sea-scorched eyes and the fault lines of his scars which were always alluring.

The freighters he worked on carried grain or tumbled *akavit* the whole way around the world, making it fire. Aleksei sailed under frozen skies. He watched his laundry dry on ships' decks making certain nobody stole it. He sailed in blistering heat, in terrible storms that swung even the flat bulk of a grain carrier like a toy. He was only frightened, though, when he stared into the huge darkness of an empty hold.

Then for the first time he came to America. Seeing a newspaper, he found he knew English. This was in Buffalo where a bumboat pulled alongside his freighter and he bought toothpaste and the *New York Times*. He was wary of America. He assumed any women he met would have AIDS; he assumed there would be efforts to entice him into spiritualism or buying a revolver. The newspaper, though, challenged his ideas. He was fascinated by the advertisements, by black faces in pictures.

By the fifth time he had travelled through the locks of St Lambert and Côte-Ste Cathérine, heading west through the snaked route of seaway and lakes, he had lost his surprise. True, it still felt odd to be sailing between countries too alike to fight, odd to be on a freighter that needed a second set of load lines for water that was fresh. (How, he still wondered, could vast seas with giant waves not be salt?) But he had his own notion of America now, his own experience of it, and when, in December, his ship passed to the east of the aerial bridge in Duluth, Minnesota, and entered its slip on the Wisconsin side of the harbor at Superior, he had his own places to go.

An icebreaker had cleared the harbour. Aleksei, with his duffle bag on his shoulder and a cigarette warming his mouth, left the ship by himself. He was feeling oddly tired, even in the bracing cold. There was a pulling pain on the inside of his right knee, and he wondered if he had twisted his leg somehow, if in leaning back to shout the answer of where he was going to his shipmates he had caught his foot on the ladder in the engine room. He did not think that he had. But his knee hurt and he favoured it, limping as he walked up the snow-covered dock.

It was afternoon under a grey sky which dulled the lake. Aleksei had meant a brisk walk to a coffee-house. In his duffel bag he had a book of poems, a collection of Greek lyrics in English translation, and he had wanted to read and drink coffee until it was dusk, until the lighthouse which, in summer, rolled up in the morning fog, silted light on to the dark benign sky. But today he was no swift Idaios of the strong legs. The cold had settled in his knee. He was shivering with fatigue.

He stopped. He could hear the tin sound of Christmas carols playing from speakers, see decorations mounted on streetlamps. For a moment he had no idea what to do. It was a long walk farther to where he was going and a longer walk still to return to the ship. Then a BudLite sign with a length of burned-out neon caught his eye and, shoving his duffel ahead of him, he opened the door of the bar which it illuminated and went inside.

The bar was not the kind of bar he was used to, not a sailor's bar with a pool table and with the smell of dust and beer dried into the wood of the floor. It was a place with silent, big-screen TVs and a horseshoe-shaped footrail that was brassy new. Aleksei stopped in front of a bar stool and then changed his mind. He braced his knee, which was actually his hip now and even his shin when it came to the pain. He worked himself backwards into a booth. A chill cut from his groin down his leg, chattering an aftershock in his nerves.

He saw the waitress coming to take his order. She was broad-faced and freckle-nosed, and she was wearing blue jeans and a t-shirt. 'Brandy,' he told her. The pain twisted like an augur inside his leg.

Two shots later he was still focused on his leg and on the alive skin above it and below his waist. Oddly, he felt calm. He was in a bar that was strange to him, no sailors in sight, and he had a strange illness – he was sure he did – but he was not really worried. In his experience there was always a nurse in American bars. And, if this one time there wasn't, in America, there was still 911. Safety. Aleksei ordered another brandy.

When the girl brought it she was watching the screen, which had switched from a ball-game to ice-skating.

She put his drink down. 'She is so good. I've seen this five times.'

Aleksei looked up at the screen. 'Praha' he saw on a wall in the picture. He watched as a skater spun from a leap to her skates. He winced, felt his leg clench at the impact. 'Who is it that's so good?'

'A Russian or something. She won. She's amazing.'

'This Prague is now?'

The girl shook her head. 'They've played it for months. Since I've worked here.' She picked up his empty glass. 'When I get drunk I can remember her name. Bayou? Odessa Bayou? No, maybe that's her town.'

Odessa. Aleksei stared at the screen. He was stunned with excitement. The skater was young, maybe fifteen. She was bowed to the audience and she was sitting, now, between a man and a woman, and holding a bouquet of flowers in her arms.

He searched her face. She was delicate in colour but with dark lines under her eyes and, though the smile was radiant, the look that replaced it belonged to the lines. In repose her face was hungry. It was, he decided, the face of an orphan.

The screen blanked and went to an ad. Aleksei drank his brandy straight down. A quarter of him was in acute, intensifying pain.

He could feel his face whitening while he did not scream. His leg shrieked, and in the planet which was the rest of him and which lived as far away as the sun, he could feel the cracked seal on the anguish that stayed in his heart. He motioned for the waitress.

'Are you a nurse?' he said, his voice an inhaled whisper. She shook her head. 'Then please. Call the number. The 911.'

When he thought about it in the next weeks in his hotel room – after the ride to the emergency room in a pickup truck, after the morphine shots, and the three nights in the hospital with the antiviral drugs that kept him retching in the bathroom – Aleksei was certain he had been sick before he ever left the ship, that his leg had been nagging him across the whole of Lake Superior and that he had been a little crazy once more, this time with fever. Why else would he have quoted the 'Wedding of Andromache' to the man in the cowboy hat who drove the pickup? (*And the virgins sang a loud heavenly song whose wonderful echo touched the sky.*) Why indeed? And why, feeling flu-ish, would he have taken shore leave when he knew his freighter was leaving in the morning with its load of wheat? The last run of the season. The urgency to avoid heavy ice and running aground in the St Mary's River, though now he was the one who was run aground.

It had not been an easy thing getting a diagnosis. He'd been CAT-scanned and MRI'd, had given blood, given urine, given blood again. When finally the doctor stood in his room, looking affirmative, Aleksei had made his job easy. There was an eruption of blistered sores that marked his backside and which was progressing down the inside of his leg.

'The good news,' the doctor said, 'is you're not positive for HIV and you don't have this because you're weakened from chemotherapy. It's right that you haven't had chemo? You don't have cancer?'

'No cancer.'

'It's shingles.'

'Excuse?' Aleksei was thinking fast, that this was an American deal. He got treatment; he roofed the doctor's house.

'You had chicken-pox. Sometime in your life you had it, and now – nobody could say why now – some crack in the immune system and the virus woke up in the nerve root and gave you shingles. But you get it in only one nerve path. You picked a long one. Sometimes that spreads out the impact, dilutes it. You weren't that lucky.'

'I do what, then?'

'You leave here. Take the pain pills. Sleep a lot. In a few weeks you're well. And the drugs we gave you – they keep you from neuropathy and chronic pain syndrome. You'll be fine.'

Shingles then. That was the diagnosis and the new homonym and quirky new transit of pain in Aleksei's life. To be released from the hospital he had signed an avalanche of papers, most of them promising the payment of apparently large but unspecified sums. Then he'd been wheeled to a taxicab, his head still in a dancy swoon. He loved the cold air, the sunlight. He rode with the window half-down until the cabbie swore at him to roll it up or be out on the pavement: *You fucking better or you fucking will.*

In a room in the hotel in Superior that he knew to be the cheapest Aleksei had sagged on to the bed and fallen asleep in his jacket and boots. It was the start of the self-monitored portion of his illness and recuperation. He had not stopped being hungry and, every day or so, he used what energy he could pry from himself to go out and buy food. The skin of his groin and leg were so tender that finally he gave in, ripped open the sash of red silk he had bought in Hong Kong for a gift – for someone, sometime – and wrapped it around himself. At odd times he cried, which was new for him. He did not remember crying. Tears, perhaps, but not racking sobs. He would lie on the stained bed-cover and listen through the walls to the rhythmic banging of bodies hitting the headboard in the next room and he would cry not for those bodies or his own but from the sheer need to cry. Then he craved chocolate. For three days he ate Hershey bars and boxes of drugstore candies he pretended were truffles. When he began to itch he scratched every bit of his leg that was not covered with sores and, once, just once, in a bath he scratched away the old layer of skin and then, drying himself, covered his leg with lotion which, for a full minute, felt glorious.

And he dreamed. He had two dreams. The one was that the captain of his ship had come to the hospital on the first night and said, 'Well, keep him then. It's not as if there's a real country that requires him home.' The other dream was of a skater circling the ice in the darkness like a small plane teasing a ship. But this dream was a happy dream, and when he woke from it it was always with a feeling of joy. And this second dream he trusted; the first one he did not, though his sea-bag, with the name Ukrrichflot Shipping Company of Odessa stamped on its side, had appeared at the hospital and had left with him, though he had not taken it there. Somehow, in the vacuum left surrounding the morphine, contact had been made.

When the pain in his leg began to lessen Aleksei went through the bag. Nothing was missing. He had his books, his balalaika. Everything he owned was here in his room behind the flimsy door with its uncertain lock and loose frame. The effort of taking stock, however, had exhausted him. He lay on the bed, staring at the ceiling, listening to his alarm clock tick. He had no desire to read nor any energy even to worry about money. He felt enveloped by lassitude, filled with a sadness that lacked any focus.

He drifted this way through a replay of his symptoms, which moderated slowly as the days passed. When he had first taken his room the television had no sound, only snow for a picture. Occasionally there were vague shadows that passed across the screen, companions of sorts. They required no attention and, as he had none to give, the situation suited him. As he began to feel better, though, he tried to make sense of the fleeting images. Tentatively he would identify a man, perhaps a child, but then the snow would return and the story he'd started for himself would disappear. He played with knobs, rattled the table the television sat on. Finally he complained to the maid, and this assertiveness and the vexation which prompted it startled him. He had, he realized, presumed himself more or less dead. Now, though, there were definite signs of his life returning. He was excited, in fact, when the night desk brought him a television which had sound and a black and white picture with only a slight double image.

'Hell of a way to spend Christmas Eve,' the clerk said.

'Merry Christmas to you,' Aleksei said carefully, quoting the greeting he'd heard on his trips to buy groceries.

'A fucking merry Christmas to you, too,' the man answered.

Aleksei found this funny. When the man left he laughed out loud. Then he flipped channels eagerly, but there was no skating on this TV; churches and choirs, a stirring liturgical voice that was, even in his state of non-practice, two weeks too early for the Christmas he knew. He listened awhile, and then he was very tired and slept a long time into the morning that was American Christmas Day.

When he awoke the day after this Christmas he felt almost strong. His reaction was panic. His illness had drugged him into indifference, but for a man now capable of concern his situation was clearly alarming. He hopped one-footed out of bed and got his wallet from his pants. He turned his pockets out and, dumping everything on to the bed, counted what he had. $84.60 American. There was not a coin or bill of any other currency, though he had only the vaguest memory of making an exchange. He sat back against his pillow and went through his papers, receipts. For an hour he studied them, trying to piece things together. Finally he had the outlines of his predicament; in another three days more rent was due on his room and by January fifteenth he was obligated to pay the hospital whatever it asked. He did not know where he stood legally as a documented resident of Ukraine who had overstayed his shore leave; he was stranded until spring.

Aleksei sat upright. Clearly he was headed for jail, but, in America, was he required to pay for that too? He leaned back slowly into his pillow, back into the exhaustion that moved over him once more.

In the morning, though, he felt better again. He bathed carefully and shaved. He opened his sea-bag and began to sort. A few of his books might be worth something, a few of his trinkets from the Orient. The handle of his knife was inlaid with mother-of-pearl and his watch had a gold chain. There was his fur hat. There was also his balalaika.

Aleksei packed all these things, well wrapped, into his duffel bag. He needed a nap first, but when he woke up he went straight out to find a pawnshop.

As he walked the wind blew up puffs of white from the snow banks along the street. The cold travelled in his leg. He wanted to run. Instead he limped. He felt the bite of the wind on his face and in his fingers, felt the fever chill that made its own bitter ice inside him.

The cold was steamed and frosted on the windows of the pawnshop. He went inside to the dank air and dim light and he was still cold. He bit his lips quiet so he could talk.

'How much?' he asked. He opened the duffel and put everything on the counter.

The pawnbroker sat on a chair, looked idly at the counter, picked at his teeth. 'Not this,' he said finally, moving the balalaika away from the other things. He was paunchy and had thin hair and smelled of smoke. He pushed himself up from the chair and opened the cash register. He laid two twenties on the counter, wrote on the tickets and gave Aleksei the stubs.

'For this all?'

'Take it or leave it.'

Aleksei put the stubs and the money in his wallet. He wrapped the balalaika and settled it carefully back inside the bag. Walking again, he was looking for a place to eat when he saw the BudLite sign with its dark curve on the 'u'. *The skaters*, he thought. *The child with the blue-lined eyes.*

He went straight to a booth, stationed himself in front of a

TV. On the screen there were women in bathing suits lifting weights. He looked around the bar, hunting for the girl with the freckled nose, for the cowboy. Nowhere. Neither of them. A different waitress, much older, came to the booth and he ordered a beer and a corned beef sandwich.

'You want a pitcher?'

He shook his head. 'The skaters are on?'

The waitress looked blank. Aleksei continued. 'Prague. Skaters in Prague. What time?'

'These babes don't do it for you?' The waitress was tapping her pencil eraser on her pad. She stared at him. 'I don't know about any skaters.'

'A waitress is having spots?' He pointed to his nose.

'If you're talking about a kid, she'd be home for Christmas. You want your beer or not?'

Aleksei nodded. He put a bill and his coins on the table. The name '69 Mets' flashed on the screen and he lifted his foot up on to the far bench and felt next to him for the balalaika in his duffel.

The waitress brought his beer and then came back with his sandwich. 'I talked to the bartender,' she said, pushing her hair back, showing some interest. 'With reruns, its whatever they put on the feed. No skaters. Tonight, it's Bulls. Live.'

Aleksei nodded and purposely looked away. Reruns. Feed and bulls. Livestock. He thought he understood. He was feeling very disappointed, though. Empty.

When he got back to his hotel and had wrapped his leg in the sash, he lay face down, grasping the bed, and slept from fatigue and from loneliness. But in the dream he dreamed he was a man in a spotlight. He was in a darkened amphitheatre with a floor of prismed ice, and he played his balalaika and sang of a coachman with a leather lash and gloves, of a frozen heart that burst into flame, while, around him, a faceless skater in a shimmer of a cloth skated spirals, tightly, ever more tightly.

Later, he woke in the darkness, his mind jumbled with thoughts. He reached for a pen.

In the morning he read this: *Go to the bar where picture has sound. Can't sailors make friends? Survivors survive. Who is Harold Rydell?*

Disgusted, he crumpled the note. He had wanted directions. He had wanted answers. The name, though, nagged at him. He pulled his shirt on, zipped up his jeans. He combed his hair. In the blackened silver of the mirror and in the window light he looked young. All this sleep. He sat down on the bed to pull his socks on.

And then he knew where the name was. He leaned back on the bed and pulled his hospital papers from the table. In the morass of signatures there was one stamped Harold Rydell. Attorney-at-Law. Aleksei folded it and put it into his wallet. Then he took it out again and, mentally, he paced the room. What did American lawyers do? Why had one signed his papers? Did he need to find out?

At the least, he thought, he needed to talk to someone. He lay on the bed and stared at the ceiling. But who? Somebody at the coffee house where, in the life that never was, he read Pindar and Simonides? Or perhaps the new waitress at the BudLite bar? He didn't think so.

But a sailor's bar? Even in the off-season there might be someone who would be all right. He clasped his hands, not in prayer but in hope. He thought that there would be.

In the late afternoon then, the sun just warming the bar stools, Aleksei Andreiovitch Smirnov, still feverish, was in a bar where he felt at ease. There were dust motes in the air, in the sunlight. There were depressions in the stools and a slant and squeak to the floor. The beer foamed from the tap and the bartender, slim in her jeans and faintly wrinkled around her eyes and her mouth, swore in loud English.

Aleksei settled himself into a booth. He had brought his bala-laika with him. He was not sure why, but since the pawnbroker had rejected it he had felt more need of it, more attachment. There were other customers, two men at the end of the bar, a couple shooting pool, a table of old men, bristly with stubbly beards, playing pinochle. He heard the loud crack of the pool ball.

This time he got his beer at the bar and took it back to the booth. He was eyeing the customers, sizing them up under cover of the newspaper he'd found lying on the street. What he didn't expect was to hear his name, but that is what happened.

'Aleksei, you too damned good to sit at the bar?'

He felt a fleshy hand on his shoulder and looked up into a big, smiling face. He stood up quickly, pushing his weight on to his good leg and put his hand out.

'You miss the boat?' He was in a bear hug from Don Lachine, who worked the docks loading grain and was the last man to close the bars and the first man to win a sailor's money when the mood hit him and he wanted to play. He was a big Chippewa with black eyes and a ponytail and his jeans low in the seat.

'I miss the boat.' Aleksei was laughing and grinning. 'Yes. Not shanghaied. Shingle leg.'

'Ouch. So take the weight off.' Don went to the bar and got a beer and a glass of something else. He pushed the beer across the table and fit himself into the booth. 'Pepsi,' he said, answering Aleksei's look. 'My boy died drunk in a car. I been on the wagon.'

Aleksei put his hand on the table.

'Yeah, it's rough. He was the smart one. So you got beached.'

'You know Harold Rydell?' Aleksei reached for his wallet and took the paper out.

Don glanced at it, shook his head. 'You look in the phone book? I'll look.' He walked with his paddling walk to the phone on the wall. He stood there, leaning over the phone book and then he got a pencil from the bar and wrote something down. 'Here,' he said, coming back. 'He's on Mesaba Avenue. You got a problem with the law?'

'I don't know.'

'You hit somebody?'

'No, but I am of limited means.'

Don gazed down at him, sipped at his Pepsi. 'If you want, I'll look over your paper.'

'Yes, please.' Aleksei pushed it across the table and waited.

Don squinted, studied. In a while, he pushed it back. 'You owe the hospital money.'

'And tomorrow for my room. I can pay American some, but money at home, worth is not much. Or how to get it. Does he put me in jail?'

'What you do is find another lawyer. Not this one. Take a name from the phone book. They don't charge for the first time. You sure you didn't hit somebody?'

Aleksei pointed at his leg. He was feeling a lack of language to say what he felt. 'I am hitting nobody. And I am sorry so much for your son.' He put his hand on his heart. 'I too am losing a child.'

Don nodded long and seriously. 'We'll find you a lawyer.'

On January sixth, the day he knew as Christmas Eve, Aleksei was at Meryl's on the lake, playing his balalaika and singing. He was well, almost entirely well with barely a limp, and he had his watch back, his room paid up, and he had made the first instalment on his hospital bill. And he was very clean in his narrow black pants and open white shirt. He was wearing a Ukrainian belt he had bought in a store and he had a temporary green card in his wallet which he checked very often. It allowed him to wait on tables, which he did in the day, and to perform in the bar in the evening or to play background music in the restaurant. Making money, he thought, was making him well. And he was understand-ing the American dream – that impossible things were often possible; that not every bureaucracy had the self-sustaining exist-ence of a worm; that a big, quick-thinking Chippewa could save your life if he told a lawyer with a part-share in a restaurant that you had performed on the balalaika professionally in the Kremlin. For Aleksei this was all a kind of happiness and he sang it in his songs, plucked it from his balalaika, even in minor keys. He was saying Happy Christmas, though nobody knew.

And then the television sets were suddenly full of skaters. There was the girl crying, bashed on the knee, and the championship of America won by the hard-jumping blonde. Aleksei took his breaks in front of a TV set. In his hotel room he set his alarm clock to go off for the morning news shows and, in his hunt, turned his TV from channel to channel. On his afternoons or evenings off he sat at a bar with Don Lachine and watched for skaters through the noise of Tonya Harding this, Tonya Harding that. Even the pool players used their sticks in Tonya Harding's name.

In his room he had seen an ad that drained his face white. The girl from Odessa had skated on to the Olympic stage; Oksana Baiul, world champion at sixteen years old. Her mother was dead. She was an orphan abandoned by a father presumed to be dead, a father who left when she was two.

Aleksei looked at his army papers, looked at himself. He had taken the age of Aleksei Smirnov – thirty-seven – and no one had ever questioned it, but he did not know his real age any more than he knew his real name; he could be older, perhaps somewhat younger. But these were all facts: in 1980 he had been in the army; Odessa was his home; he had left his child. In the smoke and mirrors that were his life these certain memories and realities did not change. What he could not know was if another man from Odessa had done what he had, if a whole fraternity of Odessa men had abandoned young daughters one year and were lost. He could not know, that is, if this child was his.

His life, though, had gained a great clarity. Whether he was working or in his room, whether he was walking to make his weekly payment on his hospital bill or drinking a beer to Don Lachine's Pepsi, he was watching Oksana – watching for her, reading whatever he saw that mentioned her name. Like a sailor attuned to a coming storm he was fully alert, at times so secretly thrilled he thought his fever was back.

Some of this excitement entered, unbidden, into his music. With fervour and tenderness he sang the Pushkin texts he had set himself. He played, too, from a past of peasants and gypsies, their plaintive tunes, their dances, their dreams summoned with a clear sung note and tremolo of string. Sometimes at full break he raced horses across a steppe and held, in his balalaika, the jangling, rough drumming of their stride.

This drew a crowd. In the bar girls gathered near the raised chair where he sat. They did not know to throw flowers, but they asked him home or to their rooms. Especially when the music stayed in his nerves this tempted Aleksei to a serious consideration of American safe sex. And yet he stopped. The West, he had seen, had no secrets. He had read of Arkansas troopers and of the father of Steffi Graf who embarrassed his daughter into depression. If he was the real father of Oksana Baiul desertion was enough. He would not touch her name with scandal.

'I have a bad leg,' he would say, pointing to his trousers, including the article for the noun as he was learning to do. The girls would laugh, tease him a little with sly remarks, and finally let him alone.

This left him, as he wished, to his job and to his dogged watching of TV and reading of newspapers and magazines. He had learned the name of Oksana's coach – Glina Zmievskaya – and he said it to himself often, relishing the comfort of its familiar sounds and lingering particularly over the 'skaya'. He wanted to see the orphan ad again, but it seemed to have disappeared. There were no new ones. Oksana was invisible.

Aleksei asked Don Lachine if he had seen the ad. 'They tell her hardships,' Aleksei said. 'Her mother dead and her father is disappeared long ago and supposed to be dead. She is from my city Odessa. Oksana Baiul. She is the champion skater of the world.'

'I didn't see it. I'll bet you though, Tonya Harding wants to kick her butt.'

Aleksei was suddenly brave. 'She is the age of my daughter in Odessa. I, too, am presumed dead and this child I am losing was very young then, like Oksana.'

'You name your girl Oksana?'

'That part I don't know. My own name even is gone. Afghanistan in the war.' Aleksei struck his head. 'Holes. Empty spots.'

Don turned to him on the bar stool and shook his hand. 'Vietnam,' he said. Then he was quiet and even his face went still. 'You think this girl is yours?'

Aleksei shook his head. 'No,' he answered. 'Many people in Odessa. Many, many people.' Yet even as he shook his head the ideas ran through him like a freshet that she was.

By the Wednesday that she was to skate Aleksei was almost sick again, this time for nervousness. He paced in front of the window with the BudLite sign, nearly spilled his vodka. He heard her name and sat down at the bar next to Don Lachine and stared mutely at the television and looked at an unfamiliar picture of a very young Oksana. He recognized nothing about it, nothing of the background or her clothing, or her. He did not recognize her dead mother, either, the round faced woman in a black and white photo, but he could not say with any certainty that, younger, she had not been his wife. He didn't know.

But the Oksana of sixteen the television showed haunted him. She had the orphan's blue-tinted face. He could not deny this – even when her smile seemed to banish everything but joy – even when she danced, so pliantly and shockingly seductive of a discotheque. Staring at the Black Sea, at his sea and the sea of the mythical past, her sadness was transparent.

And then she skated in Olympic time, and Aleksei was all attention. He was struck by the oddness of her skates, the way they matched her legs in colour, almost as if they were part of her. Her head-dress was unexpected, too; a cap of black feathers that did not so much suggest the swan she portrayed as a woman who was wizened and old. And though her smile cancelled the effect, made her young just as it had erased the orphan, the impression of age stayed with him as she skated. His face grew tight. There was an uncanniness in her movements, a sort of preternatural agility that vied with awkwardness. This scared him.

He held his breath. As she moved though, curling deeper into a spiral of unquestioned grace, he began slowly to nod his head. She was performing, describing the movement of emergent beauty, showing the swan's freedom from enchantment through her own power to enchant. She was creating before his eyes.

Aleksei pressed his fingers to his mouth. He recognized the moment in his head and in his muscles. This was ballet. For all the announcers' talks of jumps and combinations this was a body in the act of revelation. He watched, transported, transfixed.

Oksana made her bow.

'She skated good. I'll buy you a beer.' Don leaned over the bar. 'You ever see Wonder Woman in the comic books?' He stretched one hand in front of him and one behind, his head down. 'Like this. Superman too. Phony flying. Kerrigan does it, but not this one.'

'American angular and coarse chilly elements. Alexander Herzen saw this. Long ago. Russian view. Not Ukrainian.'

'If you say so.'

Aleksei nodded, he was watching Oksana again, listening to her answers to questions and to the stumbling translation of Viktor Petrenko. Son-in-law of her coach, hah! He did not trust this man. Perhaps her saviour, as they said on American TV. So as a fellow skater he had begged her a home. But Oksana was only a child and Aleksei did not like at all the looks between them. And why hadn't her mother made sure she learned English?

Aleksei stood up from the bar. He was angry, and he went outside and flung snowballs into the curb across the street.

He was setting tables after lunch the next day when he heard of Oksana's collision with the German girl in practice. He rushed out of the dining room to find a television, almost skewering the cashier with the forks he was carrying.

'Sorry,' he said, 'very sorry.' But he hurried on into the restaurant bar to check the TV. He flipped the channels himself. Nothing. There was no news on the radio, either, and no one in either the bar or restaurant could answer his questions. He finished the tables in a state of near panic. When he finally saw the accident footage on the evening news he was watching with a tray of drinks in his hands and had to sit down. A gashed leg and an injured back. As bad as shingles. Maybe worse. How could she skate? Should she skate? Who was taking care of her? Aleksei waited on his tables and did his sets in a cloud as heavy as fog on the lake.

He did not sleep the whole night. He gave up on the bed and tried lying on the floor and then sitting in a chair with his legs up. Finally he turned the light on and read the sports pages from the papers he'd bought. He read poems, half a mystery, then the sports pages again. He listened to head-bangings and panting laughter behind the wall and a train in the night. In the frozen dawn he went out and bought coffee and rolls.

By late afternoon the radio had made him ecstatic. Oksana had not only skated but *won*. Aleksei was jubilant, all but ready to do back flips through the dining room. But the evening news began without skating; a massacre of Muslim worshippers on Purim by an Israeli settler from Brooklyn, and Aleksei thought how American, that Americans killed their enemies in public.

He was playing only the late set, and so at seven he was on his stool next to Don Lachine.

'You know?' Don asked.

'I know,' Aleksei said. He shook his hands in the air, beaming. 'I know she won!'

'You should think about this,' Don said. 'That brother that showed up for Clinton? You could be famous. Maybe this girl needs a father, and you are him.'

'No, no,' Aleksei answered. 'But we're watching her skate. A girl from Odessa.'

There were the other skaters first and Tonya Harding's shoelace. The bar was crowded with patrons who grew rowdier with everything that Tonya Harding did. When she began her routine she appeared to Aleksei as if she were posing to start a war dance. Don scowled and spit on the floor. 'She think she's Indian now? Miss Native America?'

When Oksana finally took the ice Aleksei had stopped drinking beer and stopped being nervous. He looked at the bandage on her leg, looked for a sign of the back pain the announcers said she's had injections for. She seemed all right, fine, and since she'd won, he thought she must be. He was not sure, though, about her frizzy ponytail or her costume. He didn't like the pink or the phony fur and he didn't like the show tunes. Why American? He watched to see if she was vamping, the word a skater had hurled against her in the paper. But she was only flirting, playing, and she was dazzling on her feet. Aleksei felt himself melting, ceasing to be cross or a worried papa.

But when she had finished the bar crowd was ugly. There were loud complaints of double-footed landings and missing triple combinations, talk of crooked eastern judges and clean Nancy Kerrigan. Of course she had skated clean, Aleksei thought. Weren't all these skaters immaculately clean?

He looked through the smoke to find the loudest voice, and then Oksana was on again in her own voice and in Viktor Petrenko's.

The loudmouth was shouting over them: 'Look at that prick. For sure he's balling her.'

Aleksei was off his stool and elbowing hard past bodies. He reached for the man's collar, saw the hair in his nostrils and the hole for his earring. He threw a hard jab. Air. A hand on his shoulder had pulled him back.

'My friend likes his young skaters too much. Excuse us,' Don said, and Aleksei did not think there could be so much strength in the flesh hand, but there was. He could not get loose from Don pushing and shoving him toward the door.

Outside Don handed him his jacket. 'Don't mess up my favourite bar, Aleksei,' he said. His face was sombre, but then he laughed. 'Those skate boys couldn't even ball a hooker.'

For the last night of skating – the exhibition of all the winners, all the champions – Aleksei was tired of working an extra shift. He was waiting on tables until his first set at nine, and he kept his eye on the television as he went back and forth with his orders.

Most of the skaters he hadn't seen before. Now he was interested, especially in the couples – in what they did together, the terrifying moves or the astonishing ones that made the ice white heat. Aleksei was behind in his orders, rushing to catch up.

When he finished his shift in the dining room he sat at the bar and watched. And then he fell a little bit in love. Gordeyeva and Grinkov were on the ice in their airy blue costumes, Grinkov's face with a hint of Slavic complexity, Gordeyeva with a simple and classic loveliness. Aleksei knew who they were, that she had been a child when they first were partners, that now she was his wife. They flowed in a pure line across the ice, so achingly beautiful together that they seemed in union prelapsarian, Adam and Eve without the apple.

Aleksei saw this and heard Gordeyeva speak in her good English. But he could not keep his feelings for himself. Katya Gordeyeva, he thought, was exactly the kind of person for Oksana to admire. A role model, as Americans said.

Aleksei got up and went to change for his first set. When he came back he moved his chair so the television was in his line of vision. He told the bartender to keep the picture on. When he began playing the crowd was already quite large, and more people drifted in from the dining room. He started with the song of the young peddler and went on to his Pushkin arrangements and to the songs about bells that he had found were very popular – 'Odnozvuchno Gyremit Kolokolchik'. 'Vercherniy Zvon'. He saw Nancy Kerrigan fall and get up, fall once more.

When it was Oksana's turn to skate she was a swan again, this time in white, and this time Aleksei was with her from the start. She skated to his balalaika, to the melodic, plangent strains that were his story of the swan. When she finished, he was startled to see his audience rising with loud applause – for him. Aleksei bowed, as Oksana did, and put his balalaika away. He sat at the bar in front of the TV and drank a glass of water. Oksana had flipped the skirt of her costume off. She was hurrying towards the dressing room and then she was back on the ice, wearing a ruffled skirt and colourful top over her white dress. She was skating with Viktor Petrenko in a sort of child's version of pairs, both of them smiling and relaxed. Perhaps it was all right, Aleksei thought, that he could put to rest what, were he American, he would certainly call murder in his heart. Maybe Viktor Petrenko was nothing more than a surrogate older brother, protective and kind. Really, it was as if he and Oksana were playing together. It was not the fusion of the other pairs, the two parts making a whole.

And then all of the televisions were empty of skaters and Oksana was gone. Aleksei read the last newspaper stories, clipped one last picture to keep up with his books. When he walked in the streets he felt cold. The weather was milder, but there was a greyness that crept inside him, even when he took the bus to Minneapolis on his day off and bought his ticket at the Target Centre for the Olympic skating tour coming in May.

When he got back to Superior he found Don Lachine in a poker game. Aleksei sat down to wait. In two hands Don folded his cards and got up. Aleksei looked at him. 'It's OK,' Don said. 'Without drinking I don't think so good playing cards.'

They went outside. They walked down towards the lake and stood on the shore listening to the big ice floes cracking far out in the harbour. 'You get your ticket yet?' Don asked.

Aleksei didn't answer.

'Me, if I had a chance to see my boy back from the spirit path I'd be in the front row.' Don sighed. He moaned a little or the ice did. 'Maybe she is your girl, maybe not. If it needs proving they can do it now with DNA.'

Aleksei said nothing. He knew this from Geraldo or Connie Chung – all that slipping of channels.

'You think maybe you are no good, taking pride for what you didn't do, but that is her choice, right? Or you worry about scaring her, or a bad reunion, that she tells you no.'

Yes, Aleksei thought – American stalking, American reunions of parents and children that want a happy ending for something impossible from the start. American dreaming which is fine for something like shingles, but not life.

The ice boomed and echoed on the lake. 'The ships will come soon. The ships will come always. What have you got to lose, Aleksei, that is not already done?'

Aleksei was quiet, touching his daydreams; he saw Oksana whirling on the dark ice. He stood before her, gave her flowers as her father, took the blue lines from beneath her eyes and held her very close.

'It is decided. No,' he said aloud. For a second he was back in Minneapolis, clutching the purchased ticket inside his palm. He had held it, then sat on a bench staring at it and memorizing the number of his seat. And then he had released it, letting it flutter in the breeze to find a puddle, a rivulet that softened it and floated it away for this; to keep, for Oksana, to save for her her green sapling growth.

The Experiment

CATHERINE MERRIMAN

Catherine Merriman has had three novels published, the first of which won the Ruth Hadden Memorial Prize. 'The Experiment' first appeared in a small limited edition of her stories published by Honno in Wales.

Thursday 26 October

I shall start this diary where it all began, by saying that I have for years regarded myself as an unlucky person. Let me explain immediately that I am not suggesting by this that terrible things have happened to me, or that my life has been more than usually tragic, because it hasn't. I am divorced, it is true, but then so are a lot of women my age; the children didn't die cot deaths or fall victim to child molesters, and neither grew up to be drug addicts or homosexual, which these days probably counts as positively lucky. Jennifer is married and lives in Canada now, and perhaps it's a pity Geoffrey wasn't the adventurous one as we've never had much time for each other, but that has very little to do with luck. It's just one of the normal, mildly regrettable imperfections of everyday life. No, what I mean by 'unlucky' refers quite simply to my extraordinary record where games, competitions, whatever, involving chance are concerned, and since this entry is intended as an explanatory preamble, I shall give brief examples.

First, my experience with raffles. These are extremely numerous, as I have been buying raffle tickets – upwards of twenty a year – for the last thirty-five years. Yet I have never, even at informal, draw-on-the-night occasions, won a prize. Of course I realize that in most cases the chances are slight; the Christmas Pensioners' Draw, for instance, sells over 10,000 tickets and offers only twenty prizes, giving my five tickets only the slimmest of chances. All the same, I have been buying for years and whilst I know that the likelihood of winning in an individual draw cannot be enhanced by past failure, I nevertheless believe the law governing probability to be a trifle rigid in this respect, particularly since I have discovered that of the ten of us in the office (I work for Bowdens, the plastic cutlery people) I am the *only one* who has never won anything. Given that I am the oldest by five years, and move in more raffle infested circles than any of them, this has to be remarkable.

Second, from the past, my luck at Monopoly. (Ridiculously trivial I know, but still perfectly illustrating my point.) Years ago I used to play this game regularly with the children. It was however an accepted feature of play that any property on which I bought houses was henceforth landed on by no one except myself (unless I was in gaol and unable to collect rent) and that if I bought more than one hotel I would immediately be assessed for crippling repair bills and summarily bankrupted. In one game, I recall, I passed Go only once without forfeiting my two hundred pounds four spaces on in Income Tax. I am by nature a uncompetitive person and thus a good loser, especially with children; I seem to remember my fate upsetting them more than me, and the game is permanently associated in my memory with childish and genuinely pitying cries of 'Poor Mummy!'

And finally, very briefly, there is the office Grand National sweepstake. In this case I have simply dropped out altogether; again, not because I'm a poor loser, but because I like horses and couldn't take the responsibility. I chose a namesake horse once, Brave Vera I think it was called, and it had to be shot.

So, I have for some time thought of myself as unlucky, in this limited respect, but it was only a little over a year ago – soon after the first anniversary of my divorce, I remember – that I decided to stop merely thinking it, in some nebulous, unsubstantiated way, but actually to start recording evidence of it. This decision, I should add, was taken not in morbid spirit, far from it; I saw it rather as an entertaining diversion, and a welcome sign that I was emerging from mild depression following the divorce into a much more positive frame of mind. Because the fact is that I have always found numbers fascinating and figurework a joy; it has been one of life's minor disappointments, how little is actually needed to survive. Moreover, besides a love of figures, I have some expertise with them, having worked for several years as secretary to the Statistician for the Area Health Authority. I borrowed extensively from his library and I think I could claim that by the time I left, when the Authority was abolished, I was at least as proficient statistically as he. (Where he had the edge was in his ability to communicate such concepts to the laity; I'm afraid I've never had that kind of patience.)

So it was with real enthusiasm that I began my 'luck' book, and in my eagerness to provide data for it I undoubtedly bought more raffle tickets, sent off more unsolicited Prize Draw Numbers, and participated in more office sweepstakes (excluding the National) than ever before. And it was when I reviewed the year's entries that the idea came to me, the idea that in development – which I'm coming to shortly – inspired this account. Because study of the pages of data, and acknowledgement of my inability to achieve any measure of success whatsoever, raised in my mind for the first time the possibility not just that I was unluckier than most people, but that this result was, in a statistical sense, *significant*. That is, I was contemplating for the first time the notion that my bad luck was NO ACCIDENT.

Now after the initial revelatory excitement a certain resistance to this idea crept in, simply because it didn't seem to lead to anywhere sensible. I also made the mistake of mentioning it to some of the women at work, whose reactions reinforced my hesitance. They weren't willing, quite honestly, even to look at the figures, but were inclined to pooh-pooh the suggestion out of hand, and in one instance, actually find it terribly funny. So for quite a long time I fought against it, because no one likes to go out on a limb, intellectually speaking, and besides, even I could see difficulties in the idea. However I did continue to maintain my records, and so of course every so often the urge to tidy up the figures would come upon me, because there really is nothing messier than uncollated data; and then it came into my mind – in fact it was a conversation with Cheryl at work that provoked it – how generally *stupid* most other people are. I showed her a letter I had written to the Department of Employment criticizing their use of the Mean when calculating Average Wages Figures. In it I had pointed out that the Mean was a most misleading statistic to draw from a skewed distribution such as earnings, and only spread resentment among ordinary workers, most of whom could with justification claim that they didn't earn that much, since thanks to the distorting effect of the few very high earners, most of them wouldn't. Much better, I stressed, to use the *Median*; not only was it statistically sounder; but since it would be lower, and by definition half the work-force exactly would feel prosperous beside it, the political benefits would be enormous. Cheryl, however, had great difficulty grasping the difference between a mean and a median, and when I explained in words of one syllable, said, 'Oh, you mean like a plimsoll line?'

It was at that moment, I'm sure, that I resolved to ignore what other people thought, and trust the figures. And just a small step from trusting them to pursuing them. So we come, finally, to what all this has been leading up to; my decision to design an EXPERIMENT. After all, I have been telling myself, I could go on filling my notebook forever with data that may well suggest and support my theory, but is never going to be able to prove it. It's time to take the initiative. I haven't worked out the methodology yet, but I can't believe it beyond me, and I must say that I'm looking forward to the whole exercise enormously. A great intellectual weight has been lifted from me; it's so gloriously simple, just to let the facts decide. Indeed, if it doesn't sound ludicrously extravagant, I might almost say that in this project, anticipating the hours of planning I shall have to put into it, and the mathematical rewards I am bound to reap from it, that whatever the result, I have discovered some Purpose in Life again.

Wednesday 8 November

The experiment is designed. As I suspected, it wasn't difficult, once I had identified the prerequisites of the exercise. These are:

1. It must be simple, and the results easily understood. There is no point proving something if no one grasps you have proved it.

2. It must provide definitive results. Obviously I can't predict what these will be, and dealing with probabilities means no absolutes, but the confidence levels must be as rock-solid as I can make them. This means overkill, in a statistical sense.

3. It must involve other people who are strangers to me. The more the better, to discourage conspiracy charges.

4. There should be an element of actual gain or loss, so as to reproduce as faithfully as possible the real-life experience I am investigating. However, the gains/losses can be trivial, as they are in real life.

So, here is the plan. After work next Monday I shall drive up to the Broadlands estate, which appears well-lit and of course is highly respectable, so I am unlikely to get mugged, and knock on doors until I have found twenty volunteers to help me. (As long as they are unknown to me they don't have to be randomly selected, since this isn't a sample survey.) I shall say that I am conducting research into probability and explain that over the next fortnight I would like to visit them a total of four times, for no more than a few minutes on each occasion, during which they will roll a die six times, after first making a written guess at the result. Then I will roll the die once, after likewise, in their presence, recording my guess. For any correct result they will win fifty pence, unless I guess right, which cancels their win. (This is the nearest I can get to a gain myself, since I can hardly ask them to reward me!) Fifty pence seems about the right level; just enough to tempt, without being ruinous for me. I have calculated that at the outside, assuming they're right one-sixth of the time and I'm not right at all (which even with the worst luck in the world is surely unlikely) I should lose no more than ten pounds an evening, forty pounds in total, which seems an eminently reasonable price for settling it once and for all. I shall take a tape recorder with me to record all our exchanges (unnecessary, but this is part of the overkill) and I shall ask the volunteers to witness the written records with their signatures as we go along. By the end each volunteer will have made twenty-four guesses, of which one would predict four would be right, and I will have made eighty, of which with 'normal' luck one would expect thirteen to be right. Results deviating from these averages will have definite probabilities associated with them. No need to go into the mathematics of it now; suffice to say that if one of my volunteers made no correct guesses this would have a probability of $\frac{5}{6} \times \frac{5}{6}$ twenty-four times, which is 0.0125, or a chance of one in a hundred. Pretty unlikely, in fact.

So, it is designed, and although I'm nervous about Monday, it is an excited kind of nervousness and I'm still looking forward to it. This must be apparent to others, because Cheryl has accused me of being uncharacteristically chirpy (I'm sure I've never chirped in my life) and has demanded to know 'what I'm up to then?' There is a quite unwarranted degree of suspicion in her tone, and it seems to me that there is no satisfying some people.

Monday 13 November

I have just returned from my first visit to Broadlands and it has all gone remarkably well. I have made myself some Horlicks but even so I anticipate a late night; the adrenalin is running high.

The estate is really most attractive. The houses are detached and mature-looking, all mellow red brick, and turned at angles to each other along curving roads, creating a delightfully rural feel to the place. In fact the only straight section of carriageway is the access from the main road up to the estate; deliberate policy I should imagine, since it is surprisingly steep. There was a builders' skip on the tarmac half way up, the only blot on an otherwise immaculate landscape, though even this has been positioned with obvious thoughtfulness under a street lamp and well in to the kerb. All in all, the place glows with responsible citizenship.

I had no problem parking. All the houses have at least one garage, leaving the roads clear, and it took me only twenty-four house calls to select twenty volunteers. Nobody was rude to me. One guttural youth with the word 'Cocaine' inexplicably daubed across his t-shirt said, 'Yeah' at me a few times, but then couldn't promise to be in regularly over the next fortnight so I dropped him, and at one house the door was opened by two young children who said Mummy was out but would be back soon. I was a little concerned for them but the inside of the house looked monied and well cared-for (as to be honest did the children) so in the end I decided not to inform the authorities and merely let the woman next door know, who promised to check up on them later. The other two failures were empty houses. I would guess that twenty out of twenty-four is an exceptionally high success rate, and that the prospect of winning fifty pences, which I mentioned early on in my spiel, was a strongly positive point.

In the event I have lost seven pounds tonight. Two of the volunteers were right twice, ten right once, and eight wrong each time. Almost, I would imagine, a text-book spread. On the other hand my results were fairly unusual, because I wasn't right once either, and of course I threw twenty times. Probability 0.026 or one in forty. (Unusual but extraordinarily unlikely.) In fact at the time it felt more like good luck than bad, considering the aim of the exercise, and I don't expect it to hold.

There should be no trouble with the follow-ups. Human beings are born gamblers; most of them seemed to regard it as a treat, and only one woman asked any questions about the methodology of the Experiment. She wanted to know why it was being carried out like this when matters of probability must be solved mathematically, so I played the dumb researcher and said well yes, but I only knew what I'd been told, and sometimes it was necessary that the people in the field weren't in full possession of all the details. Ah, she said knowingly, you mean a double blind. We had a most interesting conversation subsequently, and I hope the acquaintanceship deepens over the next fortnight, as she sounds just my sort of person.

So altogether a satisfying evening, but above all relieving, since the preparations have been a strain. I was very nervous about tonight – silly as it turned out – and I haven't been sleeping well. Also because I went to Broadlands straight from work and didn't want to leave my recorder and notebooks in the car I had to endure some mild banter in the office. I haven't confided the exact nature of the Experiment, but I did say that I was undertaking some private research, and Cheryl immediately piped up with 'Going to prove how everybody's out to get you?' which temporarily shook my faith in her stupidity. And with having to leave everything by the desk all day I couldn't forget about it. As with other semi-automatic activities typing is extraordinarily affected by nerves; I actually had to give up with carbons and use the photocopier for file copies instead.

Tuesday 14 November

No empirical results to record (next visit not till Friday) but I am making this entry after being struck by a philosophical, rather than mathematical, aspect to the matter. Indeed, an aspect, now I come to think of it, that harks back to a remark made to me months ago, at the time I foolishly aired my hypothesis in the office, and Cheryl said, 'So what on earth do you think's so special about you?' What I am asking myself now, but hedging around, because I haven't yet followed it through, is WHAT IF I AM RIGHT? In fact the question is written in rather larger capitals in my mind. I shall press on with the Experiment, naturally, but I can see that I must apply myself to this, and that it was most remiss of me not to earlier, since in terms of investigative logic this surely should have come first. In the very first entry, I suddenly remember, I commented on the idea 'leading nowhere sensible'; and yet here I am, going there! And it is all very well saying 'let the facts decide', but ultimately, I have to ask myself, decide what? I have a horrid feeling that this oversight stems from reluctance, and that since the question has always existed, but merely remained unaddressed (or more accurately avoided) that I have been guilty of acting with two discrepant minds, one – dominant till now – which wants urgently to develop, pursue and prove a hypothesis; and the other, hitherto muted, which intuitively foresees, and has no desire to face up to, the consequences. This is not good enough. So I am going to make myself tackle it, despite sensing fairly momentous conclusions. I will report further, when they're clarified.

Thursday 16 November

Here is the further report. It is going to be difficult, so I will take it step by step.

First, let me say that I have just reread Tuesday's entry, and realize that the 'two minds' figure of speech showed extraordinary prescience. I am of course still one person, but I do feel that since I started exploring this question my mind has split into two operating modes; one firmly prosaic and practical and still keenly investigative (I have, for instance, just prepared report sheets for tomorrow with real, and almost innocent, enthusiasm) and the other . . . well, rather overcome, to be honest, by the issues it has been grappling with. I understand much more fully now that earlier sense of reluctance, and I have to confess that merely entering this mode induces in me a muddle of conflicting emotions. It is as if I am being fragmented yet again; on one level there is a deep disturbance, almost an apprehension; yet on the other a tremendous excitement, and sense of awed anticipation. And this is without taking into account the natural inclination of mental revolt, produced by such a challenge to the rational brain. Because cutting the argument to its essence – and we might as well go straight there, though I dithered around it for hours yesterday before biting the bullet – to claim that one is significantly more unlucky than others is to suggest either that there is something special about oneself – and it would have to be very special indeed, to influence natural law – or . . . and I scarcely like to write it, though I must . . . that there is some purposeful force outside oneself – outside everyone, indeed – that has ordained one to be treated so. I almost feel I should apologize for writing that, but I have thought about it all day, and I see no alternative. The very word 'significant' implies cause, or reason; if it cannot lie in other humans, and in this case it cannot, then it must lie in me, or in fate itself. And since I do not feel, and cannot believe that I am in any crucial sense different from my fellow man – certainly not on a scale capable of distorting the laws of probability – then if my hypothesis proves correct it is with fate, i.e. the purposeful force, that I am left.

At that point I have rather stuck. It has been effort enough, frankly, committing it to paper. My only solace, I suppose, is that I would appear to be falling into good religious company, though that would come better from someone who hadn't always claimed to be a non-believer. And even if I do suspend disbelief and entertain it, it raises nothing but questions. Why, for instance, should this purposeful force, God, whatever you like to call it, be behaving like this? What is the point? One could almost accept a divine bolt from the blue, in appropriate circumstances, but mischief at Monopoly? And if there is no point, and it is hard to see how there could be, why be so petty, and childishly malicious? And why, above all, to me? There, I've said it, and of course that's it, I felt the hurt as I wrote it. In heaven's name, why me?

But then again – and even as I contemplate it I sense the upsurge taking over – if I succeed, just think what I will have proved! In my head I hear a voice, tremendously excited. 'Have faith,' it urges. 'Go on, don't back away now, DO IT!' Gracious, I can scarcely grip the pen! Just think! It would be momentous, cataclysmic! An irrefutable, scientific proof! Surely, I tell myself – and the voice agrees, so enticingly – what the whole world has waited for!

That was foolish to write. Extremely foolish. I am letting excitement run away with me. Anyone would think it already proved. Also speculation along these lines sounds mad, whatever the logic. I think that for the present I should concentrate on the Experiment, and on preparing my results as professionally as possible. If it comes to a point where I want to share it with the world, well, the figures will say it for me, and others can draw their own conclusions.

I wish, rather, that I had not made myself tackle this at all.

Friday 17 November

Just the facts tonight and no speculations. I am too tired for more anyway.

I found all the volunteers in for this second visit. One old gentleman had actually delayed a social engagement for my sake and was rewarded by winning a pound. I have lost nine pounds fifty altogether tonight. He was right twice, seventeen were wrong once, and two wrong every time, though both were winners on Monday. There is an increasing tendency for volunteers to stick to the same number for their guesses, in the intuitive (though erroneous) belief that this improves their chances, and the six is by far the most popularly chosen. I had to decline seven cups of tea (all from winners, which may say something encouraging about the human psyche) but regretfully wasn't offered one where I had hoped for it, because she had to dash off to her Soroptimists' meetings. She seems on second acquaintance a very practical, busy sort of person, and made me feel slightly tired. Though I didn't call on her until towards the end, and twenty house calls takes nearly three hours, so perhaps it was just me.

As far as my results are concerned I wasn't right once, but I'm not going to calculate the probability of this, or say anything more about it. I still have forty throws to go.

I hope I am not sickening for something. I do not recall feeling so weary after the first visit, and just writing this short report has left me quite exhausted.

Monday 20 November

I have now made three visits. I know I said I was going to leave calculations till the end but I can't. I don't know how to describe the intensity of emotion gripping me at the moment, which makes my hand tremble even as I attempt to write this, but an approximation would be to say that I am appalled. Some coalescing process between states of mind has been creeping up on me for days, but only unified, stark and terrifying, tonight. Because I have now made sixty guesses on the roll of a die, in the presence of impartial witnesses, and I have not been right once. The volunteers have made only eighteen guesses so far, but everybody has been right at least twice. The probability of my result, no wins out of sixty, I have just calculated as 0.0000174, or less than one in 50,000. There scarcely seems any point in continuing, though I suppose I must. Absolute certainty may not exist where probabilities are concerned, but I think I have come near enough, and that is why I am recording the result now, because whatever happens, it is proof.

This evening was a terrible ordeal. The tension I experienced preparing for my throws are almost disabling. Two of the volunteers asked me if I was all right, and I had to invent a story about drinking too much coffee before I came out to explain why my hands were shaking so violently. I haven't been in to work today and shan't again, till this is over. It is a horrible feeling, to be convinced beyond doubt that one has been deliberately singled out for bad luck. That one is, putting it bluntly, the object of divine spite. I feel on the edge of something terrible now, not something tremendous. I cling to the hope that when I publish, or otherwise get these results into expert hands, someone will be able to suggest a different explanation, but I fear they won't.

And I am haunted by new questions. Desperate, thought-numbing questions. Why, I keep asking myself, if I am able to prove what I have so easily – and it has been easy, ludicrously so, in the scale of things – hasn't anyone done it before? If this is a divine game, I cannot be the first to be so played with – God, I can't – and if I, a humble, only moderately educated woman with no previous interest in theological certainties can devise an experiment that conclusively proves what I have, then why haven't others? Or if they have, why don't we know about them? And if they truly haven't, why in heaven's name has this force, God, what you will, let me do it? That is the crux. WHY HAS HE LET ME DO IT? If he has the power to spite, he has the power to choose not to spite, surely? Does he suddenly want to be exposed? I can't believe it, not after all this time. Does he, for some unthinkable reason, place spiting me above protecting himself? Or does he simply not realize what I have done? Is he – most dreadful thought – not just a childish, malicious God, but a stupid one too?

There are no answers, and I am frightening myself.

Tuesday 5 December

Nurse Frinton says it's a miracle I survived. It doesn't feel much like a miracle to me, attached to all these tubes and equipment, but little Nurse Rose claims it's impossible to look at anything positively with a catheter inserted, and assures me I'll feel quite different next week, when it comes out.

I don't remember anything about the accident. I recall the drive to the estate, and the evening's house calls, but nothing at all about the drive home. They tell me the car hit the skip at more than forty miles an hour, and that a male passer-by, happily ignorant of every emergency First Aid rule, dragged me bodily from the car and several yards down the pavement, thereby saving me from certain incineration when the petrol tank exploded. Apparently this occurred with such force that several objects in the boot, including parts of my tape recorder, were found imbedded in the wooden wall of a garden shed twenty yards away. All other contents of the car, mostly paper of course, were destroyed in the subsequent conflagration.

The police have examined the remains for evidence of mechanical failure and found both the brakes and steering in their words 'severely defective'. However, and here I quote more extensively, 'while failure in both could have been present before the collision, and thus been the cause of it, it was equally likely that they were in fact a result of it, since the impact had been considerable'. The 'equally likely' is, I think, a kind understatement on their part, as I received the impression from the Inspector who visited me that he thought the chances of a simultaneous brake and steering failure, at the one spot of my journey where the result would be catastrophic, unlikely in the extreme, and although he was too polite to say so, that I had, for reasons unspecified, deliberately rammed the skip.

I suspect Cheryl thinks this too; she has visited with one of the other secretaries nearly every day, and it would explain her ingratiating and apologetic manner. All these visitors from Bowdens' seem to consider it their duty to pop in and assure me that my work has been taken in hand, so I'm Not to Worry About It (as if, in my condition, I would) and it was a great relief when Jennifer finally got her flight sorted out and I could tell them not to bother as my daughter would be here every day. (I have hazy memories of Geoffrey visiting, in the early days, but now he knows I'm not going to die he has confined his sympathies to letters.) Jennifer arrived a week ago, and apart from the pleasure of seeing her it has meant that I have at last got my personal possessions at the hospital, such as, thank goodness, my night-dress and towels, and of course this notebook. (Regarding this, and in passing only, I should say that both the police and my own doctor have apparently read it, though Jennifer, I think mercifully, has not.)

Really there is little else to say. I'm already strong enough to write, and now Jennifer is here they're talking about discharging me within a fortnight. I think, even with the catheter removed, I will still be dubious about Nurse Frinton's 'miracle' (it seems somehow entirely the wrong word) but I believe I know enough about misfortune to recognize when I have indeed been lucky, and the folly of pushing it.

Cautiously, I would say only that the questions I asked in the previous entry have in my own mind been answered; and on that note of restraint I therefore close this diary.

The Hostages

NAOMI MITCHISON

*One of the most celebrated women of her day, Naomi Mitchison died in 1992
aged ninety-five. She was an intrepid traveller, and wrote travel books as well
as some fiction.*

There were only three of us left now; the others had been hung
over the ramparts, one every morning. Elxsente was still sick and
we didn't know what to do with him; he was only a child and
cried for his mother at nights; some of the others had done that,
and I would have too, but I was fifteen and had to set a good
example. They used to take us out on to the walls, and whip us
where the men from our own cities could see us; of course they
had the right to do it, but some of us weren't very old and used
to cry even at the thought of it, which was hard for everyone. But
we could look out when we were taken up, and there was our
camp, spread and shining below us; once there was an attack
while we were there and we all cheered, but the Romans paid us
back in kicks for that. I saw the banner of Mireto from time to
time, and thought I could make out my father at the head of the
spearmen, and my big brother with him; and once I saw a herald
whom I knew and called out to him, but he didn't hear me. Every
day we hoped the town would fall, though we should very likely
have been killed before anyone could get to us; still, it was a
chance, and better than being dragged out and choked like dogs
at the end of a rope. We knew our people were pressing hard and
might soon starve the town out; for the last week they had given

us nothing but water and a very little bread; the one who was chosen to be hung every morning used to leave his share of the bread to anyone he liked. There wasn't too much water, either; the last day Teffre and I had given it all to Elxsente; we thought we should be able to eat his bread – he wouldn't touch it – but we were too thirsty.

I was awake all that night, though Teffre slept for a little. I leant up against the wall at the back, with Elxsente's head on my shoulder; he seemed easier that way. I thought about home, and tried to imagine I was in my own room; I wondered if they were looking after my pony properly, and I tried to remember whether I'd mended the bridle before I was sent away as a hostage to the Romans; I couldn't be sure and it worried me.

When it was just light Teffre woke me and said he heard shouting; we both listened and I heard it too. He went over to the slit, but of course he could see nothing; he used always to think he might see something some time. But certainly there was cheering, and Teffre said he was sure we'd taken the town; but it wasn't the first time he'd thought that, and I wasn't hopeful, particularly as nothing else happened for hours. My back was very sore from the beating, and we'd had no chance of a wash for weeks. Elxsente was better after his sleep, and thirsty, but the water was all gone.

Then the door opened, and the man we called the Boar – we all hated him – came in. I wondered which of us he was going to take, and rather hoped it would be Teffre, because I was much better at looking after Elxsente – I didn't want it to be *him* anyhow. Teffre asked him what had happened – he never could learn not to – and the man hit his hand with the iron key, and then said, 'The General's come, and your people have all run away.' That was hard hearing for us; we knew it wasn't true about our army having run, but we supposed they'd withdrawn, and we were very unhappy, but we said nothing and waited. He went on, 'You dogs, you ought to be hung, but the General's begged for your lives and you've been given to him.'

We didn't quite understand at once, and then a great tall man came in, all in armour, with a golden helmet plumed with a black horse-tail; he could only stand upright in the middle of the arch; he looked at us and asked, 'Are these all that are left?' The Boar stood at attention and said, 'Yes, sir,' and then to us, 'Down on your knees before your master!' I don't remember what Teffre did but I simply sat and stared at the General; one can't think very quickly after one hasn't slept all night. The Boar came over and hit me and I was afraid he was going to hurt Elxsente; so I knelt, and Elxsente knelt, leaning against me, and Teffre knelt in the other corner. The light came in through the doorway, behind the General, and he looked very big, as if he could tread us into the ground; a little wind came in too and I heard the horse-hairs rustling against the bronze.

He was speaking to us, but I didn't hear it all; I was thinking that we were going to live, and I was glad and thankful, and then I thought that our army was beaten, and perhaps my father and brother were killed; I felt that I loved Mireto, my city, terribly, and that it would be awful if the Romans were to take her; and then I thought it might be better to die after all. I heard the General saying that our lives were forfeit, but that he had asked that we should be spared, and then about how wicked it was of the League of Cities to have broken the treaty; I was wondering if it was any use my telling him that bad treaties ought to be broken, but just then Elxsente slipped forward and I had to catch him; he felt very hot and was breathing fast. The General came up to us and stooped over him; Elxsente threw his arms round my neck and held on tight with his face pressed into my shoulder; the General said, 'Don't be frightened,' and lifted his head quite gently; he asked how long he'd been like this, and I told him ten days, and said could we have some water for him. He asked if we had not had any, and I said yes, but that Elxsente had had his share and our share too, but he was all burnt up and always wanted more. He turned round to the Boar and the metal plates on his kilt swung against my face; he told him to get us water, and then felt Elxsente's head and hands, and told me he thought he would live. When the water came Elxsente let go of me with one hand and drank and looked up at the General, and Teffre drank, and then I drank; I've never tasted anything as good as that water; I felt quite different at once, and I would have spoken to the General to justify our cities, only he went out.

That day we had dried figs with our bread, and in the evening they brought some milk for Elxsente. We heard how the General had marched up secretly and surprised and scattered our camp and relieved the town; a few days afterwards the Boar told us peace had been made; some of the cities were given up to Rome, and the walls of Mireto had to be pulled down. Teffre and I talked it over; we wondered whether we ought to outlive the disgrace – *his* city was to pay tribute and have Rome for overlord – but finally we made up our minds to go on living for a little longer at least; we didn't quite know how to kill ourselves, and besides there was Elxsente; his city had to pay tribute too, but he didn't understand the shame of it like we did.

By the time they let us out, Elxsente was much better, but we were none of us very strong. They tied us into a wagon; we sat on the bottom, out of the sun, and saw the tops of the trees that we passed under along the road, but not much else. The journey took three days, and then we stopped outside the walls of Rome. There was dust all over everything, dust in our hair and ears and eyelashes, dust caked on our hands and feet, white dust on the bread and fruit we ate. The wagon was drawn up on the inside of a square, and we sat on the edge trying to see what was happening; prisoners – our own men – were brought in under guard, formed up, and chained; of course we all looked hard to see if there was anyone we knew among them; often we thought we saw faces of friends, but they never were. Then one of my father's men was marched past and I shouted to him; he turned and called to me that my father had escaped, but he didn't know about my brother; still, that was something. There were women prisoners too, from the towns that had been taken, and armour and horses and gold cups from the altars of the Gods. Teffre saw one cartload from his own city and raged at being so helpless. And then Elxsente cried out and said he saw his cousin among the women, a white-faced girl with eyes swollen from tears and dust; we all called, but she didn't hear or heed, and Elxsente was terribly disappointed.

Then we were taken out of the wagon over to a heap of chains and one of the soldiers found light ones for us. Then we waited at the edge of the road till our turn came. The Roman soldiers went by first, crowned and singing; after them our prisoners, chained together; and more Romans; the trophies of swords and spears, and the pick of the cattle that had been taken; and more Romans; and a great line of women and children, and pictures of the battles, and ox-carts full of gold and silver, well-guarded; and more Romans still, and more prisoners; and we were bitterly angry and sad. Then there was a place for us, and we joined the march with Roman soldiers in front of us and at each side. At first there was nothing but choking dust, until we got to the suburbs, where the streets had been watered, which kept the dust down and was pleasant to the feet. But then the crowds began, crowds of shouting enemies at the two edges of the road; they frightened me more than anything; we were so helpless and alone in the middle of them, and sometimes the noise would suddenly swell up into a road all round us, and Elxsente would shrink up close to me; once or twice they threw things at us, but nothing sharp enough to cut. A man who walked in front of us kept on repeating in a shout that we were the hostages from the cities who were spared by order of the General and that the rest were hung. He said it over and over again like a corncrake; I would have given a lot to kill that man. We must have had seven or eight miles to walk in the sun at the pace of the slowest oxen; at first I looked about me and whispered to the others from time to time and sang our marching song under my breath, but later I was too tired to do anything but stumble along with my head down. My hands were chained behind my back so that I couldn't even wipe the sweat off my forehead or the dust out of my eyes. About half-way, Teffre cut his foot on a sharp stone and fell, but one of the guards picked him up and helped him along. I was miserable about Elxsente; he wasn't well yet and the sun was burning on our heads; he knew he must go through the day without whimpering for the honour of his city, and he did it well, but I could feel how much it was costing him and I could do nothing to help him; I was thankful when the soldier on his side said, 'I've a child of my own,' and took him on to his shoulder for part of the way. The day seemed endless, but suddenly we were halted in a great square place where someone was speaking from the top of a flight of steps. I saw the General a long way off, wearing a laurel wreath and a purple robe, but I was too tired to see much; all those great white buildings were swimming in the heat and there wasn't a breath of wind to blow away the smell, that seemed everywhere, of leather and onions, and the hot crowd.

When the Triumph was over and our chains were taken off, we were locked up in a little barred room, a prison of some sort, with straw on the flagstones. We lay there, thankful for the dark and quiet, and slept like the dead all night. The first day a woman, who seemed too dazed to speak, brought us food; the second day another woman brought it; she was Elxsente's cousin. He rushed up to her with 'Where's mother?' and she burst into tears and put her arms round him. She had seen his father dead of wounds and knew his mother and the baby sister were burned in a house with some other women who'd tried to escape from the soldiers. But she could hardly speak about it; something terrible must have happened to her too; and she mightn't stay with us. Elxsente cried all that day, and even while he slept he was sobbing and calling, 'Mother, mother'; I couldn't bear it, I put my hands over my ears so as not to hear, but I knew it was going on all the time and I couldn't sleep at all. Teffre was very much upset; he seemed to have thought that when it was all over he could go back to the old life, but this showed him that he couldn't; perhaps it was lucky for him that his mother was dead years before; Mireto had not been sacked, so my mother and sisters should have been safe, and I knew my father had escaped, but my brother might have been killed or anything; and besides, I was the oldest and I realized it all better; how this was the end of the League of Cities, our Gods were powerless, and our hope and honour in ashes.

The next morning we were taken away again; we were used to obeying orders now. An old soldier with a black beard was in charge of us; he wouldn't answer questions or let us talk among ourselves much. As we went through the streets a woman recognized us and threw a dead rat; it hit Elxsente; but I was glad it wasn't a brick. We had a long way to walk (though we got a lift for a few miles on a wagon that was leaving the town empty), first along one of the big main ways that went out between gardened houses and under arches, right into the country, and then along a lane with deep ruts, beside vineyards and cornfields; it was past noon when we came to a long low house with a walled garden where there were pomegranate trees. There was no one to be seen, and the soldier stopped, sat down on the bottom step of the ones that led up to the house door, and ate bread and onions. We sat on the ground beside him and waited, and the afternoon got hotter and hotter; we were all very tired. We'd had nothing to eat since early that morning – we hoped the soldier would give us something, but he didn't and of course we couldn't ask. Teffre was complaining of his foot, which was badly swollen; I tied it up with fresh grass and a strip torn from my own tunic. Elxsente was crying all the time, quite hopelessly; his face was streaked with dirt and tears, and his hair was tangled into grey knots all over his head. I was unhappy enough myself; I tried to tell them stories, but that reminded us of home and made it all worse. Elxsente put his head down on my knee, and I felt his hot little face, wet against my skin. Teffre cried every time he moved his foot, and I was near to it myself, but I thought of our being among the enemy and that we must show we were men. Still nobody came; sometimes we heard a cock crowing behind the house, and once a reaper passed through the trees in front of us with a sickle under his arm, but he never looked our way.

Then we heard voices inside the house and a lady came out on to the steps, with a maid carrying a basket behind her. The soldier saluted and spoke to her; she was all in blue, and the western sun on her face and hair. She ran down the steps and saw us. 'Oh,' she said, 'Oh – you children! You poor children!' and in a moment she was beside me and had gathered Elxsente up into her arms; he lay there limp with his eyes half-shut still crying. 'Have you been here all day,' she asked, 'with nothing to eat?' I nodded and she called up to the maid to bring food and drink quickly. I was glad to see how angry she was with the soldier; she sent him away and sat down on the steps with Elxsente on her knee, sobbing a little less. The maid brought milk and barley cakes and pears and grapes; we ate everything and she fed Elxsente herself. Then the General came round from the other side of the garden; I knew him at once, though he was wearing a woollen tunic and sandals instead of armour, the bailiff (though we didn't know who he was until afterwards) was at his side. I stood up, and his wife stood up holding Elxsente to her breast.

He looked at us kindly enough and told the bailiff to take Teffre and me down to the pool to wash. We went with him, Teffre limping badly; it was a broad, shallow, stone basin, with sunflowers growing round it. We stripped and went in and washed off layers and layers of dust and sweat, and swam among the lily pads till he told us to come out. They brought us clean clothes and we put them on with our hair dripping; he took us back to the house, to a clean, light room with blankets spread on the floor for us, and Teffre sat on a table while someone bandaged his foot properly. Then Elxsente came in and told us how the women of the house had washed him and dressed him and been kind to him, and he lay down on the blankets and I covered him, and he went to sleep almost at once. Then the General sent for me; he was sitting alone in a tall chair, with candles behind him. He asked me if I thought we should be ransomed; I said I believed Teffre and I would be, but that Elxsente's father and mother were killed, so I couldn't tell about him. He sent me away, and the mistress met me in the hall and asked if Elxsente was asleep.

The next day we were left alone for most of the time, to eat and rest, but after that, when Teffre's foot was better, we were given work to do about the farm and garden, under the bailiff; it wasn't hard -- getting in the grapes and apples, feeding the geese, driving the cows home, and so on. Elxsente got well wonderfully quickly, and forgot about his mother for hours together, the mistress petted him a lot and the General spoke to him whenever he saw him.

But the weeks went on and the autumn was going; there were frosts at night; once round the pond and out was as far as we cared to swim. But none of us heard anything from our homes. And then one day the General sent for Teffre to tell him he'd been ransomed, and his uncle was waiting to take him away. In an hour he'd said goodbye to us and was gone; I've never seen him since. Of course Elxsente and I were glad for his sake, but it made me wonder what was going to happen to me; I thought of all sorts of things; perhaps the soldier might have been wrong about my father; perhaps he was dead and my brother was dead, and all our money was gone; perhaps I should never see Mireto and my mother and our house again. Everyone was good to us, but of course we were no more free than any of the slaves and I didn't like to think of all my life being like that. At one time I thought of running away, but I should probably have been caught, and anyhow I should have had to leave Elxsente; I had a plan that my father should ransom him too and he should come back alive and live with us and be my little brother, now that he had no one of his own kin left. We used to talk about that in the evenings.

But it was winter now. We were busy pruning the vines and fruit trees; Elxsente worked with me, but of course I worked longer hours and did more. After it was dark the mistress used often to have us in and we sat with them, making withy plaits, while the General talked about farming and wild beasts and told us all his adventures. Sometimes he talked about Rome, things she had done in the past, things he said she would do in the future. I thought about Mireto and said nothing, but Elxsente seemed to believe it. We worshipped with them too; the country Gods are the same all the world over. Sometimes we went out after wolves and once I was in the thick of it, when either a hound or a wolf bit me in the arm. Looking back on it all now it seems such a waste of time that I didn't really enjoy it; but then I didn't know what had happened at home.

One day I was coming up to the house with my pruning knife and a great bundle of prunings to burn; Elxsente had gone in but I had stayed to finish the row, and it was nearly dark. I heard hoofs behind me, turned, and there was my father! I threw down the bundle and ran to him, and he was off his horse and had me in his arms, all in a moment. The horse grazed by the roadside and we talked. Of course I asked first about mother and everyone. 'My little son,' he said, 'you didn't hear all this long time! All's well at home, but you know I'd spent all the money we had in arming my men. There was nothing left and I had all I could do to raise enough to buy you both back. Did you know your brother was taken prisoner during the siege? I couldn't find him for months; he had been sold as a slave in the Roman market, and I bought him back first; he was having a bad time. But I thought you would be well treated here – they've not been unkind to you, son?' He looked at the bundle of wood and then at the bound place on my arms where I'd had the wolf-bite. I told him they'd all been kind and what sort of life it was; he put me up on his horse – it was fine to be in the saddle again – with the prunings behind, and we went up to the house. The General met my father and took him in, and I led the horse round to the stables and bedded him down.

When I came in they'd settled my ransom, and father said we should go home the next day. I was so happy I could hardly think, and then, with a jump, I remembered Elxsente. 'Oh Father,' I said, 'can't you buy my friend back too? He's got no one left, and I told him I'd take him home with me.' Father looked miserable and said he couldn't – I found out afterwards how hard the ransom money had been to come by – but that he'd try to later, for the honour of the Cities. But the General said, 'I don't want to have Elxsente ransomed; I've another plan for him; call him and we'll see.' He came in, and the mistress with him; he ran over to me and took my hands. 'Oh, you're going,' he said, 'you're going back to your mother and I shall be left all alone.' But the General leaned forward, saying, 'Elxsente, you know I've no children of my own. Will you come and live with me always and be my son?' and the mistress spoke softly to him: 'Stay with us, dear,' and Elxsente looked at them and looked at me and then looked down on the floor, wondering. And I said, 'Think of your city, Elxsente! Don't put yourself into the hands of the enemy!' And he said to me, 'Would it be very wrong to stay? I think I'd like to stay.' I would have spoken but my father stopped me and spoke himself: 'You know that I'm of the Cities, child, on your side; so you can trust me; I advise you to stay.' Then Elxsente went over to the mistress and put his arms round her neck and she and the General kissed him, and called him son. And the General gave back the ransom money to my father and said to me that while there was peace I should always be welcome in his house.

The next day father and I set out for home. Elxsente came with us as far as the main road, and there we said our goodbyes. Elxsente went back to the house, and father and I struck out over the hills for Mireto. We were back within the week and everything was right again. I found I hadn't mended my pony's bridle, but my brother had done it for me after he came home.

Under the Rose

JULIA O'FAOLAIN

Julia O'Faolain was born in London and brought up in Dublin. Her novels include The Obedient Wife, No Country for Young Men *and, most recently,* The Judas Cloth. *Her short stories have appeared in various journals, including* The New Yorker, *where 'Under the Rose' was first published. It is included in her new collection of stories,* The Corbies Communion.

Dan said . . . to be sure, there was only his word for this; but who would invent such a thing? . . . that, in their teens, his brother and he had ravaged their sister on the parsonage kitchen table. Their father was a parson, and when the rape took place the household was at Evensong. Dan described a fume of dust motes sliced by thin, surgical light, a gleam of pinkish copper pans and, under his nose, the pith of the deal table. Outside the door, his sister's dog had howled. But the truth was, said Dan, that she herself did not resist much. She'd been fifteen, and the unapologetic Dan was now twenty. It had, he claimed, been a liberation for all three.

'The Bible's full of it,' he'd wind up. 'Incest!'

The story was for married women only. Dan specialized in unhappy wives. *Mal mariées.* He sang a song about them in French, easing open the tight, alien vowels and letting the slur of his voice widen their scope; *ma-uhl mah-urrr-ee-yeh.* It was a Limerick voice, and those who resisted its charm said that the further Dan Lydon got from Limerick the broader his accent grew. The resistant tended to be men; women always liked Dan. To hear him lilt, 'My lo-hove

186

is lo-oike a r-red, r-red r-ro-ose' was, as respected matrons would tell you, like listening to grand opera. His vibrancy fired them. It kindled and dazzled like those beams you saw in paintings of the Holy Ghost, and his breath had a pulse to it, even when all he was ordering was the same again, please, and a packet of fags. Words, moving in his mouth like oysters, put town-dwellers in mind of rural forebears of the damp, reticent lure of the countryside.

The parsonage of Dan's youth lay in grasslands watered by the River Shannon, flat country shadowed by those cloud formations known as mackerel backs and mares' tails ... arrangements as chameleon as himself. He was a bright-haired, smiling boy, who first reached Dublin in 1943, a time when the Japanese minister rode with a local hunt and the German one did not always get the cold shoulder. Dan's allegiance was to the noble Soviets, but he was alive too to sexual raciness blown in like pollen from the war-zones. Change fizzed; neutrality opened fields of choice, and values had rarely been shiftier.

'So where is your sister now?'

Mrs Connors did and did not believe his story. 'Tea?' she offered. Tea was his hour. Husbands tended to be at work. Mr Connors was a civil servant.

Dan took his tea. 'She had to be married off,' he admitted. 'She has a sweet little boy.'

Mrs Connors dared. 'Yours?'

'Or my brother's? I'd like there to be one I *knew* was mine.' His eyes held hers. Putting down the cup, he turned her wrist over, slid back the sleeve, and traced the artery with a finger. 'The blue-veined child!' he murmured. 'Don't you think children conceived in passion are special? Fruits of wilfulness! Surely they become poets? Or Napoleons?'

Phyllis Connors was sure Napoleon's family had been legitimate. On her honeymoon, before the war, she had visited Corsica. 'Their mother was addressed as Madame Mère.'

'Was that the model Connors held up to you? Madame Mère – ?' Dan teased. 'On your honeymoon! What a clever cuss!'

The teasing could seem brotherly; but Dan's brotherliness was alarming. Indeed, Phyllis's offer to be a sister to him had touched off the nonsense . . . what else could it be? . . . about incest.

Nonsense or not, it unsettled her.

He was predatory. A known idler. Wolfed her sandwiches as though he had had no lunch . . . and maybe he hadn't? The *parson* had washed his hands of him. But Dan had a new spiritual father in a poet who had stopped the university kicking him out. Dan's enthusiasm for poetry . . . he was, he said, writing it full-time . . . so captivated the poet that he had persuaded the provost to waive mundane requirements and ensure that the boy's scholarship (paid by a fund for sons of needy parsons) be renewed. Surely, argued Dan's advocate, the alma mater of Burke and Sam Beckett could be flexible with men of stellar promise? Talents did not mature at the speed of seed-potatoes, and Ireland's best known export was fractious writers. Let's try to keep this one at home.

The poet, who ran a magazine, needed someone to do the legwork and, when need be, plug gaps with pieces entitled *Where the Red Flag Flies, A Future for Cottage Industries,* or *Folk Memories of West Clare.* Dan could knock these off at speed and the connection gave him prestige with the undergraduates at whose verse-readings he starred.

It was at one of these that Phyllis Connors had first heard him recite. The verse had not been his. That, he explained, must stay *sub rosa.* Did she know that Jack Yeats, the painter, kept a rose on his easel when painting his mad, marvellous pictures of horse-dealers, fiddlers, and fairs? Art in progress was safest under the rose.

After tea, Dan talked of procreation and of how men in tropical lands like Ecuador thought sex incomplete without it. That was the earth's wisdom speaking through them. RCs . . . look at their Madonnas . . . had the same instincts. Dan, the parson's son, defended the Pope whose church had inherited the carnal wit of the ancients. 'The sower went out to sow his seed.'

Talk like this unnerved Phyllis, who was childless and unsure what was being offered. What farmer, asked Dan, would scatter with an empty hand? 'Your women are your fields,' he quoted, from the Koran. 'Go freely into your fields!' Then he extolled the beauty of pregnant women . . . bloomy as June meadows . . . and recited a poem about changelings. 'Come away, O human child.'

Phyllis, thinking him a child himself, might have surrendered to the giddiest request. But Dan made none. Instead he went home to his lodgings, leaving her to gorge her needs on the last of the sandwiches.

He came back, though, for her house was near the poet's, and after drudging with galleys would drop by to cup hands, sculpt air, praise her hips, and eat healthy amounts of whatever was for tea. Refreshed, he liked to intone poems about forest gods and fairyfolk. 'And if any gaze on our rushing band,' he chanted, 'We come between him and the deed of his hand. We come between him and the hope of his heart.'

Why did he not come after what he implied was the hope of his own heart? Wondering made her think of him more than she might otherwise have done, and so did seeing him in The Singing Kettle, eating doughnuts with the poet's wife. Peering through trickles in a steamy window, she thought she saw the word 'love' on his lips. Or was it 'dove'? His motto, 'Let the doves settle!' meant 'Take things as they come.'

Phyllis decided that some doves needed to be snared.

Soon she was pregnant, and when she went into the Hatch Street Nursing Home to give birth Dan brought her a reproduction of Piero della Francesca's Madonna del Parto, with the pale slash where the Virgin, easing her gown off her round belly, shows underlinen more intimate than skin. His finger on Phyllis's stomach sketched an identical white curve. He teased the nurses, relished the fertility all about, and was happy as a mouse in cheese.

It turned out that the poet's wife was here too, and for the same reason. Her room was on another floor, so Dan yoyo'd up and down. Sometimes he brought gifts which had to be divided;

fruit, for instance, from the poet, who still used Dan to run errands. Or books, review copies from the magazine. When a nurse let drop that the poet's wife had the same Piero Madonna on her side table Phyllis wrapped hers in a nappy and put it in the trash. If there had been a fireplace, she would have burned it, as she had been trained to do with unwanted religious objects.

Her baby received her husband's first name, and the poet's baby the poet's. Dan . . . though neither couple asked him to be godfather . . . presented both infants with christening mugs. One had been his and the other his brother's, and both were made of antique Dublin silver. Early Georgian. The official godfathers, fearing odious comparisons, returned their purchases to Weirs Jewellers and bought cutlery. Phyllis wondered if Dan's brother knew what had happened to his mug. Though the war was now over, he was still overseas with the British Army.

'He'll not be back,' Dan assured her, and revealed that the parsonage had been a dour and penurious place. Its congregation had dwindled since the RC natives took over the country in '21, and attendance some Sundays amounted to less than six. Pride had throttled Dan's widowed father, who did menial work behind the scenes and made his children collect firewood, polish silver, and dine on boiled offal.

'He wouldn't want the mug,' said Dan. 'Too many bad memories!' The brothers had left as soon as they could, and getting their sister pregnant had been a parting gift. 'If we hadn't she'd still be Daddy's slave.'

Some years went by and Dan declared that his poetry, though still under the rose, was coming along well. Cherishing a belief that different sorts of fertility reinforced each other, he carried photographs of three toddlers which he showed, selectively, to women. The three faced the camera with Dan's own smile. 'Under the rose!' was his motto, and . . . punningly . . . 'Mum's the word!'

He was a student still, of a type known to Dubliners as 'chronic', a ragged brigade which, recoiling from a jobless job market, clung to a rank which harked back to the tribally condoned wandering scholars of long ago. This connection was often all that raised the chronics above tramps or paupers, and, as in nightmares where you overfly a chasm, the lifeline was frail.

Out of the blue, opportunity came Dan's way. The poet, who had to go into hospital, asked him to bring out an issue of the magazine bearing on its masthead the words 'Guest editor: Daniel Lydon.' Here was challenge! Dan toyed excitedly with the notion of publishing his secret poetry which he yearned, yet feared, to display. These urges warred in him until, having read and reread it, he saw that it had gone dead, leaking virtue like batteries kept too long in a drawer. Stewing over this, he fell behind with the magazine and had, in the end, to ghostwrite several pieces to pad the thing out. Giddy and frustrated, he now did something foolish. As part of the padding, he decided to publish photographs of A CHANGING IRELAND. Hydrofoils, reapers-and-binders, ballpoint pens and other such innovations were shown next to neolithic barrows. The Knights of Columbanus in full fig appeared cheek by jowl with an electric band. Portraits of 'the last Gaelic storyteller' and some 'future Irishmen' rounded out the theme. The future Irishmen, three small boys with their heads arranged like the leaves of a shamrock, were recognizably his nephew and the recipients of his christening mugs . . . and what leaped to the eye was their resemblance to himself. The caption 'Changelings' drove the scandal home.

The poet, convalescing in his hospital bed after an operation for a gentleman's complaint, told his wife, in an insufficiently discreet hiss, that he had paid Dan to do his leg work, not to get his leg over. Reference was made to 'cuckoo's eggs' and it was not long before echoes of this reached the ear of Mr Connors, the proverbial quiet man whom it is dangerous to arouse. Declan Connors who, in his bachelor days, had done a bit of hacking, had a riding crop which he now took to the student lodgings where Dan lived, and used it to tap smartly on his door. When Dan opened this, Connors raised the crop. Dan yelled, and his neighbour, a fellow-Communist who was on the Varsity boxing team, came hurtling to the rescue. Assuming the row to be political and Connors a member of the Blue Shirts, the rescuer proposed beating him to a pulp and Dan's stuttering rebuttal only reinforced his zeal. Shoving ensued; Connors fell downstairs; gawkers gathered and the upshot was that an ambulance was called and the opinion bandied that the victim had broken his back. Some genuine Blue Shirts were meanwhile rustled up. Men whose finest hours had been spent fighting for Franco, singing hymns to *Cristo Rey* and beating the sin out of Reds, they were spoiling for a scrap and, but for Dan's friend spiriting him out the back, might have sent him to join Mr Connors – who, as it would turn out, had not been injured after all and was fit as a fiddle in a couple of weeks. By then, however, Dan had prudently boarded the ferry to Holyhead, taking with him, like a subsidiary passport, the issue of the magazine bearing his name as 'guest editor'. It got him work with the BBC which, in those days of live programming, needed men with a ready gift of the gab, and was friendly to Celts. Louis MacNeice and Dylan Thomas were role-models, liquid stimulants in high favour, and Dan recruited straight off the boat.

So ran reports reaching Dublin. Pithy myths, these acquired an envious tinge as his success was magnified along with the sums he was earning for doing what he had formerly done for free; talking, singing and gargling verse. Others too were soon dreaming of jobs in a London whose airwaves vapoured with gold. Hadn't Dubliners a known talent for transubstantiating eloquence to currency? Think of Jimmy Joyce! And couldn't every second one of us talk at least as well as Dan Lydon?

Declan Connors doubted this. Despite himself, he'd caught snatches of what nobody had the indecency to quote quite to his face; a saga featuring Dan as Dispenser of Sweet Anointings to women. These, Connors understood, had needed preparation. Persuasion had been required; a process whose boldness had grown legendary, as an athlete's prowess does with fans. The gossips relished Dan's gall and the airy way he could woo without promise or commitment, arguing – say – that, in a war's wake, more kids were needed and that his companion's quickened pulse was nature urging her to increase the supply. Nature! What a let-out! Any man who could sell a line like that in Holy Ireland could sell heaters in hell.

'He's a one-man social service!' A wag raised his pint. 'Offers himself up. Partake ye of my body! He'd rather be consumed than consume!' The wag drained his glass. His preferences ran the other way. So did those of the man next to him whose tongue wrestled with ham filling from a sandwich. All around guzzled males – women, in this prosperous pub, were outnumbered ten to one. Connors thought, 'No wonder Lydon made out. We left him an open field!'

He could no longer regret this, for now, after ten barren years of marriage, Phyllis had had three children in quick succession. It was as if something in her had been unlocked. He supposed there were jokes about this too but didn't care. His master-passion had turned out to be paternal and Declan Junior was the apple of his eye. The younger two were girls and, as Phyllis spoiled them, he had to make things up to the boy.

For a while after the scandal, the couple had felt shy with each other, but had no thoughts of divorce. You couldn't in Ireland and it wasn't what they wanted. They were fond of each other – and besides, there was Declan, of whom it was said behind Mr Connors' shrugging back that he used his blood father's charm to wind his nominal one around his little finger. A seducer *ab ovo*.

Smallmindedness! Envy! Anyway time heals and when the boy was picked, surprisingly early, for his elementary school soccer team and later won ribbons for show jumping, Connors – a sportsman – knew him for his spiritual son. Even if the kid was a Lydon, he was a better one than Dan – whose brother had been decorated for gallantry in the war. Skimming the entry on Mendel's law in the encyclopedia, Connors learned that hereditary character was transmitted chancily and, remembering the poltroonish Dan draped over armchairs and cowering during their fight, decided that Declan Junior had nothing of his but his looks.

He still took an interest, though, in the news trickling back from London where Dan's free-lance was said to be cutting a swath. In his days of working for the poet, who had a haughty disdain for Dublin's pubs, Dan had often had the job of touring distinguished visitors around them. He had beguiled several; and these contacts now proved so useful that he was soon the protégé of a literary pundit who, though married, was partial to a handsome young man.

It was now that Connors noted an odd thing; admiration was ousting envy and Dan's stature in the saga growing. Needless to say, Dan's news was slow to reach Connors since nobody who remembered their connection would wish to re-open old wounds. It came in scraps and, by the time he got them, these were as spare and smooth as broken glass licked by recurring tides.

As Connors heard it then; Dan's new patron's marriage, though possibly unconsummated, was harmonious, for his wife had money. The couple were fashionable hosts and Dan was soon glowing in their orbit, singing ballads, referring to his secret *oeuvre* and enlivening their soirées with tales of Irish mores. In between, he did jobs for the BBC helped by the pundit's wife who, in return, made use of him for what the Dublin poet had sourly described as 'leg work'.

She was a handsome, angry woman who, having hated her father but agreed to inherit his money, would make no further concession to men and slept only with those she could pity or control. As her husband didn't fit the bill, she had lovers who were all, in some way, impaired. So, presumably to her mind, was Dan, for he was soon servicing both her and the husband who, being both jealous and smitten, did not know this.

Here the story fractures. In one version she 'gets preggers' which so shatters the husband that his violence leads to a miscarriage and Dan's flight to Paris. But there is an implausible symmetry to this, as though running dye from the Dublin episode had coloured it, and a likelier account has no pregnancy and the jealousy provoked by someone's indiscretion. Deliberate? Careless? Either way, Dan left. The marriage collapsed and the husband, till now a rather nerveless knight of the pen, who had, in his own words 'failed to grapple with his subjectivity', did so in a book which raised him several rungs up the literary ladder. It was before the Wolfenden Report. Homosexuality was a painful subject and the grappling brave. Dan, as midwife to his lover's best writing, could be said to have done him a good turn.

Meanwhile Declan Junior was in his teens and his mother, noting that if you cut the heart from his name you'd be left with 'Dan', feared leaving him alone with his sisters; an idle fear. Girls bored him, and so did poetry, to her relief. Not that Dan himself had yet produced a line, but the appellation *Poète Irlandais* clung to him who had now – wonder of wonders – married and settled in Paris. The word about that was that an old Spanish-Civil-War hero, whose memoirs Dan had been ghost-writing while sleeping with his daughter, had, on catching the pair *in flagrante*, sat on Dan's chest and said 'Marry her' – so Dan did. A bad day's work for the girl, tittered those Dubliners who still remembered Dan. One or two had looked him up on trips abroad and reported that he was doing something nowadays for films. Script-doctoring, was it? And his wife had published poems before her marriage but none since. Maybe she didn't want to shame him? Closer friends said the marriage was a good one and that no forcing had been needed. Why should it have been? Marisol was bright, young, had a river of dark hair and gave Dan the tribal connection he had always coveted. His ravenous charm came from his childhood in that bleak parsonage in that empty parish. Marginal. Clanless. Left behind by the tide. Catholics – whose clan had dispersed his – did not appeal, but the Left did. The Spanish Civil War had been Dan's boyhood war and the more romantic for having been lost. Dan loved a negative. What, he would argue, was there to say about success? The surprise was that the Anglo-Saxon ruling classes could still talk and didn't just beat their smug chests like chimps. If it wasn't for their homosexuals, he claimed, they'd have no art. Art was for those whose reality needed suborning. It burrowed and queried; it – etcetera! Dan could still chatter like a covey of starlings and the Limerick accent went down a treat in French being, as people would soon start to say, *mediatique*.

Then along came the Sixties. The Youth Cult blossomed just as Dan – in his forties – began losing his hair. Juvenescence glowed in him though, as in a golden autumn tree. His freshness was a triumph of essence over accident and he became an acknowledged youth-expert when he made a film about the graffiti of May '68. The graffito being, like pub talk, insolent, jubilant and an end in itself, was right up his street and he was soon in Hollywood working on a second film. It came to nothing – which confirmed the purity of his response to the pop and ephemeral, and he continued to fly between Paris and California, dressed in light summery suits, and engaged in optimistic projects, some of which did throw his name on to a screen. Briefly. For a fleeting shimmer.

One evening in Paris he and the Connors came face to face in a brasserie where, being at different tables, they could have ignored each other. As their last encounter had led to Connors' departure in the ambulance and Dan's from Ireland, this might have seemed wise. Sportingly, however, Dan came over. Shiny and aglow, his forehead – higher than it used to be – damp with sweat. It was a hot night. Hand outstretched. A little deprecating. He had heard their news, as they had his, and congratulated Connors on a recent promotion. Family all well? Grand! Great! He was with *his*. Nodding at a tableful of Spaniards. Laughing at their noise. Then, ruefully, as two of his wrestling children knocked over a jug of sauce, said he'd better go and cope. He left, but soon the waiter brought the Connors two glasses of very old cognac with his compliments. They accepted, toasted him and, watching his gipsy table, remembered hearing that 'the poor bastard' – their informant's words – had saddled himself with a family of idlers whom he had to work overtime to support. The old hero, it seemed, had emphysema. Dan's brother-in-law yearned to be a pop star and

Marisol kept producing children. How many had they? The Connors counted three who, being dark like their mother, did not look at all like Declan Junior. As they left, the couple thanked Dan for the cognac.

Afterwards, they discussed the encounter half sharply, half shyly. Looking out for each other's dignity. Not mentioning Declan Junior. Phyllis, her husband guessed, thought of *him* as having two fathers. Blame could thus be moved about or dissolved in the whirligig of her brain. Romance, too, he suspected. He suspected this because – this evening had brought it home to him – he too had an imaginative connection with Dan and had not liked what he saw in the brasserie. It had depressed him. Spilled gravy and domesticity cut Dan down to size and a life-sized Dan was a reproach, as the saga-figure hadn't been at all. That connection had, somehow, aureoled Connors' life and added a dimension to his fantasies. For a while it had even made Phyllis more attractive to him. An adulterous wife was exciting, like a Scarlet Woman, or a whore, and he had often wondered whether it could have been that extra zest which had led to his begetting the two girls. Water under the bridge, to be sure! The Dan Saga had not stimulated his sex-life for years. What it did do was make him feel more tolerant than might have been expected of the sober civil servant he was. Broader and even more passionate. It was as if he himself had a part in Dan's adventuring. That, of course, made no sense, or rather the sense it made was private and – why not? poetic. Dan, the unproductive poet had, like Oscar Wilde, put his genius into his life; a fevering contagion. Or so Connors must have been feeling, unknown to himself. How else to explain the gloom provoked by the sighting of the brasserie? Phyllis didn't seem to feel it. But then women saw what they wanted to see. Connors guessed that for her Dan Lydon was still a figure of romance.

It was now that Declan Junior began to disappoint his parents. A gifted athlete who handled his academic work with ease, he had come through university with flying colours and Connors, convinced that he could star in any firmament, had looked forward to seeing him join the diplomatic corps or go in for politics or journalism. Something with scope. Instead, what should their affable, graceful boy do on graduating but take a humdrum job in a bank and announce that he was getting married! Yes. Now. There was no talking him out of it and it was not a shotgun wedding either. Indeed, Declan Junior had been rather stuffy when asked about this. And when you met the girl you saw that it was unlikely. She was limp-haired, steady and, well, dull. It was ironic. Here was their cuckoo, thought Connors, turning out too tame rather than too wild. If there was a Lydon gene at work the resemblance was more with the family man he and Phyllis had glimpsed in Paris than with the satyr whose heredity they had feared. Had they worked too hard at stamping out the demon spark?

That, they were to learn, was still riskily smouldering in the vicinity of Lydon himself. Connors heard the latest bulletin by a fluke, for he had grown reclusive since Declan's wedding and more so after the christening which came an impeccable ten months later. He was, to tell the truth, a touch down in the mouth. Brooding. Had Phyllis, he wondered, been cold with the boy when he was small? Could guilt have made her be? And might there be something, after all, to Freudian guff? Till now Connors had dismissed it as projection; the bid of an urban Jew with a bad conscience to prove that he was just like the rest of us. And how could he be? We might be no better, but how could we be the same? Us? Weren't we Catholics? Farmer-stock? Healthy. Simple. Healthily simple! Yes, but . . . There was Declan married to a surrogate Mum. Born to be a Mum, she was pregnant again and had tied her limp hair in a bun. Cartoonish, in orthopaedic shoes, she wore a frilly apron and loved to make pastry. Declan was putting on weight! Ah, well.

The latest about Lydon was that, hungry for money, he had agreed to be a beard. A what? 'You may well ask,' said Connors' source, a man called Breen, who swore him to secrecy. Breen was on leave from our embassy in Rome which, said he, was in a turmoil over the thing.

'But what *is* a . . .'

'Shush!' Breen looked over his shoulder – they'd met in the Stephens Green Club – 'I can't tell you here.'

So Connors brought him home and settled him down with a whisky, to tell his story before Phyllis came in. She was babysitting Declan III, known as Dickybird, who was at the crawling stage and tiring. His mother needed a rest.

Breen's hot spurts of shock revived Connors' spirits. The Dan Saga thrilled him in an odd, outraged way, much as the whisky was warming and biting his mouth. Recklessness, he thought welcomingly, a touch of folly tempered the norms and rules.

Lydon, said Breen, had been acting as cover for one of the candidates in the upcoming US election, a married man, who was having it off with an actress. Needing to seem above reproach – 'You know American voters!' – the candidate had engaged Dan to pretend to be the woman's lover. 'He's what's called a beard – travelled with her, took her to parties etc. then left the scene when the candidate had a free moment.'

The beard's function was to draw suspicion. For the real lover to seem innocent, the beard must suggest the rut. And Dan did. Though he was now fifty, an aura of youth and potency clung to him. 'It's all in the mind!' said Breen, shrugging.

Outside the window someone had turned on a revolving lawn sprinkler and the Connors' labrador, a puppy called Muff, was leaping at its spray. That meant that Phyllis and the child were back from their walk.

Breen said that what Lydon's wife thought of his job nobody knew. The money must have been good. Or maybe she hadn't known – until she was kidnapped. Kidnapped? Yes. Hadn't he said? By mistake. At the Venice Film Festival. By Sardinian kidnappers who got wind of the story but took the wrong woman. 'The candidate's rich and they'd hoped for a big ransom.' This had happened just three weeks ago.

Connors was stunned. A changeling, he thought and felt a breath of shame. Play had turned dangerous and he felt angry with himself for having relished Lydon's tomfoolery.

'The Yanks came to us,' Breen told him, 'asking us to handle the thing with discretion – after they'd got the actress back to the US. You could say we're *their* beard!' He grew grave, for there was a danger that the kidnappers could panic. 'Sardinians feed their victims to their pigs, you know. Destroys the evidence. They're primeval and inbred! Islanders! No, *not* like us. More basic. Crude. Their life-way was easy to commercialize just because it was so crude. With them vengeance required blood as real as you'd put in a blood sausage. Quantifiable! Material! We, by contrast, are casuists and symbol-jugglers, closers of eyes . . .'

A flick of embarrassment in Breen's own eye signalled a sudden recognition that this could seem to refer to the story – had he only now remembered it – of Connors and Dan; a case of eyes closed to lost honour. With professional blandness, he tried to cover his gaffe with an account of the embassy's dilemma; on the one hand the papers must not learn of the thing. On the other, the kidnappers must be made to see that there was no money to be had. Breen castigated Lydon whose sins were catching up with him. His poor wife though – Poor Marisol!

Connors tried to remember her face in the Paris brasserie but could not.

'That louser Lydon!' Breen, intending perhaps to express solidarity with Connors, threw out words like 'parasite' and 'sociopath'. When you thought about it, a man like that was worse than the kidnappers. 'He breaks down the barriers between us and them. He lets in anarchy. He sells the pass.'

Connors tried to demur but Breen, warming to his theme, blamed society's tolerance for which it – 'we' – must now pay. 'Bastards like that trade on it.' Someone, he implied, should have dealt with Lydon long ago.

Connors ignored the reproach. Off on a different tack, his mind was cutting through willed confusions. The eruption of menace had shrivelled old camouflage and he recognized that what he felt for Dan was love or something closer. So far from being his enemy, Dan was a part of himself. Luminous alter ego? Partner in father and grandfatherhood? Closing his ears to his companion's sermon, he looked out to where Phyllis and Dickybird had caught up with the golden Lab on whose back the child kept trying to climb. Shaken off, he tried again, a rubbery putto, bouncing back like foam. The wild Lydon heritage had skipped a generation and here it was again.

Excited by the whirling spray, the puppy scampered through its prism while the infant held on to its tail. The child's hair was as blond as the dog's and, in the rainbow embrace, the two gleamed like fountain statuary. They were Arcadian, anarchic, playful and propelled by pooled energy.

'It's a terrible thing to happen,' Connors conceded. 'But I wouldn't blame Lydon. Blame the American candidate or the Italian state. Hypocrisy. Puritanism. Pretence. Lydon's innocent of all that. Blaming him is like, I don't know, blaming the dog out there.' And he waved his glass of whisky at the golden scene outside.

Angelfish

WENDY PERRIAM

Wendy Perriam is a full-time writer. She has published twelve novels and is the author of a forthcoming book of short stories.

On three nights out of seven Mr Chivers dreamed of purple candlewick. Sometimes they wrapped him in it as his winding sheet; other times it formed the fabric of the universe and, everywhere he wandered, little purple tufts tripped him up or tugged at him like burs. Occasionally they served it up as bacon with his rubberized fried egg. He often woke screaming. He switched his torch on underneath the blankets and prayed to a purple God that Miss Lineham hadn't woken up as well. Miss Lineham slept with her door open. Maybe she didn't sleep at all, but she retired to her room at ten o'clock sharp, with a purple hairnet and a cup of cocoa and demanded silence until seven.

Mr Chivers crept out of his tangled bed into the bathroom. There it was – living, breathing candlewick – no dreamstuff, this. Purple candlewick bathmat lying exactly parallel to the cold white bath; purple candlewick toilet-seat cover, masking the shameful business that went on underneath it. Even the toilet roll was ruched and frilled in purple candlewick.

Mr Chivers stumbled over to the basin and inspected his tongue in the mirror. It was shaggy grey, as if a fine mould had settled on it in the night. His bladder was kicking him in the gut, demanding to be emptied. He hitched up his pyjama bottoms, tied the cord more tightly. He dared not risk the jet of water on white porcelain, not at three a.m. Even in normal daylight hours, he preferred to use the public convenience. Miss Lineham's lavatory was a decorative item. He doubted if she even used it herself. She was too refined to pee. He presumed she must evaporate off her waste-products in some noiseless, odourless form of celestial dialysis. Even the cistern was shrouded in candlewick. Miss Lineham had turned a cesspool into an ornamental lake. Little matching doileys, hand-crocheted in purple, smirked at him from every surface, standing guard beneath the Harpic, cushioning the Vim. The bathroom boasted little else. Toilet articles were strictly banned. No toothbrush was permitted to flaunt its dripping nakedness in public; no bar of soap to wallow in its own slime. After-shave was decadent, bathsalts an indulgence. Flannels, toothpaste, sponges, razors – all must be locked away in strictest purdah. In the early days, before Mr Chivers realized the perils of exposure, he had rashly left his nail-brush by the basin. It had seemed the sensible place for it, at the time. Miss Lineham said nothing. But four mornings running, he found the damply accusing object cringing by his breakfast egg. Four mornings running, he suffered with tension headaches and indigestion.

Now, he never quitted the bathroom without a thorough scrutiny. He went down on his hands and knees searching for stray hairs or slops of water; re-positioned the bathmat dead centre. Not that he ever dared take a bath. His feet would print obscene naked splodges on the purple candlewick; his city dirt might even leave a tidemark impossible to remove. The cleaning rag was folded so squarely on the canister of Vim, it would be sedition to disturb it.

He ran just a piddle of water into the basin. If he turned the taps full on, the geyser roared in accusation – Miss Lineham's private spy. He dabbed at his face, then at his private parts, gazing upwards at the prim white ceiling, so he wouldn't get excited. Arousal made the bed creak. He couldn't even eat an apple in bed. The very first bite brought a warning cough from Miss Lineham's open door. There were ways and means, of course, if you were desperate. It was dangerous to chew, but you could graze your teeth very gently, up and down, up and down, against the skin, until the flesh gradually succumbed. Then you held it in your mouth and sucked. The saliva did the rest. It took an hour to dispose of one small Orange Pippin. Granny Smiths were more or less impossible. Mr Chivers stuck to Jonathans.

'I do not consider it hygienic, Mr Chivers, to store perishable foodstuffs among your underclothes. Nor would I have deemed it necessary to supplement the more than adequate diet I supply.'

He couldn't even hide a Jonathan. Miss Lineham inspected everything in his room, including his underpants. She called it cleaning. She lined his cufflinks up in twos, sprayed his shoes with foot deodorant.

'Tabloid newspapers, Mr Chivers, are *not* encouraged in this establishment.'

'I have found it necessary, Mr Chivers, to invest in a new front door mat, and I should like to draw your attention to the fact.'

He never saw her smile. The nearest she got to it was at nine o'clock every other evening, when she fed her angelfish. The bevelled tank stretched its tropical turquoise luxury along a table in the hall. Jungle plants trailed soft green fingers through the water. Broad-backed leaves and ferny fronds rippled in an effervescent spume of bubbles. And through them glided the celestial colours and fairy fins of three exotic angelfish, one gold, one silver, one marbled black and cream. Their glowing opalescence seemed almost blasphemy in Miss Lineham's fawn and frowning hall. No one else in the house was indulged as were those fish. While the lodgers shivered in their fireless rooms, the angels basked in a constant eighty degrees Fahrenheit. Mr Chivers ate frugally off melamine, but the twelve varieties of vitaminized, freeze-dried fishfood lorded it on a silver tray.

Feeding time was a sacred ritual; hall lights turned low, front door locked, parlour blinds drawn down. Mr Chivers watched through a crack in his bedroom door, peering down through the banisters, awaiting that magic transformation in Miss Lineham's granite face. As the angelfish darted to the surface and nibbled at her dead white fingers, her face turned from stone to petals, the corners of her mouth lifting slightly, so that he could see the tips of plastic teeth.

'My pretty angels,' she whispered, sprinkling Magiflakes like manna. 'My pretty pretty angels.'

Mr Chivers' pulse raced. There was something about the way her cold blue eyes sparked and softened, the almost flirtatious flurry of her hand across the water. He never heard that velvet voice at any other hour; it was sackcloth and hessian when she was snapping at her lodgers.

'Some of us are born to work, Mr Chivers, and some are born to idle.'

'I do not wish Princess Margaret's name to be mentioned in this house again.'

She was even uncharacteristically generous with the fishfood. True, her angels were fed only on alternate nights, but she flung in fresh pink shrimp and bite-size worm with almost an abandon. Everyone else was rationed. Mr Chivers' scant teaspoonful of breakfast marmalade was apportioned out the evening before and sat stiffening in a plastic egg-cup overnight. He never saw the jar. Bacon rashers were cut tastefully in half. And when he had swallowed the last morsel of his one barely-buttered piece of toast (thin-sliced from a small loaf), Miss Lineham whisked every comestible swiftly out of sight. Not a crumb nor tealeaf remained to give promise of future sustenance. Even the smell of food crept cravenly away at the touch of Miss Lineham's Airfresh. Five minutes after breakfast, the kitchen looked like a morgue or a museum – shining tiles and dead exhibits in sterilized glass jars.

Mr Chivers started eating out. He sprawled in Joe's Caff or Dick's Diner, elbow-deep in chips; baked beans tumbling down his chin, wallowing in ketchup, gnawing chicken bones. ('Dogs eat bones, Mr Chivers, not Civil Service gentlemen.') He ordered both cream and custard on his syrup sponge, relished every mouthful as he slurped it down. Delirious contrast to those tight-lipped breakfasts when Miss Lineham jumped and blinked her eyes every time his teeth made contact with the toast.

He spent more and more time away. He added the public baths to the public convenience, running the bath full to overflowing and shouting above the Niagara of the taps. He set up floods and cataracts, slooshing the water over the side of the cracked white tub. He bought a plastic duck and spent reckless hours torpedoing it with the bar of municipal soap. He flung in whole cartonsful of bathsalts and turned the water as blue as Miss Lineham's fish-tank. He left hairs in the plug-hole and a rim around the bath. Nobody cared. Nobody pinned crabbed little notes on his door, saying 'Water costs money, Mr Chivers, were you aware?' No one slipped a purple crocheted doily underneath his pink soapy bottom.

He discovered a bath with a toilet beside it, for only tenpence extra. Now he ruled the world. He jetted his urine at the stained, un-Harpicked bowl, aiming at the central 'C' in the maker's name, his own initial. Sometimes he took risks or invented games, standing further and further back and still not missing, or stopping and starting the stream, or tracing patterns with it as if the jet were a golden pencil. That done, he sat on the cracked and germy toilet seat (which had never known the chastening caress of candlewick) and strained and groaned in thunderous ecstasy. He even returned to prunes.

Whatever his excesses in the Baths, he was always back in the house by 8.55. Nine p.m. was the angels' feeding time – the high spot of his day. Miss Lineham was often prowling by the door.

'Good evening, Miss Lineham. Lovely weather.'

'Good evening, Mr Chivers. It won't last.'

'Good evening, Miss Lineham. Nice bit of rain for the garden.'

'Good evening, Mr Chivers. They forecast floods.'

He rarely glanced at her. His whole attention was fixated on the fish. He dawdled past their tank as slowly as he dared, watching their perfect gills pant in and out, their sweepingly dramatic ventral fins flowing like fancy ribbons from their underbodies. There were other inhabitants of the tank, inelegant and drably coloured small fry, creeping things which slimed and gobbled on the bottom, the proletariat of snail and loach. Mr Chivers hardly noticed them – only the wide wings and golden eyes of the angels, weaving in and out of each other's shadows, haloed by their own enchanted fins. He longed to know more about them, what sex they were, what age, their parentage, their origins. He dared not ask. He dared not even loiter by the tank. Only in his fantasy did he lay his cheek against the cold compress of the glass and feel his fingers caressed by foraging mouths, the tickle of peacock tails against his palm.

Cold reality shoved him briskly up the stairs, to cower all evening, a prisoner in his room. He could only watch the feeding in breathless secrecy, craning his neck, peering through the crack, rigid with terror that Miss Lineham's eye would swivel in its socket and meet his own. It never did. She had eyes only for her angelfish, her concrete brow flushing and softening as they flicked their fins and flirted with her hands. Mr Chivers' heartbeat almost cracked the walls. He could feel his supper singing through his veins, jam on the semolina centre of his soul. This was his finale, his golden climax to a sallow day, his after-dinner port, his nuts and wine.

At 9.05 it was over. Gloom descended like a dust-sheet. Miss Lineham disappeared and was stiff and grey again by the time she re-emerged. Mr Chivers drooped in his room, dressing-gown atop his pinstripes. The one-bar fire was removed on March 1 and did not reappear until the last day of October.

'Overheating the system can be dangerous, Mr Chivers.'

'Yes, Miss Lineham.' Three inches of snow recorded at the Kew Observatory.

Mr Chivers sat and read (TV and radio were forbidden in the house). He bought every aquarist magazine on the market and squandered his Christmas bonus on a Pictorial Encyclopaedia of Tropical Fish. He always turned first to the angelfish: studied their breeding habits, learned their Latin names. He traced their showy outlines on sheets of greaseproof paper and coloured them in with a set of Woolworth's crayons. And when at last he fell asleep, marbled bodies and gossamer tails plunged through the spaces in his purple candlewick nightmares and turned them into gleaming silver mesh.

'SILVER JUBILEE FESTIVAL OF ANGELFISH'
April 15–21

Mr Chivers was reading in bed, his torch concealed beneath the blankets. ('Lights out at eleven, Mr Chivers. Electricity is not a gift from God.') He peered more closely at the print – a full-page advertisement in the glossy new issue of *Fishkeeper's Weekly*. Never before had so much money and attention been lavished on the species. An eccentric Yorkshire millionaire with a passion for *Pterophyllum Scalare* was sponsoring a festival in Doncaster, devoted exclusively to angelfish. Special breeds, rare specimens, unheard-of colours, generous prizes. All the local pet shops and aquaria had promised back-up displays and exhibitions for the week of the festival. Yorkshire would be awash in angelfish.

Mr Chivers had never been up North. His Easter holiday was due; he was tired of Littlehampton. He stared at the magazine with trembling hands. He would book on Inter-City direct to Doncaster and spend an enchanted week among the angels.

April 22. He alighted at King's Cross with an empty wallet and a suitcaseful of dirty shirts. His soul was still in Doncaster. He jumped on the tube and plunged through rocky clefts and tangled weed. His suburban train was packed with angelfish. Ghostly albinos plopped between the pages of his newspaper; aggressive all-blacks jostled his elbows and bumped against his knees; foamy lace angels swooped past the windows and swam along the rails. When he got off, water-snails were clinging to his suitcase, bubbles streaming from his nose.

He trudged from the station to the cropped and pollarded trees of Hilldon Close. Miss Lineham met him in the hall.

'I took the liberty, Mr Chivers, of moving you to a different room. A new gentleman lodger has arrived, who particularly requested a location facing front.'

He jumped. Her voice had startled the rare and fantastic Liu Keung angelfish, whom he had just persuaded to nuzzle at his hand. 'Yes, Miss Lineham,' he muttered. He was counting the bars on majestic marbled torsos, admiring the damask splendour of stately tails.

She ushered him into a cold cramped cubicle which looked out across the dustbins. He saw only verdant water-fern reflecting the light from darting silver fins.

'As one of my longest-standing lodgers, Mr Chivers, I knew I could count on your co-operation. The new gentleman is decidedly artistic and requires a room with good light. I also took the opportunity of replenishing your Airwick and have added the 55p to your rent.'

'Thank you, Miss Lineham,' he murmured, as she closed the door. He was smiling at two flirtatious silver veil-tails rubbing noses on the ceiling. He could see their spiky back-bones gleaming through the diaphanous silk of their flesh. He sank smiling on the bed.

Two hours later, Doncaster was fading. Supper had been sausages – the cheaper beef variety with a high percentage of rusk, and mortar-mix potatoes. He crunched on a lump in his custard, swilled it down with tea, and returned upstairs to the beige disapproval of his new back-room. Silver fins and shot-silk tails had vanished, blue water leaked away, leaving only sludge-coloured lino, purple crocheted water-lily leaves stranded on bare wood. All his possessions had been lined up in rows like orphans awaiting transport to an institution. His chewing-gum was confiscated, his thirteen books (eleven of them on fish) banished to a damp cardboard box marked 'NO DEPOSIT, NO RETURN. LEMON BARLEY WATER'.

Mr Chivers changed into his pyjamas and sat staring at his bunions. Miss Lineham would have thrown his feet away if he had been rash enough to leave them in his room. Miss Lineham liked things straight. In his jacket pocket was the crumpled entrance ticket to the Festival. He dropped it in the waste-bin.

Nothing left but bed. He slunk into the bathroom to clean his teeth – stopped dead before the bath. Something was different, dangerous. He glanced around. The toilet seat was up! In all his years at Miss Lineham's, it had never been left up. If some new inmate in his raw foolishness forgot to replace the cover, Miss Lineham would dart into the bathroom after him and snap it shut. Four or five repeats and the trembling tenant was completely cured. Candlewick became part of defecation.

The same with toiletries. An untrained lodger's first few breakfasts were often egg-and-flannel or sausage-and-loofah, the table littered with hang-dog razors and confiscated shaving sticks. Cure was always swift. Or had been up till now. Mr New-Boy Gordon had been in residence a week, so what was his orange flannel doing draped across the bath – flagrant, dripping, not even folded . . . ? Miss Lineham was at home, so why had she not removed this blushing flag of revolution? Why had no contemptuous note been pushed beneath the offender's door? As far as he could ascertain, she was still in her right mind. Or had been so at supper.

'Since you appear to be having so much difficulty in disposing of your second sausage, Mr Chivers, I shall apportion it to Mr Gordon in future.'

He saw the offending sausage, wreathed in Coleman's mustard and Miss Lineham's smiles. She never smiled. He clutched at the basin for support. How could he have been so blind? The new Artistic Gentleman had changed her, softened her, found the flinty remnants of her heart and swathed them in his shameless orange flannel. An upstart, a greenhorn, stinking out the house with aftershave, taking artistic licence with the purple candlewick . . .

He strode back to his room and stared in fury at the stag at bay. One picture per room. 'Nothing, I repeat nothing, is to be stuck or pinned onto lodgers' bedroom walls.' He hated stags - all their vaunting headgear. It had been a Victorian flower-girl in his previous room – tyro Gordon's room – with nothing on her head but blonde curls and a circlet of roses, a froth of white pantaloons teasing beneath her skirt.

He opened his wardrobe and stared at his row of ties, all limp, all drably coloured. He took out a bar of Cadbury's Wholenut chocolate, hidden in a slipper, put it back again. Wholenut was the riskiest confection on the market. If you bit into a hazelnut, it made a crack to wake the dead. And Miss Lineham was very much alive. He had noticed it at supper. She had hovered over Mr Gordon all through the bread-and-butter pudding, offering him Jersey cream from a silver jug. Melamine and custard had always been the rule.

He could hear her now, her brown no-nonsense lace-ups phat-phatting from kitchen to hall. Mr Chivers sprang up from his chair. Feeding time! Every other night at Doncaster he had tuned in, in mind and spirit, to that magic ritual, hearing Miss Lineham's fin-enchanted voice winging after him on Inter-City. 'My pretty angels, my pretty pretty angels.'

He crept to his bedroom door and opened it a crack. Useless. His new room was stuck away round a corner. He was cut off, shut out, excluded from those holy rites. No longer could he peer down through the banisters and share the azure mysteries of the tank. He heard the brogues shuffle to a stop, and then the sound of voices. Voices? He slunk out of his room onto the landing; could see only squiggled lino and stripey wall. His full-frontal view of the hall had departed with the roses and the pantaloons. He tiptoed along the passage, round the corner to the top of the stairs. Peered down. Miss Lineham was there, the flushed-and-radiant-feeding-time-Miss Lineham, lingering almost coquettishly by the tank. But she was not alone. Standing beside her, almost leaning against her, was Mr Basil A. F. Gordon; black eyes, white hands, topiary moustache. Four eyes staring at the fish, four hands trailing in the torrid water, two heads almost joined as one.

The largest angelfish was nibbling at Mr Gordon's index finger. Chivers could feel the throb and tingle in his own. The new

Artistic Gentleman was making stylish patterns with rose-coloured shrimp flakes on turquoise water. All three angels swooped to the surface and kissed his hand. Mr Chivers' palms vibrated with the tiny pressure of their worshipping mouths. Miss Lineham was pointing at a fin. He could hear the husky murmur of her voice, confiding those intimate details she had always denied to him – the personal histories of the angelfish, their weaknesses, their gender, their little fads and foibles. He could see her own pale mouth opening and shutting almost in time with theirs, the flush on her opalescent skin, her strange gold eyes.

'My pretty angels,' she was murmuring. 'My pretty pretty angels.' But it was Basil Gordon she was looking at.

'May I help you, sir?' inquired the salesman.

'Yes,' said Mr Chivers. 'I want three angelfish. One gold, one silver, one marbled black and cream.'

'Certainly sir.' The salesman led him over to the corner. The fish were smaller than Miss Lineham's.

'Don't worry, sir; they'll grow to fit the tank.' He made a little flurry with his net. 'You'll be wanting a tank as well, I presume?'

Mr Chivers shook his head.

'You've *got* a tank? Right, how about a heater? Or a piston pump? Or an under-gravel filter unit?'

'No,' said Mr Chivers. 'Thank you.'

'All right for fishfood, are you?'

'I won't be needing food.'

'Growlux lighting? Stimulates plant life. Choice of pink or blue.'

'Just the fish,' repeated Mr Chivers.

He carried them on the bus in a polythene bag fastened with a rubber hand, his capacious sponge-bag in the other hand. People stared.

'Not so bright this morning, is it?' remarked the woman at the public baths who issued him with his ticket and his towels.

He didn't answer. He needed all his concentration to conceal the bag of fish beneath his raincoat. His usual cubicle was free.

He double-locked the door, slipped the polythene bag into the basin. He didn't release the angels; time enough for that. He ran his bath, tipping in almost half a bottle of Blue-Mist Foam, so that azure bubbles frothed above the sides. He unwrapped his plastic duck, littered the floor with sponges, brushes, flannels, then turned back to the angelfish, wrenching off the rubber band, tossing the bag on the floor. It landed on its side, jarring the writhing bodies. Slowly, the water leaked away. The fishes flowed out with it, marooned and slithering on the shiny tiles. The gold angel twitched and palpitated, leaping six inches in the air, then somersaulting down again with a sickening thud. Mr Chivers paused a moment to admire the markings on the marbled angel, almost identical to Miss Lineham's specimen. Its mouth was opening and shutting in a wordless plea, its feeble tail flailing on the tiles.

He climbed into the bath. The water was armpit high. He could hear the overflow gurgling down the pipe. He picked up a sponge and slapped his thighs with it. He stuck a crooked foot through a tower of foam. There were so many bubbles you could lose whole limbs. Steam was rising from the water, falling again in streams of condensation down the walls. He leaned over the edge of the tub and saw the silver angelfish plunging and zigzagging in a frenzied attempt to reach the water, its gills pistoning in and out in panic, its eyes almost starting from its head.

Mr Chivers began to sing. The marbled angel had fallen into a drain-hole and was floundering on its back. Mr Chivers loofahed his upper arms. The soap was lost and melting at the bottom of the tub. He stretched and yawned in the benison of steam. He could see the fishes through his half-closed eyes, the marbled angel growing feebler now. Its mouth gaped open, as if it had been unhinged. Its eye were glazing over.

He ran more water, laughing aloud as the hoarse hot tap thundered between his feet. Every time he moved, the bubbles frothed and flurried over the sides. He turned on his belly and lost his chin in foam. The silver angel was only a pale splodge on the tiles. Its eyes were still open, but the gills were shuttered and inert. The gold angel kept on fighting. Its leaps were lower now, but it still struggled to save itself, panting and throbbing with each agonized contortion. Mr Chivers wallowed in his tub, rocking backwards and forwards on his bottom, so that the water sloshed and seesawed from one end to the other. Bubbles were pricking and popping all along his limbs; a soft pink flush pyjamaed him from brow to bunions. When he sang, the words resounded off the walls, adding a choir and organ to his voice.

The brave gold angel was singing along with him. He could see its mouth gasping open, wheezing out the words, its once-majestic tail trailing like a broken rudder. The other two fish were motionless. Only their eyes stared upwards, as if they were praying for deliverance.

Chivers pulled out the plug, listening to the water chuckle down the waste-pipe. He stepped out onto the tiles, careful to avoid the corpses, dried himself on stiff municipal towels, then flung them wet and soggy in a corner. He picked up the three small bodies and placed them in the toilet bowl. They floated on the top, their colours still unfaded, their eyes beseeching. There was a flicker of life in the golden angel still. It twitched in shock as it felt itself fall on water. Slowly, it spread its tail, jerked its fins, struggled between triumph and extinction. Mr Chivers stood above it, legs astride. He watched the jet of golden urine strike and shatter it. Three broken bodies whirled and plummeted in their porcelain goldfish bowl, colliding with each other as the gilded waterfall spewed on.

'My pretty angels,' he murmured, as he traced an 'L' with the last slowing dribble. 'My pretty pretty angels.' He pulled the chain and watched them churn and rupture down the bend.

He was humming as he trudged back to his lodgings, his hair slicked down, his shoes high-shined with a wad of toilet paper. The nail-brushes were dried, the flannels folded, the plastic duck caged safely in its sponge-bag. Miss Lineham had never approved of toys.

She met him at the front door. His quiet grey raincoat was neatly belted, his nails were double-scrubbed with coal tar. A spruce white handkerchief burst into late-spring flower from his top right pocket.

'Good evening, Miss Lineham. It looks like a storm.'

'Good evening, Mr Chivers. I'm afraid you're wrong. The barometer is rising. Set Fair it says and Set Fair it's going to be. Now, will you kindly go upstairs and wash your hands. I am serving supper early. Mr Gordon has most kindly invited me to see his Exhibition and I don't wish to be late.'

Mr Chivers paused by the fish-tank. The golden angel was spiralling lazily towards him, flaunting its outrageous tail, gills throbbing, mouth insolently open. He could see its topaz eyes smiling at him, smiling . . . He turned away.

'Yes, Miss Lineham,' he whispered. And went upstairs.

The Unclouded Day

E. ANNIE PROULX

E. Annie Proulx's most successful bestselling novel is The Shipping News, *published in 1993, which won the Pulitzer Prize for Fiction, the Irish Times International Prize and the American National Book Award. She is also the author of the novel* Postcards, *for which she became the first ever woman to win the Pen/Faulkner Prize. She lives in Wyoming.*

It was a rare thing, a dry warm spring that swelled into summer so ripe and full that gleaming seed bent the grass low a month before its time; a good year for grouse. When the season opened halfway through September, the heat of summer still held, dust lay like yellow flour on the roads, and a perfume of decay came from the thorned mazes where blackberries fell and rotted on the ground. Grouse were in the briars, along the watercourses, and, drunk on fomenting autumn juices, they flew recklessly, their wings cleaving the shimmering heat of the day.

Santee did not care to hunt birds in such high-coloured weather. Salty sweat stung the whipped-branch welts on his neck and arms, the dog worked badly and the birds spoiled in an hour. In their sour, hot intestines he smelled imminent putrefaction. The feathers stuck to his hands, for Earl never helped gut them. Noah, the dog, lay panting in the shade.

The heat wave wouldn't break. Santee longed for the cold weather and unclouded days that lay somewhere ahead, for the sharp chill of spruce shadow, icy rime thickening over osier twigs and a hard autumnal sky cut by the parabolic flights of birds in the same way pond ice was cut by skaters. Ah goddam, thought Santee, there were better things to do than hunt partridge with a fool these burning days.

Earl had come to Santee the year before and begged him to teach him how to hunt birds. He had a good gun, he said, a Tobia Hume. Santee thought it overrated and overpriced, but it was a finer instrument than his own field-grade Jorken with the cracked stock he'd meant to replace for years. (The rough walnut blank lay on the workbench out in the barn, cans of motor oil and paint standing on it; kids had ruined the checkering files by picking out butternut meats with them.) Santee's gun, like its owner, was inelegant and long in the tooth, but it worked well. Earl had come driving up through the woods to Santee's place, overlooking the mess in the yard, nodding to Verna, and he had flattered Santee right out of his mind.

'Santee,' he said, measuring him, seeing how he was inclined, 'I've talked to people around and they say you're a pretty good hunter. I want to learn how to hunt birds. I want you to teach me. I'll pay you to teach me everything about them.'

Santee could see that Earl had money. He wore nice boots, rich corduroy trousers in a golden syrup colour, his hands were shaped like doves and his voice rolled out of his throat like sweet batter. He was not more than thirty, Santee thought, looking at the firm cheek slabs and thick yellow hair.

'I usually hunt birds by myself. Or with my boys.' Santee gave each word its fair measure of weight. 'Me'n the dog.' Noah, lying on the porch under the rusty glider, raised his head at the sound of 'birds' and watched them.

'Nice dog,' said Earl in his confectionery voice. Santee folded his arms across his chest rather than let them hang by his sides. Hands in the pockets was even worse, he thought, looking at Earl, a wastrel's posture.

Earl oiled Santee with his voice. 'All I ask, Santee, is that you try it two or three times, and if you don't want to continue, why then I'll pay for your time.' He gave Santee a smile, the leaf-coloured eye under the gleaming lids shifting from Santee to the warped screen door, to the scabby paint on the clapboards, to the run-down yard. Santee looked off to the side as though the muscles in his own eyes were weak.

'Maybe give it a try. Rather go on a weekday than a weekend. You get away Monday?'

Earl could get away any day Santee wanted. He worked at home.

'What doin'?' asked Santee, letting his arms hang down.

'Consulting. I analyze stocks and economic trends.' Santee saw that Earl was younger than his own oldest son, Derwin, whose teeth were entirely gone and who worked up at the veneer mill at Potumsic Falls breathing fumes and tending a machine with whirling, curved blades. Santee said he would go out with Earl on Monday. He didn't know how to say no.

The first morning was a good one, a solid bright day with a spicy taste to the air. Noah was on his mettle, eager to find birds and showing off a little for the stranger. Santee set Earl some distance away on his right until he could see how he shot.

Noah worked close. He stiffened two yards away from birds in front, he pointed birds to the left, the right. A single step from Santee or Earl sent partridge bursting out of the cover and into straightaway flight. He pinned them in trees and bushes, scented them feeding on fallen fruit or dusting in powdery bowls of fine earth, marked them as they pattered through wood sorrel. He worked like two dogs, his white sides gliding through the grass, his points so rigid he might have been a glass animal. The grouse tore up the air and the shotguns bellowed. Earl, Santee saw, didn't know enough to say 'Nice dog' when it counted.

Santee held himself back in order to let his pupil learn, but Earl was a slow, poor shot. The bird would be fifty yards out and darting through safe holes in the air when he finally got the gun around and pulled the trigger. Sometimes a nervous second bird would go up before Earl fired at the first one. He couldn't seem to catch the rhythm, and had excuses for each miss.

'Caught the butt end in my shirt pocket flap,' he'd say, laughing a little, and 'My fingers are stiff from carrying the gun,' and 'Oh, that one was gone before I could get the bead on him.'

Santee tried over and over again to show him that you didn't aim at the bird, that you just threw up the gun and fired in the right place.

'You have to shoot where they're going, not where they are.' He made Earl watch him on the next one, how the gun notched into place on his shoulder, how his right elbow lifted smoothly as his eyes bent toward the empty air the bird was about to enter. *Done!* went the shotgun, and the bird fell like a nut.

'Now you do it,' said Santee.

But when a grouse blustered out of the wild rose haws, Earl only got the gun to his hip, then twisted his body in an odd awkward contortion as he fired. The train of shot cut a hole in the side of a tamarack and the bird melted away through the trees.

'I'm sure you need a lot of practice,' said Santee.

'What I need *is* practice,' agreed Earl, 'and that is what I am paying for.'

'Try movin' the stock up to your shoulder,' said Santee, thinking that his kids had shot better when they were eight years old.

They worked through the morning, Santee illustrating swift reaction and tidy speed, and Earl sweating and jerking like an old Vitagraph film, trying to line up the shotgun with the bird. Santee shot seven grouse and gave four to Earl who had missed every one. Earl gave Santee a hundred dollars and said he wanted to do it again.

'I can practice all the rest of this week,' he said, making it sound like a piano lesson.

The next three Mondays were the same. They went out and worked birds. Earl kept shooting from the hip. With his legs straddled out he looked like an old-time gangster spraying the rival mob with lead.

'Listen here,' said Santee, 'there are six more weeks left in the season, which means we go out six more times. Now, I am not after more money, but you might want to think about goin' out a little more often.' Earl was eager and said he'd pay.

'Three times a week. I can go Monday, Wednesday and Friday.'

They tried it that way. Then they tried Monday, Tuesday and Wednesday for continuity. Earl was paying Santee three hundred dollars a week and he hadn't shot a single bird.

'How's about this?' said Santee, feeling more and more like a cheating old whore every time they went out. 'How's about I come over to your place on the weekend with a box of clay pigeons and you practice shootin' them up? No charge! Just to sort of get your eye in, and the gun up to your shoulder.'

'Yes, but I'm not upset about missing the birds, you know,' said Earl, looking in the trees. 'I've read the books and I know it takes years before you develop that fluid, almost instinctive response to the grouse's riding thunder. I know, believe me, how difficult a target these speedy fliers really are, and I'm willing to work on it, even if it takes years.'

Santee had not heard shooting birds was that hard; he had the reflexes of a snowman. He said to Verna, 'That Earl has got to get it together or I can't keep taking his money. I feel like I'm goin' to the salt mines every time we go out. I don't have the heart to hunt any more on my own, out of fear I'll bust up a bunch of birds he needs for practice. Dammit, all the fun is goin' out of it.'

'The money is good,' said Verna, giving the porch floor a shove that set the glider squeaking. Her apron was folded across her lap, her arms folded elbow over elbow with her hands on her shoulders, her ankles crossed against the coolness of the night. She wore the blue acrylic slippers Santee had given her for Mother's Day.

'I just wonder how I got into it,' he said, closing his eyes and gliding.

*

Santee bought a box of a hundred clay pigeons and drove up to Earl's house on a Sunday afternoon. It was the kind of day people decided to go for a ride.

'I wish I hadn't come,' said Verna, looking through the cloudy windshield at Earl's home, an enormous Swiss chalet with windows like tan bubbles in the roof and molded polystyrene pillars holding up a portico roof. She wouldn't get out of the truck, but sat for two hours with the window ground up. Santee knew how she felt but he had to go. He was hired to teach Earl how to shoot birds.

There was a big porch and on it was Earl's wife, as thin as a folded dollar bill, her hand as narrow and cold as a trout. A baby crawled around inside a green plastic-mesh pen playing with a tomato. Earl told them to watch.

'Watch Daddy shoot the birdy!' he said.

'Beady!' said the baby.

'Knock those beadies dead, Earl,' said the wife, drawing her fingernail through a drop of moisture that had fallen from her drink on to the chair arm.

Santee cocked his arm back again and again and sent the clay discs flying out over a garden of dark shrubs. His ears rang. The baby screamed every time the gun went off, but Earl wouldn't let the woman take him inside.

'Watch!' he cried. 'Dammit, watch Daddy shoot the beady!' He would get the gun to his hip and bend his back into the strange posture he had made his trademark. Him and Al Capone, thought Santee, saying, 'Put it to your shoulder,' like a broken record. 'It won't backfire.'

He looked to see if Earl shut his eyes behind the yellow spectacles when he pulled the trigger, but couldn't tell. After a long time a clay round flew into three black pieces and Earl shrieked, 'I got it!' as if it were a woolly mammoth. It was the first object he had hit since Santee had met him.

'Pretty good,' he lied. '*Now* you're doin' it.'

*

Verna called all the kids home for dinner a week later. There was home-cured ham basted with Santee's hard cider, baked Hubbard squash, mashed potato with Jersey cream spattered over each mound and a platter of roast partridge glazed with chokeberry jelly.

Before they sat down at the table Verna got everybody out in the yard to clean it up. They all counted one-two-three and heaved the carcass of Santee's 1952 Chevrolet in with the torn chicken wire, rotted fence posts and dimpled oil cans. Derwin drove the load to the dump after dinner and brought back a new lawn mower Verna had told him to get.

The next day she waded the brook, feeling for spherical stones of a certain size with her feet. Santee carried them up to the house in a grain bag. When they had dried on the porch she painted them snow white and set them in a line along the driveway. Santee saw the beauty of it – the green shorn grass, the gleaming white stones. It all had something to do with teaching Earl how to hunt, but aside from the money he didn't know what.

After a while he did. It was that she wouldn't let him quit. She would go out into the yard at the earliest light of hunting days – Santee had come to think of them as work days – walking in the wet grass and squinting at the sky to interpret the character of the new day. She got back into bed and put her cold feet on Santee's calves.

'It's cloudy,' she would say. 'Rain by noon.' Santee would groan, because Earl did not like to get his gun wet.

'Won't it hurt?' Earl always asked, as though he knew it would.

'Don't be no summer soldier,' said Santee. 'Wipe it down when you get back home and put some WD-40 to it, all good as new.' It took him a while to understand that it wasn't the gun. Earl didn't like to get rain down his neck or on to his shooting glasses with the yellow lenses, didn't care to feel the cold drops trace narrow trails down his back and forearms, nor to taste the salty stuff that trickled from his hatband to the corners of his mouth.

They were walking through the deep wet grass, the rain drumming hard enough to make the curved blades bounce up and down. Earl's wet twill pants were plastered to him like blistered skin. Something in the way he pulled at the sodden cloth with an arched finger and thumb told Santee he was angry at the rain, at Santee, maybe mad enough to quit shelling out three hundred dollars a week for no birds and a wet nature walk. Good, thought Santee.

But the rain stopped and a watery sun warmed their backs. Noah found tendrils of rich hot grouse scent lying on the moist air as solidly as cucumber vines on the garden earth. He locked into his catatonic point again and again, and they sent the birds flying in arcs of shaken raindrops. Earl didn't connect, but he said he knew it took years before shooters got the hang of it.

The only thing he shot that season was the clay pigeon, and the year ended with no birds for Earl, money in Santee's bank account and a row of white stones under the drifting snow. Santee thought it was all over, a bad year to be buried with the memory of other bad years.

Through the next spring and summer he never thought of Earl without a shudder. The droughty grouse summer held into September. Santee bored the replacement stock for the Jorken. He bought a new checkering file and sat on the porch after dinner making a good job of it and waiting for the heat to break, thinking about going out by himself in the chill October days as the woods and fields faded and clods of earth froze hard. He hunched toward the west on the steps, catching the last of the good light; the days were getting shorter in spite of the lingering heat from the baked earth. Verna fanned her damp neck with a sale flier that had come in the mail.

'Car's comin',' she said. Santee stopped rasping and listened.

'It's that Earl again,' said Verna, recognizing the Saab before it was in sight.

He was a little slicker in his talk, and wore an expensive game vest with a rubber pocket in the back where the birds would lie, their dark blood seeping into the seams.

'My wife gave me this,' he said, and he showed them the new leather case for his shotgun, stamped with his initials and a design of three flying grouse.

'No,' Santee tried to say, 'I've taught you all I can. I don't want to take your money anymore.' But Earl wasn't going to let him go. Now he wanted a companion with a dog and Santee was it, with no pay.

'After all, we got to know each other very well last year. We're a good team – friends,' Earl said, looking at the fresh paint on the clapboards. 'Nice job,' he said.

Santee went because he had taken Earl's money. Until the fool shot a bird on his own or gave up, Santee was obliged to keep going out with him. The idea that Earl might ruin every fall for the rest of his life made Santee sick.

'I've come to hate partridge huntin',' he told Verna in the sultry night. 'I hate those white stones, too.' She knew what he was talking about.

Derwin heard Earl bragging down at the store, some clam dip and a box of Triscuits in front of him on the counter. Earl's new game vest hung open casually, his yellow shooting glasses dangled outside the breast pocket, one earpiece tucked through the button hole.

'Yes,' he said, 'we did quite well today. Limited out. I hunt with Santee, you know – grand old fellow.'

'He didn't know who I was,' raged Derwin, who had wanted to say something deadly but hadn't found any words until he drove up home and sat on the edge of the porch. 'Whyn't you tell him where to head in, Pa? At least quit givin' him birds he makes like he shot hisself.'

'I wish I could,' groaned Santee. 'If he would just get one bird I could cut loose, or if he decided to go in for somethin' else and quit comin' around. But I feel like I owe him part of a bargain. I took a lot of his money and all he got out of it was a clay pigeon.'

'You don't owe him nothin',' said Derwin.

Earl came up again the next morning. He parked his Saab in the shade and beeped the horn in Santee's truck until he came out on the porch.

'Where you want to hit today?' called Earl. It wasn't a question. In some way he'd gotten ahead of Santee. 'Might as well take your truck, it's already scratched up. Maybe go to Africa covert and then hit White Birch Heaven.'

Earl had given fanciful names to the different places they hunted. 'Africa' because there was long yellow grass on the edge of a field Earl said looked like the veldt. 'White Birch Heaven' because Noah had pointed six birds in twenty minutes. Santee had taken two, leaving the rest for seed after Earl shot the tops out of the birches. They were grey birches but Santee had not cared enough to say so, any more than he pointed out that the place had been called 'Ayer's high pasture', for generations.

It was breathlessly close as they climbed toward the upper fields of the old farm. The sky was a slick white colour. Noah lagged, the dust filling his nose. Santee's shirt was wet and he could hear thunder in the ground, the storm that had been building for weeks of drumming heat. Deerflies and gnats bit furiously at their ears and necks.

'Gonna be a hell of a storm,' said Santee.

Nothing moved. They might have been in a painted field, walking slowly across the fixed landscape where no bird could ever fly, nor gree fall. The leaves hung limp, soil crumbled under their feet.

'You won't put no birds up in this weather,' said Santee.

'What?' asked Earl, the yellow glasses shining like insect eyes.

'I said, it's gonna be a corker of a storm. See there?' Santee dropped his arm toward the west where a dark humped line illuminated by veins of lightning lay across the horizon. 'Comin' right for us like a house on fire. Time to go home and try again another day.'

He started back down, paying no attention to Earl's remarks

that the storm was a long way off and there were birds up there. He was dogged enough, thought Santee sourly.

As they went down the hill, slipping on the drought-polished grass, the light thickened to a dirty ochre. Little puffs of wind raised dust and started the poplars vibrating.

'You might be right,' said Earl, passing Santee. 'It's coming along pretty fast. I just felt a drop.'

Santee looked back over his shoulder and saw a black wall of cloud swelling into the sky. Bursts of wind ripped across the slope and the rolling grind of thunder shook the earth. Noah scampered fearfully, his tail clamped between his legs, his eyes seeking Santee's again and again.

'We're goin', boy,' said Santee encouragingly.

The first raindrops hit like birdshot, rattling down on them and striking the trees with flat smacks. White hail pellets bounced and stung where they hit flesh. They ran into a belt of spruce where there was a narrow opening in the trees like a bowling alley. Halfway down its length a panicky grouse flew straight away from them. It was at least eighty yards out, an impossible distance, when Earl heaved his shotgun on to his hip and fired. As he pulled the trigger, lightning struck behind them. The grouse dropped low and skimmed away, but Earl believed he had hit it. Buried in the sound of his crashing gun he had not even heard the lightning strike.

'Get it!' he shouted at Noah, who had pasted himself to Santee's legs when the lightning cracked the spruce. 'Make your dog get it!' yelled Earl, pointing in the direction the grouse had flown. The rain roared down on them. Earl ran for evergreen shelter in the direction his bird had vanished, still pointing through the bursting rain. 'Fetch! Fetch! Oh, you damn thing, fetch my bird!'

Santee, trusting the principle that lightning never strikes twice in the same place, went under the smoking spruce. The bolt had entered the pith and exploded the heartwood in a column of live steam. White wood welled out of the riven bark. Almost at his feet, lying where they had fallen from the needled canopy of the top branches, were three dead grouse. They steamed gently in the cold rain. The hard drops struck the breast feathers like irregular heartbeats. Santee picked them up and looked at them. He turned them around then upside down. As soon as the rain had slackened he pulled his shirt up over his head and made a run for Earl's tree.

'You don't need to yell at my dog. Here's your birds. Three in one shot, mister, is somethin' I never seen before. You sure have learned how to shoot.' He shook his head.

Earl's eyes were hidden behind the rain-streaked yellow shooting glasses. His thick cheeks were wet and his lips flapped silently.

'Something felt right,' he gabbled, seizing the birds. 'I knew something was going to happen today. I guess I was ready for this breakthrough.'

He talked all the way back to Santee's truck, and as they drove through the woods, the windshield wipers beating, the damp air in the cab redolent of wet dog, explained how he'd felt the birds were there, how he'd felt the gun fall into line on them, how he saw the feathers fountain up.

'I saw right where they went down,' he said. Santee thought he probably believed he had. 'But that dog of yours . . .'

Santee pulled up in his yard beside Earl's Saab and set the hand brake. The rain flowed over the windshield in sheets. Santee cleared his throat.

'This is the parting of our ways,' he said. 'I can take a good deal, but I won't have my dog called down.'

Earl smirked; he knew Santee was jealous. 'That's okay with me,' he said, and ran through the hammering rain to his car, squeezing the grouse in his arms.

Santee woke before dawn, jammed up against Verna. He could see the pale mist of breath floating from her nostrils. Icy air flowed through an inch of open window. He slipped out of bed to close it, saw the storm had cleared the weather. Stars glinted like chips of mica in the paling sky, hoarfrost coated the fields and the row of stones along the drive. The puddles in the road were frozen solid. It was going to be a cold, unclouded day. He laughed to himself as he got back into the warm bed, wondering what Earl had said when he plucked three partridges that were already cooked.

The Bishop's Lunch

MICHÈLE ROBERTS

Michèle Roberts is half-English, half-French, and lives in London. Her novel Daughters of the House *won the W. H. Smith Literary Award and was shortlisted for the Booker Prize.*

The angel of the resurrection has very long wings. Their tips end in single quills. The angel of the resurrection has three pairs of wings that swaddle him in black shawls then unwrap him when he needs them, nervous and strong. The angel of the resurrection flies in the darkness. He is invisible and black. His feathers are soft as black fur.

That is what Sister Josephine of the Holy Face was thinking early on that Wednesday morning of Holy Week four days before Easter. Uncertain whether or not her picture of the angel was theologically sound, she decided that she would record it later on in her little black notebook, the place where she was required to write down all her faults. These were confessed at a weekly interview with the Novice Mistress and were then atoned for by suitable penances. The little black notebook was one of the few items Sister Josephine had been allowed to bring with her from home when she entered the convent seven months previously. Her mother had put it in her suitcase herself, along with a new missal and four pairs of black woollen stockings.

A thought which Sister Josephine of the Holy Face knew she would not write down in the little book was that she ought to be called Sister Josephine of the Holy Stomach. At home on the farm eight kilometres from Etretat she had drunk her breakfast *café au lait* from a china bowl stencilled with blue flowers. She had eaten warm crusty bread fetched half an hour before from the village bakery. On Sundays there was hot chocolate after High Mass, with brioche or galette, and a hearty appetite seen as a good thing. Here in the convent on the outskirts of Rouen the day-old bread was always stale, and the thin coffee bitter with chicory and drunk from a tin cup.

Angels, having no bodies, were not tormented by memories of *saucisson* and cold fresh butter, of thick sourish cream poured over cod and potatoes, over beans, over artichokes. Yet the black feathers of the wings of the angels of the resurrection were very soft.

Sister Josephine was down on her hands and knees in front of the cupboard under the big stone sink of the convent kitchen groping inside it for the bread-knife she had unaccountably mislaid. Her fingers closed over a bunch of silky plumage. It wasn't an angel's wing, she discovered when she brought it out, but the feather duster she had lost a month ago. Her penance for that had been to kiss the ground in the refectory before breakfast every day for a week. The taste of floor polish. She shivered as she remembered it.

The bell rang for chapel. Sister Josephine spotted the bread-knife hiding behind a bucket of washing soda. Squatting back on her haunches, she flung it, with the feather duster, on to the wooden table behind her. Then she straightened up, untied the strings of the heavy blue cotton apron, and hung it on the nail behind the door. Not *my* apron, she reminded herself; *ours*.

She glided along the dark cloister as rapidly as she dared. She wasn't supposed to begin her kitchen duties so early, but she'd wanted to get on with slicing up the long baguettes into the bread-baskets ready for breakfast. There was too much work in the kitchen for one person to do, even in such a small community, but to complain would be a sin against obedience. Putting Sister Josephine in sole charge of the cooking, the Novice Mistress had announced six weeks earlier, was a real test of her faith. And of the nuns' digestion, Sister Josephine had muttered to herself.

She knelt in her stall, amongst the other novices, yawning as she tried to follow the still unfamiliar Latin psalms. Her empty stomach growled, and she clasped her hands more tightly together. They were chilblained, and smelt of carbolic soap. Now they looked like her mother's hands; red, roughened by work. Her mother's hands were capable, quick and deft for the labour of farmyard and house. They were expert at cooking, too. She was famous among the village women for the lightness of her choux pastry, the gougères and eclairs she turned out on feast-days. Sister Josephine had resisted all her mother's attempts to teach her the domestic arts. She had refused to believe that God had wanted her to serve Him through topping and tailing beans, peeling potatoes. She'd hungered for transcendence, for the ecstasy of mystical union. She hadn't come to the convent to *cook*.

What in heaven, Sister Josephine asked herself for perhaps the hundredth time that Lent, am I going to do about the Bishop's lunch?

It was an ancient tradition in the convent that every year on Easter Sunday the Bishop of the diocese would say High Mass in the convent chapel and then join Reverend Mother, the Novice Mistress and the other senior nuns at their table in the refectory for the midday meal. To celebrate the end of the rigorous fasting of Lent and the presence of such a distinguished guest, and, of course, the resurrection of the Saviour from the dead, an elegant array of dishes was always served. Sister Josephine knew that the Bishop, like all holy men of the cloth, had renounced the pleasures of the flesh, but she knew too that nonetheless he would expect to be given exquisite food just so that he could demonstrate his indifference to it as he ate.

Help me, she prayed; please help me.

Normally she did not bother God with problems over lost feather dusters and bread-knives and how to turn a few cabbages and turnips into a nourishing soup for twenty hungry nuns. God, being male, was above such trivia. But the Bishop's lunch was an emergency, to go straight to the top.

The smell of incense, pungent and sweet, made her open her eyes. Morning Mass had begun and she hadn't even noticed. Daydreaming again. Another fault to note down in her little black book. Sighing, she reached into the skirt pocket of her habit, drew it out and opened it hastily at random. Her stubby black pencil hovered over the page. She drew in a sharp quick breath, and then released it.

Maundy Thursday passed peacefully, apart from the gardener mentioning to Reverend Mother had someone had taken his old and rusty rifle from its usual place in the shed, and that someone else had thoughtfully weeded all the wild sorrel from under the apple trees in the orchard. On Good Friday the gardener told Reverend Mother he'd heard rifle shots coming from the field backing on to the kitchen garden. Also, the traps he'd laid for rabbits, all three of them, had been sprung by some poacher. And when he went to investigate a great squawking in the chicken shed, he found that the best layers among the hens had been robbed of all their eggs. There would be none to take to market the following week.

Reverend Mother sighed. She was getting old and tired, and did not want to be faced with all these practical problems. She consoled the gardener as best she could. Then she went for Sister Josephine. How, she enquired of the young novice, was she going to manage to make a lunch on Easter Sunday fit for a Bishop to eat? Well, Sister Josephine explained, I have been praying for a miracle.

All through that Good Friday afternoon the nuns knelt in the gloomy chapel, all its statues shrouded in purple and its candles extinguished, following the Passion of the Saviour as he was stripped and scourged, crowned with thorns, and then forced to carry his heavy cross up the hill to Calvary. Finally he was nailed to the cross and hung from it. The nuns sang the great dialogues of the Church, taken from the Old Testament, between Christ and his God, Christ and his people. *My people, what have you done to me? Answer me.* Rain beat at the chapel windows. Christ cried out for the last time and then died. The nuns filed from the chapel, ate their frugal supper, the only meal of the day.

On Holy Saturday Christ was in the tomb and Sister Josephine was in the kitchen. Swathed in her blue apron, she scrubbed the sink, the table, the floor. Then, on the table, she laid out certain items from her *batterie de cuisine*; a wooden spoon, an egg whisk, several long, very sharp knives.

The rabbits she had taken from the gardener's traps were hanging in the pantry. Swiftly she skinned them, one by one, then cut them up and threw them into the pot with a bunch of herbs and half a bottle of communion wine. Next she fetched the pigeons she had shot two days earlier, plucked and trussed them, and arranged them on a bed of apples in a well-buttered dish. Finally she prepared a small mountain of potatoes and leeks, washed a big bunch of sorrel and patted it dry with a cloth, and checked that the two dozen eggs she had removed from the hens were safe in their wicker basket in the store-room.

When the knock came on the back door of the kitchen she was ready. Opening it, she smiled at the boy who stood there, at the silvery aluminium churn and squat bottle he clasped in his arms. The boy's eyes were as blue as hers, his nose as aquiline, his chin as determined. Sister Josephine took the churn and the bottle, smiled as the boy again, and shut the door on him. Now everything was at ready for tomorrow as it could be.

Very early next morning, just before dawn, the nuns gathered outside the chapel to see the New Fire lit in the cold windy courtyard. Now the great candle, symbol of the risen Christ, could blaze in the darkness. Easter Sunday had arrived. Now the chapel could be filled with flowers and lights, the dark coverings taken off the statues, and the altars hung with lace and white brocade.

The Bishop, with his retinue, arrived to say High Mass. The organ peaked, the nuns stood up very straight in their stalls and sang a loud psalm of praise; Christ is risen, Christ is risen, alleluia.

This miracle of the Resurrection was repeated in the Mass; through the actions of his chosen one, his priest, Christ offered his body, his blood, his faithful children. The Bishop's hands moved deftly amongst his holy cutlery. He wiped the chalice, picked up the silver cruets of water and wine, attended to the incense boat. Meanwhile, in the kitchen, Sister Josephine's choux pastry leapt in the oven.

The Bishop's lunch, all the nuns later agreed, was a great and unexpected success. The rabbit pâté, scented with juniper, was exquisite. So too was the dish of roasted pigeons with apples and calvados, the sliced potatoes and leeks baked in cream, the poached eggs in sorrel sauce. But, they unanimously declared, the *pièce de résistance* of the entire banquet was the creation which ended it; the figure of an angel sculpted from choux buns stuck together with caramel and then coated with dark bitter-chocolate cream. His arms were held out wide, and his three pairs of black wings extended behind him. A very noble confection, said the nuns; truly, a miracle.

After finishing the washing-up, Sister Josephine went upstairs to her curtained cell in the novices' dormitory. This was forbidden in the daytime, but she didn't care. She sat on her bed and took out her little black book. She opened it, and leafed through the recipes so carefully written out in her mother's handwriting in its centre pages. Perhaps, Sister Josephine thought, my vocation is to leave the convent, train as a chef, and open my own restaurant.

Mr Sumarsono

ROXANA ROBINSON

Author of the novel Summer Light, *and of the biography of painter Georgia O'Keeffe, Roxana Robinson's short fiction has appeared in numerous American magazines and journals.*

Oh, Mr Sumarsono, Mr Sumarsono. We remember you so well. I wonder how you remember us?

The three of us met Mr Sumarsono at the Trenton train station. The platform stretched down the tracks in both directions, long, half-roofed, and dirty. Beyond the tracks on either side were high corrugated-metal sidings, battered and patched. Above the sidings were the tops of weeds and the backs of ramshackle buildings, grimy and desolate. Stretching out above the tracks was an aerial grid of electrical power lines, their knotted, uneven rectangles connecting every city on the Eastern Corridor in a dismal industrial way.

My mother, my sister, Kate, and I stood waiting for Mr Sumarsono at the foot of the escalator, which did not work. The escalator had worked once; I could remember it working, though Kate, who was younger than I, could not. Now the metal staircase towered above the platform, silent and immobile, giving the station a surreal air. If you used it as a staircase, which people often did, as you set your foot on each moveable, motionless step, you had an odd feeling of sensory dislocation, like watching a color movie in black and white. You knew something was wrong, though you couldn't put your finger on it.

*

Mr Sumarsono got off his train at the other end of the platform from us. He stood still for a moment and looked hesitantly up and down. He didn't know which way to look or who he was looking for. My mother lifted her arm and waved; we knew who he was, though we had never seen him before. It was 1961, and Mr Sumarsono was the only Indonesian to get off the train at Trenton, New Jersey.

Mr Sumarsono was wearing a neat suit and leather shoes, like an American businessman, but he did not look like an American. The suit was brown, not grey, and there was a slight sheen to it. And Mr Sumarsono himself was built in a different way from Americans; he was slight and graceful, with narrow shoulders and an absence of strut. His movements were diffident, and there seemed to be extra curves in them. This was true even of simple movements, like picking up his suitcase and starting down the platform toward the three of us, standing by the escalator that didn't work.

Kate and I stood next to my mother as she waved and smiled. Kate and I did not wave and smile; this was all my mother's idea. Kate was seven and I was ten. We were not entirely sure what a diplomat was, and we were not at all sure that we wanted to be nice to one all weekend. I wondered why he didn't have friends of his own age.

'Hoo-oo,' my mother called, mortifyingly, even though Mr Sumarsono had already seen us and was making his graceful way toward us. His steps were small and his movements modest. He smiled in a non-specific way, to show that he had seen us, but my mother kept on waving and calling. It took a long time, this interlude; encouraging shouts and gestures from my mother, Mr Sumarsono's unhurried approach. I wondered if he too was embarrassed by my mother; once he glanced swiftly around, as though he were looking for an alternative family to spend the weekend with. He had reason to be uneasy; the grimy Trenton platform with its corrugated sidings and aerial grid did not suggest a rural retreat. And when he saw us standing by the stationary escalator, my mother waving and calling, Kate and I sullenly silent, he may have felt that things were off to a poor start.

My mother was short, with big bones and a square face. She had thick, dark hair and a wide mobile mouth. She was a powerful woman. She used to be on the stage, and she still delivered to the back row. When she calls 'Hoo-oo' at a train station, everyone at that station knows it.

'Mr Su*mar*sono,' she called out as he came up to us. The accent is on the second syllable. That's what the people at the UN had told her, and she made us practice, sighing and complaining, until we said it the way she wanted; Su*mar*sono.

Mr Sumarsono gave a formal nod and a small smile. His face was oval, and his eyes were long. His skin was very pale brown, and smooth. His hair was shiny and black, and it was also very smooth. Everything about him seemed polished and smooth.

'Hello!' said my mother, seizing his hand and shaking it. 'I'm Mrs Riordan. And this is Kate, and this is Susan.' Kate and I cautiously put out our hands, and Mr Sumarsono shook them limply, bowing at each of us.

My mother put out her hand again. 'Shall I take your bag?' But Mr Sumarsono defended his suitcase. 'We're just up here,' said my mother, giving up on the bag and leading the way to the escalator.

We all began the climb, but after a few steps my mother looked back.

'This is an escalator,' she said loudly.

Mr Sumarsono gave a short nod.

'It takes you *up*,' my mother called, and pointed to the roof overhead. Mr Sumarsono, holding his suitcase with both hands, looked at the ceiling.

'It doesn't work right now,' my mother said illuminatingly, and turned back to her climb.

'No,' I heard Mr Sumarsono say. He glanced cautiously again at the ceiling.

Exactly parallel to the escalator was a broad concrete stair-case, which another group of people was climbing. We were separated only by the handrail, so that for a disorientating second you felt you were looking at a mirror from which you were missing. It intensified the feeling you got from climbing the stopped escalator – dislocation, bewilderment, doubt at your own senses.

A woman on the real staircase looked over at us, and I could tell that my mother gave her a brilliant smile; the woman looked away at once. We were the only people on the escalator.

On the way home Kate and I sat in the back seat and watched our mother keep turning to speak to Mr Sumarsono. She asked him long, complicated, cheerful questions. 'Well, Mr Sumarsono, had you been in this country at all before you came to the UN or is this your first visit? I know you've only been working at the UN for a short time.'

Mr Sumarsono answered everything with a polite unfinished nod. Then he would turn back and look out the window again. I wondered if he was thinking about jumping out of the car. I wondered what Mr Sumarsono was expecting from a weekend in the country. I hoped it was not a walk to the pond; Kate and I had planned one for that afternoon. We were going to watch the mallards nesting, and I hoped we wouldn't have to include a middle-aged Indonesian in leather shoes.

When we got home my mother looked at me meaningfully.

'Susan, will you and Kate show Mr Sumarsono to his room?'

Mr Sumarsono looked politely at us, his head tilted slightly sideways.

Gracelessly I leaned over to pick up Mr Sumarsono's suitcase, as I had been told. He stopped me by putting his hand out, palm front, in a traffic policeman's gesture.

'No, no,' he said, with a small smile, and he took hold of the suitcase himself. I fell back, pleased not to do as I'd been told, but also I was impressed, almost awed, by Mr Sumarsono.

What struck me was the grace of his gesture. His hand slid easily out of its cuff and exposed a narrow brown wrist, much narrower than my own. When he put his hand up in the *Stop!* that an American hand would make, this was a polite, subtle, and yielding signal, quite beautiful and infinitely sophisticated, a gesture that suggested a thousand reasons for doing this, a thousand ways to go about it.

I let him take the suitcase and we climbed the front stairs, me first, Kate next, and then Mr Sumarsono, as though we were playing a game. We marched solemnly, single file, through the second-floor hall and up the back stairs to the third floor. The guest room was small, with a bright hooked rug on the wide old floorboards, white ruffled curtains at the windows, and slanting eaves. There was a spool bed, a table next to it, a straight chair, and a chest of drawers. On the chest of drawers there was a photograph of my great-grandmother, her austere face framed by faded embroidery. On the bedspread was a large tan smudge, where our cat liked to spend the afternoons.

Mr Sumarsono put his suitcase down and looked around the room. I looked around with him, and suddenly the guest room, and in fact our whole house, took on a new aspect. Until that moment, I had thought our house was numbingly ordinary, that it represented the decorating norm; patchwork quilts, steep, narrow staircases, slanting ceilings and spool beds. I assumed everyone had faded photographs of Victorian great-grandparents dotted mournfully around their rooms. Now it came to me that this was not the case. I wondered what houses were like in Indonesia, or apartments in New York. Somehow I knew; they were low, sleek, modern, all on one floor, with hard gleaming surfaces. They were full of right angles and empty of allusions to the past; they were the exact opposite of our house. Silently and fiercely I blamed my mother for our environment, which was, I now saw, eccentric, totally abnormal.

Mr Sumarsono looked at me and nodded precisely again.

'Thank you,' he said.

'Don't hit your head,' Kate said.

Mr Sumarsono bowed, closing his eyes.

'On the ceiling,' Kate said, pointing to it.

'The ceiling,' he repeated, looking up at it too.

'Don't hit your head on the ceiling,' she said loudly, and Mr Sumarsono looked at her and smiled.

'The bathroom's in here,' I said, showing him.

'Thank you,' he said.

'Susan,' my mother called up the stairs, 'tell Mr Sumarsono to come downstairs when he's ready for lunch.'

'Come-downstairs-when-you're-ready-for-lunch,' I said unnecessarily. I pointed graphically into my open mouth and then bolted, clattering rapidly down both sets of stairs. Kate was right behind me, our knees banging in our rush to get away.

Mother had set four places for lunch, which was on the screened-in porch overlooking the lawn. The four places meant a battle.

'Mother,' I said mutinously.

'What is it?' Mother said. 'Would you fill a pitcher of water, Susan.'

'Kate and I are not *having* lunch,' I said, running water into the blue and white pottery pitcher.

'And get the butter dish. Of course you're having lunch,' and my mother. She was standing at the old wooden kitchen table, making a plate of deviled eggs. She was messily filling the rubbery white hollows with dollops of yolk-and-mayonnaise mixture. The slippery egg-halves rocked unstably, and the mixture stuck to her spoon. She scraped it into the little boats with her finger. I watched with distaste. In a ranch house, I thought, or in New York, this would not happen. In New York, food would be prepared on polished man-made surfaces. It would be brought to you on gleaming platters by silent waiters.

'I told you Kate and I are *not* having lunch,' I said. 'We're taking a picnic to the pond.' I put the pitcher on the table.

Mother turned to me. 'We have been through this already, Susan. We have a guest for the weekend, and I want you girls to be polite to him. He is a stranger in this country, and I expect you to *extend* yourselves. Think how *you* would feel if *you* were in a strange land.'

'Ex*tend* myself,' I said rudely, under my breath, but loud enough so my mother could hear. This was exactly the sort of idiotic thing she said. 'I certainly wouldn't go around hoping people would *extend* themselves.' I thought of people stretched out horribly, their arms yearning in one direction, their feet in another, all for my benefit. 'If I were in a strange country I'd like everyone to leave me alone.'

'Ready for lunch?' my mother said brightly to Mr Sumarsono, who stood diffidently in the doorway. 'We're just about to sit down. Kate, will you bring out the butter?'

'I did already,' I said virtuously, and folded my arms in a hostile manner.

'We're having deviled eggs,' Mother announced as we sat down. She picked up the plate of them and smiled humorously. 'We call them "deviled".'

'De-vil,' Kate said, speaking very loudly and slowly. She pointed at the eggs and then put two forked fingers behind her head, like horns. Mr Sumarsono looked at her horns. He nodded pleasantly.

My mother talked all through lunch, asking Mr Sumarsono mystifying questions and then answering them herself in case he couldn't. Mr Sumarsono kept a polite half-smile on his face, sometimes repeating the last few words of her sentences. Even while he was eating, he seemed to be listening attentively. He ate very neatly, taking small bites, and laying his fork and knife precisely side by side when he was through. Kate and I pointedly said nothing. We were boycotting lunch, though we smiled horribly at Mr Sumarsono if he caught our eyes.

After lunch my mother said she was going to take a nap. As she said this, she laid her head sideways on her folded hands and closed her eyes. Then she pointed upstairs. Mr Sumarsono nodded. He rose from the table, pushed in his chair, and went meekly back to his room, his shoes creaking on the stairs.

Kate and I did the dishes in a slapdash way and took off for the pond. We spent the afternoon on a hill overlooking the marshy end, watching the mallards and arguing over the binoculars. We only had one pair. There had been a second pair once; I could remember this, though Kate could not. Our father had taken the other set with him.

Mother was already downstairs in the kitchen when we got back. She was singing cheerfully, and wearing a pink dress with puffy sleeves and a full skirt. The pink dress was a favorite of Kate's and mine. It irritated me to see that she had put it on as though she were at a party. This was not a party; she had merely gotten hold of a captive guest, a complete stranger who understood nothing she said. This was not a cause for celebration.

She gave us a big smile when we came in.

'Any luck with the mallards?' she asked.

'Not really,' I said coolly. A lie.

Kate and I set the table, and Mother asked Kate to pick some flowers for the centerpiece. We were having dinner in the dining room, my mother said, with the white plates with gold rims from our grandmother. While we were setting the table my mother called in from the kitchen, 'Oh, Susan, put out some wineglasses too, for me and Mr Sumarsono.'

Kate and I looked at each other.

'*Wine*glasses?' Kate mouthed silently.

'Wineglasses?' I called back, my voice sober, for my mother, my face wild, for Kate.

'That's right,' said mother cheerfully. 'We're going to be festive.'

'*Festive!*' I mouthed to Kate, and we doubled over, shaking our heads and rolling our eyes.

We put out the wineglasses, handling them gingerly, as though they gave off dangerous, unpredictable rays. The glasses, standing boldly at the knife tips, altered the landscape of the table. Kate and I felt as though we were in the presence of something powerful and alien. We looked warningly at each other, pointing at the glasses and frowning, nodding our heads meaningfully. We picked them up and mimed drinking from them. We wiped our mouths and began to stagger, crossing our eyes and hiccuping. When Mother appeared in the doorway we froze, and Kate, who was in the process of lurching sideways, turned her movement into a pirouette, her face clear, her eyes uncrossed.

'Be careful with those glasses,' said my mother.

'We are,' said Kate, striking a classical pose, the wineglass held worshipfully aloft, like a chalice.

When dinner was ready mother went to the foot of the stairs and called up, 'Hooo-oo!' several times. There was no answer, and after a pause she called, 'Mr Sumarsono! Dinner. Come down for dinner!' We began to hear noises from overhead as Mr Sumarsono rose obediently from his nap.

When we sat down I noticed that mother was not only in the festive pink dress but that she was bathed and particularly fresh-looking. She had done her hair in a special way, smoothing it back from her forehead. She was smiling a lot. When she had served the plates, my mother picked up the bottle of wine and offered Mr Sumarsono a glass.

'Would you like a little *wine*, Mr Sumarsono?' she asked, leaning forward, her head cocked. We were having the dish she always made for guests; baked chicken pieces in a sauce made of Campbell's cream of mushroom soup.

'Thank you,' Mr Sumarsono nodded and pushed forward his glass. My mother beamed and filled his glass. Kate and I watched her as we cut up our chicken. We watched her as we drank from our milk glasses, our eyes round and unblinking over the rims.

We ate in silence, a silence broken only by my mother. 'Mr Sumarsono,' my mother said, having finished most of her chicken and most of her wine, 'do you have a *wife*? A *family*?'

She gestured first at herself, then at us. Mr Sumarsono looked searchingly across the table at Kate and me. We were chewing and stared solemnly back.

Mr Sumarsono nodded his half-nod, his head stopping at the bottom of the movement, without completing the second half of it.

'A wife?' said my mother, gratified. She pointed again at herself. She is not a wife and hasn't been for five years, but Mr Sumarsono wouldn't know that. I wondered what he did know. I wondered if he wondered where my father was. Perhaps he thought that it was an American custom for the father to live in another house, spending his day apart from his wife and children, eating his dinner alone. Perhaps Mr Sumarsono was expecting my father to arrive ceremoniously after dinner, dressed in silken robes and carrying a carved wooden writing case, ready to entertain his guest with tales of the hill people. What did Mr Sumarsono expect of us? It was unimaginable.

Whatever Mr Sumarsono was expecting, my mother was determined to deliver what she could of it. In the pink dress, full of red wine, she was changing before our very eyes. She was warming up, turning larger and grander, glowing and powerful.

'Mr Sumarsono,' said my mother happily, 'do you have photographs of your family?'

There was a silence. My mother pointed again to her chest, plump and rosy above the pink dress. Then she held up an invisible camera. She closed one eye and clicked loudly at Mr Sumarsono. He watched her carefully.

'Photo of wife?' she said again loudly, and again pointed at herself. Then she pointed at him. Mr Sumarsono gave his truncated nod and stood up. He bowed again and pointed to the ceiling. Then, with a complicated and unfinished look, loaded with meaning, he left the room.

Kate and I looked accusingly at our mother. Dinner would now be prolonged indefinitely, her fault.

'He's gone to get his photographs,' Mother said. 'The poor man, he must miss his wife and children. Don't you feel sorry for him, thousands of miles away from his family? Oh, thousands. He's here for six months, all alone. They told me that at the UN. It's all very uncertain. He doesn't know when he gets leaves, how long after that he'll be here. Think of how his poor wife feels.' She shook her head and took a long sip of her wine. She remembered us and added reprovingly, 'And what about his poor children? Their father is thousands of miles away! They don't know when they'll see him!' Her voice was admonitory, suggesting that this was partly our fault.

Kate and I did not comment on Mr Sumarsono's children. We ourselves did not know when we would see our father, and we did not want to discuss that either. What we longed for was for all this to be over, this endless, messy meal, full of incomprehensible exchanges.

Kate sighed discreetly, her mouth slightly open for silence, and she swung her legs under the table. I picked up a chicken thigh with my fingers and began to pick delicately at it with my teeth. This was forbidden, but I thought that the wine and the excitement would distract my mother from my behavior. It did. She sighed deeply, shook her head, and picked up her fork. She began eating in a dreamy way.

'Oh, I'm glad we're having rice!' she said suddenly, gratified. 'That must make Mr Sumarsono feel at home.' She looked at me. 'You know that's all they have in Indonesia,' she said in a teacherly sort of way. 'Rice, bamboo, things like lizard.'

Another ridiculous statement. I knew such a place could not exist, but Kate was younger, and I pictured what she must imagine; thin stalks of rice struggling up through a dense and endless bamboo forest. People in brown suits pushing their way among the limber stalks, looking fruitlessly around for houses, telephones, something to eat besides lizard.

Mr Sumarsono appeared again in the doorway. He was holding a large leather camera case. He had already begun to unbuckle and unsnap, to extricate the camera from it. He took out a light meter and held it up. My mother raised her fork at him.

'Rice!' she said enthusiastically. 'That's familiar, isn't it? Does it remind you of *home*?' With her fork she gestured expansively at the dining room. Mr Sumarsono looked obediently round, at the mahogany sideboard with its crystal decanters, the glass-fronted cabinet full of family china, the big, stern portrait of my grandfather in his pink hunting coat, holding his riding crop. Mr Sumarsono looked back at my mother, who was still holding up her fork. He nodded.

'Yes?' my mother said, pleased.

'Yes,' said Mr Sumarsono.

My mother looked down again. Blinking in a satisfied way she said, 'I'm glad I thought of it.' I knew she hadn't thought of it until that moment. She always made rice with the chicken-and-Campbell's-cream-of-mushroom-soup dish. Having an Indonesian turn up to eat it was a lucky chance.

Mr Sumarsono held up his camera. The light meter dangled from a strap, and the flash attachment projected from one corner. He put the camera up to his eye, and his face vanished altogether. My mother was looking down at her plate again, peaceful, absorbed, suffused with red wine and satisfaction.

I could see that my mother's view of all this – the meal, the visit, the weekend – was different from my own. I could see that she was pleased by everything about it. She was pleased by her polite and helpful daughters; she was pleased by her charming farmhouse with its stylish and original touches. She was pleased at her delicious and unusual meal, and most important, she was pleased by her own generosity, by being able to offer this poor stranger her lavish bounty.

She was wrong, she was always wrong, my mother. She was wrong about everything. I was resigned to it; at ten you have no control over your mother. The evening would go on like this, endless, excruciating. My mother would act foolish, Kate and I would be mortified and Mr Sumarsono would be mystified. It was no wonder my father had left; embarrassment.

Mr Sumarsono was now ready and he spoke. 'Please!' he said politely. My mother looked up again and realized this time what he was doing. She shook her head, raising her hands in deprecation.

'No, no,' she said, smiling. 'Not me. Don't take a picture of me. I wanted to see a picture of your wife.' She pointed at Mr Sumarsono. 'Your wife,' she said, 'your children.'

I was embarrassed not only for my mother but for poor Mr Sumarsono. Whatever he had expected from a country weekend in America, it could not have been a cramped attic room, two sullen girls, a voluble and incomprehensible hostess. I felt we had failed him, we had betrayed his unruffled courtesy, by our bewildering commands, our waving forks, our irresponsible talk about lizards. I wanted to save him. I wanted to liberate poor Mr Sumarsono from this aerial grid of misunderstandings. I wanted to cut the power lines, but I couldn't think of a way. I watched him despondently, waiting for him to subside at my mother's next order. Perhaps she would send him upstairs for another nap.

But things had changed. Mr Sumarsono stood gracefully, firm and erect, in charge. Somehow he had performed a coup. He had seized power. The absence of strut did not mean an absence of command, and we now saw how an Indonesian diplomat behaved when he was in charge. Like the *Stop!* gesture, Mr Sumarsono's reign was elegant and sophisticated, entirely convincing. It was suddenly clear that it was no longer possible to tell Mr Sumarsono what to do.

'No,' said Mr Sumarsono clearly. 'You wife.' He bowed firmly at my mother. 'You children.' He bowed at us.

Mr Sumarsono stooped over us, his courtesy exquisite and unyielding. 'Please,' he said, 'now photograph.' He held up the camera. It covered his face entirely, a strange mechanical mask. 'My photograph,' he said in a decisive tone.

He aimed the camera first at me. I produced a taut and artificial smile, and at once he reappeared from behind the camera. 'No smile,' he said firmly, shaking his head. 'No smile.' He himself produced a hideous smile, then shook his head and turned grave. 'Ah!' he said, nodding, and pointed to me. Chastened, I sat solemn and rigid while he disappeared behind the camera again. I didn't move even when he had finished, after the flash and the clicks of lenses and winding sprockets.

Mr Sumarsono turned to Kate, who had learned from me and

offered up a smooth and serious face. Mr Sumarsono nodded, but stepped toward her. 'Hand!' he said, motioning toward it, and he made the gesture that he wanted. Kate stared but obediently did as he asked.

When Mr Sumarsono turned to my mother, I worried again that she would stage a last-ditch attempt to take over, that she would insist on mortifying us all.

'Now!' said Mr Sumarsono, bowing peremptorily at her. 'Please.' I looked at her, and to my amazement, relief and delight, my mother did exactly the right thing. She smiled at Mr Sumarsono in a normal and relaxed way, as though they were old friends. She leaned easily back in her chair, graceful – I could suddenly see – and poised. She smoothed her hair back from her forehead.

In Mr Sumarsono's pictures, the images of us that he produced, this is how we look.

I am staring solemnly at the camera, dead serious, head-on. I look mystified, as though I am trying to understand something inexplicable; what the people around me mean when they speak, perhaps. I look as though I am in a foreign country where I do not speak the language.

Kate looks both radiant and ethereal; her eyes are alight. Her mouth is puckered into a mirthful V; she is trying to suppress a smile. The V of her mouth is echoed above her face by her two forked fingers, poised airily behind her head.

But it is the picture of my mother that surprised me the most. Mr Sumarsono's portrait was of someone entirely different from the person I knew, though the face was the same. Looking at it gave me the same feeling that the stopped escalator did; a sense of dislocation, a sudden uncertainty about my own beliefs. In the photograph my mother leans back against her chair like a queen, all her power evident, and at rest. Her face is turned slightly away; she is guarding her privacy. Her nose, her cheeks, her eyes, are bright with wine and excitement, but she is calm and amused. A mother cannot be beautiful, because she is so much more a mother than a woman, but in this picture it struck me, my mother looked, in an odd way, beautiful. I could see for the first time that other people might think she actually was beautiful.

Mr Sumarsono's view of my mother was of a glowing, self-assured, generous woman. And Mr Sumarsono himself was a real person, despite his meekness. I knew that; I had seen him take control. His view meant something; I could not ignore it. And I began to wonder.

We still have the pictures. Mr Sumarsono brought them with him the next time he came out for the weekend.

Somewhere Out of This World

TERESA WAUGH

Teresa Waugh lives in Combe Florey, Somerset, with her husband, the critic and columnist Auberon Waugh. She has written a number of successful novels, including Painting on Water.

It had been all right while she was in India. Or so it had seemed at the time. At least until those horrible French people had arrived. They had spoilt it all. If they hadn't come she'd probably have been there still, and still been happy.

Perhaps she hadn't been happy in India at all so much as just not unhappy. She'd gone there, she supposed when she looked back, to escape from all the horror of England where she had no job, no lover, no husband, no children, no future as far as she could see; no anything. All she had in fact was a little money and one rich and successful brother. He was a barrister and a Conservative MP. He had a flat in London and a house in Hampshire and a pretty wife with a loud voice and four children. Another reason to escape. But she didn't like children, she didn't want children. She didn't want a house of her own with all the responsibility it entailed; neither did she want a boring job to tie her down, but she did want, she thought, a lover – a husband – someone. Yet whenever the chance presented itself, she shied away from it. Her rich sister-in-law was wont to say in her loud voice that it was because she was afraid of being hurt. She didn't know that herself and put it down to the fact that she had never found anyone that she could really trust.

So she had gone to India, taking her paint-box with her, a little fearful, but buoyed up by a dreamy kind of hopefulness. There she had wandered around for a while, visiting the Taj Mahal by moonlight, handing out alms to the occasional beggar, eating saag and dal which she could have found just as easily and better cooked in London, painting a few pictures and reading – in a desultory fashion – *The Raj Quartet*. In India, in those leisurely early days, she imagined she understood the country and that she had found her soul. Perhaps she had just adopted the Hindu philosophy of acceptance, or perhaps the heat, the dirt, the distance from home and from her own reality just made her indolent.

After a while she settled in a town in the north, in a faded hotel which had once been an elegant dependency of a maharaja's. Next to her bedroom she had a bathroom with a huge bath on claw-and-ball feet into which, if she was lucky, cold water would trickle very, very slowly.

There was a dining room with a stone floor and a large table at which all the guests at the hotel sat together. That was how she had met the French people. But until they appeared she had been happy, or at least not unhappy. The days had passed peacefully and uneventfully by. She spent them carrying her easel around the town and setting it up to paint a crumbling building, a monkey that soon leapt away, a group of dark and ragged children playing cricket in the dirt with a makeshift bat, an old man squatting on his hunkers. This, she felt, was life. Or as close to it as she was ever likely to get.

Back in London and in Hampshire her rich brother and her loud-voiced sister-in-law told everyone that she was blissfully happy, she adored India and was having a perfectly marvellous time. They joked about her coming home with a fellow in a dhoti – or perhaps a fabulously rich maharaja. Restore the family fortunes. They were glad that she was far away where they had no need to worry about her.

She was sometimes lonely, but in a strange, detached sort of way, so that it didn't really hurt. Then she would talk to the night-watchman who lay in the dust outside the hotel entrance, or to the kitchen-boy, or to the women who squatted on the grass behind the hotel, cutting it with what seemed like nail scissors. But this was more difficult as they rarely spoke English and she had to brave her few words of Hindi. The women would crowd around her and smile and giggle and stop working.

Then she found the dog. Poor little thing. And it was when she found the dog that she changed her mind about the Indians. Until then she had invested them with every quality, found them poetic and patient and beautiful, philosophical and kind, had found no fault in them. They had filled her with wonder, with awe, with pity or with admiration, but she never imagined them as 700,000,000 individuals, some of whom were less likeable than others and none of whom saw the world through her eyes. Then came the dog. And then she realized how cruel and heartless Indians were. She had thought that their religion taught them to love animals because a rat, a snake or even a stray dog might be the reincarnation of someone's granny. But the reality proved to be different. Even the night-watchman said, 'We are not liking this dog.' She couldn't understand why. Poor little dog.

The dog was white and black and brown and scrawny, with pointed ears and thin haunches and sores on its hindquarters and around its eyes and it came to the kitchen door begging for food and the kitchen-boy kicked it and said, 'I am not liking this dog.' She smuggled the dog into the hotel and smuggled it up to her room where she kept it for days. The poor little thing was so hungry. She began to abandon the saag and dal and to order meat dishes – chicken stews and lamb or goat – so that she could take some upstairs to the little dog. She gave it water to drink from an empty face-cream jar. It lapped it up and licked her hands and face in gratitude. Perhaps she was really happy then because she loved the little dog so much and because she was there to care for it. The cruel Indians would have kicked it out of the hotel and left it to starve.

But despite all the care she lavished on the little dog, it did not seem to flourish. It grew nervous and irritable, even depressed, and it developed a overwhelming thirst, yet when presented with the jar of water it appeared to gag. It began to refuse the little offerings she brought up from the dining room. It lurched about her room, lowering its head and weaving from side to side. Eventually she decided that she would have to take it to the vet. There must be a vet in the town. In fact the vet lived on the other side of the town and she would have to take the little dog to him. She wrapped the trembling creature in a shawl, gathered him up in her arms and set out to find a bicycle rickshaw. But no rickshaw man would take her and the dog. They were not liking that dog. She was appalled by the lack of heart, and clasping the dog to her breast she crossed the hot town on foot.

The vet was tall and good-looking and polite and he took one look at the little dog and explained that it was in the penultimate stages of rabies and he ordered it to be destroyed at once and she thought that he was too cruel and walked back to the hotel through the heat and the dirt with tears streaming down her cheeks.

The next day the French people appeared in the hotel. They were there when she went down to supper, sitting at the big table in the dining room. She was glad of their company and wanted to tell them about the little dog and about how cruel the Indians were. But she lived to regret it.

The French woman had been sharp and rather assertive. She talked good English and was intelligent and educated. Her husband was quieter, but he too spoke English. She liked them until she told them about the dog. Then she decided that they were just as heartless as the Indians, for not only did they express no sympathy for the little dog, but they entirely sided with the hotel staff who refused to let it indoors, with the rickshaw man and even with the vet. They wanted to know if she had had the anti-rabies injections, were horrified when she hadn't, amazed when she dismissed the idea as quite unnecessary. The little dog, she said, wouldn't have bitten a fly. Then they told her horrifying stories of how death from rabies is long and painful, how you die from exhaustion caused by muscular spasms, and yearn – yearn – for water, but in the last stages, the mere sight of it gives you an intense pain in the back of the throat, causes you to foam at the mouth and to gag. In some countries they tie you foaming to a cartwheel to prevent you from running around and biting everyone in sight.

The following morning, they marched her off to the doctor. The doctor confirmed everything the French people said and even reprimanded her for having had anything to do with the little dog. Then she had the injections. Those were still the days of injections in the stomach. One every day for fourteen days and more afterwards at weekly intervals. Never in her life had she experienced anything so disagreeable. The doctor remained throughout cold and unsympathetic.

The French people had gone long since, she had had her last injection, she was lonely, and had begun to hate India – the smells, the sounds, the sights, the taste, and she had nothing left to say to the night-watchman who lay in the dust at the hotel entrance. She had gone there to escape, perhaps to avoid confronting the reality of her existence at home and had, in the end, found nothing to replace it. She no longer felt like painting. India had lost its magic. She would have to go home again.

She wondered if she might kill herself, and began to think about how she would do it. Desperately her sister-in-law tried to enthuse her to live. 'You could have a horse, go hunting, breed Pekingese, take bridge lessons in Basingstoke, do some voluntary work,' she suggested. None of these things seemed remotely tempting; in fact she could think of a hundred good reasons for doing none of them. She continued in secret to plan her death.

Then one day an old school friend turned up out of the blue, a woman who had just been abandoned by her husband and who was trying to pick up a few threads, to build a new life. This woman stayed for a while in the flat above the stables, pouring out her heart, confiding. 'You're so lucky,' she said, 'never to have tied yourself to some selfish man, to have your independence –

and your pictures – your paintings of India, they're marvellous. What are you doing now?'

She was ashamed to say that she was doing nothing and suddenly something miraculously stirred inside her which made her think that she might postpone death for the moment and do some more painting first. But above all, she had to get away from Hampshire. Right away.

Her friend left and she took out an atlas.

It would have to be somewhere very beautiful, somewhere peaceful, somewhere where there were not too many tourists, somewhere where she could be at one with herself, somewhere out of this world. After all, she had been all right in India, until the French people came.

And there it was, an island in the middle of the ocean, a tiny dot on the map somewhere to the south of the Tropic of Cancer and to the north of the Equator. Somewhere out of this world.

The travel agent told her that the scenery on the island was beautiful, the food delicious – fresh tropical fruits, fresh fish from the ocean – and that there was a brand new hotel on the beach, up to date and comfortable, bathroom en suite. She would take her paint-box and settle there.

So she managed to gather up what energy she had left, to look forward with apprehension and hope and finally to take off for the island of her dreams, where she would live in peace, gaze at the ocean pounding the shore, paint, eat tropical fruits and above all escape from the horrors of modern England and nothingness of her life.

The rickety little plane that flew to the island from the continental mainland circled the airport two or three times as she looked down at her Shangri-la. She had to admit that on first sight it looked a little disappointing. The ground was black and she could see no trees. She supposed that it would be like this just around the airport, and looked forward to the drive across beautiful countryside to the hotel on the other side of the island. In fact her main concern on the bumpy ride across was fear lest the taxi, which coughed and spluttered its way along, should break down altogether, leaving her abandoned in the middle of what was literally nowhere. The exquisite landscape promised by the travel agent was slow to materialize. There were no trees at all. Nothing grew anywhere. The land was black and dusty. An extinct volcano. It was like driving across a very large hearth which hadn't been swept.

The hotel stood on the end of a village of sprawling huts where little half-naked, brown-skinned children swarmed in the dust. The taxi hooted at them as at chickens to get out of the way, and jolted on towards the hotel. She felt infinitely depressed and rather angry. The hotel itself was a shabby, jerry-built affair which looked unfinished, with no glass in the windows but only mosquito nets tacked to the frames. The en-suite bathroom was not yet in working order. In her room she pushed aside the mosquito netting and looked out of her window at the sea. It was amazingly beautiful. She decided to stay.

The next morning, as she sat on the beach, she thought that if she could keep her back to the hotel, to the poor little village, to the infertile land, to the world, and just look out to sea, she would be all right. Life might be bearable. Then, as she gazed along the shore, she suddenly saw something strange, a dark blob, jerking and drawing gradually nearer. She could not make out what it was, but it didn't look like a child. Perhaps it was an animal. It came closer and closer and little by little became recognizable as a dog. She stood up in horror as it weaved its way across the beach towards her, its neck stretched out, its body shaken by violent spasms, foaming at the mouth.

The Key

EUDORA WELTY

Eudora Welty, one of the influential band of writers from the Deep South, was born in Jackson, Mississippi and has done most of her writing in the short-story form.

It was quiet in the waiting room of the remote little station, except for the night sounds of insects. You could hear their embroidering movements in the weeds outside, which somehow gave the effect of some tenuous voice in the night, telling a story. Or you could listen to the fat thudding of the light bugs and the hoarse rushing of their big wings against the wooden ceiling. Some of the bugs were clinging heavily to the yellow globe, like idiot bees to a senseless smell.

Under this prickly light two rows of people sat in silence, their faces stung, their bodies twisted and quietly uncomfortable, expectantly so, in ones and twos, not quite asleep. No one seemed impatient, although the train was late. A little girl lay flung back in her mother's lap as though sleep had struck her with a blow.

Ellie and Albert Morgan were sitting on a bench like the others waiting for the train and had nothing to say to each other. Their names were ever so neatly and rather largely printed on a big reddish-tan suitcase strapped crookedly shut, because of a missing buckle, so that it hung apart finally like a stupid pair of lips. 'Albert Morgan, Ellie Morgan, Yellow Leaf, Mississippi.' They must have been driven into town in a wagon, for they and the suitcase were all touched here and there with a fine yellow dust, like finger marks.

Ellie Morgan was a large woman with a face as pink and crowded as an old-fashioned rose. She must have been about forty years old. One of those black satchel purses hung over her straight, strong wrist. It must have been her savings which were making possible this trip. And to what place? you wondered, for she sat there as tense and solid as a cube, as if to endure some nameless apprehension rising and overflowing within her at the thought of travel. Her face worked and broke into strained, hardening lines, as if there had been death – that too explicit evidence of agony in her desire to communicate.

Albert made a slower and softer expression. He sat motionless beside Ellie, holding his hat in his lap with both hands – a hat you were sure he had never worn. He looked homemade, as though his wife had self-consciously knitted or somehow contrived a husband when she sat alone at night. He had a shock of very fine sunburned yellow hair. He was too shy for this world, you could see. His hands were like cardboard, he held his hat so still; and yet how softly his eyes fell upon its crown, moving dreamily and yet with dread over its brown surface! He was smaller than his wife. His suit was brown, too, and he wore it neatly and carefully, as though he were murmuring, 'Don't look – no need to look – I am effaced.' But you have seen that expression too in silent children, who will tell you what they dreamed the night before in sudden, almost hilarious bursts of confidence.

Every now and then, as though he perceived some minute thing, a sudden, alert, tantalized look would creep over the little man's face, and he would gaze slowly around him, quite slyly. Then he would bow his head again; the expression would vanish; some inner refreshment had been denied him. Behind his head was a wall poster, dirty with time, showing an old-fashioned locomotive about to crash into an open touring car filled with women in veils. No one in the station was frightened by the familiar poster, any more than they were aroused by the little man whose rising and drooping head it framed. Yet for a moment he might seem to you to be sitting there quite filled with hope.

Among the others in the station was a strong-looking young man, alone, hatless, red-haired, who was standing by the wall while the rest sat on benches. He had a small key in his hand and was turning it over and over in his fingers, nervously passing it from one hand to the other, tossing it gently into the air and catching it again.

He stood and stared in distraction at the other people; so intent and so wide was his gaze that anyone who glanced after him seemed rocked like a small boat in the wake of a large one. There was an excess of energy about him that separated him from everyone else, but in the motion of his hands there was, instead of the craving for communication, something of reticence, even of secrecy, as the key rose and fell. You guessed that he was a stranger in town; he might have been a criminal or a gambler, but his eyes were widened with gentleness. His look, which travelled without stopping for long anywhere, was a hurried focusing of a very tender and explicit regard.

The color of his hair seemed to jump and move, like the flicker of a match struck in a wind. The ceiling lights were not steady but seemed to pulsate like a living and transient force, and made the young man in his preoccupation appear to tremble in the midst of his size and strength, and to fail to impress his exact outline upon the yellow walls. He was like a salamander in the fire. 'Take care' you wanted to say to him, and yet also, 'Come here.' Nervously, and quite apart in his distraction, he continued to stand tossing the key back and forth from one hand to the other. Suddenly it became a gesture of abandonment; one hand stayed passive in the air, then seized too late; the key fell to the floor.

Everyone, except Albert and Ellie Morgan, looked up for a moment. On the floor the key had made a fierce metallic sound like a challenge, a sound of seriousness. It almost made people jump. It was regarded as an insult, a very personal question, in the quiet peaceful room where the insects were tapping at the ceiling and each person was allowed to sit among his possessions and wait for an unquestioned departure. Little walls of reproach went up about them all.

A flicker of amusement touched the young man's face as he observed the startled but controlled and obstinately blank faces which turned toward him for a moment and then away. He walked over to pick up his key.

But it had glanced and slid across the floor, and now it lay in the dust at Albert Morgan's feet.

Albert Morgan was indeed picking up the key. Across from him, the young man saw him examine it, quite slowly, with wonder written all over his face and hands, as if it had fallen from the sky. Had he failed to hear the clatter? There was something wrong with Albert . . .

As if by decision, the young man did not terminate this wonder by claiming his key. He stood back, a peculiar flash of interest or of something more inscrutable, like resignation, in his lowered eyes.

The little man had probably been staring at the floor, thinking. And suddenly in the dark surface the small sliding key had appeared. You could see memory seize his face, twist it and hold it. What innocent, strange thing might it have brought back to life – a fish he had once spied just below the top of the water on a sunny lake in the country when he was a child? This was just as unexpected, shocking, and somehow meaningful to him.

Albert sat there holding the key in his wide-open hand. How intensified, magnified, really vain all attempt at expression becomes in the afflicted! It was with an almost incandescent delight that he felt the unguessed temperature and weight of the key. Then he turned to his wife. His lips were actually trembling.

And still the young man waited, as if the strange joy of the little man took precedence with him over whatever need he had for the key. With sudden electrification he saw Ellie slip the handle of her satchel purse from her wrist and with her fingers begin to talk to her husband.

The others in the station had seen Ellie too; shallow pity washed over the waiting room like a dirty wave foaming and creeping over a public beach. In quick mumblings from bench to bench people said to each other, 'Deaf and dumb!' How ignorant they were of all that the young man was seeing! Although he had no way of knowing the words Ellie said, he seemed troubled enough at the mistake the little man must have made, at his misplaced wonder and joy.

Albert was replying to his wife. On his hands he said to her, 'I found it. Now it belongs to me. It is something important! It means something. From now on we will get along better, have more understanding . . . Maybe when we reach Niagara Falls we will even fall in love, the way other people have done. Maybe our marriage was really for love, after all, not for the other reason – both of us being afflicted in the same way, unable to speak, lonely because of that. Now you can stop being ashamed of me, for being so cautious and slow all my life, for taking my own time . . . You can take hope. Because it was I who found the key. Remember that. I found it.' He laughed all at once quite silently.

Everyone stared at his impassioned little speech as it came from his fingers. They were embarrassed, vaguely aware of some crisis and vaguely affronted, but unable to interfere; it was as though they were the deaf-mutes and he the speaker. When he laughed, a few people laughed unconsciously with him, in relief, and turned away. But the young man remained still and intent, waiting at his little distance.

'This key came here very mysteriously – it is bound to mean something,' the husband went on to say. He held the key up just before her eyes. 'You are always praying; you believe in miracles; well, now, here is the answer. It came to me.'

His wife looked self-consciously around the room and replied on her fingers, 'You are always talking nonsense. Be quiet.'

But she was secretly pleased, and when she saw him slowly look down in his old manner, she reached over, as if to retract what she had said, and laid her hand on his, touching the key for herself, softness making her warm hand limp. From then on they never looked around them, never saw anything except each other. They were so intent, so very solemn, wanting to have their symbols perfectly understood!

'You must see it is a symbol,' he began again, his fingers clumsy and blurring with excitement. 'It is a symbol of something – something that we deserve, and that is happiness. We will find happiness in Niagara Falls.'

And then, as if he were all at once shy even of her, he turned slightly away from her and slid the key into his pocket. They sat staring down at the suitcase, their hands fallen into their laps.

The young man slowly turned away from them and wandered back to the wall, where he took out a cigarette and lighted it.

Outside, the night pressed around the station like a pure stone, in which the little room might be transfixed, and, for the preservation of this moment of hope, its future killed, an insect in amber. The short little train drew in, stopped, and rolled away, almost noiselessly.

Then inside, people were gone or turned in sleep or walking about, all changed from the way they had been. But the deaf-mutes and the loitering young man were still in their places.

The man was still smoking. He was dressed like a young doctor or some such person in the town, and yet he did not seem of the town. He looked very strong and active; but there was a startling quality, a willingness to be forever distracted, even disturbed, in the very reassurance of his body, some alertness which made his strength fluid and dissipated instead of withheld and greedily beautiful. His youth by now did not seem an important thing about him; it was a medium for his activity, no doubt, but as he stood there frowning and smoking you felt some apprehension that he would never express whatever might be the desire of his life in being young and strong, in standing apart in compassion, in making any intuitive present or sacrifice, or in any way of action at all – not because there was too much in the world demanding his strength, but because he was too deeply aware.

You felt a shock in glancing up at him, and when you looked away from the whole yellow room and closed your eyes, his intensity, as well as that of the room, seemed to have impressed the imagination with a shadow of itself, a blackness together with the light, the negative beside the positive. You felt as though some exact, skilful contrast had been made between the surfaces of your hearts to make you aware, in some pattern, of his joy and his despair. You could feel the fullness and the emptiness of this stranger's life.

The railroad man came in swinging a lantern which he stopped suddenly in its arc. Looking uncomfortable, and then rather angry, he approached the deaf mutes and shot his arm out in a series of violent gestures and shrugs.

Albert and Ellie Morgan were dreadfully shocked. The woman looked resigned for a moment to hopelessness. But the little man – you were startled by a look of bravado on his face.

In the station the red-haired man was speaking aloud – but to himself. 'They missed their train!'

As if in quick apology, the trainman set his lantern down beside Albert's foot, and hurried away.

And as if completing a circle, the red-haired man walked over too and stood silently near the deaf-mutes. With a reproachful look at him the woman reached up, and took off her hat.

They began again, talking rapidly back and forth, almost as one person. The old routine of their feeling was upon them once more. Perhaps, you thought, staring at their similarity – her hair was yellow, too – they were children together – cousins even, afflicted in the same way, sent off from home to the state institute . . .

It was the feeling of conspiracy. They were in counterplot against the plot of those things that pressed down upon them from outside their knowledge and their ways of making themselves understood. It was obvious that it gave the wife her greatest pleasure. But you wondered, seeing Albert, whom talking seemed rather to dishevel, whether it had not continued to be a rough and violent game which Ellie, as the older and stronger, had taught him to play with her.

'What do you think he wants?' she asked Albert, nodding at the red-haired man, who smiled faintly. And how her eyes shone! Who would ever know how deep her suspicion of the whole outside world lay in her heart, how far it had pushed her!

'What does he want?' Albert was replying quickly. 'The key!'

Of course! And how fine it had been to sit there with the key hidden from the strangers and also from his wife, who had not seen where he had put it. He stole up with his hand and secretly felt the key, which must have lain in some pocket nearly against his heart. He nodded gently. The key had come there, under his eyes on the floor in the station, all of a sudden, but yet not quite unexpected. That is the way things happen to you always. But Ellie did not comprehend this.

Now she sat there as quiet as could be. It was not only hopelessness about the trip. She, too, undoubtedly felt something privately about that key, apart from what she had said or what he had told her. He had almost shared it with her – you realized that. He frowned and smiled almost at the same time. That was something – something he could almost remember but not quite – which would let him keep the key always to himself. He knew that, and he would remember it later, when he was alone.

'Never fear, Ellie,' he said, a still little smile lifting his lip. 'I've got it safe in a pocket. No one can find it, and there's no hole for it to fall through.'

She nodded, but she was always doubting, always anxious. You could look at her troubled hands. How terrible it was, how strange, that Albert loved the key more than he loved Ellie! He did not mind missing the train. It showed in every line, every motion of his body. The key was closer – closer. The whole story began to illuminate them now, as if the lantern flame had been turned up.

Ellie's anxious, hovering body could wrap him softly as a cradle, but the secret meaning, that powerful sign, that reassurance he so hopefully sought, so assuredly deserved – that had never come. There was something lacking in Ellie.

Had Ellie, with her suspicions of everything, come to know even things like this, in her way? How empty and nervous her red scrubbed hands were, how desperate to speak! Yes, she must regard it as unhappiness lying between them, as more than emptiness. She must worry about it, talk about it. You could imagine her stopping her churning to come out to his chair on the porch, to tell him that she did love him and would take care of him always, talking with the spotted sour milk dripping from her fingers. Just try to tell her that talking is useless, that care is not needed . . . And sooner or later he would always reply, say something, agree, and she would go away again . . .

And Albert, with his face so capable of amazement, made you suspect the funny thing about talking to Ellie. Until you do, declared his round brown eyes, you can be peaceful and content that everything takes care of itself. As long as you let it alone everything goes peacefully, like an uneventful day on the farm – chores attended to, woman working in the house, you in the field, crop growing well as can be expected, the cow giving and the sky like a coverlet over it all – so that you're as full of yourself as a colt, in need of nothing, and nothing needing you. But when you pick up your hands and start to talk, if you don't watch carefully, this security will run away and leave you. You say something, make an observation, just to answer your wife's worryings, and everything is jolted, disturbed, laid open like the ground behind a plough, with you running along after it.

But happiness, Albert knew, is something that appears to you suddenly, that is meant for you, a thing which you reach for and pick up and hide at your breast, a shiny thing that reminds you of something alive and leaping.

Ellie sat there quiet as a mouse. She had unclasped her purse and taken out a little card with a picture of Niagara Falls on it.

'Hide it from the man,' she said. She did suspect him! The red-haired man had drawn closer. He bent and saw that it was a picture of Niagara Falls.

'Do you see the little rail?' Albert began in tenderness. And Ellie loved to watch him tell her about it; she clasped her hands and began to smile and show her crooked tooth; she looked young; it was the way she had looked as a child.

'That is what the teacher pointed to with her wand on the magic-lantern slide – the little rail. You stand right here. You lean up hard against the rail. Then you can hear Niagara Falls.'

'How do you hear it?' begged Ellie, nodding.

'You hear it with your whole self. You listen with your arms and your legs and your whole body. You'll never forget what hearing is, after that.'

He must have told her hundreds of times in his obedience, yet she smiled with gratitude, and stared deep, deep into the tinted picture of the waterfall.

Presently she said, 'By now, we'd have been there, if we hadn't missed the train.'

She did not even have any idea that it was miles and days away. She looked at the red-haired man then, her eyes all puckered up, and he looked away at last.

He had seen the dust on her throat and a needle stuck in her collar where she'd forgotten it, with a thread running through the eye – the final details. Her hands were tight and wrinkled with pressure. She swung her foot a little below her skirt, in the new Mary Jane slipper with the hard toe.

Albert turned away too. It was then, you thought, that he became quite frightened to think that if they hadn't missed the train they would be hearing, at that very moment, Niagara Falls. Perhaps they would be standing there together, pressed against the little rail, pressed against each other, with their lives being poured through them, changing . . . And how did he know what that would be like? He bent his head and tried not to look at his wife. He could say nothing. He glanced up once at the stranger, with almost a pleading look, as if to say 'Won't you come with us?'

'To work so many years, and then to miss the train,' Ellie said.

You saw by her face that she was undauntedly wondering, unsatisfied, waiting for the future.

And you knew how she would sit and brood over this as over their conversations together, about every misunderstanding, every discussion, sometimes even about some agreement between them that had been all settled – even about the secret and proper separation that lies between a man and a woman, the thing that makes them what they are in themselves, their secret life, their memory of the past, their childhood, their dreams. This to Ellie was unhappiness.

They had told her when she was a little girl how people who have just been married have the custom of going to Niagara Falls on a wedding trip, to start their happiness; and that came to be where she put her hope, all of it. So she saved money. She worked harder than he did, you could observe, comparing their hands, good and bad years, more than was good for a woman. Year after year she had put her hope ahead of her.

And he – somehow he had never thought that this time would come, that they might really go on the journey. He was never looking so far and so deep as Ellie – into the future, into the changing and mixing of their lives together when they should arrive at last at Niagara Falls. To him it was always something postponed, like the paying off of the mortgage.

But sitting here in the station, with the suitcase all packed and at his feet, he had begun to realize that this journey might, for a fact, take place. And after his first shock and pride he had simply reserved the key; he had hidden it in his pocket.

She looked unblinking into the light of the lantern on the floor. Her face looked strong and terrifying, all lighted and very near to his. But there was no joy there. You knew that she was very brave.

Albert seemed to shrink, to retreat . . . His trembling hand went once more beneath his coat and touched the pocket where the key was lying, waiting. Would he ever remember that elusive thing about it or be sure what it might really be a symbol of? . . . His eyes, in their quick manner of filming over, grew dreamy. Perhaps he had even decided that it was a symbol not of happiness with Ellie, but of something else – something which he could have alone, for only himself, in peace, something strange and unlooked for which would come to him . . .

The red-haired man took a second key from his pocket, and in one direct motion placed it in Ellie's red palm. It was a key with a large triangular pasteboard tag on which was clearly printed STAR HOTEL. ROOM 2.

He did not wait to see any more, but went out abruptly into the night. He stood still for a moment and reached for a cigarette. As he held the match close he gazed straight ahead, and in his eyes, all at once wild and searching, there was certainly, besides the simple compassion in his regard, a look both restless and weary, very much used to the comic. You could see that he despised and saw the uselessness of the thing he had done.

EDITED BY SUSAN HILL

The Penguin Book of Modern Women's Short Stories

Marriage, motherhood, the battle for self-realization, bereavement, the louring of old age – women's particular preoccupations thread in and out of our literary history.

Susan Hill's collection of short stories by British women reveals the consolidations made during the post-war period as women became more confident about articulating their desires and intimate thoughts. Taken together, the stories drive a tap root into different aspects of the feminine psyche; A. S. Byatt's agonizing cry for a dead child in 'The July Ghost'; the encounter with self-knowledge seen in Patricia Ferguson's nurse on night duty; the tyranny exerted by food which many women will recognize in Angela Huth's 'The Weighing Up'; Fay Weldon's sparkling, blackly funny view of a middle-class marriage.

Including contributions by, among others, Penelope Lively, Edna O'Brien, Sara Maitland, Margaret Drabble, Georgina Hammick, Rose Tremain and Elizabeth Jane Howard, this stimulating, entertaining and many-layered collection shows women writing easily, confidently and superbly well.

'Almost without exception the stories in this collection are powerful and enthralling' – *The Times*

PUBLISHED IN PENGUIN PAPERBACK

SELECTED AND INTRODUCED BY SUSAN HILL

The Penguin Book of Contemporary Women's Short Stories

With dazzling originality and wit, the writers in this anthology examine a range of themes, from domesticity and love, to lust, childhood and loss. They are unified by their excellence, their sensitive attention to detail and their intuitive understanding of life. Each story has a timeless quality that makes Sylvia Plath's story about tattooing as much of the moment as Candia McWilliam's 'Sweetie Rationing' or Janet Frame's 'Swans'.

In making her selection the acclaimed novelist and writer Susan Hill has cast her net widely around the world from London to New Zealand, from Alice Munro to Angela Carter to Helen Simpson and Leonora Brito. Her contributors offer 'sheer interesting, exciting, good writing. Several have already stood the test of time, the rest will quite surely do so.'

'Satisfyingly wide-ranging, evidence that women are our remembrancers . . . remarkable feats of story-telling' – *The Times*

PUBLISHED IN PENGUIN PAPERBACK